MEMORY OF SNOW AND OF DUST

ff

BREYTEN BREYTENBACH

Memory of Snow and of Dust

Farrar Straus Giroux

NEW YORK

First published in Great Britain by
Faber and Faber Limited, 1989

Library of Congress Cataloging-in-Publication Data

Breytenbach, Breyten.
  Memory of snow and of dust/Breyten Breytenbach.—1st American ed.
    p.   cm.
  I. Title.
PR9369.3.B67M46   1989 823—dc19   89–1202

Printed in Great Britain

First American edition, 1989

CONTENTS

PART ONE
UTÉROPIA

'Little by little the egg grows its feet.'

ETHIOPIAN SAYING

A Kind of Telling

Memory is a strange thing
all by itself. Through which
words, incidents, people will
move like snow or like dust.
Words giving surface to memory
in the present, or remembered
as the fall-out of past writers;
incidents modifying the meandering
   remembrances
of memory people, my people.
I am the memory of a kind
of artisan novelist. The biography
I am repeatedly in the process of
writing is always the same one,
and it may be described
as a variously sliced-up or torn-apart
book of myself as the essential
apocryphal memory.

This is where your story starts.

I am sitting in this enormous and cold and grey and luminous cathedral. By my reckoning, birds should be fluttering under the roof, swooping down from the belfries, but there are none. The winter city's distant sounds are muffled – you could imagine a lost flock of sheep wandering down black trails among cliffs with the colour of sadness. It is lonely to be an animal in a city of no birds. The light out there is subdued and yet objects are intensely outlined.

In a somewhat similar fashion, I want to outline for you some experiences and some people. I know that evoking memories is a way of imagining the world and, strangely enough, that the search for clarity extends the areas of uncertainty and diffuseness, like fog swallowing up the hollows, whilst also etching the shadows deeper. I am still not a writer, only a part-time journalist, but ever since I set out describing the events for your benefit, I realized that I carry a book in me, and that I could not rest until I gave birth to it.

Thus, as a reporter of lost time, I fashioned your past, chapter by chapter. Barnum – your father sometimes laughingly referred to him as his *older ego* – was kind enough to encourage me. When I was through blackening a sheaf of papers, I would submit them to him and he then read the notes and made a few professional comments. He filled me in on some things that I could not have known. He said I should try and be objective, that personal feelings and opinions on a page do not yet constitute a book-world which, by definition, ought to have a life of its own if it were to survive, and that I should therefore attempt to project myself in the third person singular. Even more important, he said, is to write about events where I could not have been present – doing this will give breath to the book, and it is also a way to heaven. This string of breathing is furthermore the only lifeline, to his mind, which can help transform pain into pleasure. Writing must be metamorphosis.

Why am I writing to you in this place? How should I know? Except that I announced your existence to the absent one for the first and only time out there, on the steps just outside that door. Cold had set in, autumn had stripped the lanes of their leaves and the square was empty. I can't remember trees in Africa ever getting that bare. The sky was low on that day too, the streets had a sheen of humidity, the light was a banked fire.

The contrast! I knew I had another life inside me. You were one month old. It was difficult to mask the trembling of my lips. I told him, the absent one, about you, and his expression was stern, the irises around the pupils went dark the way they sometimes did when he was moved by anger or fear or nostalgia, but then they softened as he took me in his arms to comfort me. Or was he doing this so as not to have to look into my eyes? Against his shoulder I said, I couldn't help myself: 'Please don't tell me not to.'

I so much wanted him to be proud, happy, enthusiastic. Maybe he was. Maybe he just couldn't show it. But he will certainly love you, my little blackbird. I know that he needs you even more than I do. He held me close for a long time. What were the images coursing through his mind, what cracks did he fear, what shifts in the subsoil of his anguish? You see, we were already separated because of a silly quarrel. He was due to leave the very next day for that horrible country in his mind – 'to go into the geography of absence' was the way he referred to it. Was it unfair of me to tell him about you just before his departure? Was it a desperate throw to try and hold him back? I wanted to give him hope (or rope enough?), a reason for believing, a motivation for coming back to us. We have nothing left but hope.

With his arm across my shoulders he led me into the cathedral down the nave to the apse where the high altar is. On the side there's always an open book for lonely people to come and scribble their messages asking for prayerful intervention because of a dying parent, an absconded husband, a child with an obstinate cough, an operation, hunger, undefined sadness, loneliness. 'Are you sure?' he asked me. Yes, I was certain, the doctor had confirmed it that very morning. About a month. 'I know it is there already.'

'Poor child,' he sighed. Why? 'Why, it must have ah-come about in the theatre!' he smiled. 'It is not exactly a propitious start in life, you know – the father a knockabout, a hack actor, a stateless unemployed marginal, a *shifta*, and then to be conceived off-stage in the wings between acts!' I reminded him that ah-it was in a loge, and most exciting. Also it ah-happened during a rehearsal not a real play. He said it only goes to show what magic even a bad play can do.

There, just beyond that sea of votive candles where the darkness

6

lies in wait, he kissed me. 'Not here,' I protested. He put his hand on my belly and with his lips in my hair he said he could neither detect any movement nor feel a thing. Stupid! Then, he said, surely you should be in bed now, and I laughed. 'Let's return to Africa,' he whispered. 'Let's not stay in this land of selfish and superficial people,' and it was as if a crow had swallowed his voice raw. I put my finger on his lips: 'You know it's not possible. Africa? Which Africa? Yours or mine?'

We continued walking past all the dark paintings of suffering and torture, past the chilly alabaster-faced madonna locked up behind rails as if in a cell, past the depiction of man's downfall in waterfalls of stone. Our feet rang over the big flagstones underneath which the bishops and the rich patrons lie buried. 'You do know that I have to go?' he said. Yes, I know. 'But I swear to you that I shall return, and sooner even than planned.'

'Go do what must be done, but be careful and please come back safely to us,' I comforted him. Already he was on the run, always running away. The seconds went by slowly.

By this side-chapel we stopped. He pointed out the life-size figure of a man seemingly hooked to a cross on the wall. 'It is the most beautiful one I know,' he said. 'Look how graceful yet humble his limbs are. So smooth, no blood. Can't make out for sure whether it's marble or some other stone. Skeleton of flight. It shines, don't you think so? Lips and eyes closed, calm head tilted slightly to the left shoulder. No contortion, no agony there. It is not a crucified dead god, just a beautiful sculpture. Look at the smoothness of the patina.' There was awe in his voice. 'And so light, so effortlessly stretched – like a bird about to take off . . . It's not bad, it's not bad . . . Do you remember that church in Mont Aigu where we first met? I never told you that I went back there the next day, and that I lit a candle for you before the blackest virgin mother in the place. Ridiculous, no? Do you think it might have the opposite effect because I'm not a believer?'

I smiled and stroked his cheek. It was days since last he'd shaved, his chin and cheeks were stubbly. I remembered how he once joked that only Whites have the time to grow beards, that the others are too busy making revolutions. My tears were burning just below the eyelids. 'Don't you see it's already worked?' I asked. 'That the miracle did take place?'

'But I wanted you to be happy whatever happens. Although I

7

couldn't get myself to pray. That would have been preposterous blasphemy.'

'I *am* happy. I *am* happy' – I repeated several times, and I wanted him to stay and to go then before he saw me crying. I was afraid I'd end up telling him the terrible news about his father.

'Do you think I'm mad?'

'No, of course not, it is only natural that you should be on edge before leaving for *that* place. You *will* be careful?'

'I think I must be mad,' he said with a mocking voice. 'But since I don't know who I am, or who is doing the thinking for that matter, we shall pretend it is the other, right?' Quickly he kissed the beauty spot in the palm of my hand – his sun, he always claimed – and then he was gone.

Here I sat down for a long time. In the end I was shivering violently even though I had on the same coat I'm wearing now. Made it myself, you know. My mother showed me how to cut patterns and sew when I was still very young. It's one of the few things she bothered to teach me. One day I shall pass on the knack to you. Even if you are a boy. But I'm sure your father would prefer you to be a girl.

See, already I'm talking to you: somebody has to tell you who you are. Soon I'll feel you moving in my body. You will still be small and wrinkled, the doctor told me, hardly bigger than a brown penis, and I don't even know if you are girlchild or boychild. What is it like to be so little? How hard you must be working to make your hands, your feet, your sex! You are a serpent, a fish with gills and swollen eyes; during these few months you will grow your way through millions of years of evolution until you are bird. You will always be part of the sea. I prefer to think of you that way so as not to focus on the 'concept' *man* or *life*. I don't want to be writing to an abstract idea.

The bells are quaveringly booming the quarter-hours, amplified by the grey acoustics of this place. Can you also hear them? I feel the reverberation of sound through my body. Perhaps this is the kind of sea of sounds in which you now live, a sac of breakers strung to the tolling of my heart. I shall be your sea. Had there been birds roosting in the clock-towers, they would all have been shaken loose by these waves of fright. I don't know of many birds in Paris. Up the hill in the Luxembourg Gardens there are sparrows and blackbirds and also, for a few years now, some crows. The crows are the bad thoughts surfacing from our subterranean history, but I close my mind to evil memories. You will be a dolphin dreamed by your father and me, and you will be beautiful. Pigeons aren't birds, your father always says; they are rats with wings.

But of course I know why I'm here: superstition. Three days after your father's departure I received one of those yellowish, ready-made post office parcels through the mail, with the name of the sender illegible. I should have known it was from him – he was never any good at wrapping up and tying strings around things. It was much too big for what it contained: a toy lion of some fluffy brown material with one ear chewed off. See, I have it here with me. There was a note in the box which read:

> This is for the small magician. He will guard our dream and frighten off the evil spirits. His name is Fanuel and he hunts mice and crows. So don't worry if he goes off at night. My love . . .

The lion has been living in my bag ever since that day, and thus I had him with us when I came to the appointment with Walser across the square in the Café des Anciens d'Afrique.

I don't know how Walser got hold of *my* number. I'd only seen him once before, in the company of Mano, your father. That was in another café, in the Chinese Quarter. Now he was sitting with his back to the wall facing the door.

When I arrived he was slurping his tea through a big moustache. His eyes were obscured by thick-lensed dark glasses. I'd been warned about his eyesight, though Mano wasn't sure and thought his blindness was something of a mystery. On the table there was the folded evening paper and a small pile of coins. He'd already paid his bill and when he noticed my presence he pretended to be looking at his watch.

I apologized for being a few minutes late but he waved my words away and smiled, wiping the wing-like growth under his nose. He gave me to understand that I was not to take any notice of it, that it was an old underground habit to be so painfully punctual ('that is why we never miss the date with our killers'), as also to pay immediately for what you had so that you could leave quickly and unobtrusively if ever the need arose. They are like Boy Scouts, these people. I thought it was certainly a joke for him to be setting up appointments in such a place – this hang-out for maudlin 'African hands' and other reactionaries – because I knew, from Mano, that

Walser had been engaged in subversive goings-on in several African countries. Still, he seemed at ease even though his eyes never stopped roaming the room. That's the impression I had: a hoary head swivelling slowly from left to right. How much could he actually take in? Shadows trespassing on the retina? Was he using his eyes like vibration captors?

He ordered a beer for me and quite automatically paid the waiter despite my protests. 'Don't be upset now,' he said, enunciating firmly but gently from the side of his mouth. 'We've had some disturbing news. Your friend has been arrested. No, no, take hold of yourself! Don't jump like that. We never know who may be watching us. Don't let them see. I'm positively sure it's not serious. It can't be. It rather seems to be a case of mistaken identity, and he should be out of there quickly enough. But we can't afford to let on. Don't do anything, whatever you do. It is the best way for us to help him. Ahem, we didn't want you to hear about this by some other means. Naturally we shall keep you informed, you must trust us. Do you understand? There's nothing to worry about. When and if I call you again I shall say: "How about going to Africa?" which will be the signal that we must meet here again, but always exactly half an hour earlier than the time I mention on the telephone. Is that clear?' I could only nod my head.

I asked him how he'd learned about the arrest but he said he couldn't tell me, that it was better not to know more. It is always better not to know any more than the strict essentials. The barest bones. Then he all of a sudden looked embarrassed and got up to go without even finishing his tea. He gave me his hand, I noticed that it was frail and warped like time-freckled parchment, and he bowed over mine in an old-world fashion. It was impossible to guess his age. I imagine that the only way to recognize him would be by his stooped, slightly hesitant shuffle, and the moustache riding like a frightened monkey on his upper lip – if it is a real one!

Instinctively I returned to the cathedral as if for asylum and I found that I was clutching Fanuel in my fists. At what moment did I take him from my bag? I can't remember. Now I have a crazy urge to deposit the limp little beast at the feet of the man floating calmly on his cross. As a kind of offering I suppose – some sacrifice so that my fright may be taken into consideration. Of course it is a stupid idea. It would have been giving in to the need for a barbaric ritual. What would your father have said had he known? He always scoffed

10

at all these sanctified images and icons. Abject obscurantism, he'd have exclaimed.

I am alone. Walser's news and the secrecy of it made me feel my isolation even more. Then I remembered you. You are my family, my confidant. I said to myself that you would have to know about the rest of us, that you must know where you come from. We are your past. This, the telling of your past, will be my present to you. Perhaps – my throat is tight – perhaps he will not be around then to give you all the stories which in time should colour your world. But no, I refuse to despair: *you* will be the magician bringing him back to us.

And so I started this letter. It is getting longer and darker already. Here and there old ladies in threadbare coats with trembling heads and thin thighs, sit on their uncomfortable kneeling chairs, staring through dim adoring eyes at the distant altar with its panoply of morbid statues. I shiver so much that you must certainly also be feeling the cold.

It is time for us to go home, my blackbird.

2

The best moments of the day are during the morning at about five and then again in the afternoon at eleven. In Ethiopia, from time immemorial, we start counting the hours of the day from what would actually be six o'clock in the morning here in Europe. Five in the morning is the equivalent of the white man's eleven o'clock, eleven in the afternoon is therefore his five p.m. Those are the ritual times when coffee is prepared and served.

All activity in the neighbourhood comes to a standstill and friends and family gather for the ceremony around the hearth which is always near the back door. The green coffee beans together with a few handfuls of grain are grilled on a big metal plate over the flames. With their fans the women of the house will be wafting hot air over the beans. When ready, the beans are pounded and ground in a mortar and the powder boiled with water for a long time. This strong beverage is drunk scalding, and flavoured with greyish crystals of rough salt. Maybe there will be enough for two rounds, sipped whilst lost in thought and tongue-smacking appreciation. The grilled cereals are chewed. Sometimes there will also be *injera*, our pasta, eaten with fiery spices. The air will be scented by the smoke from incense and, on holidays, sheaves of odoriferous herbs spread over the floor. The priests – they are always present – will softly intone their prayers. The delicious smells of incense, coffee, burnt wheat and sweet grasses are to please and to nourish the deities of the house, the prayers are to ward off evil spirits.

Then the latest tidbits of gossip are bargained for, deals are made and commented upon, marriages are arranged, the family history passed along to the younger members. Everyone will be present, and no distinction is made between houseboys and masters. Old men sit there wrapped in thin white shawls, flicking away flies with their cow-tail whisks. They all have long forked sticks. As on early mornings before dawn, or at mass, some will be standing balanced on one leg, the foot of the other resting on the knee, cupping their chins in the cleft of their sticks. Thus they can sleep in the upright position. The children are as quiet as mice in the presence of owls, shifting on their heels and tails. The women have huge doe-like eyes. They are demure, but make no mistake, they are certainly not weak.

The women of your family – grandmother, great-aunts, cousins – were forceful characters to a man. In our country family relationships go far and deep. Even cousins of the seventh degree remain 'brother' and 'sister'. We do not really have the notion of 'cousin' or 'niece'. That is why you will one day have so many brothers and sisters.

Listen. The Emperor sent his grand-daughters to Paris for schooling and your great-uncle Ganen magnanimously took them in. He was the one of our family who had left for Europe quite young and by now he was living the bohemian life in an enormous but ramshackle flat in Saint-Germain. He may have been an artist, but he also had opportunistic ambitions. So of course he seduced and married the eldest of the three. Not for love, I should add, but presumably for the money or the standing. Wasn't she a princess, after all?

When the couple returned to Ethiopia to take possession of her heritage, the Emperor summoned them. He had a gentle way of doing so, beckoning one with a soft but imperious hand. He always spoke just above a whisper and expressed his ideas gently. You cannot be married to your own sister, he told Ganen. Our customs will not permit it. I hereby dissolve your union. In any event, Western civil weddings mean nothing to us.

And that was that. To understand this you must know that your great-grandmother's father was the brother of Makonen, the King's father. He was a great warrior, this maternal great-great-grandfather of yours. With his vassals he had conquered and pacified the region around Harrar. It must have been about then that the French boy, Rimbaud, trafficked his arms in the area. Maybe he even flogged some guns to the family!

Your great-grandmother, though, had spent her youth in the vicinity of the more recent capital, Addis Ababa ('the new flower') where at 8000 feet above sea level, another conquering king had rested his horses and his eyes. There she was brought up by one of her uncles and his wife. They were warlords all, and the vast stretches of land they administered had also been won in some war or other. When she was only twelve years old, the elders promised her in marriage. It was the done thing then, to ensure that the bride is still a virgin. Usually a first divorce followed shortly afterwards; the marriage could be repudiated easily enough by either party, and if there was sexual incompatibility it could even be dissolved on the very night of the blood-letting.

Some time during that period your future great-grandfather arrived in the country from his native land. No one knows for sure why he came there, nor from where exactly. Maybe he had something of the sea in his veins. I must warn you that there is a streak of lawlessness staining your lineage. We think, family lore has it, that he was an exile, that he had to leave his native climes because of a murder he'd committed, thus besmirching the soil of the ancestors. If so, he would have been obliged to become a roving penitent abroad, dragging his guilt from village to village until such time as he could earn enough money to go make amends to the victim's next of kin.

It is said that when the vagabond finally had the necessary blood money in hand, he returned to his home village only to find it deserted. A terrible drought – so endemic to our part of the world – had swept over the land, killing fowls and livestock and shepherds, blackening vine and wheat and making skeletons of the olive trees. A dry wind played in the dust of the empty courtyards. Only one very old blind man still lived under a lean-to, and the prodigal son was too horrified to even approach the ancient survivor. Never was he going to be allowed to pay off his guilt. He left the land of his birth for good.

Anyway, during his wanderings the unfortunate sinner one day came to present himself to your great-grandmother's ward, the uncle, and asked for land to start a dairy for making cheeses and yoghourts – a trade he'd learned in his faraway youth. The country-side thereabouts is docile and hospitable. The hills are green and fat. Permission was granted readily enough. He was the first really light-coloured man your great-grandmother ever laid eyes on.

She was with the cows in the pastures when he passed by on his horse, sitting mighty and straight like a god. So impressed she was – she thought he must be a god – that she shied away under the rumbling belly of one of the ruminants. (I remember her telling us that cows have waterfalls in their stomachs.) The man never even noticed her. Remember, she was about to be given away in wedlock, she was only a child still, and beautifully bashful.

Then something else occurred, nobody knows what. She must have done something wayward, perhaps angering a house deity, which would certainly have been inexcusable. We have all forgotten what caused the incident. There are shadows in the family tree, rotten fruit swinging in the breeze, bats and the skeletons of bars, which we all pretend not to notice. Whatever it was, and maybe she simply baulked at the prospect of being wed, she decided to leave home. Away she ran, her feet jumping like frogs after the rain.

During that time, once every three days, a serf took two big containers of milk to the pale-faced horseman's cheese factory – a distance of fourteen kilometres. Our hapless migrant had in the mean time established a flourishing business. The servant used to carry the containers on a pole slung over his shoulders. Your great-grandmother was small of stature. And she went up to the slave and said: 'Please take me with you to the god's house.' He was aghast, stood there trembling as big as he was, because he knew that he'd surely be run through with a sword if it were ever to become known that he'd helped the child bride abscond. But your great-grandmother was mulish. She pleaded with him, promising him all her gold jewellery, and he hid her in one of the containers and carried her fourteen kilometres. There he left her sitting in the pot like a foetus waiting to be born.

Half a day and a night passed and a new morning dawned with the flushed indignation of roosters. Soon it was one o'clock (your seven a.m. in Europe), and the farmer heard a plaintive whimpering coming from his barn. He knew that no new-born calf was due, located the sobs echoing in a jar, went up for a closer look, and to his dismay discovered the small girl-woman inside. He lifted her out and she fell at his feet, clinging to his trousers to implore his protection. What was he to do? Had he sent her back to her uncle for chastisement the family history would have taken a completely different course and I would not have been here to write your story. Who is to know what went on in this wistful foreigner's mind? Could he have interpreted the event as divine intervention, God's beckoning finger showing him the means by which finally to atone for his sins, at last to expiate to his fellows on this earth his own debt of blood?

He took her into his house. Surely, in due time, however guiltily, also into his bed. She had small rough feet. It was only months later, once your great-grandmother was starting to show the swellings of a well-churned happiness, that the pale god decided (was prevailed upon, I'd think) to find a way of normalizing the spilt milk about to become cheese. He put her on the back of a mule, mounted his horse – traditionally only the men are allowed on horseback, the women straddle mules or donkeys – and off they set for the homestead of her uncle and her aunt.

The complicitous slave saw them coming over the horizon, was petrified, shook himself like a wet dog, grabbed stick and *couta* and fled into the hills. The menfolk in the family had come out on to the veranda. They wore daggers hidden under their *netelas* – the fine and embroidered lengths of cotton which the rich wrap around their bodies. Your great-grandmother demurely sat her mule some way off while the lord and benefactor went to palaver with her kinfolk. (But her dark eyes must have flashed keenly from the shadow hooding her face.)

Sunlight dappled the bluegum leaves, ricocheted from the rich apparel of the steeds in the farmyard. Certainly the talks took a considerable time doing the rounds of many mouths, and hinged upon the matters of compensation for insulted honour as also upon that of religion. These and other sensitive sentiments had to be smoothed over before matters could take a turn for the better. Nobody knew very much about the comings and goings of this man – there is a tradition, for what it's worth, that the family never really took to liking him – but he was more than old enough for marriage, and evidently a hard worker. Tradition also has it that he was a dandy, so particular about his appearance that he changed his white suit every day, a clean silk handkerchief flowering from the top pocket, and the horse had to be groomed to a shimmer as well. To his honour it must however be said that he was one of the rare palefaces willing to legalize his bedship with a native woman. (But she was an aristocrat, and left him no choice!) Once he'd convinced the clan that he too was a Christian, the *fait accompli* was sealed by handclasps to be duly followed by a wedding ceremony and a feast. Within weeks the pact thus entered upon became rapidly more visible.

Your great-grandmother was called Ioubit, the beautiful one. As for your great-grandfather, he entered the clan's annals as Mikael. He must have doted on his young wife – he would do anything to make her life more attractive and less boring. He bought European shoes for her tiny chapped feet.

The slave, Tsahai, who'd fled so precipitously when he saw Ioubit and Mikael coming to within shouting distance at he time of the negotiations, after some days was seen roaming around the outhouuses. He was too scared to ake a clean breast, but sat hiding behind some shrubs quite near by where he could clear his throat and whistle like a bird, hoping that someone would come and investigate and find him as it were accidentally. Already he was as thin as a stick from hunger. Ioubit lured him forth with a promise of butter. On the day of the wedding he duly changed owners as part of your great-grandmother's dowry, and he was promptly put in charge of the household.

Master Mikael instructed Tsahai to look after the young mistress while he was away inspecting pastures and barns – as closely as if he were looking after his own eyes, he said. To Ioubit Mikael entrusted the keys to pantry and storehouse, and he told her that everything he possessed was henceforth hers to use with the discretion of responsibility.

On the night of the first day Great-Grandfather Mikael returned home and asked Tsahai for news of his young wife, how the day had been, was she happy, was she sad, and was told that the jewel of his eyes was upstairs. But, Tsahai said, she spent all her waking hours in one room, seemingly pining for something nobody knows. Mikael climbed the stairs and found your great-grandmother sitting facing a big locker in the room where he kept the few personal relics of his past. He clucked his tongue, straightened his waistcoat and said something like: 'Now, now, little bird of my heart, what are you doing all alone up here in the dark?' She most likely replied that she was no warbling fool like Tsahai, and asked: 'What do you have in this chest?' And he would have answered: 'Oh, this and that only. Nothing really, come now.' And certainly she then pouted her lips and became miserable and kicked off her shoes.

The days woke up with the speechmaking roosters and went to bed with the long-horned cattle mumbling their evening prayers as if chewing the cud, and the chest – big enough to have been a coffin – became the only obsession of the pregnant bride. She even neglected the ceremony of the coffee. Neighbours and servants alike took to whispering behind their hands. At night, when your great-grandfather returned from his labours, he'd find her sitting with speechless lips in the greening dusk. So he took an old key from the watch-chain in his pocket and without a word laid it on the lid of the chest. But when evening once more folded its tent he found Ioubit in the same position in the same chair with the very same dully shining key lying untouched on the dark wood.

Next morning he called Tsahai and together they carried the heavy chest down the steps to the bottom of the garden. Your great-grandmother in her white nightdress, her hair wild and her hands folded over the belly, watched, from an upstairs window. Tsahai dug a hole as deep as his superstition and the two men lowered the chest on ropes. Your great-grandfather took his hat in his hand and stood very silent for a long while – although the early wind fluttered his lips – before throwing the key on top of the unopened box, and Tsahai shovelled red soil into the hole.

Ioubit has come down the breath of our telling as a headstrong woman with a flame-like mind. There is an old photo showing the set of her beautiful lips, her high brown forehead and the straight no-nonsense look of her eyes – and two bandoleers crossing her breasts! It was not uncommon for a woman of her station to take part in the skirmishes pitting a king against his usurpers. When the Italians invaded the country (which they knew as Abyssinia, Arab for 'land of the mixed-bloods'), she retreated to the mountains with her elder sons, from there to sally forth in pitiless guerrilla sorties against the occupant, screaming defiance, and leaving Mikael on his estates to his cheeses.

It is recounted that the first batch of Italian soldiers who came to steal our land soon merged with the population, taking up quarters with its beautiful females. Ethiopian girls have lovely shoulders. Mussolini learned of these lackadaisical mores so unbecoming to a race of conquerors (what? getting straddled by the natives!), had a jowl-quivering fit, and promptly sent in his Black Shirts to go separate the wheat from the chaff and root out the rot. As his shock troops entered Addis with a cadenced step, women ran ahead of them through the streets shouting *soldati! soldati!* to warn their lovers to take refuge with local families in loft and garden-shack and at the bottom of wells where water is a black mirror. To this day we say *soldati* for 'coward' in Amharic.

Mikael leaves our story as he entered it, at a dignified gait – a well-dressed but effaced old gentleman, he was so much older than her, sitting a straight horse and wiping his chin. From his union with Ioubit five children were born, four boys and a girl – the last one was to be your grandmother, Wolete Mikaele.

All of this I was told by our grandmother who has one all-important principle in life: never to tell a truth. She believes in evil and in magic, and that the only way to keep bad luck and envy and the bulging blue eye of terrible intentions away from reality is to change same constantly.

(In which Barnum, the ghost writer, comes to the fore and nudges an elbow to present figures for a book and the beginning of a relationship.)

There is an international congress of writers in the town of Mont Aigu, in Switzerland. Meheret flies there on a grey morning, winds buffeting the tiny aircraft, the door leading to the cockpit banging open, the pilot fighting the controls to keep the plane from yawing, over the border and suddenly the rim and the run of sharp white peaks, down through valleys, dark lakes. The town is stretched along the edge of a dark lake.

The town is not pretentious. In the centre, around arcaded squares, the houses are big with heavy leaded windows behind balconies, but around the frames one sees the delicate tracery of patterns in stone. Some houses have a Nordic yellowish colour, others are stained ochre. The people who dwell here speak Italian but they behave like Swiss. They are calm and ponderous, they drive carefully, obeying the traffic signals. It is as if having come into a town where the locals have taken to the hills or are cowering in the cellars, the immigrant Italian squatters are now trying hard to be on their best behaviour. Provided you keep to a decent pace you may perhaps escape drawing undue attention to yourself and thus avoid being expelled to the poor South. They are still a mite stiff in the staid clothes of the original inhabitants. Only their speech betrays the origins: with palate and tongue they fashion words as if enjoying a meal where the one dish must build into the voluptuous delectation of the next.

The place is seedy, dated, a bit mournful. End-of-an-epoch feeling in the air. Cavernous hotels with ballrooms lit by chandeliers. Off the lake the light comes in low. Geese sweep over the water. Dogs bite back their barks and trot responsibly, tail at the correct bourgeois angle, alone or at the clicking heels of their mistresses, down the promenade. An old man sits by himself on a bench, gently reminiscing with his walking stick. His mind is a walking stick. The ghosts of counts are kissing the hands of ladies wearing loops of pearls and long dresses. The ladies play whist in the polished halls and wait in vain for mail from distant places. Their estates are hocked, their underclothes darned, they have flat feet and their lovers suffer from the wasting disease. Restaurants are roomy and empty, the waiters solicitous with their moustached smiles, the fish from the lake and the fresh asparagus from the valleys tenderly prepared. The white wine is worth twirling your lips at. The white

19

wine sings of the bottled liquid sun of another season. The white wine sings a time-fugue leaving as echo a pale liquid.

She comes to the conference with the intention of meeting and talking to Farrah, a Somali writer now exiled to Khartoum. She is gathering material for a thesis on the role of the intellectual in fractured African societies. Maybe she will even write a book about the question, or about closely related matters. Maybe she will write a diary, or develop the need to write letters.

The meeting turns out to be a crashing non-event. Delegates with angry cheeks debate heatedly behind closed doors on policies which cannot in any way impinge upon the real world. They have to make up their minds whether they ought to go to Seoul next for their annual meeting. The first thing you do at a meeting is to decide where next to meet. The South Koreans are ubiquitous. A hefty delegation of buxom ladies in colourful traditional garb and gentlemen with grey-suited double breasts bow and scrape to hand out stacks of free publications intended to woo the votes of brother and sister countries. Their faces are frozen in gentle snarls. It so happens that a few hand-stroked presidents of national chapters of the organization – known individually for their thick-skinned and paranoid anti-communism – had fortuitously already been to the land of Early Blossoms, there to be wined and dined and woman-numbed and discreetly to be provided with financial arguments. With these arguments in mind they will now democratically insist that Congress vote to go to Seoul. Why on earth not? Could one so heinously slight gentle Korean faces by disdaining the invitation? Democracy? Did I hear the honourable colleague say democracy? But isn't it generally understood that the niceties of that admirable system (to which we *all* subscribe or aspire) be provisionally left in abeyance when faced by a totalitarian onslaught? Elsewhere, in another mouth, in another country, it will turn out to be: individual freedom stops where the interests of the state commence.

The open sessions are harangued by sententious 'experts' or 'witnesses'. The theme: 'The Writer and Frontiers'. Speakers and stupefied audience alike seem to have old-fashioned hand-trained moustaches or blushing fish-naked pates. Even clean mouths hold forth with the well-chewed authority of hirsute lips. Men and women are draped in the ample layers of the well-fed bookworm. Those too poor or too young for moustache or cranial mirror can at least sport a literary paunch or library buttocks. Most women wear shapeless dresses of an immemorial fashion. A few in the front row have fingers blued by jewellery, fur coats camouflaging the bulging strategic regions now seldom coveted by imperialists, dark glasses to go with the shady upper lips. The speakers get themselves entangled in lines of linguistic or religious or regional demarcations of the decadent and morose world of a criss-crossed Europe. Afternoon drones on with its furry body getting progressively more sluggish. The mind relinquishes its anxious need to know whether it is day or night outside.

It is probably good for such a congregation to exist. The fuddled-minded ones, the charitable hearts, the never-never authors also need their very own whacky club.

At least they are off the streets and don't risk messing up the bumpers of the cars they may have been run over by.

A man called Barnum takes his turn behind the microphone on the stage. Meheret knows about him because she'd gone to test his views at the time of the publication of his first book, following upon an early release from a South African prison. It was like waiting for the angel to finger the water. Many people seem to spend time in captivity and they all want to write books about it. Therefore she is familiar with the story he is spinning now, and pays only half an ear of attention. He is reading a paper called *Tortoise Steps;* he seems cocksure up there. Ostensibly he is flaying the liberal sentiments in the hall, and they are lapping it up with small sighs caressing civilized tongues. When he concludes they applaud him with the enthusiasm of couch-broken patients, happy to be proved guilty. A few fur coats go over to congratulate his fingers and an old body who had died somewhat during the performance now comes to a spotty imitation of life, cups a shell-like claw behind one hard ear to inquire in a querulous whine: 'What? Which young man? What did he say?' Barnum leaves the hall in the company of someone who'd been sitting at the back.

A while later she comes upon the two of them in the ground floor cafeteria where over beers they seem to be indulging in animated conversation. When Barnum sees her he gets up, and in his best French he invites her to join them.

'Put down your machine,' he says, motioning to her recorder. He is still flushed with the success of his peroration. He laughs: 'Please, no interviews.' (Vain idiot, she thinks; as if I'd be interested in hearing a replay of the obvious!) 'Let me introduce you to a countryman of mine, Mano. He's from the Cape. Mano, this pretty lady works in publishing, eh –'

'Meheret. I don't work for anybody.'

'I beg yours?'

'Meheret. My name is Meheret. It means *miséricorde*.'

'Of course, I know. As you can see, she's from Africa too.'

Mano smiles a lazy eel of a smile at the self-evident observation. Their eyes touch looks. His is quizzical, slithering over her neck, her breasts, her wrists, her belly, but he doesn't say anything. Her glance takes in the man with the mop of wiry hair, the broad potato nose and the judge-like cheekbones, the pebbly green eyes set in the olive skin. He could pass for an Arab, but she recognizes the hesitation, the touchiness, the false bravado of someone ill at ease with his identity. He must be what is known as a Cape Coloured. Barnum has pulled up a chair for her.

'Are you a writer too?'

Mano doesn't answer. He grimaces, picks up his mug for another swig of foam-lipped beer. Like an eel hitting brown river-water.

Barnum looks from the one to the other, as proud as Punch, as if he'd pulled the two of them from a hat. 'He's an actor. Theatre actor. We're working together on the project for a film. That's why we are here together, isn't it so, Mano? To try and make contact in Switzerland. This is where the big black money is, if you can make them cough it up.'

'If banks can spit, you mean.'

Soon they are joined at table by a jovial Swedish publisher bringing two crinkly blue eyes, a blond quiff sticking up in front of his face, and two intricate cufflinks hampering his handshake. Barnum and Per – he is called Per – swap views on the people and the proceedings. They laugh a lot. More beer is ordered. When Per bulges his neck to laugh, his face becomes red and shiny and a silver tooth winks in his mouth. If the tooth is a lighthouse, the mouth is a moth.

'Oh dear,' Per sighs, taking out an old pocket-watch and squinting at it through his blue tears. 'I'll have to go. I have this appointment with *ja-ja* the Djerman delegation. They want my advice. Do you *ja-ja* think I have anything I can tell them? What should I suggest?' Between two segments of a phrase he inserts the periods of *ja-ja* produced as if from a finger stuck deep down the throat. Like chewing the tongue to hide a slight shakiness of the words.

'But, I say, why don't we meet for supper?'

It is agreed that they will all get together at eight cuckoos in a restaurant on the lake front. Barnum suddenly remembers that he too has an interview appointment. Mano gives her a long rippling look, and asks: 'Will you walk with me?'

He lifts the straps of her recording machine over his shoulder and they start walking through the narrow streets winding up the hill. The grey morning has been softened to the haze of a silverish afternoon.

Here then are the two protagonists alone together for the first time. This is the beginning when two people who don't know one another, who already know without knowing that they are going to be lovers – in fact they'd be shocked by the suggestion of that knowledge – are sensitive to the contours of words and of eyeflight. She thinks that she can find no reason to like this stranger, she's not missing a man in her life or her bed, he doesn't stimulate any dream image. He doesn't even look as if he could have a dagger strapped to his leg. He would be no comfort against the snow, no security when the policeman knocks. There is little in him to remind her of Africa except perhaps for his rather prominent buttocks worn high and a faint odour impregnating his shirt. He finds her exotically beautiful with her shiny brown skin, the slim figure and the proud undulating bearing of the people of the Horn, her very short hair combed to a halo, the eyebrows urgently growing together to meet in a frown. But not sexy, no. He thinks: she is not sexy at all. Already he is sad that she will lose her mysteriousness to him, and he is sorry because he is going to hurt her. Knowing is hurting. Leave the flowers alone.

Their words touch and shy away. They point out to one another things they like or find funny in the shop windows. They agree that the Swiss must be the funniest people on earth. She tells him about the town – she's been here before – the old centre and the yellow colours of the house fronts; the merchants with their aprons and their white hand-wringing, their solid ideas, their placid lives, their smooth forearms; the careful people living on tip-toe in their cellars. She doesn't ask about his country nor does she probe into the reasons for his living abroad. He thinks she must of course be intrigued by his origins but that she doesn't dare ask; he dreads the moment when she will break the charm and start mouthing the platitudes people always do when they know you are from the land of blood and shame. He will have to slip away into the water. An exile lives abroad as a moon does in a lake.

He says he would quite like to live in a town like this, far away from the mainstream, the notion of edge-life attracts him, it must be calm and rich. The centres have become too self-absorbed, harried, imploding to madness and soot and broken bottles. Edges are more authentic. 'Would you want to stay for ever in Europe?' he asks.

'Why ever not? I have left nothing in Africa. The revolution . . .'

He looks at her. 'Tell me.'

She shrugs and turns her eyebrows away. Now he shifts her recording machine to the other shoulder. The noses of his shoes are scuffed. He says to her that it is all very well to be an individualist. It probably allows one to develop your talents to the full. The world needs strong creators, iconoclasts, the selfish and the self-absorbed. Even the Three Continents do, so as to have their own Cultural Role Figures. But what is the case ultimately? A man severed from his own community becomes inoperative. Depending on which community, evidently. 'I mean, one must decide which community you belong to. Where I come from –'

He coughs. He very nearly succumbed to the temptation of telling her he has the feeling of having a choice. Would she understand that? And the excruciating sense of guilt this brings about? Because it implies rejection, surely. 'I am attracted by opposites. That may be why I am a strolling player. You see, an actor must fashion his life around that of the character or the ideas or the tradition he's trying to portray. He must make an abstraction of himself, like the chameleon. He is the imitator moving over foreign territory in such a way that his life will not be endangered. The actor as a person must become invisible. Just a situation of view, a transit point, an impersonation – better still, a translation. For me this raises the fascinating relationship between illusion and reality. And the fact that illusion is not less real than reality, indeed it can even be more real since one apprehends reality through an imitation or a reconstruction thereof.'

Here he stops to laugh, and then he says it explains why the actor is an egomaniac, a part-time god. 'The more you suppress the ego, the stronger it manifests itself. You cannot keep a good man down. Because he is, of course, also a real person. I mean, I am real. With my own emotions, desire, history.' He says he is sorry to get carried away like that on the wings of thinking, that he must be boring her to tears. She protests no, no, not at all.

'Not at all,' she says.

Again she doesn't ask him about his history, nor about the emotions he may have to handle while living the imitation (mutation) of a normal life so far from his natural environment. He doesn't get the chance to quote to her his favourite aphorism, the one about exile being the living proof that death doesn't kill.

The road takes them to the top of a hill. A church is built there, imposing its grey baroque front on the skyline. At their feet, beyond the parapet, the city swoops away with red roofs and yellow walls, further back there is the sullen lake with a dark depth to it, further still the green mountain slopes which seem to back up the lake. The sinking sun precipitously plunges through the cloud cover and dramatically paints the whole scene in garish colours as if to decorate some theatre for a tear-jerker. 'No, I don't think I could live here after all,' she muses. 'The landscape is too pretty to exist. I should think one would become very languid, covered with moss, sitting by the lake-side to throw pebbles at the ducks and waiting for a letter from a far-away lover.'

'And it probably gets as cold as hell in winter,' he adds.

The scene below them is bathed in an emerald glow. A flock of birds – geese? – fly in line over the water, their wing tips nearly touching the surface to disturb the mirror-face. He points out a distant rooftop which looks flat. A little girl seems to be figure-skating there, spinning, running, throwing up her arms. 'Probably dreaming about becoming a famous ballerina,' he chuckles. 'Don't you think people invent themselves that way? When you are young you spend at least half your time in a dream world. Everything is still possible. Is it a biological necessity to dream that much, stretching the awareness in order to get to understand the world? Or blunting the horrors of it? I wonder if we are not the result of our dreams, and the world the sum total of our awareness? Have you noticed the way little boys walk about, oblivious of the real world, with hats too big for them falling over the eyes? They go *bang! bang!*, firmly believing they're Gary Cooper.'

The light is starting to leak ink, the first street lamps are turned on.

'Maybe Gary Cooper thought he was a small boy,' she smiles.

Slowly, now speaking to himself, he continues: 'In Africa there's a warrior called Soundiata. The man of the many names, son of the buffalo and son of the lion. It is said that he founded the Mandingue empire, that he was a stout fighter, conquering all, never beaten . . . I think of him as a bird with blue and green and red feathers. His shoulders are heavy and his feet are dusty and he has a piece of skin tied around the forehead. He moves in the night, sometimes in the deep shadows on the ground, sometimes very high in the

25

sky, sliding like a blemish over the face of the moon. He always turns up when people are really in need, when they are down-trodden. He was in the Congo with Lumumba, in Guinea-Bissau with Amilcar Cabral, in Burkina Faso with Sankara. He likes beer and women. When he shows up the cattle start lowing and it even happens that they break from the enclosures of thorny branches. He's not evil though – people are only afraid of his virtue. And many women claim to be pregnant by him! When he disappears he leaves behind a single red or green feather. This is the feather that will turn into a boy child or a girl child.'

'I have a parrot in Paris,' she says in the dusk.

'Then you must watch out not to become pregnant!'

'No danger! Did you grow up in the country?'

'No. I'm a city boy. Rather, a suburb boy. Better still, a location kid. And the only stories I heard as a child were about ghosts, or bad people changing themselves into baboons to put a jinx on innocent folk and their houses. It rained stones in the night, I swear! And the moon would be red with blood. Must have been our Malay legacy. We had a wide range of traditions to choose from.'

'But Soundiata?'

'A nice story. Actually part of a script I once had to learn, a play called *The Earth Speech*. You learn and then you unlearn, your self becomes a slippery eel. Still, I believe in Soundiata the bird who goes to battle with his scarred body for the miserable, miscreant Africans. Don't you?'

In the gathering gloom they try to have a closer look at the church façade. It is decorated with satanic motifs – people in the cusp of fire, people coupling with mythical beasts, severed heads offering thick protruding tongues. She stands on tip-toe to see better. He inhales the oily smell of her hair, feels the smell in the back of his throat, feels the warmth of her body close to his chest. 'A man dreams the perfect woman,' he murmurs. She turns around, sur-prised to find herself within the circle of his arms. With one hand he lifts her chin and then he brings his lips down on hers. They are exchanging breaths. They hear somebody clearing a throat, they break apart and notice two old ladies in black hobbling by, not turning their heads, but their eyes are stiff and walled white.

'I'm getting cold,' she says, 'and the others must be waiting.'

'There will be a moon tonight. Wouldn't it be wonderful to forget them and go rowing out over the lake, you and I alone?'

They are nevertheless the first ones to reach the restaurant. They laugh and joke and study the menu very attentively so as to hide their unease from one another. There is a shyness between them as of an apprehensive moon rising over the lake, playing hide and seek with thickening clouds.

Then Per comes in in a rush, flustered at being late. He'd lost his way between Djermany and the lake. He loosens his tie and suggests ordering some ice-cold Polish vodka. 'I am the host *ja-ja*,' he insists. And to the waiter: 'What kind of vodka you haf?' The waiter salutes with one finger laid next to the moustache, enters into the third depth of meditation, calls over his wine list colleague who bends an attentive ear and gets all confused over Per's no-no *ja-ja* order. Barnum arrives as they are about to decide what nosh they'd like, looking a bit pooped. He must have been waylaid by some other highway interviewers.

Per fishes up a pair of quaint half-glasses to study the menu, scratches his head, goes all red in the face, laughs. They finally settle for lake fish to be served with fresh asparagus and cooled white wine from the region. Would anyone like an eel? No? There are helpings of light banter. From time to time Per sits back, lays down knife and fork, looks at them with his kindly blue eyes and says: 'Oh, but I'm *ja-ja* so happy!' He is genuinely surprised that a man as reticent as he could have such a warm glow of well-being.

Over coffee Per arranges his features and takes from a wallet three snapshots of his first grand-daughter. There is one of him smiling all his teeth at her over her cot, inviting her to the coast of affection. Her name, he says, is Elise *ja-ja*. He is as proud as only a grandfather insanely in love with life and its mysteries could be. But sad too, because he senses that he is already on the downhill scuttle, and curious to imagine the universe she will grow up to. 'How the world would have changed when she's twenty,' he sighs, 'And she will never know *ja-ja* what our world was. Isn't it fantastic?' And he sits back again, torn between sentiments of puzzlement and happiness.

The theme is taken up by the others and soon Barnum and Per are enthusiastically discussing the makings of a book. Several writers will be approached to write a summing-up of their world, or a projection of the one they expect to exist twenty years hence. These writings will be collected and printed as *A Letter to Elise*. They are even now drawing up a list of names of writers. Barnum has taken off his jacket and is noting down spiders and flies and moths which he will certainly lose.

After the meal they decide to go to the reception for congressists in the Hôtel du Lac. Meheret is not very keen; she's not dressed up for it. But you will be Alice in Wonderland, they tell her. When they arrive at the hotel, rain has started slipping from the dark skies.

In the halls with their glittering chandeliers from high ceilings, old gentlemen with waxed pates are kissing the hands of mummified ladies encased in long dresses and loops of pearls. A band starts up. Now the *Titanic* will sink all over again. Mano turns to her and says, as if inviting her to follow the ways of the eel: 'Will you dance with me?'

The rigmarole of lights as Mano twirls Meheret over the floor. The shared joy of hot blood coursing through two young bodies. The strangeness and the familiarity of discovering each other's rhythms. At a central table a late hobnobbing of writers is in full session. Food is still being served. People look at the dancers and purse their smiles, afraid to lose their small change, nod their heads, judge their knees briefly. Most have forgotten all about syncopation. Many of them are mourning the demise of European Culture. Some, including a delegation of very hungry, shiny-suited Polish authors, have drawn up their chairs as close as possible to that of Milosz. They have respectful necks and doleful eyes and they nod their heads in sage enthusiasm at the grunts falling from the great man's lips. When the heads don't nod, they tremble. Then their eyes follow the movements of the fork shovelling food back into the mouth of wisdom to replenish the grunts. Barnum too has edged his chair up to the outer reaches of this magic cluster. He must assume that his grey hair is giving him access to the age of respectability, and he hopes thus by association unobtrusively to identify with the great wordmasters.

In another hall, empty now but for a few obstinate roisterers and waiters walking by with huge white napkins in their hands (they are clearing glasses off the tables, pouring left-overs in one tumbler, rapidly gulping same down from a crouched position behind a bar or a table hoping not to be seen), Per lifts his glass high to drink to happiness. 'Don't take *ja-ja* the bottle away yet, my good man,' he says to one of the white-vested scavengers. He pats his hair into place and laughs. He would have liked to share his hard-won insights on the function of intellectuals with the girl, Meheret, but through the open doors he sees her in a swirl of light among the dancing couples. They will be grinding their hips. Anyway, his eyelids are becoming lazy. His chest is swollen with warmth and the bulge of the wallet in an inside pocket. Better to live today than to die tomorrow.

Much later still, when Mano and the young woman leave the Hôtel du Lac to look for a taxi, the rain has become a rustling thick grey curtain darkening the stage of night. The walk-on actors have gone home. The lake is invisible, the moon eclipsed. It must be somehow just across the road, black and brooding. The mountains will be getting thoroughly soaked.

In the taxi she mentions the name of the hotel she's staying at, and he gives the address of friends putting him up. She says: 'I've lugged this heavy machine around the whole day and I haven't fed it a single word. I haven't even met Farrah, the man I came here for. If I'd kept it running I could at least have taped our silences.'

He says: 'I think the moon is taking a midnight dip in the lake.'

She asks: 'In the rain?'

The car is swishing like an eel through the watery night. He says: 'There's nothing nicer than swimming in the rain.' And then: 'You have a pretty name, but I'm not sure I like it. You are so distant, so difficult to reach. Let me dream . . . I think I'll call you . . . Greta. Do you mind?'

Later he says: 'Exile is the living proof that death doesn't kill.' A pause. Then he puts his hand over hers: 'Will you stay the night with me? I'm afraid of the moon.'

(Where I, Barnum, put myself in Meheret's position to write a reflection called 'A Touch of the Moon'.)

I think I've written this scene before, but I'll write it once again. In a boat, midway upon the lake, sit a man and a woman. High above in the dark sky stands the moon. The night is still and warm, just right for this dreamy love adventure. Is the man in the boat an abductor? Is the woman the happy, enchanted victim? This we don't know; we only see how they both kiss each other. The dark mountain lies like a giant on the glistening water. On the shore lies a castle or country house with a lighted window. No noise, no sound. Everything is wrapped in a black, sweet silence. The stars tremble high above in the sky and also upward from far below out of the sky which lies on the surface of the water. The water is the friend of the moon, it had pulled it down to itself, and now they kiss, the water and the moon, like boyfriend and girlfriend. The beautiful moon has sunk into the water like a daring young prince into a flood of peril. He is reflected in the water like a beautiful affectionate soul reflected in another love-thirsty soul. It's marvellous how the moon resembles the lover drowned in pleasure, and how the water resembles the happy mistress hugging and embracing her kingly love. In the boat, the man and the woman are completely still. A long kiss holds them captive. The oars lie lazily on the water. Are they happy, will they be happy, the two here in the boat, the two who kiss one another, the two upon whom the moon shines, the two who are in love? They are happy. The light in the window of the country house has been switched off. It's marvellous how the lover resembles the moon drowned in pleasure and the mistress is like water lapping around the thighs of her kingly love. The bed is a boat midway through the night. No noise, no sound. A long kiss holds them captive. Their limbs lie lazily on the sheets as white as the blood of the moon. I think I've written this scene before, but I'll write it once again. 'Are you afraid?' the lover asks his mistress. Everything is wrapped in a black, sweet silence. Her lips tremble in the dark space above him and also upward from far below where an oar has penetrated the water. It is like putting the moon to the sword. The moon has impaled her trembling on the oar. The oar is the friend of the moon, it has pulled it down to itself, and now they kiss, the boyfriend and the girlfriend, like moon and water. Water flows from her mouth. Slowly the boat of the bed is rocked into motion until moonlight drips from the oar. The dark pleasure lies like a giant on the glistening water. In the boat, the man and the woman are completely still. High above the moon has been swallowed by the dark sky. Are they happy, will they be happy for ever, the two here in the bed, the two who kiss one another, the two who have eaten the dark and soft moon of love? This we don't know; we only see how they both kiss each other. When they wake in the morning it is still drizzling outside. The empty boat floats on the mirror. Down by the lake rubber-clothed policemen are dredging the dark depths for the sodden corpse of the moon.

3

Last night I dreamed that I was travelling on the back of a beautiful lion. I had on my flowery dress and my belly was flat. His name was Fanuel. On and on we went, fast as the wind over the soft green hills of my motherland. The landscape was so delightful, with sun-flecked glades and trees spreading dark-blue perfumed shadows, it was Africa all over, as in a dream. All at once our path was blocked by another lion, a big wild one, an African one (of the kind known as *Panthera leo, bonega* or *gigemdé* in Moré, *dyara* in Dioule, *biladde* or *rawandulade* in Fulani), who immediately wanted to join battle with Fanuel. What was I to do? Although Fanuel was bigger and much more impressive than the other, he would never survive a scrap with the snarling and scarred interloper, I just knew it. The other stood high and taut on its padded paws, the claws being revealed slowly and yellowishly, and light was only a wet veneer on its terrifying fangs. Fanuel had simply become too accustomed to being dreamed about, had gone soft like the tissue of sleep . . .

My belly has grown. Now, when I dream, I am afraid for you. You are vulnerable and blind like a very small lion inside me, and I need to protect you. Dreams can be big black vultures, powerful enough to drop from the sky with the sound of silk being torn, to flutter off with you in their claws, mewing and rubbing your eyes. I am starting to waddle like a bird without wings, pointing the toes of my feet outward, pramming my swollen abdomen in front of me. My back has become straighter, the small hollow more arched. I think I can sense how the cavity in which you are growing is being expanded. You are making your nest. My diaphragm must be lifted higher, because I seem to take less food, to be sated quicker – or is it my imagination? At night I feel my ribs being pushed apart, to make room for you. Am I dreaming? There are painful swellings under my breasts. I think I can hear a creaking and a cracking. Am I the ark and you the black whale slowly getting bigger until you can burst asunder the joists of my body to break free into your native element, dive and gambol among the floating debris?

Your grandfather, my father, also had a lion for many years . . .

I cannot tell you much about Guebre Gsiaber's parents. They were of emigrant stock, having moved to the capital from somewhere on the coast. It is certain that they weren't of the Highlands. Both died when I was still very small and before my brother, your uncle, was born. I have a childhood memory snapshot of arriving at a house with a big garden. Weeds are lining the path and ants are swarming over the dark-red calyxes of the hibiscus bush. On a veranda, sitting back so as to be in the shade, an old couple – thin, black, leathery, a fly as big as a winged thumb crawling over the white shawl covering the old woman's head, moving down in invisible writing over her forehead. The upper part of her bust, from the breasts to the sagging jaw-line, is tattooed in an intricate dark-blue pattern. The eye too could be a fly getting lost in the labyrinthine byways of beauty.

In our part of the world women really run the show, the more so when they have to live on the dark side in the shadow of visible society, not part of men's public prancing and dancing. For each woman, even the poorest, the household is a kingdom to be admin-istered with a severe hand. I am talking now of the real rulers of the Three Continents. Before, during the time of feudal privileges, they could organize the estates of their husbands; now, in our modern states of unemployment, and so often in exile, they still express that same urge to exercise power in a much more limited territory – they command what's left of their families. In so doing they become capricious, like fat, caged lionesses. When they were part of the ruling caste in a poor country (and their richness was a matter of status only – their world a heady mixture of corruption, misery, duplicity, obscurantism, illiteracy, superstition, just like that of the lowly serfs), the women turned their husbands and particu-larly their sons into ne'er-do-wells. The sons were reared for gaming, gambling and playing the cock among the females. Now that the mothers have been dispossessed and live in more straitened circumstances, they cosset their sons, allow them to satisfy their puerile whims, do everything possible to have them escape the 'normal' strictures of society; they make of their male offspring spoilt drifters. In fact they themselves have always been marginal and now they live out the last glow of a non-existent glory in genteel decadence. We are the end of the line. After us oblivion. After us the West.

Guebre Gsiaber grew up poorly. I want to tell you that he was maimed in early life, he never talked about what happened, so that he had one leg shorter than the other. It could have been a defect of birth. This weakness, this handicap – he must have lived it as a curse – definitely shaped his later experiences. Now that I am by the day becoming more conscious of my own way of walking, carrying you like some prayer in my stomach, I often put myself in his place. How the limp must have haunted him. He was a beautiful man. I hope you inherit his dimpled smile, the crinkling of his eyelids against the sun.

At the age of seven he ran away from home to the harbour town of Assab on the Red Sea. Can you imagine what it must be like to be alone in a strange environment at so young an age? Probably he made friends with some of the other rag-tailed kids then living in the streets. Assab was at the time still a busy seaport, often teeming with foreign sailors searching for liquor and dope and easy women or boys. He was a shoe-shine boy. He was a small drug trafficker, running errands for older dealers. His face was grimy and his hands prematurely tough. All the time he had but one obsession: to some-how have his crookedness straightened.

The reason for his going to Assab, of course, was the presence in that town of a distant relative, one of Ethiopia's very first orthope-dists. Maybe a word dropped into the fire in his parents' house alerted him to this wondrous fact, and made him fashion a dream of running. Ultimately he succeeded in tracking down this uncle living in that part of town where houses behind high walls and locked gates climb the gentle slopes of the hill above the sea in a search for healthier air and the cool breezes of evening. He watched the gate, he tried to scale the wall, eventually he wormed himself into the garden and forced his way into the consultation room of his father's 'brother'. He demanded to be operated upon. The doctor refused. Could this madly intense ragamuffin really be related to him?

Guebre Gsiaber went on a hunger strike just outside the gates to the magician's magnificent residence. This was intolerable! The doctor was going to become the subject of scandal! The one and only local newspaper was sure to catch wind of it! What a story it would make! Thinking that he could in this way rid himself of the nuisance, perhaps also already feeling some stirrings of sympathy with the stubborn boy, the doctor told him that nothing could be done without the written permission of his parents. And so Guebre Gsiaber returned to the capital, to the garden overgrown with weeds and the ants mining the sweetness of the hibiscus flowers (a chameleon clung quiet like a leaf to a branch of the bush), to the veranda where his father cleared a raspy throat and spat a sudden streak of liquid and his mother waved the fly away from her forehead. He hobbled towards the house and respectfully went to kiss his ancestor's shoulder.

The orthopedist certainly never expected to see the boy return. But scarcely a week later he was back, thinner in the face, with a sheet of paper duly signed. The doctor effected the first operation of its kind on Guebre Gsiaber: he grafted the bone of a calf on to the shorter leg. I know, it once came to me in a revelation, that the secret formula of memory was engraved on that length of bone which was to be folded over with my father's flesh.

And the slow years of horror started. The hospital, even in the fairly prosperous seaport Assab, was primitive. The wards were overflowing with wailing cast-offs dying without any dignity. In summer (it was always summer) the blue heat engulfed the inadequate buildings and made one's head buzz with the agony of a fly unable to die. A thumb was being screwed into one's head. There was death and the indifference to death. From the age of nine until the age of sixteen Guebre Gsiaber lay in the oven, the wound suppurating, the stench of pus and blood and urine and aseptics becoming part of the grain of his skin. But the graft took! He was going to dance! (He would draw a veil over those years. Sometimes, rarely, when he was in the mood to, he'd smile until his eyes half-closed and a dimple appeared in his cheek, and say: 'Before I was born I was a guinea pig.')

When he walked out of hell he was mad. He had a fiercely flowering star in his head and the permanent smell of decay in his nostrils. Worse – he was poor. First he learned the trade of cobbler. He was to wear a built-up shoe till the end of his days. Maybe, too, his hands remembered the deftness of the shoe-shine boy. One is always served best by oneself. A polished shoe is better than a naked foot. Then he learned how to dance.

At the age of twenty he was the tango champion of all Ethiopia. He could play the guitar and sing. He would dribble smoke from his lips, dangling the cigarette from the corner of his mouth and closing one eye against the curlicues. Then he would take a deep draw before removing the fag to hold it close to the palm between third and fourth finger, the other digits stretched. He danced his way from ballroom to ballroom, from one competition to the next championship. He spoke seven words of Italian and wore a tie-pin.

35

Wolete Mikaele, allowed to go partying primly with her brother, Ganen, saw this light-stepping debonair young man, narrowed her eyes, smiled to herself, turned her face away and fluffed out her hair. He was a good catch, he could be tamed, he would make money, there would be no flies on him but he wouldn't be too clever, his family couldn't have too much of a hold over him. This is how they got married. This is how I was born in the dueness of time, and many years later your uncle, Tekle Haimanot, too.

I cannot possibly situate his life for you. It was too fluid, he was always on the move. He had an itchy foot and a fly like a flame in the head. Maybe there was once a political dimension to his preoccupations. It must have been before the stirrings of liberation turned Africa upside down, our country was already free, the Lion of Judah on the throne, but even so there were activists in the hotels of the capital who talked about colonialism, maybe even about revolution. According to my father a European round about then tried to recruit him for a leftist political cause. This European was a first-class dancer. My father, always game for a bet, suggested that they should settle the matter of recruitment during a dancing competition at the local Armenian Club. He must have won, Guebre Gsiaber, because he never did become involved in politics. Escaped by the skin of his teeth though, he'd say, because had his opponent, the foreigner, not been so weak-sighted, had he not bumped into the ballroom wall, it might well have ended differently with him, Guebre Gsiaber, at the end of time looking into the long black eyes of a firing squad or at the hairy snake of the hangman's rope.

He gambled, he danced, he got mixed up in the craziest schemes. For a time he was the trainer of our first national bicycle team. Just think – cycling at that altitude! The house started smelling of Vaseline and rubbing oil, and multi-coloured jerseys flew from the washing-line. Often he disappeared into the interior, for weeks on end, hunting crocodiles and collecting chameleons. He brought home the knobbly skins of the giant predators, the yard stank of rotting flesh, the chameleons never survived for very long. He had money. He lost money. He made some more money. He wore beautiful dove-grey suits and black shoes so well made you never noticed the hesitation of a difference. My mother, your grandmother, became sleeker. She was more Amhara than Guebre Gsiaber could ever hope to be, she swore. The provincials are fly-farmers, she said. She walked like a nobleman sitting his horse. She started smoking in secret and spent long hours away from home, either at the

Armenian Club (where there was a swimming-pool) or gossiping with her sisters-in-law.

Two gentlemen turned up at our house. Their hair was of a glistening sleek-blue colour, nearly black; they had vigorous moustaches nesting in their red cheeks underneath the noses, completely covering their mouths so that when they spoke one had the impression of people respectfully standing behind screens to whisper low-intensity obscenities. Anyway, they spoke a foreign tongue. They had flashing black eyes. They wore overalls and striped caps. They were his 'guests', my father said, engine drivers, and together they were going to plan and build an extensive railway system all over the country. Heaven was to be brought within reach. There were going to be locomotives steaming through the mountains, white smoke plumes appropriating the skies, my father boasted. He screwed up an eye against the smoke of his cigarette. And once they'd done with the Horn of Africa, he claimed, they were going to do the same all over again in China. It was impossible to distinguish the one 'locomotist' from the other. They were Turks, my father declared. Or perhaps Afghans. These countries were very similar most of the time. In his enthusiasm he even described them as Chinese. There was a fortune to be made: he had the entrepreneurial knack and they the know-how of furnace and piston. One was going to be able to transport crocodiles live to the coast. People could go into the interior to study chameleons and the maturing of clouds. One could imagine a mobile casino, hooked behind an engine, criss-crossing the country. Many stops would be foreseen. At night there would be dancing competitions in the smallest towns. Civilization was on the march . . . The bicycle racing team had disappeared, leaving behind one cannibalized bicycle. For a week the two steam engineers worked at putting it together again. Then they too left for other stations. The dismantled bicycle ended up in Tsahai's quarters.

By then my own memory had taken shape. One of the first people to stand out in my mind, as if moving forward out of that night from which we all emerge – how endlessly dark our past is, an unremembered night filled with dreams, the dreams where all time is already measured out, the dreams we then make true by giving our lives as lining, as substance, dark except for a moon so big it is invisible – one of the first people I remember clearly is Tsahai. He was old and fat and greedy and cunning. Wolete Mikaele had inherited him from Ioubit, again he was part of the dowry. By now he was no longer a slave – slavery had been officially abolished although the nobles carried on as if no such decision had ever been made – but he'd stayed on with the family of his own free desire, and because of his enormous appetite.

He had a terrible weakness for butter. Wolete Mikaele, your grandmother, who showed little interest in running the house, did finally notice that too much money was being spent on buying butter. 'A thief,' Tsahai muttered darkly. He was the overseer of the house, you see, the real boss of the servants. He advised my mother to buy a lock for the big dark cupboard in the storeroom, to keep the butter there. My mother gave him the money and he went to market to buy the lock. He pocketed the change. My mother wore the key to the cache on a chain around her waist. And still the stock of butter kept on melting alarmingly. 'Clever thief,' Tsahai gritted his clenched teeth furiously. 'If I get him . . .' It was quite an unexpected day when Zera Jacob, my sister (not really – she only grew up in our house, but was always considered a child to the family), supposed to be at school, returned home to find Tsahai before the open cupboard, his black hands glistening yellow with butter. It was as if he'd managed to get his paws on the hiding place of the sun. He had a second key all along! A deal was struck. Zera Jacob would say nothing to Wolete Mikaele, and Tsahai would turn a blind eye and a deaf ear to the untimely 'surprise parties' Zera Jacob and her chattering of friends were already interested in. I was too little to participate, but as I grew up a confidante of my sister, I too eventually benefited from the deal made with the butter thief.

The older he became, the more eccentrically Tsahai behaved. When I was about five it started happening, once a month, that the old man would go on an outing and return all bleeding and bruised to his quarters. It took us some time to realize what was up. The whole month long Tsahai would be repairing and pressing an immaculate white suit. Ribbons were cut from bits of coloured cloth and sewn to the breast-pockets, medals fastidiously fashioned from bottle-tops and other metal discs and pinned to the jacket. Came the last Saturday of the month and Tsahai would dress up with his pay in his pocket and go into town with a white colonial helmet, two sizes too big, on his head. There he played the role of the Emperor. He firmly believed himself to be incarnating the Emperor, that he himself was in fact the Emperor. Disdainfully he would strut up and down the market and summon people to come and kiss his buttery fingers. What would at first be fun and games with people pretending to pay homage to His Highness, bowing whilst giggling behind their hands, soon turned nasty. Kids ran up and teased him, rocks were thrown at him, people set upon him with their sticks, the excited curs joined the fray and he was driven off with barking and squealing in a cloud of dust as if he were some ancient sacrificial goat. It might even have been a ritualistic way of revolting against the real ruler . . . It took a month for the cuts and weals to heal, for the regalia to be repaired, for the megalomania to again build to a peak.

What finally got Tsahai's goat (if I may say so), what made him leave our service and probably hastened his death, was when Guebre Gsiaber, my father, returned from one of his expeditions to the South with a small lion. He'd found the cub abandoned by its parents, he said, and he couldn't just leave it to die there in the flaming heat. The little animal used to mew and when sleepy would rub its face and folded ears. Guebre Gsiaber decided to call it Fanuel after the angel protecting us with fire against the demons. 'When you are big, you will roar with the fiery breath of Africa,' he told Fanuel – 'your voice will be the furnace that makes people jump and dance!'

But Tsahai was frightened out of his wits. 'Bad day, bad day,' he grumbled. And he prophesied sombrely: 'Small cats grow up to be big wild beasts which catch and eat cooks and overseers!' A few days later when Fanuel had started mauling the furniture and devouring the slippers of the house, he solemnly asked my mother – he never considered my father to be the decision-maker – for permission to be discharged and to return to his native village in the hills. He had grown a lot thinner over the previous months, his skin no longer shined. Maybe the preposterous and compulsive intake of butter had in the long run upset his guts. He left for his ancestral home and died not long afterwards. He returned to the night of dreams, to the big dark cupboard, to hide from the *zar* – his intimate devil – and from lions. We found a broken-down bicycle and a soiled white suit in his room.

Wherever my father travelled, Fanuel went with him. They were an inseparable couple. One could see my father coming down Churchill Avenue in his automobile, and the surprised head of the lion on the back seat would be just visible above the window. During this period he was often absent from home. Maybe Wolete Mikaele was not exactly happy to have a *ménage à trois* with a lion, however docile, and that could have been the reason for his frequent trips. But there was also some ambient political turmoil. I was still small, your uncle not yet born, and I remember the raging arguments my parents had – about 'that animal, Fanuel', about 'those two anarchist friends of yours', meaning the engine drivers now based in Cairo whom my father went to visit 'to advance the planification of mankind's march', about his extravagant gambling orgies, most of all about the local political situation and his lack of interest in the matter.

I have said that my father was certainly never politically motivated, but he had an inbred sense of justice and a memory of what it was like to be poor. Whenever he returned home in his car, Fanuel serenely and imperturbably sitting in the back, all the little spindle-legged kids of the neighbourhood would rush out of doors and run after the dust-cloud of the car, frantically waving and shouting in their strident voices: 'Geta Babi! Geta Babi! Geta Babi!' 'Mister Father' would stop to fondle their heads and to hand out sweets and small coins.

No one in the family realizes how many of these children he helped obtain some schooling. Every month he would be gone for days, discreetly doing the rounds with little envelopes of money to the families of his 'orphans'. At night he sometimes walked the narrow streets of the poorest quarters (you could hardly perceive the limp), and when he came upon some destitute person sleeping in a porch he would have the man or the woman taken to hospital for a check-up, for care if necessary. These down-and-outers with their fly-gathering sores were the people he employed to work in his various business ventures. Unfortunately the business ventures never lasted very long. They had a way of folding. But most of all he went to extraordinary lengths to try and have as many children as possible wear shoes. This was his obsession – that every child should have a pair of shoes. He equated wearing shoes with being civilized, if not exactly educated yet.

He in turn accused my mother of not taking enough care of the house and of me, of disdaining his friend, Fanuel ('Your animal is scaring off all our servants, their buttocks are too sore to sit down!' my mother would shout), of not having a correct appreciation of the importance of his projects with his Turkish (or Afghan) collaborators, of spending too much time with other female chatterboxes doing nothing, of having too well-exercised a tongue. He suspected her of smoking. He thought she came from a spoilt and snobbish family. These quarrels must have affected me – no, it was the mad love for my father which was too much for me – I remember how often I thought I was going to die, how I climbed on to the table at night and stood there gasping for air, for breath. I heard the whirring of the flies against the ceiling. The asthma attacks continued until I was seven. Now I know that I was, and remain, totally and blindly attached to him.

The night was peopled by shadows. My mind was swarming with stories I'd heard around the fireplace during the frying of the coffee beans. I never went to visit my paternal grandparents – the spirits living in the house with the veranda were strangers to me. (Guebre Gsiaber, I suspect, didn't ever go either.) Maybe there had been a burial during the day and in my ears I still had the wailing and the ululations of the Yuyu people. They, the Yuyu people, had it as their job to mourn at funerals; no one else, not even the family, was supposed to weep and shout, the Yuyu people did it for them, and this they accomplished with total conviction and evident delight. They did cartwheels in the street, slapping their feet like whips on the hard surface. Or it might have been a night of full moon, and from time to time I heard the destitute ones going by our house. The custom, it is said, was started by Emperor Lalibela: at full moon the bums were expected to parade in rags and tatters, chanting psalms, carrying a very heavy stone in each hand. People would open a window and chuck alms at the poor beggars. This ceremony of the penitents was supposed to be a protection against the jealousy of the gods, and particularly to ward off leprosy. It was supposed to work on condition that you never looked the recipient of your largesse in the face . . . I used to wake up at night and the world was a pale death-like shimmer, I'd be shivering and crying. How hauntingly beautiful it all was. I'd listen to the holy songs and then I'd be afraid of one day also becoming a *clochard*. Often the house was quiet because my father would not be home. I'd slip my hand under my pillow and find the sweet he always managed to leave for me, and I never saw him putting it there. Now we are exiles. There is nothing to stop our downhill slide. No poor people to take on our load of sins. No Yuyus to weep in our place. No emperor to steal our butter. No beggars to carry our stones.

Still, I think it would be unfair to say that Wolete Mikaele's family was snobbish. Maybe they were just a little strange and living on the outer edges of society, but this might have been inevitable given their strong-willed mother and their weak father. My mother's four brothers were all relatively forceful men; even so at least two of them married domineering women who promptly set about taming them and using them up. They never showed themselves in public with their husbands, as if they were ashamed of their husbands' diction and their noses.

In fact all of my uncles, your maternal great-uncles, were artistically inclined, except for Talsam who became a merchant. My uncle Ayna Tela, for instance, made his life as a house-painter. He was strikingly tall and always dressed in grey. He was also nearly blind. One always saw him walking the street after the first coffee of the morning, in no hurry to get to his place of work, swinging a pot of paint in his hand. His handyman would precede him, carrying the ladder. Nobody understood why he employed this half-witted helper who was quite incapable of putting three words in a row, but when asked Ayna Tela would reply: 'Who else will buy him his cigarettes then?' And at night, all alone at home – his room was tall and narrow with grey walls and five blue birds painted on the ceiling – he would devote himself to his real passion: painting religious pictures for the church. He painted biblical and apocryphal scenes for the Ethiopians, the saints and the bishops with the angels for the Armenians, icons for the Greeks. Silence was mixed in with his pigments and fixed for all eternity in the folds and the frowns of his figures. When the first cock crowed sleepily, a bit upset at the treacherous paling of the sky, Ayna Tela would sigh contentedly and go to bed for a few hours before getting up to set out food for the handyman who soon was to come puffing morosely up the hill with the ladder on his back.

Your great-uncle Asmat I didn't know very well. I knew his wife, my aunt, better. They married under bizarre circumstances. She had been corresponding with a pretender to her hand. At the time she was living in a far-off province. The problem was that her suitor could neither read nor write and so my uncle, still a student, and a friend of the husband-to-be, was hired as a kind of travelling scribe. The relationship flowered; once a month Asmat would leave the capital for the province with his little bag of letters. There he would spend the time needed for the answers to be thought up and shaped into missives of love, wash the dust of the journey from his sandals, have some tidbits in the shaded house of the courted one, and return. And then, just as the protracted affair was at last to be concluded – the lady bagged, as it were – he did not return at all.

Not for quite a few months. When he finally did, it was with the lady as his bride . . .

She must have been from a family of merchants, I think she (and Asmat) went into partnership with Talsam and his wife because I often heard the two old women bickering bitterly years after both their husbands had turned to dust and eternal smiles. One of the men had been the travelling salesman ('he even drank Arabian tea!'), the other ran the shop trading in cloth for making shawls, and safety pins. 'I brought the capital,' Asmat's widow said. 'Your Asmat was a useless dreamer, my husband had to employ him, he even lost the shop's money, it was we who made you rich,' Talsam's widow would hit back. 'What?' Widow Asmat would howl – 'You were nothing when we started, and anyway I was more pretty than you. You're just jealous!' Widow Talsam would then remind her sister-in-law about some early adultery, and about people who swap the mail for the mailman. And thus they would continue shouting to keep each other alive.

Apparently Asmat did once lose a large sum of money belonging to the partnership. He was travelling back to the capital from his wife's province, with two employees and a bag stiff with coins and notes of several currencies. About fourteen kilometres from the city the party of travellers came under attack from a band of highway robbers. Asmat's companions did not know about the money. Shots were being fired, birds rose squawking from the branches, dropping red and green feathers, there was a lot of confusion, and Asmat suddenly clutched at his stomach. Ooh! Ooh! What an inopportune moment to have cramps! Maybe the situation did impress a certain urgency upon his bowels. He grasped his luggage, slipped off his horse and started running crab-wise up the wooded slope of the hill, ducking from tree to tree while undoing his trousers. Somewhere up there he hurriedly buried the moneybag before making his way back to the road. His two employees had meanwhile made enough noise to drive off an army of thieves. And now poor Asmat had to find some lame excuse to return up the hill, that he'd dropped his glasses where the needs of nature had brought him to his heels, but his two solicitous assistants insisted on helping him look. Needless to say that no glasses were ever found among the droppings, and no bag of money either.

But the only true businessman of the family was your great-uncle Talsam. He never gave up on a good deal or an outstanding debt. Only the other day I received a letter from him, penned in the careful spidery script of an old man's hand, in which he reminded me that as inheritor of my father's liabilities and assets I still owed him the price of one stout wooden coffin. The debt goes back to well before my birth . . .

It must have been a particularly hot year in Addis, and some epidemic, perhaps the Spanish flu, was decimating the population. Guebre Gsiaber was once again in hospital with fever and delirium. He died there, or was thought to be dead, so many people died at the time, worse than flies, he was at the very least in a coma as cold as death, and he was taken to the morgue. The family, his young wife, his family-in-law, were informed of the sad event and my uncle Talsam immediately decided to do what must be done under the dolorous circumstances. It was a hot day and the morgue then still a little way out of town, but he courageously set off with two bearers carrying a fresh coffin for the victim. Guebre Gsiaber had in the mean time come to his senses, absolutely flabbergasted to find himself alive but weak in a hall full of dead people. He got up and staggered to the door, in the corridor he bumped into a supervisor, giving the poor fellow such a fright that he had a heart attack and died on the spot, and your grandfather made his way to the yard and the shade of a bluegum tree. There were fewer flies about outside. The sun shifted, the shadows trembled, the birds were quiet, and not long afterwards your great-uncle Talsam entered the dusty courtyard wiping rivulets of perspiration from his brown brow. At first he didn't recognize the man under the tree – Guebre Gsiaber had lost all his hair and he must have been as thin as a walking stick. A dialogue was struck up between the two men, Talsam asking after the director and declaring that he'd come for the mortal remains of his brother-in-law, poor man, and the latter saying that he'd never heard of such a person, at least not among the dead. When Talsam eventually realized who he was speaking to, he got all hot and furious. He felt he'd been made a fool of, worse – cheated! Guebre Gsiaber assured him that he hadn't come in vain at all – there was one dead orderly, collecting flies in the corridor, in pressing need of a coffin. The problem was one of paying for the box. This my father naturally refused, seeing as how he wasn't just then needing one. For years Uncle Talsam kept on sending the bill to our house, valiantly hoping to make a point.

Poor Uncle Talsam! He is known as the stingy one of the family, and yet it was more a question of hard work and being in the good books of the right people. Of having strong shoes and good legs.

He lost his fortune during the revolution, but then so did my father. Talsam was an unconditional supporter of *Ganhoy*, the *Negus*, the wily old dummy, Haile Selassie. Being himself an aristocrat from his mother's side, it was only normal for him to be of the King's party. He did go out of his way to prove it however. Once, when the Emperor returned post haste from a trip abroad to squash the beginnings of an uprising, Talsam was among the loyalists who went to the airport to welcome him. The small King of Kings walked his cape through the crowd and got into a jeep. Talsam rushed forward to greet his lord, grabbed him by the hand, and the jeep started moving off. The old ruler, whether inadvertently or absent-mindedly or out of sheer malice, kept hold of Talsam's hand. He asked after his health, the family's news, the country's health and then again after his health and that of the family. With the other hand, and with his enigmatic smile lost like a wet thought in the beard, he saluted the throngs along the road. And Talsam trotted next to the slow-moving jeep, his hand held in a firm greeting by the King, all of the fourteen kilometres between the airport and the palace.

Ganen was the one who got away. He was the artist, the film-maker. Maybe he did not really escape: so much of his work finally turns around the central wound of exile. I remember a film of his I saw many years ago: the story of a young man who kills his betrothed without intending to, of how he is exiled – it was the customary retribution – to go wandering abroad, a bird without a tree, working until he's earned enough to buy the pardon of the bereaved family, to buy back acceptance by the community, and when he finally returns he finds his native village demolished by droughts and locusts and other plagues, everybody dead except for one blind old seer. Then there was another film: a boy leaving his country to go work abroad, inventing relations with 'home' to give him standing in the eyes of his exiled comrades. One lie leads to another invention which leads to reality. Pain must be wrapped in beautifully embroidered cloth. He passes off the photo of a luscious young woman advertising some product as being that of his sister, imagines a correspondence with this sister, becomes the go-between between her and a friend, a fellow migrant labourer, who wants to marry her. The sister must now be produced since the wedding feast is ready. Inevitably there is a rendezvous with death . . .

Guebre Gsiaber, my father, your grandfather, never did get away, although he was so often absent on some journey or errand or scheme. One fatal day he came back from Italy without Fanuel. He became sombre and irritable. It was only when I was about to leave for Paris that he told me the story of how it came about. (It was also one of the last times he communicated with me.) Apparently he'd obtained permission – and cooperation from a friendly captain – to take Fanuel to Europe with him. He'd met up with his two Turkish (or Chinese) co-conspirators in Milan. From there they all took the train to Rome where they were to meet with prospective financiers for their plans. Their arrival at Rome's Central Station caused a scandal. The two 'locomotists' had found a way of flying red flags out of the windows of the carriage, and they deployed a huge banner demanding the return to full duty of steam engines. In the resultant ballyhoo my father never got to meet the 'contacts'. He had a flaming row with the Turks, they separated – 'the two anarchists flashed their eyes and rolled their moustaches,' my father related – and he went to live with Fanuel in an acquaintance's flat in the Via Capo d'Africa. The building, like so many of Rome's apartment blocks, had a terraced roof. The acquaintance was a small man with bad, clumsy feet. There, it would seem, Fanuel one night jumped or fell to his death on the pavement below. Maybe he was just lonely, maybe he felt out of place there, a live lion watching bad television in a private house in Rome, maybe he thought he was the last of his kind. Or perhaps he wanted to fly. Television induces an experience of the void. He wasn't so very old, and he still had the folded floppy ears of a kitten. Mano, your father, once told me of an old Khoi woman in the country of his birth, the last one alive of her tribe, the last one on earth to speak her language, waiting for death in the hut of a foreign family – and I thought of Fanuel.

After that trip Guebre Gsiaber acted stranger by the day. He was to become a foreigner in his own house. Tsahai was gone. Nobody stole any butter any more. He'd started another gambling establishment which was doing quite well, judging by the pools of smoke drifting along the ceiling. My mother became more modern, more inclined to wearing tight skirts, more emancipated by the day. And then Guebre Gsiaber started talking to himself in the street, or talking to the absent lion. To the lion he confided his anger and his fears, his disgust of poverty, his troubled relations with his partners. He complained of the heat, of the terrible sun in his head. He said he felt like someone lying inside his own head, incapable of walking, with the sun beating down on the roof. He said he saw flies as big as thumbs. He became afraid of being killed. He sent two letters to his Afghan partners in the dream. He refused to take his shoes off, from fear of having his orthopedic boot stolen. Then there was the revolution.

I'd been sent to Paris for higher education. Now I know Guebre Gsiaber wanted me to go away so that I may not witness his downfall. At one stage he ordered me back to come and marry his best friend's son. I refused. I wanted to stay in Europe to become a journalist. My father was furious. He never again wrote to me. This putative 'fiancé' of mine was anyway soon after killed by his own father. It was during the revolution: an opposing faction had come to take away the young man and the father shot him down on the veranda rather than let him be tortured by his enemies. Ethiopians can't take the shame of being humiliated physically.

Your grandmother, Wolete Mikaele, joined the neighbourhood revolutionary committee. Their job was to make up new words to fit the new political concepts. Your grandfather had his casino nationalized. He went to court against the *Derg* to appeal against the expropriation, and won his case. Then, out of his own free will, he nevertheless handed over his gambling halls to the revolutionary government. 'When my country is rich one day, you will repay me,' he said. Those must have been terrible times, dog-days of blood and flies and rumour and fiery wind, each dawn revealing its harvest of moist corpses in the streets. Great-uncle Ayna Tela stopped painting houses, his helper disappeared, and the ladder too. Great-uncles Asmat and Talsam had died, their widows moved into the same house, shouting at one another. Ganen was abroad: he started denying being Ethiopian. My mother still had at home her adopted elder daughter, her son, and a young girl – my sister – born many years after myself and Tekle Haimanot. (She was only five years old at the time.)

Guebre Gsiaber entered the paradise of grandiose railway projects and crocodile dictionaries all alone in a poor, run-down hotel room down-town. He'd left home a few weeks earlier. Much later I learned that they found a set of cobbler's tools under the bed, a new pack of cards, a picture of a lion with me on its back and he as a young father smoking a cigarette in the background, his eyes drawn to slits against the sun. Also an old record of tango airs, a clean pistol, a promissory note addressed to his brother-in-law for one coffin to be paid from his gambling gains, a sheet of paper nearly falling apart with dim writing giving permission for an operation, and a book on chameleons.

He died peacefully, the wind fluttering the curtains. I was told that he had a most impressive funeral procession despite the times of upheaval and internecine fighting. There were then restrictions on public meetings, but all the poor and the lame and the halt and the blind of Addis Ababa followed the cortège anyway. Traders along the route rang down their heavy metal shutters. I heard that the mood was quiet and mournful. It had rained and the sky was lying fractured in puddles on the street. They couldn't have buried his smile. He'd inherited it from a distant ancestor, passed it along to your uncle, and I'm sure it will be yours soon. Maybe you will have his dimple, his way of holding a cigarette, his love for dancing as well.

I wrote the death of my father and then I had an agitated night. I dreamed that I was mad, a white object emitting a high, thin shriek, enclosed in a white sack – which must have been a placenta. I woke up, fell asleep, dreamed that I was the corner of a table, continually breaking up to float away and yet always present. Absence is no relief. I woke up and looked at the window above the bed, the night was white, there were raintears against the pane. I slept and dreamed that I'm on my way home in the back of the car – my father had taught me to drive with one nonchalant elbow outside, the hand on the steering-wheel holding a cigarette although I don't smoke, he wanted me to be 'a lady of the world'. We pass through a beautiful leafy tunnel, I point out the landscape to Tekle Haimanot, but the road becomes muddy and the car gets stuck. We alight from the car and out of a house comes a dog shaking a head of fangs and screaming barks. There are white flowers in the snow. We enter the house. In the foyer we meet Mano who has become so thin and old and bearded, with glasses. And white! Other people are stumbling into the hall, sleepy-eyed, yawning, rubbing their faces. They borrow our toothbrushes. We go out into the yard, I'm looking at Tekle Haimanot. I wake up, or think so, and there is a telegram announcing Mano's arrival.

Last night I dreamed the death of my father, and that I was travelling on the back of a beautiful lion. I had on my flowery dress and my belly was flat. We Ethiopians believe the ferocious beasts are but the tame riding animals of the *zar*, or saints. One of our famous holy men, Abba Samuel, lived the life of a recluse in the Waldebba during the reign of Emperor David the First. It is one of the hottest parts of our country, really hell on earth, although the Takazé river spews its way through a deep gorge there, and this is the spot the hermit chose to beat and starve himself, to mortify the body for the sweetness of the soul. He wore a heavy stone helmet which can be seen in the Abrantant Monastery up to this day. It is believed that the many lions of the region used to come crawling on their pale-brown bellies to lick the dust of Samuel's feet.

Only in my dreams do I still return to that world of hunger and flies and dancing and saints. Where will I go with you, my child, in this foreign country where people have faces like terrible fists? At home we believed that one could receive divine protection by invoking Abba Samuel's memory . . . Oh, Abba Samuel, Abba Samuel . . .

(Where Barnum becomes impatient with the slow pace of the story and introduces two robust characters of his own, to ease his sore mind.)

KA'AFIR: What do you think about South Africa?

POLICHINELLE: That it must be a terrible place where nothing changes. Where the riches belong to the rich and the poor can have all the poverty they want or can afford.

KA'AFIR: You are wrong about matters not changing, about the environment, the field of reference, not being modified. You read too fast and too sloppily, that's all. But tell me, what do you think of it now?

POLICHINELLE: Nothing. I don't want to think about it. It gives me the jeebies.

KA'AFIR: Exactly.

POLICHINELLE: What do you mean 'exactly'?

KA'AFIR: Exactly that you are secretly excited by that no-man's-land, that just thinking about it gives you the shivers, and that we are lucky such a zone of erogenous and illicit pleasure exists!

POLICHINELLE: You are being indecorous.

KA'AFIR: Of course, my polivalent Polichinelle. And that is part of the pleasure! C'mon, admit to it! Let me explain. Many of these joys are shared by outsiders and insiders. For the outsiders looking in, it is vicarious, they imagine seeing their darker urges being satisfied, they envy the devils – be they revolutionary or reactionary – and the more these desires are repressed the more delicious they become. The insiders, victims of circumstance and history, can do what they have to do even when motivated by the satisfaction of clandestine excitements, and still know that the outsiders will consider them to be fighting on the barricades for humanity.

POLICHINELLE: What pleasures are you talking of?

KA'AFIR: I am coming to that. The pleasure of hate, revenge, treachery and racism. The orgiastic exercise of power. Let me explain. In the name of the struggle (for *transformation* or *survival*) you can permit yourself to hate large groups of human beings. How is it conceivable not to detest the Afrikaners? Not for nothing are they a monotheistic tribe: they are One. The mind calls up monsters with thick lips, baleful eyes, scented armpits (with revolvers strapped to them) imperfectly throwing the nose off the scent of smelliness in bourgeois clothes. The same works the other way round for Whites against Blacks. It goes further. Black can despise Brown because Brown is supposed to suffer less, and Brown can sneer at Black because he considers him to be raw and backward, and both of them can jeer at the Indian because he is the exploiter of the have-nothings, and all three of them can hate White because he is the brutal overlord, and White will look down upon all the others simply because he's not obliged not to. Communist and Black Consciousness and Liberal and Radical Revolutionary and Capitalist, irrespective of colour, can indulge their hate of one another for obvious reasons. In the name of historical vindication the oppressed can bomb and knife the masters, and in the fear of revenge the minority can gas, burn and machine-gun the majority, or ride over them in their tracked vehicles. Let loose the dogs! In the name of Purity of the Dogma of the Struggle, or the Correctness of the Strategic Line, one faction can permit itself to betray the other. Remember, we are not now speaking of France where these emotions are at best a game with boredom – we are talking of real burnt flesh, of blood and flies. How wonderful it is to be able to kill in the name of Freedom!

POLICHINELLE: Haven't we had enough?

KA'AFIR: No! Let me explain. You know that nothing can give as powerful a kick, such exquisite pleasure, as when you transgress a taboo or a convention. South Africa is dream country because the taboos are more violent, the hypocrisy is greater. Children can go to prison. A man can spend all his life behind the grey walls just because he shouted: *Enough! Freedom!* A father can wipe out his whole family to safeguard them from sorrow. You may be given a big black burning necklace to wear. Bodies may be dug up to be mutilated. The white man dreams of cruelly penetrating the black woman, or even the black man – from behind, so that he doesn't have to see the eyes. You may think, if you wish, that I'm using this metaphor for political purposes. The black man wants to assert his manhood and dreams of subduing the white woman with the powerful wingbeats of his black bird. The black woman knows that to take on the white man is to acquire secret but delicious power, or at least, by the crack of sex, to grab ahold of the floundering male. The white woman wants to be mastered and 'humiliated' by the black man. She wants to smell his shoulders and feel his saliva in her mouth.

It is called love across the colour bar. I'm telling you, what a paradise of dark painful ecstasy!

POLICHINELLE: You have a filthy imagination.

KA'AFIR: No, no, no! I am only in the process of cleaning my mind. And how else can it be done except by exercising the phantasies? I confront my mind, I undress myself to it. I'm not a voyeur like you, Polichinelle. Besides, it is true, all of this is true, you must admit it.

POLICHINELLE: You yourself are monstrously cynical.

KA'AFIR: Ah, and that is the ultimate transportment, my friend. To be exactly like the others. No snooty élitism for us. To know I am involved in the fight also. To be brave. To know that you and I also are real people of paper and ink.

4

There was a huge old tortoise which had two nests – one in a grave up by the church on the hill, the other in the school's recreation yard. Nobody could tell how old the tortoise was. On some mornings, when there was time enough, when the tortoise came slowly ambling down the hill, I got on its back for the ride to school.

I was still young when we staged our first revolt, and it had to do with your father's country, South Africa, or Azania as he insists upon calling it. The country was just the spark though. My mother, who was ambitious, enrolled me and your uncle, Tekle Haimanot, in the French *lycée* of Addis Ababa. Zera Jacob, our adopted sister, went to an ordinary school, but then she had also started much later than us. She was already nine years old and thin as a praying mantis with a rough skin from scurvy when my mother bought her for two oxen from her father Jacob, our gardener. (She quickly caught up though; she turned out to be the strongest of us all, and studied the furthest, and now she has broken off all links to the family. She must be a true revolutionary.) Guenet, my small sister, we all called her 'Paradise', was still too little to go to school.

The *lycée* was administered by lay brothers. One day, it must have been in 1967, we heard that the administration had been taken over by the Ministry of Cooperation and we found all our teachers replaced by new ones. The old system suited us fine – during the breaks between lessons we used to move along to the next classroom to the sound of opera music. All that changed with the new authorities. Bells clanged to announce the end of period. Our previous liberties were curtailed. We were fed up.

The new history teacher was a young French bourgeoise from Rennes, a Mademoiselle Poufasse. Not long after the take-over, during one of her first lessons, she started talking about South Africa, about how important and rich a country it is. We listened politely for a few minutes, but we were fed up, as I already said. Suddenly Zewd jumped to her feet, she was black and beautiful with proud buttocks standing away like that, like new pumpkins after the rain – all the boys hissed her on her way – and shouted: 'How dare you? You are in a free country here. Don't talk to us like that! Why don't you rather tell us about the struggle against oppression of our black South African brothers?' (This was just a pretext, you must understand – how much could we really have known about South Africa?) We all started twittering and cheeping like chickens in a roost when they see a skunk. Why? Yes, why, why? Do! Shame! No! Yes!

Mademoiselle Poufasse flushed an angry crimson and stalked out fliph-flaph to go fetch the *proviseur*. As one we were up and after her. The *proviseur* rushed out of his office and started flapping the dead fishes of his hands to calm the ruckus. 'She has the right,' he berated us, 'she is the teacher, she is the one to decide what's to be taught and what not!' All to no avail. We would have nothing of it. We were fed up. We shouted him down. We wanted to hear about the freedom struggle of our black brothers in South Africa. (Which we knew next to nothing about, you must understand.) Finally Zewd clamoured for attention and said, her buttocks fiercely bunched, fire in the eyes and her fist clenched: 'So we'll have a strike. All those in favour raise their hands.' As one we all voted yes.

Thus it came about that we were out on strike. Like wild-fire the news loped and lapped through all the classes and the whole *lycée* joined in the uproar. Nothing could deflect our determination. Zewd's father was a minister. That night he heard the whole story, her version of it at least, and of course everything was made more complicated and taken along byzantine corridors of whispering to the highest level – into the ear of the mummy himself. What a to-do! Hostilities were veiled, an appearance of decorum was preserved, but underneath the surface things were bubbling. It became a question of national honour. The French wouldn't give way and neither would old Emperor Stalemate. Eventually, as General de Gaulle himself was due to come on a state visit, so we were told, a deal was struck between the French and *Ganhoy* which permitted the reopening of classes.

State visits always played an important part in our history. It is not generally known that one such visit, or even just its eventuality, could in fact be considered to have sparked off the revolution. It was towards the end of 1973 and some other head of state was due to come to Ethiopia. Foreign leaders loved to be seen walking around 'the most ancient kingdom', stroking the heads of the tooth-less lions. You must know that we are a very proud people, but that we don't have the means to our ambitions. The *Neguste Negus*, the small man with the big ears, the foolish old fossil, decided that the capital must be cleared up for appearance's sake. And so he had all the beggars and the lepers and the very poor removed from the streets and taken to a disaffected army camp in the North. We had many beggars in the capital. Times were always hard.

It so happened that we were going through one of our recurrent famines. The people were simply dumped in the camp – man, woman and child – and the gates locked on them. No food, no water. The idea was that they were to be left to die. And this they duly did, like flies in the desert.

Of course there were already some rebel army officers, even if only secretly so. These brave men surreptitiously informed the student activists who went out to the place of shame and took photos. And then one day we heard a lot of screaming in the street and we flocked to the windows to see a horde of students running and brandishing placards. These placards were huge, blown-up photos of the horrors in the camp of silence – dead fly-blown babies, lepers exhibiting their death sores, mothers with flaccid dugs rocking dead children, skeletal corpses of grown men all aged beyond recognition in death's tight embrace. The city was petrified by the shame of it. We all rushed out to join the demonstration, led by Zewd of the bobbing pigtails and the muscular legs. The students were Maoists, I believe, and they went right up to the palace walls to shake their fists under *Ganhoy*'s windows.

At nightfall magnificent storms break over Addis Ababa. Water comes pouring from the white clouds which have been billowing over the mountains around the city. Steam rises from the hot-water sources, through cracks in the earth. The sky is crackling with electricity. When it is over, there is the fresh smell of warm, wet earth, the revitalized colours of red flowers and silver eucalyptus leaves. Thin children have their shirts sticking to their backs. The old tortoise glistens. The streets come to life, the station is teeming with people carrying their bundles and their sticks. On Fridays we used to go to the station for lunch – the best buffet in town, and all the fashionable people went there to be seen. The Eritrean taxi-drivers recklessly bulldoze their way through the crowds, sitting deep in the seats of their clapped-out cars, one arm dangling nonchalantly out the window.

A few months later we had a repeat performance. Same photos, only worse. More people shouting their lungs out. But this time there were shots in all directions. Forty demonstrators were killed that day. And from then on we never looked back . . . My child, will you inherit the memory of all the many dead? When you grow up and start leafing through the history books – that is, if people will still read when you are big – you will see mention there of the 'red terror', the purges and the fratricidal killings. It is true. We had at least two factions competing for leadership of the revolution, and one belonged to either one or the other depending on whether one spoke English or French. The people who'd been to the *lycée* (and you must remember that these were the sons and daughters of the aristocracy, of the feudal landlords and the rulers), and who went on to study at French universities, formed an organization called *Meison* (Pan-Ethiopian Socialist Movement); the ones who'd been to English-language schools, also from the same upper classes naturally, formed the P R P (People's Revolutionary Party). The P R P was perhaps more purist, more militant, more Maoist. The idealists turned in upon themselves and started tearing out each other's guts. And bodies littered the streets of our cities. Add to that the big-scale killings in the countryside caused by peasant uprisings, the chopping off of legs to start with, when the misery of centuries exploded in an orgy of extermination . . . Don't be surprised when you find the books soaked through with blood.

And the army? The plotting officers waited, turned group against group, played off the one faction against the other, applied a curfew and then allowed the executions to continue under the cloak of darkness. They formed the *Derg*, the 'Committee'. Our people saw that they meant well. The popular belief was that the *Derg*'s mother must be a woman of the people – how else was one to explain its concern for the welfare of the poor, its understanding of what it meant to be oppressed? Of course it was also believed that the father of *Derg* must be an aristocrat. He was a ruler, wasn't he? And so the people spoke of 'Prince Derg'.

Mengistu, it is said, is the son of a slave woman. In Amharic we call him 'the little black ant', the one whose bite is the most painful.

It was the year of my baccalaureate, and soon after we left the country for good. My father had me sent to France for further education. I think my future was all plotted as far as he was concerned. As soon as I got my *diplome d'études*, I was supposed to return and marry the son of one of his associates. My mother in the mean time had already left her husband, my father, your grandfather. Soon after she also left Ethiopia, although she sympathized with the revolutionaries. She'd given away to the landless

peasants living on her father's farm her part of the family inherit-
ance, and now she wanted to embark upon a new life as a liberated,
truly 'modern' woman. This meant, she thought, being divorced,
wearing dark glasses, playing cards for high stakes, smoking in
public and reading Russian novels. With Guenet and Tekle Haimanot she went to Rome where there was already a community of
Ethiopian exiles. But she had no money and she wouldn't let Tekle
Haimanot work, so she went out and found a job in a supermarket.
She grew heavier. In Ethiopia all was turmoil and mayhem, the
revolution in full swing.

Let me add two more paragraphs. Recently Tekle Haimanot
returned to Addis, probably on a smuggling expedition. He says
matters are now so bad, the people so poor, that he spent nearly
the whole week crying in his hotel room. There is of course the
curfew, but the few big hotels – the Ras, the Hilton, the Wabe
Shabele – have a huge turnover, they profit by allowing people to
feast and dance there the whole night through. That is where the
smart young set spend their nights. Rooms can be had for fugitive
trysts with the beautiful but desperate young women flocking like
moths to the illusion of warmth to pose as prostitutes. It is called
'to overnight'.

Before the revolution we were ground down by abject poverty,
by all the myriad illnesses of ancient times, by the wrath of the
gods and the saints and the spirits. We were all always guilty. If
you did something hurtful to a neighbour, you knew full well you'd
have to pay, or your children or grandchildren would. Came the
revolution and suddenly people had the weight of ages lifted from
their bent backs. One life became sufficient unto the travails thereof.
You could actually assume responsibility for yourself! And suddenly
everybody wanted to leave. Officers, armed with only their service
revolvers, hijacked national airliners to flee to Djibouti. You see,
we were as poor as ever, but the revolution released us from ignorance and now we thought we could flee to where there must be
some food at least – without incurring the displeasure of the
deceased deities.

5

There are moments when I fear that I shall never complete my report to you. My throat tightens – I believe it is called 'a rising of the gorge' – because I know in advance the end of the line. I am trying to convey and bequeath to you the dimension of your ancestors. I am also telling you about our love, Mano's and mine, that love which will give birth to you; and then I have to reflect what is happening while I write all of this down. The streets are dead, with a shroud of snow.

You see, Mano has been taken away from me, from us, and I believe certain people are responsible. It is so difficult for me not to let my anger and my sorrow flood these pages!

From time to time – this I already mentioned at the outset – I submit a chapter to Barnum, your father's friend and accomplice. He then reads the material and returns it to me with his comments. I have to, for he is not only my mentor as a professional writer, but there are aspects of the story which I don't know and for which I need his guidance. He must be there to steady my hand.

If I had to include all the discarded versions, the elisions and the abridgements! You would have been in the position to see for yourself how people are shaped and modified by the way in which they are looked at. The problem is that he, Barnum, also figures as a character in my pages. He has to. It is through him that I met your father, and got sucked into their literary schemes to start with. I cannot just excise him for our lives.

How shall I describe him then? Let me start with the shell, the house.

Barnum and his wife, Ms Delanoy, live in the rue Hyacinthe, in a venerable old building, at the top of a sweeping staircase. You enter their apartment through a blue door and inside it is like being in a snail's vessel – everything is spiralled or curved, the beams sculpted, the windows skew, the floor at a slant. Birds put their heads down the chimney of the fireplace to shout unimportant snippets of information at them, the moon would return from its travels and sleep on their bed for a few nights every month. Sometimes the building creaks, and since their flat is built into the roof you could say that they live at a cocky angle in the hat of the wind. In the courtyard a very old tree shelters from the vicissitudes and dangers of the street. It mumbles and groans, but in an ancient wooden tongue no longer understood by anybody.

Ms Delanoy is a quiet, reserved person. As secretive as a honey-comb. She is French, petite and pretty, with a slender body and pearly teeth. I sense that she doesn't really appreciate South Africans coming to knock at the door of their house, and she has reason not to, because they are a broken people and could therefore be dangerous. The two of them have a few friends of long standing from those distant parts, but what would the others be coming for anyway? Maybe, she thinks, maybe it is because of unsound curiosity, or just bumming, but really it must be the sadness. In any event, they are there just to chew time until all flavour itself has been lost. South Africans so much like to chew the cud of their particularness, that ungodly mixture of revolution and repression and mysticism and cynicism. They often have bad teeth. Ms Delanoy never says very much, preferring to listen and to smile and to light up her eyes, in fact to be the perfect hostess. Maybe, when the guests finally stumble down the staircase, she may quarrel with Barnum about another late night wasted in hot air. And then they will surely make up and put out the lights. He loves her, she loves him.

Barnum, on the other hand, is a much more volatile creature, often going off in all directions at once in a headlong tumble of half-finished phrases. The dykes are always being breached. At the drop of a hat, any old hat, he will vehemently tilt a lance against America, Parisian intellectuals, Party people, policemen, publishers, pavement dogs and so on. Sometimes it would appear that he will never again let anybody else dip a word in the shared broth of the subject brought to table. Even now I find it hard to keep him out of this paragraph!

When he's worked up he forgets about his maimed limb. Normally this left hand, smaller and paler than its robust partner, and seemingly paralysed, is firmly tucked away with the coins and the nuts in some coat pocket, but as the discussion heats up he starts to gesticulate with everything at hand. Then, as if he remembers the ache, or as he sails into calmer waters, he will commence massaging the numb digits with the more sinewy fingers of the healthy hand. He is tall, a little stooped, with greying hair flopping to curls in the neck as if a cup of ash had been emptied over his thoughts.

He has taken to wearing a pair of steel-rimmed spectacles, thereby enlarging the quizzical look of his blue eyes. He has a nose which has lived in close and prolonged and inquisitive proximity to wine, and a beard.

Mano says that, judging by the way Barnum is ageing now, he will end up looking like Walser in no time.

Sometimes I go along to sit in on the chats between Mano and Barnum – they grandiosely call these 'working sessions'. Mano thinks that two heads are better than one in the observation process preceding that of taking the subject apart so as to better reassemble the components in a lifelike imitation. He always sees his re-enactments as technical jobs of work, reconstituting the tics, the roll of the hips, the twist of the mouth, the frisson of the moustache, taking the mouse of a hand from a pocket and stroking it. He believes that 'the inner essence' will naturally flow to fill the void of the fabricated outer husk. This is the way we learn in Africa: by trying to be like others in an unquestioning way. We live in the eyes of others, not in a mirror. We are parrots, preening our acquired feathers.

The two of them speak together in Afrikaans. More exactly: Barnum will speak and Mano will grudgingly acquiesce to understanding. Ms Delanoy frowns upon this regression. Although it is most likely that she has more Akrikaner friends than her husband ever had, she considers it somewhat boorish of them to trot out 'that barbaric tongue', as she playfully calls it, in the presence of civilized people. It does constitute a lack of consideration to thus exclude the rest of the company. She weathered the years of Barnum's incarceration well enough but now it is as if she doesn't want to be reminded of that walk through the desert (knocking at prison gates manned by Afrikaans-speaking warders) and of the reasons which led to the impasse, foremost among which, I'd have thought were I in her position, must have been her husband's soft and confused Afrikaner *onderlyf*. The Afrikaner's underbelly consists precisely of sentimentality, insensitivity, cunning, clumsiness and guilt feeling. Why keep on bringing it all back?

It is perhaps only normal for her impatience – and trepidation? – to be focused on the language, their secret code of complicity, and on the easy, she would add raucous, way South Africans have of falling with the door into the house (one of their sayings meaning 'to trespass upon others' lives without a by your leave'). In the

60

middle of the night they are apt to scale a wall, stand under a friend's window, and warble in a poor imitation of the blackbird.

The language poses a problem for Mano. Was it not also the daily bread of his humiliation? He has long since swept the crusts and the crumbs off the table, he says; as an actor he never formally used it except perhaps to imitate or to illustrate a queer folklorism, to beard the *Boere*, or to curse properly. But it is still the only language he knew as a snothead. In a sense he has been dispossessed of the smacking of his mother's lips, the crunching of her molars, and thus also of the taste of his youth. His memory is amputated. The stump of his tongue is bleeding. He is, in some way, living a translation. I can see where it makes his exile doubly difficult, choked up as it were, spitting a reddish substance in the toilet bowls of his dreamwakes. He knows voicelessness. Most exiles take pride in their *differentness* and they squat down behind the ramparts of their native sound-castles, sucking and masticating stale bread; they take refuge, they exile themselves there as in a home away from home. Never mind the wash of a foreign sea. For Mano this is not to be. It is comical to see him mumble shamefacedly when Barnum tries to joke with him, laughing away unashamedly in Afrikaans.

This night Barnum is again trying to explain about things which are of importance to him, rituals of his youth in the Old Country, he avers – he has a ritual respect for rituals – riding hand-fashioned reed horses, stealing the neighbour's fruit from the tree, decorating a bicycle with ribbons and stickers. 'If you intend to impersonate me properly, Mano,' he says, 'we'll have to shoot at least one scene showing the wandering troops of musicians coming by to serenade each house on a New Year's morning, their banjos, their boaters and their striped blazers. There's nostalgia for you.'

Mano knows of these matters more intimately than he'd like to remember or admit. It is still there, this knowledge, in small locked-up shacks at the back of his mind, he tells me later. He had taken part as a youngster, it was transcending the misery through make-believe, he too had been a member of one of those wine-happy 'Cape coon' troops jiving and jigging to a carnival beat through the Mother City streets to go compete in some huge stadium for slave honours. They were led by bands resplendent in gaudy silk costumes, with faces painted white and black and red. It must have been a degrading spectacle, an orgy of drunken despair aped in song and shuffle and dance, and yet an apotheosis of exultation, the completion of a whole year's secret preparation of tunes and colours. This he will never talk to Barnum about.

'You tell me, Meheret, that you intend organizing your experiences and your ideas. If it is a book you'd be wishing to write' – Barnum looks at me through innocent blue eyes – 'I'd advise you to choose Africa as your subject. Where could you ever find a richer cloth, a wider field? Believe me, I'm an old hand, all writing ultimately turns only a very few major themes inside out: death, love, metamorphosis, betrayal, revenge. The unknown known and the known unknown and of how the one becomes the other, ahh-hah. And Africa has the perfect setting for it. All that magic, the rottenness, the hopes.

'I am the brother of God. Only his brother, mind you, nothing more. You could say I am his immigrant African brother. He is not African, of that we can be sure, for our continent is too deep in the shit. By this I mean that I have all the attributes of God, but none of his responsibilities. I can create people out of paper and ink, from thin air – plucking them live from some obscure chamber of the memory. There is a lascivious, cruel joy in making them dance the way I want them to, in plotting their destinies for them, in killing them off. You could say they are as many sacrificial goats dying in my place. As long as I can kill and describe that killing, I shall be alive. I shall nurture the joke of being alive.

'Naturally I write for someone just a wee bit more intelligent than I am. How else could I justify the ellipses, the obscure doctrinal points, the clogged symbolism?

'But you must know when you write' – he is still lecturing me – 'that you are interacting with life. You are bringing to life a form of communication which will be receptive way beyond you to what exists outside you. Funny items, events extraneous to your story, may suddenly be knocking for admission. Sometimes you will witness a miniature scene which may in itself suggest a complete novella, impinging on your consciousness because you happen to be in the state of writing.

'I am interested in these captured moments. No, I think you should write about Africa' – he smiles at me – 'not the vast scenes and dreams, but the intimate, even sordid everyday rituals. Recently I've been reading old man Walser, and I was struck by his marginality, the way he walks and walks through the outer regions of our awareness, consciously off-centre, along the edges of our central lake of experiences. An ancient dog, really. The more I think about it, the more I'm convinced that we are alienated because of an absence of memory. Our means to having a memory, to constituting a historical personality, have been mortgaged by our flagrantly evened-out modes of communicating. We have been introduced to the self-creating void. Perhaps also by the fact that our social problems have become insoluble and unsolvable. The Western dream of progress, of the ability of man to find solutions and to dominate his environment, has been smashed. We have become ants with a built-in echo of loss. We humans are now a foreign race, ear-marked by absence, and the absurdity of our lives reverberates in us.

'The magic of the writer is that he can shape this absence and then slip into the skin of his making. And what if writing were the art of selling the skin of absence? Suppose now that I started off writing about the two of you . . . Oh, I'd make of it a sad but romantic tale. Obviously I shall start with what I see, or think I see. To you, Meheret, I shall give a rich past robed in the security of a pastoral African setting. Already you have such a calm face, except maybe for the eyebrows. But you are here now, away from the green escarpments of your native land. So I shall imagine you as a would-be writer confiding and confessing that past interwoven with a dramatic, let us admit a *doomed*, love affair with someone like Mano sitting next to you here. As scribe you will be telling your sorrows to an unsuspecting reader somewhere in the background. Obviously I cannot imagine your reader, but it will be my task to invent your passages, to be born from your sighs and your thighs as it were.

'You, Mano, will be a restless exile – somebody imperfectly hiding the volcano of revolutionary ardour under the cold ashes of a cold actor. You will be pleased to know that I intend to put the two of you in bed together, and have you repeatedly tie the slippery knots. I am a generous man.

'Then I shall send Mano back on a supposedly political mission to South Africa, commissioned by some mysterious all-powerful organization. South Africa is the dog with bloody sores lying athwart the public mind at present – it is all too tempting not to use it as a setting, it is the ideal set-up for playing out my fantasies and my fears as also for promoting the sales of my book. I am the ruthless creator. Your parting, I'm sorry to say, will have to be a wrenching experience for the both of you.

'Down there, I'm afraid, I shall have you caught, betrayed perhaps inadvertently by a close comrade. You will be put in prison.

Not to worry – I do have some honour – I shall have you take the stand and fight right up to the most austere court the political battle that I was deprived of. Your actor's talent will be given full scope. In fact, to give the tale a twist, remember I am God's bastard brother, I shall have you actually impersonate me here and there. It will be my vindication, and I shall blur and mesh our two personalities by deft sleight of hand. There will be confusion and a gnashing of teeth. To be able to carry out my plot, I shall naturally have to insert myself, as myself, somewhere down the line. Let us not forget that we are in France, the home of Narcissus. I owe it to myself to put the writer on stage.

'Meanwhile, back at the ranch, I shall establish myself as an echo-chamber to Meheret's *récit*, to dwell in her mind and to keep the required distance. And then? Shall I polish you off? I don't know yet. Perhaps too simple a denouement. I could perhaps have you escape and return to France for an explanation, a confrontation with the confounder or the creator. Who will it be – Meheret or I? But there will be many ceremonies along the road. Small deaths. Of crickets and of flies and of spies. Still, even you must admit that you'd be useless beyond a certain point and that I myself should want to resurface to take the lines in hand. Besides, I shall want to close the circle and be back here in my own skin and shell to tease Ms Delanoy with my absurd riddles.' (At this stage he gets up, walks over to where Ms Delanoy is sitting knitting quietly and patiently – she knows her man – and then he tenderly kisses her hair.)

6

'To do all of this I need first of all to exist in the reader's mind, naturally. How do I insert myself? You tell *me*! I can't very well just stand up and snap my fingers for attention. I'd need some background, some stuffing, some shape. It is easy to change the colouring of the eyes, to add or subtract a beard, to paint on a smile and then to have it fade with the very next turn of phrase, but ultimately some substance must settle on the radar screen of the perceptive reader or word-controller.

'Maybe I shall leave this story to go elsewhere in search of specificity and substantiality. With Ms Delanoy here.' (He takes her by the hand.) 'Somewhere outside the framework of Paris and Africa. Let us go to Spain. You'd like that, Ms Delanoy? Come, there's the staging of a Passion play every Easter in a town near Ultramort. Writing about this – for through my writing I create myself – will furthermore give me the occasion to bring back to centre-stage certain themes which I'd like to carry forward as echoes. A man is being crucified. Picture him before your eyes, floating, dripping blood. The stupidity of it. It could even be a case of mistaken identity, too many instances taking him for a god. He, the god, the man acting as god, goes along with the sacrificial proceedings, as an atonement for God knows what, and *fully knowing* (my italics) that it cannot change a goddamn thing! The megalomania of the actor! This, in turn, makes it possible for me to speak about cruelty and cowardice and to philosophize in general about the state of man.

'Why Verges? This, by the way, is the town near Ultramort that we're heading for. There are similar or more spectacular performances elsewhere during those days. Simply because medieval traditions added a macabre death dance to the proceedings in that village. I like the horrific or barbaric touch.

'This is the road I shall take to get there. I shall first of all describe the general setting outside in the open air before an old church. It will be a cold, windy, star-strewn night. Then I shall bring on the principal players and have them recite their texts before a crowd of Catalans wrapped in coats and scarves. In one scene, an attractive woman, Mary Magdalene I should imagine, will tear off her ropes of jewellery and chuck these on the ground, all the while screaming and clawing at her plump breasts. Suddenly in the midst of all these goings-on, with robed apostles and a live donkey being ridden over the stage (the youth on its back will clutch a tin of pebbles to his chest), down one way, marching through the spectators to the dull throb of a muffled drum, a group of five skeletons small and big will appear. The one in front carries over his shoulder the scythe of ill repute. They wear tight-fitting black costumes with skeletons traced in some phosphorescent stuff, and where their heads ought to have been they will be crowned with bobbing life-like skulls. On they come stepping high without a word, just this drum booming the heartbeat of death, and their slightly jerky movements. It is a bloodcurdling sight – you will hear the bones of fear clicking in your minds, I promise you.

'What is mind but memory transformed? Over those hills, down the plains where it so often rains, heading for the snow-powdered passes leading to the border, the multitudes wrapped in lice-infested blankets moved slowly, painfully, on blistered feet, not so long ago, just a day's hunger march ahead of Falangist repression. *De dónde viene toda esa gente solitaria*? Whoever has been poor and lonely himself understands other poor and lonely people all the better. At least we should learn to understand our fellow beings, for we are powerless to stop their misery, their ignominy, their suffering, their weakness, and their death.

'My sentences will go snaking up the serpentine streets to a particularly narrow alley-way called Carrer de l'Orient, also known as Carrer dels Cargols or Snail Street. The edible snail is a great delicacy in Catalonia. All along this street, at the height of a tall man's eyes, snail shells are fixed to the walls with a touch of mortar, and these, each with a dab of oil and a tiny wick, will be lit as lamps when the cortège passes. The place will be packed, everybody squashed up to the walls, there being no sidewalks. Apparently the macabre dancers of death will surge from this alley when Christ comes within spitting distance.

'As the procession proceeds along the Via Dolorosa, at every station of the cross, people who'd been waiting in ambush jump out to hurl guttural curses at the poor Christ, and they whip him mercilessly. I am sure that real blood is then drawn and that the impersonator will arrive more dead than alive at the church on the knoll which symbolizes Golgotha. Whoever pretended, Mano, that acting is play-acting, is make-believe?

'But Ms Delanoy will be tired by then, as she is tonight' – and indeed, for some time now she has been expectorating small nipped-off yawns in one delicate fist; again Barnum strokes her hair, she smiles up at him – 'and besides, it will be cold. I shall be holding her tight in my arms, like this. And thus we shall be leaving Verges before the final act, the crucifixion, before the president waves his white handkerchief to accord ears or tail. On the way back I shall ask myself whether the survival urge of the species is at the root of the idea that life is an obscure suffering that must be paid for. But that too is an absurdity. The earth turns in any event, the sun also rises, stories will tell themselves, birds have wings of unconscious knowing, and we have death with us constantly in the tiniest cell and vessel. Go read the dust. There is no god, or rather, we relegated those we had to the subconscious chambers of amnesia and neglect from where they distil their unrecognized darkness. From the cellars of our plastic memory there come pale bats, and we call them dreams. A nebula of stars. Exploding nuclei.

'Enough prancing for one night! Another drink, Mano?'

It is late. We politely turn down the offer. I'm sure Ms Delanoy would like us to be on our way now. All of a sudden Barnum gets up, spilling his wine, surprising us no end, and starts rummaging in an old rolltop desk standing against the far wall of the room. He comes back towards us with a few sheets of paper. He is so excited that he gets his hands all mixed up. 'Of course! Where did I put my head?' he exclaims, striking his forehead with the limp left claw, ash drifts down and speckles the collar of his aged jacket. 'What a fool I am! But please don't quote me. I have written about all this already. I knew it! Listen, let me read to you.' He glances at his wife and then starts reading.

'We left the town of Verges before the ritual death reached its paroxysm. (*Go now!*) A cold and cynical moon rode the clearings between a race of clouds up high. We had quite a way to go. Fourteen kilometres along the road our car came out of a dark turning near the river Ter and the headlamps suddenly speared a shiny white shape. It was too late for me to avoid the collision - I swerved, but immediately sensed that the front mudguard had hit an obstacle. I backed the car up and got out. Ms Delanoy, who'd been asleep when this happened, was very shocked and kept on asking: "What is it? What happened?" In the ditch by the side of the road lay a crumpled object. It looked like a human being in a shiny overall, except that it had two big white wings, all dusty and smeared, one of which was now broken off near the shoulderblade, and oozing a viscous substance. I bent low over the dislocated being – it had on a cheap pair of running shoes – who looked at me with unbuttoned eyes. Blood, very dark in this eery light, was burbling from its mouth and nostrils. It was trying to say something – I had to put my ears close to its lips to hear: "The book . . . the book . . . careful . . . don't play with fire . . ." We decided not to move it and drove into the next village to report the accident. The *Guardia Civil* there thought it might be one of the seasonal African labourers hired, mostly illegally, for the early apple harvest, and who hadn't learned the trick of crossing roads yet. Maybe it was drunk. Or homesick. I spent two hours making a declaration in a dimly lit police station. It was like trying to write some unknown body into my life.'

(I, Barnum, drive the point home by mouth of two comedians doing their entr'acte.)

KA'AFIR: I don't see why there should be all this fuss about unemployment.

POLICHINELLE: How do you mean?

KA'AFIR: Look, the solution is simple. All you have to do is build prisons.

POLICHINELLE: Prisons?

KA'AFIR: Sure. Oh, I see your immediate objection: it is not a crime to be unemployed, so unemployed people should not be put behind bars! In abstract principle I agree, because I too am contaminated by the soft poison of humanism. But think of the alternative. Should they then be left in their holes or on the sidewalks to starve to death? Don't you know that prison at least provides you with the essentials, with free board and lodging? And that you are excused from paying taxes while there? Wait, wait – think a little further.

POLICHINELLE: I'm waiting.

KA'AFIR: First of all, to build prisons you need labour. You are creating jobs, right? Then you need guardians, nurses, social workers and such to run the establishment. Plus rehabilitation agents. Not counting the whores who service the penitentiary work-force, the doctors and special consultants who must give the penicillin jabs and the heart-to-heart talks against venereal diseases, the preachers who must combat loose morals, the judges and magistrates who have to keep up the appearance of justice while processing the cases – without the appearance of justice there can be no state. These prisoners have to eat, be clothed. Where is it all going to come from? You are stimulating production, you are creating jobs. You could go further. As the inmates start escaping you'll be needing special forces to track them down, bring them back, punish them. If people refuse the benefits of society, they have to be punished. Again you are providing work. Then there will be abuses of authority, petty thieving among the warders, drunkenness while on duty. These will have to be censured by boards of inquiry. The culprits will go inside and the ex-unemployed, the prisoners who've been discharged, can fill the resultant vacancies.

POLICHINELLE: And where are you going to find the money to finance these activities?

KA'AFIR: Easy. You don't ignore the fact that prisoners inject money into the national economy by weaving baskets, making postbags and Donald Duck souvenirs. The non-unemployed outside world will have to earn a little more money so as to afford these knick-knacks. To rationally earn more they'd have to modernize their means of production which means that more people will lose their jobs, thus providing the prisons with more potential basket-makers.

POLICHINELLE: And what do you do with the surfeit of baskets, postbags, Mickey Mouses?

KA'AFIR: You employ people to destroy them and to recuperate the parts that can be used again. You see, in fact it will be a system feeding off itself, recycling itself. The point to keep in mind is that it is more important to produce jobs than to make money. It takes only one man with a press to print money, but to fashion a society with the aim of making work is the soul-uplifting task of harnessing intangibles. Money without employment leads to idleness, you know – cock-fighting and carousing and publishing books and corruption and death. Whereas working even without money is like taking small bites out of eternity: it gives a man a sense of usefulness, it cleans his veins and stiffens his semen column, his soft bone. He can take pride in the well-stitched postbag. It is furthermore in accord with our most deep-rooted prejudices. To work is to be. The worst insult you can throw at a fellow is to say: you have no job and therefore you aren't human, you're just fit for being a politician! And wait, wait – what are prisoners best at? Building prisons, of course. They are the most expert, the ones who know best what's needed. They will be generating their own growth! From time to time they can riot and break down a wing here or burn out a refectory there. These will have to be rebuilt. I'm telling you, in this way man can accomplish his God-given mission, namely to transcend himself. It will be like the phoenix rising from his ashes to propagate fire wide and large.

POLICHINELLE: But don't you risk having more prisons than you have prisoners to fill them?

KA'AFIR: No, because our sources will never dry up. Don't forget the important production line of children born in prison to the detained unemployed. They are by nature born to the occupation. And keeping them inside until they've reached maturity will make them natural and perfectly adapted unemployable recidivists. Then also you have all those illegal or temporarily legal immigrants from the Three Continents. Luckily they have little or no education and hardly any chance of obtaining access to living papers, so that they can pass directly from the condition of slave or serf to that of unemployed. Release them and they can propagate the virtues of prison life at large with a vengeance – native Whites will even accuse the authorities of leaning over backwards to make it easier for the Black and the Browns to go to gaol. There will be demonstrations of indigenous jobless ones at the gates! People will be clamouring to get inside!

POLICHINELLE: But how do you start the cycle?

KA'AFIR: The state does. In pre-historic times you had the trinity of God, State and System. God died into State by a process of cross-breeding too complicated to explain here – once dead he was hauled down and his pants taken off him, though there's a theory he may have been killed only afterwards – and System became State's presence among men (with Media as his kept woman). The state is the Original Initiator. Or to put it more comprehensibly, State the God, State the System, and State the State. Who generated the need for prisons, who benefits from their existence? The state does, I tell you. Who is responsible for their upkeep? The state is. And naturally the state is called upon to disappear, to manifest its deepest being: to become its own projection and procreation – prison! The world will finally be one!

7

Walser leans back on the bench. The early autumn sun is still pleasantly warm. It can comfort the hands, like holding a pigeon close to the chest. Paris is beautiful at this time of the year. Small clouds course through the heavens, shading or reflecting the light, so that the city with its predominant tints of grey is suddenly decked out in hues of silver. When you take a bus from the Chinese quarter back to the centre, you come over a slight rise and you see arrayed around the slopes of the Pantheon a jumble of buildings catching the light window by window in wall after wall. You see exhibited there a sensitive range of colours, the one fading into the other like those in the feather-plated breast of a dove.

Fewer trees now line the boulevards than there used to be years ago. Many have been removed to make way for renovations, for sidewalk cafés or parking places. Others died, stifled by the pollution of the clogged city air. Those which survived are starting to show the slow reds and ochres and the burnt siennas of their annual death.

Sometimes there are high winds which bring showers. When it has rained the streets take on an oily shine and the gutters run with a rustling sound.

Walser and Mano regularly change the place of their meetings. They are nomads moving through this city-state without being part of it. Today they can be found on a bench in a public garden on the edge of Chinatown. In this sector there are nearly no trees at all, and very few birds. High-rise buildings were constructed years ago to house the poor Parisians. Arabs came to live cheek by jowl with the white natives. Then Vietnamese moved in. In their wake came the boat people, mostly Chinese, fleeing the falling dominoes of South-East Asia in overburdened barges. Flames spread over the waters. Nobody knows how many of them have since blended with this grey cement environment, but they are certainly in the majority hereabouts. There are still some Vietnamese left – Cambodians, Thais, North Africans and West Indians too. The people working in the kitchens are mostly Tamils.

Around this hub of commercial and culinary activity, the

bordering district is poor and depressed. Droves of unemployed men, some of them quite young, wander the streets or slouch on the benches of the park, in pairs or one by one, nursing bottles of cheap red wine. They are the weak birds who have replaced their wings by shoulder bags. Early in the morning elderly Chinese come here to the park with its pond and its fountain, to welcome the light of day with their *tai chi-chuan* exercises. What used to be a dusty soccer field for the neighbourhood's ragamuffins has been taken over by curving walls of rusting iron. An environmental sculpture, it is called. Because we need culture. Someone has gratified his dream by graffiti-ing big white letters on the flaky surface: 'LES VAGABONDS FONT DODO'.

In their grey, anonymous European hand-me-downs, Walser and Mano could pass for two more drifters, though somewhat less smelly than average. Walser removes his glasses. His eyes are opaque and clotted, they don't seem to alight anywhere. He rubs his nose reflectively. The nose has a moustache like a Siberian horse-trader's fur coat.

'The true trouble with philosophers,' he says, 'is not so much that they search for the absolute, but that they become absolutist in their reasoning along the byways.'

The true problem in writing about Walser is that he is such a boring old marathon mouthmover. In certain circles he is known as '*le bavard*'. To contract his discourse and to bring it down to the essentials, to blot out the dull stretches of mumble, one has to insert lashings of blah-blah-blah, with the pious wish that the reader may profit from these blank spaces to think about more important matters, about the disturbing fact that there are more pigs than human beings in Holland, for instance. One also has to cut his speeches up in chunks, to let some air into the solid mess, by bringing Mano in sideways with a sharp remark or a quick echo. That is why they are sitting so close together in the sun.

Walser shifts to an even more comfortable position. 'Let us pretend that I'm a pedantic character in a novel showing you the recesses of my wise observations. Philosophers . . . They proceed, it is said, by a system of clarification of thoughts and particularly of terms. Nothing wrong with that. Unless we sort out the important from the banal everything will become trivial. We have to keep on making choices. The problem is that they too quickly forget that their premises can only be very temporary and limited means of understanding. Blah-blah-blah.'

73

'What you are saying,' Mano chips in, 'is that philosophers are really like children. They keep on escaping into a make-believe world of abstractions, prisoners to the glitter of their own findings.'

'Thank you. You have learned your lesson well. Only recently I came across the writing of one of the bright youngsters, a "new philosopher", as they're known. You know these *princes aux petits pieds*, dandies with delicate feet who wish to fill the shoes of the great dead *maîtres à penser*. This one was discussing the nationality question. You know how there's a debate raging about that in France just now because the country, which has been living way beyond its moral means, has had to revert to its deep-seated xenophobia. It is this young man's view that France offers to the world the originality of an elective theory of nationhood as opposed to the more commonplace genetic one. Blah-blah-blah. To his mind the elective theory is based on the notion of a nation composed of people who individually consent to being members of that nation. In this way, he says, the collectivity is created daily, consciously, from a shared memory. The genetic theory, on the other hand, presupposes that the individual is fashioned insidiously, both in his consciousness and his will, by the pre-existent collectivity.'

'It sounds nice and clean,' Mano says.

'It does sound nice and clean, doesn't it? In passing he remarked quite astutely that nowadays the notion of differences in culture was replacing that of race, but that we still have the same urge to exclude the foreigners. In other words, the identical ethnocentrism with another justification. In other words, not really the shape of the nose or the blotch of the skin, but the beat of the music, the accent, the other words.

'In other words, Eurocentrism. Blah-blah-blah. People now don't talk of inferior races, but of "unassimilable cultures". He then goes on to castigate those, mainly on the Left, who demand the unquestioned *right* of anyone born on French soil to be entitled to French citizenship. The individual should have the freedom to choose, according to him. The individual born in France of foreign parents, that is.'

'The children of the immigration, as they are so euphemistically called' – Mano's hand waves in the direction of teeming Chinatown.

'What a load of bovine excretion! As if it constitutes a value to be French! He of all people should know that the struggle for equality without preconditions is a historical necessity, and a question of political emancipation for all involved. Blah-blah-blah?'

'Oh dear, oh dear,' Mano sighs.

'When all that one wishes for is the pushing back of the barriers of blah-blah and intolerance. For everybody to have access to the rights and the responsibilities of citizenship'.

'What we are really talking about,' Mano says, 'is not the opposition between elective and genetic options, but the on-going struggle between White and non-White, between rich and poor, between North and South if you prefer.'

'Indeed. Indeed.'

Here Walser himself pauses in his peroration to clear his throat and his glasses. Many of their encounters took this form of a monologue being licked into shape by the tongue. One could reproach them for holding forth on ethics or commenting upon contemporary events instead of concretely furthering the political activity, but certainly never for running out of breath. It was somehow as if Walser thought it necessary to bequeath his intellectual hobby-horses or heresies to the younger man.

After this initial, brief interlude – never long enough to cool the gums – Walser would once more pick up the cruising speed of his reflections. Seagulls would be mocking his turbulent wake. He refers far and wide to other perversions of philosophy. He has much to say about the jargon junkies who cannot see that they take and mistake the progression of logic for a lived reality, a description of flight for the realness of the pigeon, that they therefore reason within the precinct of purely mental, pre-perimetered and word-conditioned expectations. Whereas they should be flinging their wings to the wind.

'The unconnected thinking process procreates in the void and progresses unchecked . . . The blade is getting shinier and the breath more broken. Blah-blah-blah. Nothing can be made undone, at least not in our time, because we have no memory left . . . These thinkers don't realize that thinking is a hallucination induced by the drug of reasoning.'

'What would you propose in the place of this decay of mental propensities?'

'There are *other* motivations and reasons outside the boundaries of reasonableness. When a people are on the move, as during a liberation struggle, say, then the intellectual who comes along with sensible arguments, however well-fashioned, is not of much help. I'm not suggesting he should dilute the rigorousness of his principles, but that he be imaginative in helping to shape the ethics of resistance. Which demands self-abnegation, humility. This is what all of you – the poets, philosophers, writers – should be doing, and if you go down into that land of sorrows, because we are working on the preparations of your trip, then that is what you should be embarked upon. Now this involves the lucid explanation of what power and privilege are all about. I mean, we have to shuck the idea that the philosopher knows better or more than the people do. And blah-blah-blah. He may at best be more developed in the soft discipline of mental acrobatics but that doesn't make of him an authority on life. He is too top-heavy! There are more important or momentous movements than the flapping of the mind or the wagging of the tongue.'

'Are you suggesting that one must allow the unreasonable just because enough people demand it?'

'No, it's not a question of numbers. And when someone says "the people want", I know he's a hollow demagogue assuming people to be an abstract equation and wanting to think for them – for how is one to know the desires of a people except, maybe, through a representative vote based on real choices? What I *am* saying, blah-blah-blah, is that we are talking of two radically different sets of reality perception, and the tragedy may be that the powerful colonial spiders force a suicidal, or apparently self-destructive choice, on their opponents. They make them wear the same pants. If spiders ever wear pants. Perhaps they have no alternative course of action either. Could it be that conflicting interests blind people to each other's motivations?'

'What we are in fact talking about is the tragedy embedded in certain choices,' Mano says.

'Precisely. Take your country now. During a political meeting in the Ivory Coast I once listened to a mediocre political functionary, a frontman, expounding his master's doctrine of "dialogue". Mediocre, I say, because the old simian originator of the idea had other schemes up the sleeve, more blah-blah-blah, whereas this jackass was mouthing platitudes learned by rote. Nobody could fault the reasoning though! He went down the list of how people must respect one another, of how changes in the oppressor's heart can be provoked by frequenting him, of how and why dialogue is preferable to futile violence. He said it better than this, luckily, and even the hardest-hearted brute would have to agree with the principles enounced. Except that it had no base in applicable reality. Blah-blah, propagated by fools who had oodles of good intentions under their double-breasted suits and who know nothing of the history of the South African people or of the limitations of movement on the ground. The germane question ought to have been: to enter into dialogue with whom, on whose behalf, to arrive at what compromise?'

'Whom to talk to? Where to go?' Mano echoes.

'The opposites in your country are irreconcilable. There *is* dialogue certainly, the dialogue of a power relationship between opposing forces. This was so even before the present chaos. But the real way out of the horror can only be through the struggle of the majority, nourished by a rich and ancient fabric of sacrifice and spreading awareness, and a growing resistance forever inventing itself. Although you may now well be over the edge of the precipice.'

'Well spoken,' Mano concedes. 'Though partisan. And no cloth can save you from falling down the mountain. That is part of your point, am I right? That it is better to have confrontation and not to fudge the issues?'

'Yes, it is a lesson I learned from my career as a dancer: to be nimble in avoiding the horns of Dilemma, but never to imagine that it is possible to dance without a partner. To keep alive the options of resistance, from subtle to overt. But, more precisely, what we talked about this afternoon is that reasoning, or blah-blah-blah, when it is thought of as conception feeding on reasoning and not as a tool for refining action rooted in practice and in history – this needs a long breath – that such reasoning is instant rot.'

'You will however admit that the mind may also move through the domain of magic?' Mano insists. 'That it can throw up the shadows of mountain and movement?'

Walser fits the thick glasses back over his eyes, touches his big moustache with a horse thief's finger to hide the ironic smile. 'But evidently, my young friend. Sure, sure, go ahead.' (And hang yourself.)

Here we arrive at the second act of their afternoon together. Walser has held forth in a pedagogical fashion, extolling hackneyed ideas which he has given a slight twist. Mano all along has acquiesced respectfully, and now, towards the end of the session, he will try to change the drift of their talk by introducing a less rational note, but – like a good African – he will carefully commence by agreeing whole-heartedly with what his mentor has said, then

77

repeat it with small modifications in accent and emphasis, and on these supposedly shared foundations erect a different edifice.

Mano says: 'Let it be my turn to tell you two stories. I once knew an artist who had done a painting showing a black male and a white female making love on the canvas. The subjects both wore masks, like stiff faces. He had his studio in the Montparnasse of the old days, before the area was bulldozed and given over to speculators to house civil servants and the business bourgeoisie. Here, in the studio, my black friend, the painter, would prop up his works on an old couch to show them to prospective buyers.'

'Hum, hum,' Walser confides to his moustache. 'This is going to be men's talk.'

'Once an American couple came to look at his production. The man was black and his wife was white. They liked the pictures shown to them, particularly the masked one, but they couldn't make up their minds to buy. They left undecided and it was agreed that the lady would return to have another stab at decision-making. The husband had other business to attend to – smoking cigars and dealing in bonds. He was a rich Black from Chicago.'

'I once knew a Black from Boston. What happened next?' Walser asks.

'She went there several times to try and see clearly, and then, after a week, the husband telephoned the artist to clinch the deal. Seems she liked the painting after all. It was wrapped up and delivered to their hotel. When they removed the plastic sheeting they saw that the white personage on the couch had lowered her mask and her make-up and that the features were those of the buyer's wife. Likewise the black lover in the painting had had his penis blacked out and replaced by a painter's brush.'

'Thus do we rise above ourselves,' Walser says.

'The American husband let his cigar grow cold and suggested that the painting be returned to the artist's studio with the explanation that finally it didn't show up well enough outside the delicate lighting of its place of inception, but that the artist was to be allowed to keep the down payment. Why uncover more? I saw the selfsame painting on the same couch a few years later. My girlfriend, Meheret, was with me. The mask was back on the white beauty's face and the lover's hairy finger of a *pinceau* was once more a lubricated prick.'

'It is a good tale,' Walser chuckles approvingly. 'I mean, story.'

'The second one for this afternoon is about guilt by imagination.

A man called Amon lived in a land where there were two powerful political leaders in charge of the same party. Like in most countries, it was a one-party system. This Amon was a braggart and a fraud. Once, to try and draw a veil over a naked and drunken night with the whores, he claimed that he'd been mysteriously summoned to spend the dark hours discussing politics with the Number Two man of the régime. He couldn't very well pretend that it was Number One who'd consulted him: that would have been too gross to swallow. When asked what the discussions were all about, he hummed secretively and let it be known that there were certain, ah, potentially portentous differences of appreciation between One and Two, perhaps even a proclivity for dissent, who can tell? "And I have such a clear mind," he said. "Who could forgo my advice?" All of this he'd sucked from his thumb, naturally.'

'I see it coming,' says Walser, rubbing his white eyes.

'This version he repeated many times, embellishing it, the way a man would invent a mountain to decorate his travels, and he was of course basking in the aura of reflected glory of someone "in the secret of the gods". A week later, as malicious luck would have it, there was an uprising against the leader in that state, and it so turned out that the insurgents were led by Number Two. The revolt was crushed. The rebel leader died during the brief but brutal action, and his supporters scattered to hide in the wind. Rapidly an inquest was launched to sniff out the dead traitor's accomplices. Their exemplary punishment was to be ruthless.'

'Oh dear, oh dear.'

'Poor Amon was pointed out as a conspirator by several barflies. Did he not pride himself on his acquaintance with the defunct rebel? So the soldiers came to grab him one night. He protested, pleaded his insignificance, looked to his wife for an alibi, claimed to be a vulgar liar, all to no avail. He was hanged for high treason and the corpse decapitated. You must have seen something about it in the newspapers. In fact, the severed head was presented to the triumphant ruler wrapped in the newspaper which related the events.'

'Yes,' Walser comments.

The light has gone. They get up to leave. The sun is too pale now to cut out their movements on the ground. If you rub a coin for long enough it disappears. Winter has no shadows. It must hide like a lizard in the ground. The two men shake hands. On a neighbouring bench two Blacks are looking for political pies in the sky.

'I have to respect the privacy of pain,' Walser says.

8

I show the above transcription to Barnum and explain that I tried applying the lesson he taught me – putting a face on the unknown and inventing the already existent. I admit that Mano has told me a lot about the garrulous old man known as Walser who lives in many disguises under the bridge of memory, so that I have a clear picture in my mind (like looking into quiet water from a bridge). I then express the fear that these digressions may be holding up the narrative flow of my memoir. Africa is absent despite the black shadow players.

He says I should not worry. One mustn't make it too easy for the reader, not even for the commuter being shunted from suburb to city and back. He says he doesn't intend commenting on the quality of the writing – he's no critic, and how can he be harsh with others when he is so indulgent with himself? He thinks it important though to digress, to enrich the cloth by weaving in new characters or embroidering upon old ones. All of this is functional in the simulation of veracity, even when it slows down the story. For instance, the two bums on the neighbouring bench could enter the story under the names of Ka'afir and Polichinelle. But he is intrigued by the attitude to French thinking expressed by the man named Walser. Is this his real name? And is it a pure picturing of his true opinions? What a coincidence it would be!

He went through a similar process (he takes it that Walser is also an émigré? would it be possible to meet him?): from being in love with Paris right through to deception, to the cheap taste of aluminium superficiality in the mouth. One should perhaps not be too hard and fast about these matters. A large part of the disaffection lies within oneself – no civilization could live up to the inflamed dreams of youth, and ageing naturally also increases the quota of bitterness, flatulence and bile rising in the gorge. One becomes progressively greyer, more disillusioned, sadder. The old serpent loses its skin, and sometimes the snake of thinking is poisonous. There are other forces at work, elsewhere also. Europe is altogether dead, but prettily preserved in media liquids. There has been an implosion – maybe the past history is too ignominious to contemplate, the dreams of international solidarity may be too grandiose to realize. Whatever the reasons, people here are now living below the horizon of historical self-awareness and certainly are incapable of conceiving of any transforming role for themselves. The daily ambiance is indeed typified by a sort of soft fucking *à la Libération* where the birth of a supernova or the death of a people equally find expression as tired jokes only. For insiders.

He says he built nostalgic dreams around Paris when he was in prison. France was far away, veiled by longing, and he tried to walk all over it with his pockets full of words. How well one ate in that country! And the wine! In the memory of his mind he leafed through the catalogue: the speedways, the Mediterranean coast, the customs officials with their *képis* and their moustaches like small hedgehogs, the excellent evening paper and the stimulating satirical weeklies. He says he shared a cell for some time with an old gentleman named Don Espejuelo. He invited Espejuelo to visit La Coupole and Le Sélect with him, to walk by the art galleries and stroll through the public gardens which were pruned all square like the military exposés of generals with rheumy eyes. He went through all the movements of May 1968 once again, relishing the heady intoxication of carnival and insurrection – and in passing by pointed out all the young women with their nubile bodies and their tongues black with generous slogans. Too true, cornered and cut off as he found himself to be, it was only natural that he should turn his memory into a vivarium for the imagination. He had to construct an alternative world to the one in which he found himself.

Barnum says that during his absence he often thought about how he'd first encountered Paris. He didn't know a word of French at the time, but how he admired – with an open mouth – what he conceived of as a clarity of expression and intelligence. Many years passed by before he understood that the verbal fluidity more often than not drowned a generalized stupidity, that silence is not a French concept, that it was frowned upon not to have an answer to everything, all the answers, even to questions which had never been asked. The unnoticed body of silence would sometimes float by late at night.

His first years were like bones. Still, the city was so splendid, all clothed in greys and off-whites, and how lovely the smell of fresh coffee and Gauloises when the day was still pale. Remember the view from Montmartre when the city was shrouded in fog, and the banners slapping the wind during the workers' marches on the First of May? Walking their coat-wrapped carcasses down the boulevards, the *citoyens* had eyes only for the small territory of sidewalk before their noses; you could have been breathing your last on the cement and they would have fastidiously stepped over you. Riot police with machine-guns were patrolling the streets. The Algerian war had barely come to an end – owing to a lack of fresh blood – and corpses, enpurpled by death, were still being fished from the Seine. Sometimes the nights were shaken by dull explosions. There were areas in the city where Arabs gathered to listen with tilted heads to their lilting songs. When it snowed, one noticed the postcard *clochards* dying peacefully. Not for nothing were they known as knights of the naked star. Of course there are no stars in Paris – one shouldn't be too demanding. They had well-behaved little dogs with ribbons around the neck. When one of them gave himself over to everlasting stiffness under some bridge, with a frozen smile as of a mouse dead from having nibbled at the icy lips, one's heart twitched with a thought for Utrillo. Civil servants were martinets, 'cows' they were called in French, so caked with dung that you could never have scraped them clean, and at daybreak, Barnum says, he found himself with clutches of fellow-foreigners and 'developing people' trampling one another before the Préfecture gates. In the Latin Quarter art films were shown in small cinema halls filled to the rafters with cawing students. Television sets in the shop windows still broadcast in black and white the image of a big-nosed, flap-eared clown making ample gestures. His name was de Gaulle. One lived in small hotel-rooms and talked a lot to thin friends and drank cheap red wine. The madams running the hotels had mouths the colour of old blood and the smell of niggledliness, emitting smoked voices. The good-time girls wore suspenders over their knickers and the secretaries had just started discovering miniskirts. There was not yet Aids in the land, nor Japanese tourists.

Absence, that was the very presence! He once considered writing a film script about the life of an exile in Paris. He would have based the story on the experiences of a certain Serpent, a black South African painter, who came to Paris just after the Big White War. Each life is a novel. People live their lives and a hand comes to smoothe the sand of memory. No trace remains. It has been a hard century, particularly for those coming north from the Three Continents. Their family attachments have been wiped out, the villages where they grew up destroyed, the social structures within which they evolved – admittedly rotten and feudal – were torn down. And now they try and move in under the northern blanket, lying as quiet and prim as poor country cousins on the edge of the bed with a back exposed to the cold draught, pretending not to hear the snide remarks about dirty feet, snoring and fleas . . . The film would have shown this Serpent painting, continuing to paint, always depicting the same scenes: a few skeletons with the masks of youth, and the townships he knew in the land of his birth. Gradually the paintings would have been washed of all colour. Maybe it would have illustrated his life from the time of arrival. How he had to pass himself off as a black American from Boston or Chicago – black South Africans were still an unknown and unplaceable species – playing jazz piano in a cocktail club to pay for his food, a cigarette in an ashtray dribbling a tendril of smoke. It would have shown, in passing, the drinking, the descent into falling-about alcoholism. There would have been shots of a black man with a hat worn at a jaunty angle, passing the time of day at a bar counter with red-nosed Frenchmen. In fact, the screenplay would have concentrated on the notion of alienation. Serpent would be losing his language. He would have been part of the exotic fauna of Saint-Germain-des-Prés, a friend, for instance, of Ganen, the Ethiopian film-maker, but as he grew older it would become abundantly clear that he was ultimately doomed to remain a 'foreigner'. Serpent would be shown living in a small flat, painting, attached by hand and goggles to his painting like a pilot obsessively flying over a lost landscape. The shuffling presence of a woman in the flat would be indicated, always just behind the door in the next room, but she was to be voiceless. In his workroom Serpent would have a colourful African bird in a cage. He would be trying to teach the bird a few words of Sotho. Maybe the film can start with a cruel sequence – where other exiles living in Paris would have him believe that Botha is inviting all of us home, that a special plane was being chartered to take the strayed ones back to their people; and one would see his incredulity, then the mad hope, the feverish preparations, only to be told it was all a joke. Truly taken for a ride. One would see him struggling against delirium, then against the persecution of madness (because more and more he'd be living in a city of enemies), then against the degradation of old age and loneliness. Then there was to be the foreplay to death: empty room, cracked window-glass, soiled curtains, old man in ward of other old men in hospice. A studious white girl from 'home' would come and interview him about the feel of exile, and she would try to bring back images of his youth and fragments of Sotho poems. (He would curse her in French.) An affluent African writer from Soweto would come and sit by his bed, take one of the paintings stowed away underneath it, and start bargaining about the price. He'd be interested in buying it because he'd have recognized a street corner or a back-yard – *long since destroyed*. Exile could be commemorated via a detailed description of a bulldozed place of the past, who lived where, who killed whom. The soundtrack would have been the tinkling of jazz subtly shading into the African throb. The last shots would have shown *mouroir* scenes, counterpointed and interspersed with those of joyous African kids.

You must understand, Barnum says, that these sketches for screenplays are reflections, if you wish, of my work, and did not flow directly from my relationship with Paris. Besides, that love affair was interrupted by an unfortunate absence due to an unplanned stay in prison in Another Country. As you know. And a twisted history at that, it goes without saying, since it was isolating one single strain to the exclusion of the people who were part of that life.

Whether the images of prison still filtered through the prism of his obsessions? Yes and no, he says. Not long before he dreamed that he was back inside, this time for good. Somehow he knew it was for good. It was a curious complex of buildings, in fact a series of barracks fitting the one into the other – not unlike the fragmented parts of a novel, being repeated – and a desert with the colour of death starting at the barbed-wire fence. Slavering dogs, their tensely flexed bodies close to the earth, their eyes fixed on the inmates, waited on the periphery. The camp lay on a plateau. Below one could glimpse green valleys, the silver glitter of civilization, the distant broken mirror of the sea. It was that one time in the year when clowns and actors from the outside world entered the barracks, to remind the amnesiacs of carnival. His friend, Malapi, had conceived of a plan to escape, he says, by disguising himself as an angel. Malapi had a white powdered body, rouged cheeks, wings of papier mâché made from ancient manuscripts. The circus folk were withdrawing from the barracks and his friend started walking backwards with them, in this fashion trying to regress *into the past* . . . of innocence. He looked back at us with terrible sadness. In his hands he carried the rope which was to tie him to the future.

When he emerged from the tomb it was to return to Paris, he says. How changed everything was! He felt it incumbent upon him to change as well, with new times, and so he swapped his pale prison skin for that of a Frenchman. He even underwent a heart transplant although it would seem as if he now had some rejection problems.

In France the Left had acceded to power, and this made him happy. Unfortunately it rapidly became clear that this limp Left constituted a petty bourgeoisie consisting of the sempiternal political bureaucracy, draping themselves in the appearances of power and paralysed by the need to be considered 'responsible' and 'respectable'.

Later, when the Rightist *revanchards* won back the high ground, he saw that it was six of the one and half a dozen of the other. This much was certain: politicians are not human beings, but we shouldn't hold it against them. They resemble humans in many respects, and they do exist as two establishments, the Left completing the Right, but in reality they are humanoids infiltrated among us, programmed exclusively for the pursuit of power – on condition that this can be achieved through manipulation, lying and treachery.

He then made a vow to stay pure. Let's go see what gives with the intellectuals, he told himself. In all naïve sincerity he took it that the people who had married mind to morality would be like a caste of monks or clerks – this, after all, was what the propaganda said.

It was not sufficient to be a writer or a philosopher or a researcher – one also had to bray in public. He duly put on the multicoloured coat of the hired moralist, that coat which can turn with the winds. He tried to look intelligent, he embroidered on his books for whomever wanted to lend him an ear, he explained the meaning and the delightfully subtle sense of his messages, he let go of poetry – for it was no longer classy and had been reduced to the margin of seaweed cures, astral travelling and the benefits of vibration. He made sure that he had an opinion at hand to contribute on everything and anything. He started playing the games of the puppies and the old curs. What an investment to achieve the illusion of brilliance! He rushed forward and to the right with a mighty mess of words to hide the creative emptiness, the paucity of ideas, the absence of ethical responsibility. He moved down the incline in an incestuous dance with his own image!

Came the deception. What, was it really this empty? Was he also just a Paris parrot like all these surs and laydies? Was he then too in adoration before the mystique of image-fabrication? He saw them on the telly, in meaningful colour, drinking in the klieg lights the way vampires scoff blood, their hair carefully tousled and their moustaches all ready to do battle; he listened to the inane platitudes courageously laced with hoomanrights concerns – it being understood that one was breaking a lance for the hoomanrights of *homo sovieticus* and particularly for the *etiopicus* sub-category infected with marxism, meaning political Aids . . .

Quite obviously he was not going to make the grade, he then thought. One had to admit that he was not a thinker, even if it happened at times that he thought he'd been thinking, or pretending to. No, he was no intellectual, and it was already difficult enough to try and be an apprentice creator.

Ah, if only one could stop all those writers from being publishitted more than once every two years. Take for example the derisory way in which they contemplate Africa, Asia, the Americas, through the studious spectacles of their Western arrogance. Sooner or later it would have to be pointed out to these cackheads that the world did really exist *before* being 'discovered' by Europeans, that the people of the Three Continents didn't have to become slaves or kaffirs or migrant labourers in order to be touched by the grace of civilization. In short, that civilization was not a Western monopoly and the West not in any sense the navel of the world.

What could be said about Paris at present? That it is Dogshit City, accessible only to stressed joggers and their feminist spouses. That the poor are railroaded out to the suburbs where they will give birth to marginals and the permanently unemployable. The nomorerights and those left by the roadside will be invisible moles. Vacant lots will be their feeding ground of predilection. We have entered the age of instant amnesia. No more information, only staged propaganda and commentary from postmodernist city rats. Do I speak like your Walser?

We shall have silence and absence. We shall have nuclear plants. We shall generate riches by selling the tools of death, by feeding and flogging the death of others. We have consensus politics, on the Left and on the Right, about our missiles, the pretensions of our foreign policy and presence, the insularity of our culture, the control over our colonies, the structural permanence of our unemployment, our superiority over others. We watch the United States with cow's eyes, hoping to be chosen as the hired udders, the kangaroo-mothers for their culture . . . It is good to die in France, but you have to merit that privilege.

'As for me,' he says, 'I have the bleeding of a distant and ancient wound: Azania. But to be screaming against apartheid from here is only immoral moral posturing. How easy it is to cancel the debts by having a go at the *Boere*, those colonial products, foremen for the fat pigs and the good European banks swollen as tight as ticks with the blood of exploitation. Anti-racism washes whiter. This allows us to contemplate the victims with pacified consciences, to forget that the totalitarian system down there conforms to French interests in Africa, to wipe from our minds the knowledge that apartheid is the logical outcome of a history of Western "values".

'Mano is wasting his time sitting on park benches with blind old philosophical dancers. You ought to tell him that we have work to do. Somehow we must break through the screen of absence! I for my part haven't been idle – I have been working on a screenplay that I'd like him to have a look at. I call it *My brother*, or "A medieval morality play in sixteen tableaux". It is a rather crude depiction of what can and does happen in the interrogation cells down there. Those things go on day and night, perhaps especially now with the state being broken down and power slipping from the hands of the minority. We just have to be capable of picturing and facing the horrors. But why tell you about it, you may ask. Why this interruption of brutality where all has been bitter-sweet dream? Will it not be a fatal break in the tone and the voice of the book? Because that is exactly what torture is all about: the raw imprecations coming through the quiet night-hours to destroy sleep. Because it is easy and self-indulgent to be moping about a lost youth in Africa or to kick the flabby French. They are sinking quite nicely by themselves, thank you! No, what we are now telling one another springs from a shared ground, or it will become a shared experience. I want to remind and to warn Mano. My past may be his future.

'He could well play the role of one of the policemen in the story. We must try to understand each other. And inventing, shaping by means of interpretation, this is one way of understanding the other. We have to penetrate the darkness. And in the womb we are all rocked by the same placenta of words. Give this to him on my behalf and tell him not to be put off by the fact that it is a simple, straightforward story. Are we not separated, all of us, only by the thickness of a mirror from the monster in us?'

(*This is Barnum reminding Mano that it is all very well to speculate, but that reality is elsewhere.*)

My Brother
(A medieval morality play in sixteen tableaux)

1

A South African scene. Evening. Desolate. Perhaps smokestacks or haze of charcoal fires over townships in background. Middle distance a train clicking by. Hold frame for a very long time. Silent.

2

Highway in the afternoon. Black girl drives along in a small red Japanese car. She is in her early thirties, well-dressed, short hair brushed natural, wears rather out-size glasses. A white Ford Cortina with three men (two white, one black) follows her, quickly they draw level and start gesticulating for her to pull over. She looks bewildered at first, then panics. They move in front of her and force her to a halt. Two men jump out and run towards her car. She's struggling with the car door. They start dragging her out. She screams.

FIRST MAN: C'mon, you bitch!
  (*She jerks free, starts to run, loses her shoes.*)
FIRST MAN (*To black colleague*) Vang haar, man, vang haar!*
  (*Black man sprints, catches the screaming girl, violently manhandles her. Her glasses fly off to one side. They push her into the white car. Both men pile into the back with her on the floor. The third man, the driver, hurriedly gets out, goes to look for her handbag in the red car, comes back with the handbag and the two shoes, throws these on the front seat next to him. They drive off with smoking tyres. The whole scene takes only 45 seconds. Hold frame on red car, door ajar, in background vehicles whizzing past. Cars slow down slightly, anxious white faces and curious black faces peer out before the cars again accelerate. A bakkie† with two young black men stops, they run to the car and look inside, one of them picks up the pair of glasses, they get back into the* bakkie, *drive off. Hold.*)

---

* 'Catch her, man, catch her!'
† A small truck, open in the back.

3

Room, bare but for a table and two chairs, a filing cabinet against the far wall. Electric bulb with shade dangling straight from ceiling. Behind the table sits a thin white man (SWANEPOEL), with brown hair combed carefully and a small moustache adorning his rather tight upper lip. A file in front of him on the table. Propping a buttock on one end of the table, a second man (CLAASSEN), thicker set, blond hair and moustache. He swings a foot nonchalantly. Both of them are tawdrily dressed like indigent office workers. In one corner of the room a black man stands (WILBERFORCE), his heavy features impassive, his arms folded over the chest, he wears a wind-breaker zipped up to the chin. In front of the table and facing SWANEPOEL the black girl NOMZANA stands stiffly. She glares defiantly at her interrogator although she has difficulty focusing without her glasses. Next to her there's a chair. CLAASSEN has just emptied the contents of her bag on the table and is now derisively poking at the wad of Kleenex tissues, the lipstick, the wallet, the small mirror, the driving licence, the diary, the three envelopes, the ring of keys, the identity document, etc.

CLAASSEN: Nothing. All the same, women. Deurmekaar soos 'n hoer se handsak.* (*He leers at his own joke. Flips the pages of her diary.*) Hey, Sis, you're going to be late for class. Look here, Swanie, (*He leans over to point out the page to* SWANEPOEL) four o'clock, Block B, 2A.

SWANEPOEL: We must show *respect*. She teaches *African* literature. *Doctor* Kumalo.

CLAASSEN: (*With a sneer*) Doctor, hey? She'll be *professor* next. These uppity kaffirs. Eh-dew-cation! It's not going to help you here, my beauty, and it's not going to straighten your hair either. Think you're better than us, hey? Well, let's hear your story . . . Whatsa matter, haven't you read the book?
(*He starts leafing through her wallet, draws from it a small yellowed snapshot.*)
Ek sê, what's this then? Picaninnies. Mmm, I see-ee. *Sis* with her big brother. Wat 'n mooi meidjie, kyk hier Swanie. (*To her*) En nou, toe't daai pramme jou nie eers aan 'n man gehelp nie.†

---

* 'Messy as the handbag of a whore.'

† 'What a pretty girl, look here Swanie. And then your tits didn't even help you get a man.'

SWANEPOEL: Sy wag vir haar broer.*

NOMZANA: (*Furious, blindly lurching at the table*) Give that back to me, you brute! Keep your filthy hands off it! You have no right –

CLAASSEN: (*Jumps off the table, kicks over the chair, pushes her right back to the wall, his face is suddenly swollen red*) Astrant, nè? Where is he? Waar's die fokkin hond? Praat! Praat! (*He shakes her by the shoulders.*) Praat, of ek skop jou poes flinters. Where's Mfowethu? Wie gee hom slaapplek en kos?†

(WILBERFORCE *has straightened from the wall, lets his arms fall by his side. Now he takes a stick of chewing gum from his pocket, carefully removes the wrapper, pops it in his mouth, starts chewing, folds the wrapper and puts it back in his pocket. At the sound of her brother's name* NOMZANA *stiffened. She now stands very straight, looking nowhere. Quiet.*)

CLAASSEN: (*Suddenly sweeps all the articles off the table*) Tel op, doktor meid! Of is jy te fancy om Afrikaans te verstaan?‡

WILBERFORCE: (*Slurring slightly*) You better pick it up, sister.

(NOMZANA *hesitates, then bends down to grope for the scattered objects and scoops them into her handbag.* CLAASSEN *puts one heavy shoe over the snapshot on the floor and then doesn't budge.* NOMZANA *stops but doesn't look up, continues working around his feet. She rights the chair, puts her bag on it.*

SWANEPOEL *takes out a packet of cigarettes, carefully lights one, blows out a tendril of smoke.* WILBERFORCE *unobtrusively walks over to the filing cabinet, returns with an ashtray for* SWANEPOEL.

SWANEPOEL *unties the pink ribbon around the buff-coloured file. His forehead is creased. He turns over a few pages, reads, takes a deep draw from time to time. Quiet.* CLAASSEN *has resumed his perch.*)

SWANEPOEL: (*Extracts a page*) On August the thirteenth this year you received the following letter from your brother. (*He reads.*) Dear little Sister, I'm writing you this letter from somewhere not very far away. You need not worry, the person who is bringing it to you can be trusted – he is safe, and in any case he doesn't know where it comes from.

CLAASSEN: See, we know you are in contact with him. We know

---

* 'She's waiting for her brother.'

† 'Cheeky, eh? . . . Where's the fucking dog? Talk! Talk! Talk, or I'll kick your cunt to pieces . . . Who's providing him with bed and food?'

‡ 'Pick up, doctor blackwoman! Or are you too important to understand Afrikaans?'

you know where he is. And we want that terrorist before he kills again. (*Gently he kicks her bag off the chair. She doesn't budge, stares into space.*)

SWANEPOEL: (*In a flat sarcastic monotone*) I was so happy to hear you'd been appointed to the university. We still have a long way to go to free our minds, and you will help us. It can't be done abroad, I know, I've tried and I know the cynicism bred by that alienation. When this war is over I certainly want to pick up my writing again. But for the time being we have more important tasks . . . Please don't break your head about me. My health is fine and my spirit is helping me to do what must be done. I am in no danger . . . It is reassuring to know you are looking after our parents. I'm afraid there's much they haven't understood yet. I count on you to explain things to them. Do you remember how I explained poetry to you when you were still small? Please tell the parents not to worry about me. Tell them that they are always in my mind. What I'm engaged in is for the sake of all of you. I don't want you to suffer because of me. I want all suffering to stop. One day soon we shall all be together again. Please go well. Your loving brother, Ka'afir.

(WILBERFORCE *takes the wad of chewing gum from his mouth, studies it attentively, puts it back, takes up his chewing.*)

4

A nondescript arid landscape. Evening with long shadows. Wind blowing dry weeds along. Barbed wire tracing the dividing line between nowhere and nothing. No sound. Hold.

5

Office. Bare but for the essential furniture – tables, chairs, telephones, filing cabinets, wastepaper baskets. A door gives on to a corridor, another communicates with the interrogation room. Against one wall a blown-up map of Johannesburg and its immediate environment, dotted with several red pins. Above that the formal portrait of the State President. At one table, bent forward, his arms below the top so that his shoulders touch the edge, a middle-aged man (the COLONEL*) sits with a tight white face studying some reports before him. His hair is arranged to camouflage a bald patch. He is in shirt-sleeves, with a broad flowery tie, his jacket neatly draped over the back of the chair. He has no moustache. At the second table a slightly older man (*LUBBE*) with a paunch sits slouched in his chair. His eyes are small, his hands big and meaty, an unkempt moustache above his* *small pursed mouth. He wears a tracksuit and running shoes. On the table there's a typewriter, an open newspaper and some wire baskets.* LUBBE *is rolling a few pens and pencils over the table-top in a desultory fashion while idly turning the pages of the paper with the other hand. Off to one side a black man (*GLADSTONE*) sits on a chair, methodically spitting and polishing a pair of military-type black boots. The camera has made the inventory and then holds the frame. The telephone on the colonel's table rings. He picks it up, leans back in the chair, studies the ceiling, abstractedly adjusts and smooths his tie with one hand.* GLADSTONE *stops polishing the boots but pretends not to be listening.*

COLONEL: Ja . . . Wanneer? . . . Ek sien . . . Nee, ons kon nog niks uit haar kry nie en ek twyfel of sy van veel hulp gaan wees . . . Moenie jou daaroor bekommer nie. Niemand weet ons het haar nie . . . Goed, ek bel jou net sodra daar nuus is.*
(*He puts the phone down, gets up to walk to the wall-chart to study it, hands in pockets. He's a smaller than average man, rocking backwards and forwards on his heels.* GLADSTONE *has resumed his slow polishing.* LUBBE *is picking his nose.*)
COLONEL: (*As if talking to himself*) Brakpan too. The police station. Less than an hour ago.
LUBBE: Shit!
COLONEL: They threw a hand grenade. Two of our boys wounded. Blacks.
LUBBE: Hoeveel?†
COLONEL: (*Still with his back to the others, tracing a route on the map with one well-manicured hand*) Three, we think. They got away on foot. We're cordoning off the area. (*He turns around.*) That's the third attack in twenty-four hours. Dit kan nie so aangaan nie. Gladstone, wat sê jou informers?‡
GLADSTONE: (*Looks up*) Nothing definite, sir. My boys are working hard. But they tell me these are sharp cats. The word is that one of Mfowethu's comrades has been spotted near Ma Billygoat's shebeen last night.

---

* 'Yes . . . When? . . . I see . . . No, we haven't been able to get anything out of her and I doubt whether she's going to be of much use . . . Don't you worry about that. Nobody knows we have her . . . Fine, I'll ring you as soon as we have any news.'
† 'How many?'
‡ 'It can't go on like this. Gladstone, what do your informers say?'

COLONEL: Ons moet daardie vroumens aan die praat kry.*

(*The door between the two rooms is opened and* CLAASSEN *walks in.*)

CLAASSEN: Jirre, dis 'n hardegat bitch, kolonel. Sy dink sy's slim. Ek gaan my hande was. Gladstone!†

GLADSTONE: Sir?

CLAASSEN: Tee, my ou jong.

(GLADSTONE *slips on his boots, exits to go and prepare tea. The* COLONEL *is back behind his table in his previous position. He turns a very tense face to* LUBBE.)

COLONEL: Ons het nie meer tyd nie. Sersant, jy sal maar moet kyk wat jy kan doen. Ek stuur Gladstone om vir Willy af te los.‡

LUBBE: (*Getting to his feet*) Reg. Maak so.

CLAASSEN: (*Has stopped at* LUBBE's *table, is leaning over to scan the newspaper*) Jirre, ek sê, dink julle ou's Transvaal gaan more se game wen?§

LUBBE: Sure as a ton of terrie shit, my ou maat. 'Scuse me, Colonel.

(*The phone on* LUBBE's *table is ringing. He picks it up, listens, grunts, cups a hand over the mouthpiece.*)

LUBBE: Two lawyers downstairs who want to see you, Colonel. Weinstock and that coolie, Naidoo. Say they represent Kumalo's family and they have something urgent to tell you.

COLONEL: (*Leaning back, touching his tie*) Send them up. But let them come to my office, we don't want them this close. Jy beter saam met my kom, Claassen.‖

6

LUBBE *and* GLADSTONE *walk into the interrogation room. At a nod* WILBERFORCE *leaves and* GLADSTONE *takes up position in the corner. When he entered he glanced once keenly at the woman; now he's reaching down to give his boots a final dusting with his handkerchief.* SWANEPOEL *is carefully closing his file, knotting the pink tape, stubbing out another cigarette, not looking up.*

NOMZANA *is down on her knees attempting to collect the bag's belongings.*

LUBBE: (*Slaps a big hand on the table*) Hoessit, ou Swanie? (*To*

---

* 'We must get that female to talk.'

† 'God, she's a stubborn bitch. She thinks she's clever. I'm going to wash my hands.'

‡ 'We don't have any more time. Sergeant, see what you can do. I'll get Gladstone to relieve Willy.'

§ 'Lord, I say, do you guys think Transvaal will win tomorrow's game?'

‖ 'You'd better accompany me, Claassen.'

NOMZANA) Get up!

(*She gets up. Leisurely he swings around on one foot and with the heel of the other he gives the woman a tremendous karate kick in the midriff. Her breath goes out of her in a surprised sigh, she's lost the bag again, she bends over in pain. Before she can fall he hits her with the fist on the side of her head.*)

LUBBE: No, no, don't fall, my beauty. Up! Uppa-daisy!

(*The camera focuses on* SWANEPOEL *meticulously completing the tying up of his file. He doesn't look up. We hear (and see in a blur of slow motion) the methodic blows, chops and kicks, we hear the woman gasping, blubbering, screaming, wailing.*)

LUBBE: Let's – go – my – beauty. Don't – you – go – kak – on – me. Up! Up! Die's – vir – jou – moer – en – die's – vir – jou – ma – se moer – en – dié ene – vi' – jou broer. Nee – néé. Moenie gaan lê op my nie. Op! Op!*

(SWANEPOEL *pretends to ignore the action. The camera is taking a close look at* GLADSTONE's *black boots.*)

7

South African ocean view, evening, dark sea with light glancing off the swollen breakers. The churning foam and spume where they smash on the rocks. This is a long holding shot. During this sequence there is for the first time background music: the slow rhythmical chanting of dark male voices highlighted by that of a female keening in agony.

8

A consultation room, tables, chairs. One wall is glass-panelled – on the other side a corridor full of patiently waiting black families can be observed. In the room an old African couple bolt upright on two chairs, she holding a handbag in her lap, he a hat which he unconsciously keeps fumbling with. They are both neatly dressed, if somewhat incongruously. Behind them two young black men, casually clothed, wearing sneakers. One has a disfigured face, he is straddling his chair sideways to the old couple. The other is pacing the room, sometimes stopping to look out at the assembled people. Facing the couple from behind a table, his briefcase lying untouched before him, a young, very well-dressed Indian lawyer (NAIDOO).

A door opens and a stocky elderly gentleman with a silvery mane walks in. He carries a bulging briefcase and over his arm a folded black gown.

---

* 'This is for your cunt, and this is for your mother's cunt, and this one for your
  brother. No, no. Don't you go lie down on me. Up! Up!'

94

He places the gown and the briefcase on the table, exchanges a mumbled handshake with NAIDOO *who's got up, then draws up a chair close to the old couple who'd half-risen when he entered the room. He sits down. He's wearing a dark pin-striped suit, a conservative tie, highly polished, slightly pointed black pumps. He lowers his elbows on his knees, hangs his head, takes a big white handkerchief from an inside pocket and now wipes face and neck without looking up. The young man has stopped pacing. The old lady takes a small embroidered hanky from her handbag and starts twisting it.*

WEINSTOCK: (*Without looking up*) Have you told them, Esop?

NAIDOO: Not yet; we were waiting for you. (*He clears his throat.*) Last night we went to the square –

WEINSTOCK: Late.

NAIDOO: Beg yours?

WEINSTOCK: I said it was very late. Quarter to twelve to be exact. Not long after you boys had been to see Naidoo. (*He gestures vaguely to the two young men.*)

NAIDOO: Yes. We went at quarter to twelve to the square and we managed to see Colonel Williams.

STANDING YOUNG MAN: (*As if spitting*) The psychopath from Pretoria!

NAIDOO: We told him we had reason to believe your daughter had been detained by the Security Police and that we wanted to know why.

WEINSTOCK: (*Looking up*) He wanted to know why we'd come to *him*.

NAIDOO: We told him what you told us, that she knew she was being followed around by his men ever since Ka'afir left the country, probably to join the insurgents –

OLD WOMAN: (*In a stifled wail, bringing the handkerchief to her mouth*) My boy . . . My boy . . .

NAIDOO: And that the whole township knew of the vigilantes who tried to burn your house down. That her little red car was found abandoned by the road between Soweto and town, with her glasses lying on the ground.

WEINSTOCK: Williams said, well there you have it. It looks like a Black Consciousness job, doesn't it? We can't help it if the Blacks want to kill each other. Don't come and bother us, we have far more important things to do, like looking after the country's security, sir. We don't have her, we don't want her, we can't use her. She's useless. By now she's most likely got a nice necklace around her neck.

NAIDOO: He was courteous and cold as always. Cold as a snake. He had a heavy with him, though, that man Claassen, the bully.

YOUNG MAN WITH SCARRED FACE: (*Stroking his cheek*) Yeah, man. I remember that Boer. Where was Lubbe?

WEINSTOCK: (*Not taking any notice, addressing the old couple*) I apologized for coming to the wrong address. But then I asked him if we could leave the glasses there. I said Nomzana's eyesight is too weak for even signing a confession. (*Chuckles.*) I think that got to him because he went all stiff and white in the face. What did he say, Esop?

NAIDOO: Yes, he was very angry.

WEINSTOCK: He said I could leave the spectacles with him if it made me feel any happier, but that he'd expected more careful behaviour from an esteemed solicitor and, he hoped, a responsible South African citizen.

NAIDOO: Then that Claassen fellow started shouting, why don't we go and give the fucking glasses to her brother? Why don't we ask *him* what happened to that white man's whore of a Nomzana? Who is it you people are being paid to protect anyway, he asked. Terrorists!

OLD WOMAN: (*As if frightened*) My boy! My boy!
(*She dabs at the corners of her eyes with the hanky. Her old husband looks bewildered, clumsily tries to pat her hand.*)

STANDING YOUNG MAN: (*Proudly*) They'll never get to him alive!

WEINSTOCK: (*Straightening his torso*) Yes, but that's not going to be much help to Nomzana, is it?

OLD MAN: (*With fierce suddenness*) We want her body.

NAIDOO: Now, now, old father, there's no reason to believe –

OLD MAN: We want her body.

WEINSTOCK: (*Lifts a well-manicured, placating hand*) Williams reminded us about the restrictions of the State of Emergency, the usual blah-blah-blah. I'd think he was trying to threaten us, wouldn't you say so, Esop? Anyway, if you want us to we'll of course go ahead and apply for an urgent court order. The problem is that we have no proof –

STANDING YOUNGSTER: (*Brutally*) What's the use, man? A dead body is no proof in this country. And besides, where's the money going to come from? Why should we feed the system? C'mon uncle, let's go.

NAIDOO: (*Getting up*) Old father, old mother, I'm sorry . . .

   (*The door is thrown open and a young lawyer with an armful of files barges in, sees them, stops in his tracks:*)

YOUNG LAWYER: Oops chaps, I thought you were through.

   (*The scene is frozen.*)

9

South African dilapidated suburban scene. Evening streets. Light reflected in puddles where children play. In background build-up of thunder-clouds capturing last rays. Hold silence.

10

The interrogation room. We see first that the ashtray is quite overflowing with smouldering cigarette stubs. On a tray there are two empty tea-cups in their saucers, a sugar bowl. SWANEPOEL *is still in the same position, the closed file lying square before him, he is studying the yellowed fingernails of one hand.* GLADSTONE *is in the corner, his hands behind him against the wall.* LUBBE *is leaning on his fists on the table, his heavy head hanging, breathing as if tired.*

LUBBE: Go fetch me a towel.

   (GLADSTONE *leaves the room. The camera scrutinizes* LUBBE. *There are bloodsmears on his tracksuit.* GLADSTONE *returns with the towel, hands it to* LUBBE *who cleans his hands on it. He throws the towel on the table, then turns around to kick violently, again and again. We hear the thuds followed by a low whimpering.*)

LUBBE: Fok jou. Fok jou. Fok jou.

   (*We see* NOMZANA KUMALO *sprawled on the floor. She is unrecognizable, her eyes swollen tight, her mouth broken, her clothes in disarray. She is trying in vain to raise herself on her hands, rolls over, attempts to reach out for the photo not far off.* LUBBE *stamps on her hand.*)

NOMZANA: Brother . . . Brother . . .

SWANEPOEL: I'm going for a piss. (*He gets up to leave.*)

LUBBE: Why don't you sommer do it right here on the meid, man?

   (*He laughs breathlessly.*)

GLADSTONE: The man is killing you, Sis. Don't you see it? Do you hear me? The man is killing you.

LUBBE: Say ja baas! Say ja baas, damn you! (*He goes for her with flaying hands and feet in a paroxysm of fury.*) Bloody – bitch – want – to – kill – my – wife and – kids – hey – tell me – tell me – tell me – you – black – bastard!

(*The* COLONEL *walks in, stops half-way across the floor, puts his hands in his pockets, starts rocking on his feet.* CLAASSEN *follows him into the room, looks around in feigned surprise, smiles.* LUBBE *is breathing hard.*)

GLADSTONE: Hey Sis, sit up! The boss wants to talk to you.

(*He moves forward in a kind of light two-step, bends over her but makes no effort to help her, moves back to the wall. The girl has turned her face away from the men.*)

COLONEL WILLIAMS: So, Doctor Kumalo? I believe you don't want to co-operate, you don't want to tell us where your brother is hiding out? You know – Ka'afir, or however you call him. Is it Mfowethu? A pity, a great pity . . . What do you Blacks hope to achieve anyway? Do you imagine the Boere will ever get tired of killing? You should go read your Bible more carefully. It is no good bucking the system. I'm just a poor man, look at me, I have to obey the laws too. They are there for all of us even if we don't understand them. Now you come here with your foreign ideas . . . But make no mistake, we'll stick it out, don't you worry . . . Why did you let yourself be dragged into this by the communists? A nice girl like you. And where are they now when you need them? What can they do? Do you think they care? Sold you out. Half of them work for us anyway. They're not all stupid. The same way they'll sell out your precious philosopher brother when the time is ripe. Where are they, these big brave black freedom fighters and their white masters? I'll tell you where. In their air-conditioned offices overseas, with the fleshpots of Egypt. Monkey diplomats riding in big cars. Drinking their imported South African wines. And you know it's true, don't you? It's poor people like you and me who have to live in this country and face the music . . . Tell her, Gladstone, tell her what a fool she is.

GLADSTONE: You're a fool, woman.

LUBBE: Shame.

COLONEL WILLIAMS: What a waste. You had a nice job, a nice car. My own daughter certainly could never afford a car like that. And your parents. Who is going to look after them now? They even brought your glasses to me. Think of all those students now waiting for nothing . . . You know of course why I'm telling you all this, don't you? You and I are nothing. Just small people of clay in the hands of the Old One up there on the bench . . . Yes, it's a great pity, Doctor Kumalo.

CLAASSEN: (*Laughs*) The doctor's made a mess of herself, hey Colonel?

NOMZANA: (*barely audible*) Basie . . . Baas . . . Bas-tard . . . Boere-baas . . .

COLONEL WILLIAMS: (*To* LUBBE, *his face a white mask*) Jy sal maar gou moet maak, Sersant.*

11

Vast beach. Evening. Silent. From a distance we see GLADSTONE *leading a very thin old horse over the sand. When they come nearer it becomes clear that he is totally naked except for his black boots. He lets go of the nag's halter, starts walking into the dark waves, his head thrown back, his arms spread wide. Hold camera.*

12

The adjoining office. SWANEPOEL *is sitting behind* LUBBE'S *table, smoking and reading the sports pages of his newspaper. The* COLONEL *is standing, hands in pockets, before the map on the wall. In the background the muffled sounds of thuds and blows. Then silence.* WILBERFORCE *is sitting on the chair previously occupied by his black colleague.*

SWANEPOEL: (*To no one in particular, taking out a pencil to mark an item in the paper*) I'll have to ask Gladstone for a tip for Saturday's races. These kaffirs know their horses. Horses for courses, am I right, Willy?
(*The connecting door opens and* CLAASSEN *enters. His face is flushed. The door is left ajar.*)

CLAASSEN: Die bleddie meid het gevrek, Kolonel.†
(*The* COLONEL *turns around. His face is very still. Even* SWANEPOEL *has looked up expectantly.* WILBERFORCE *glances from one white to the other, then looks down at the floor. His jaws resume their chewing.*)

CLAASSEN: (*Moving across the office towards the second door*) Right, ek gaan my hande was. (*When the colonel starts talking he will stop and listen.*)

COLONEL WILLIAMS: Get rid of the body. (*Then*) No, wait. Go fetch the photographer before you take her away. I want this on record. When we catch her brother I want to show him what he's done.

---

* 'You'd better do it quickly, Sergeant.'
† 'The bloody blackwoman went and died, Colonel.'

(CLAASSEN *exits with* WILBERFORCE *following him. The* COLONEL *walks to his chair, dons his jacket, takes a pair of dark glasses from the top pocket, puts them on. He sits down.* LUBBE *walks in, his clothes stained with sweat and blood.*)

SWANEPOEL: (*Sardonically*) Jy's moeg, nè Sarge?*

LUBBE: Jy kan dit weer sê. Ek word nou te oud vir dié stories.†

13

The interrogation room. Still the same light. Through the half-open doorway the sound of male voices teasing one another, sometimes laughing. GLAD-STONE *sits on a chair in the corner, his fists on his knees, staring without blinking but also without expression at the corpse. The camera looks for a long time at the dislocated body lying in its own blood, the broken face, the trampled photograph on the floor close to one outstretched hand. Softly in the background black voices sing a slow, religious dirge.*

14

The adjacent office. We hear the dirge continuing all through this sequence, growing in volume when the door to the corridor is opened. CLAASSEN *returns with a young photographer wearing jeans who greets everybody as he walks through to the interrogation room.*

CLAASSEN: (*Goes up to* LUBBE, *slaps him on the shoulder*) Jy mors darem nie met 'n mens nie.‡

(WILBERFORCE *enters with a folded grey prison blanket over one arm. He puts the blanket on a table.*)

LUBBE: (*To* WILBERFORCE) Hoekom raas daai kaffers so in die selle? Ek het vir die poisan gesê hy moet hulle stilmaak!§

WILBERFORCE: (*Looking at no one*) Yes sir, I told him.

(*He now goes through a series of slow, methodical gestures. From the pocket of his windbreaker he produces a pistol which he lays on the table next to the blanket. He digs down again, fetches up a piece of paper from the same pocket, removes the gum from his mouth with thumb and index, carefully wraps it in the paper, puts it back in his pocket, stuffs the pistol into the same pocket, picks up the blanket and moves through*

---

* 'You're tired, hey Sarge?'

† 'You can say that again. I'm getting too old for these capers.'

‡ 'You don't mess around with a person, do you?'

§ 'Why are those kaffirs making such a racket in the cells? I told the black warder to shut them up.'

100

to the interrogation room.

The COLONEL *sits behind his table, at his back the half-opened door through which the white flashes of the photographer's camera are reflected periodically. He picks up the phone, dials, waits for an answer, absently smooths his tie with the other hand.)*

COLONEL: Generaal? Williams hier. Dis in verband met die Kumalo vroumens wat ons gehad het. Sy sal nie kan praat nie . . . Dis wat ek bedoel, ja . . . Nee, geen probleem, generaal, niemand het geweet ons het haar nie . . . Ons maak so . . . Reg . . . Dankie, generaal.*

(The two black policemen enter, carrying between them the body wrapped in the blanket. Behind them the photographer clutching his camera, very white in the face.)

LUBBE: *(Watching them pass by)* Watch nou, die outjie gaan weer kots!†

(They laugh.)

SWANEPOEL: *(Smoke curling from behind his paper)* As dit is wat 'n dooie houtkop aan jou doen dan gaan jy nog baie naar word, boetie.‡

CLAASSEN: *(When the procession reaches the corridor door)* Hey, Gladstone! Soek jy nie 'n bril nie? Why'n't you give them to your wife? It's *mos* clever glasses. So she can be the queen of the shebeen!

(They all laugh again. The two men stop in the doorway without putting down their load. They both shake their heads, smiling. GLADSTONE *shrugs his shoulders. They continue. The chant is again louder.)*

15

Evening. Silent. South African landscape with a tremendous veld fire. Smoke billowing. Flames jumping from shrub to shrub, lugubriously lighting up the evening land. Hold fire.

16

The front room of a township house crowded with people. On a trestle table an open, empty coffin. At the head of the coffin the young man with the

---

* 'It's about the Kumalo woman we had here. She won't be able to talk. That's what I mean. No problem, no one knew we held her. We'll do that. Right. Thank you, General.'

† 'Watch it, the chap is going to puke again.'

‡ 'If that is what a dead wooden head does to you, you are still going to be sick many a time, brother.'

scarred face, shouting slogans. To one side, clinging to the coffin, a handker-chief to her eyes, the keening old woman. Her husband is standing close behind her. Young women are trying to brace the old mother. People jostle their way to the coffin, each carrying a fist-sized stone. These they drop into the coffin. When the coffin is full the lid is brought in, passed overhead by many hands. The coffin is closed, the flag of the Liberation Movement draped over it. It is lifted on to the shoulders of six young men who with great difficulty carry it out of the house. Outside there's a multitude of black faces. A roar goes up. Fists are raised, the first freedom song sung from the many throats. The coffin goes through the crowd, dangerously riding over people's heads. The old couple follow. Young men try to form a protective circle around them. Hold on fists and mouths. Hold circle.

An African doesn't normally experience the need to explain. He simply is the way he is, though he may well pretend to be different, or someone else, in an attempt to fool you. Why is this so? Maybe it is because the African even now still grows up secure in a larger family context where sharing is a matter-of-fact, everyday practice, so that there's an absence of having to fight those closest to you for survival, of having to claw your way to the top; maybe because there still is an open-ended communication with the environment, animals and natural phenomena have histories and characteristics and personalities too, even when the surroundings are hostile you *fit in*, you are not isolated, you are not the master; maybe because there is an unbroken chain linking past to future, the dead are standing with wise eyes just beyond the glow of the fire; maybe because rationality has not been isolated and favoured the way it has been elsewhere in the world, there is an easier and more complete flow of sentiments too, less watertight dykes between heart and mind and liver; maybe because there is simply not such an insurmountable demarcation between 'reality' and 'illusion' and 'magic'.

An actress from the Ivory Coast, 'exiled' in Paris, tries to tell Mano about the finer points of African films. (She mistakes him for a white South African.) She is chic and svelte in a dress of 'African' cut (but from nowhere specifically) and of 'African' print (produced in Manchester or Rotterdam). Since the accent is falling on the elucidation, the need to understand, it is that – the explanation – which becomes the normative reference, and not the never-questioned Africanness. 'Understanding' – in other words, bringing the information back to a reasonable and if possible logical and controllable (if not immutable) staked-out field of mutually agreed-to conventions – however subtle, is a supremacist form of mental imperialism. Would that be the difference between African films and films about Africa? Do we Africans 'see' differently? And do we see films differently? Certainly yes, to the extent that our visual world is more round, more all-inclusive, less hierarchical. (But also more pedagogical.) Certainly yes, also, in that we relate far more immediately and directly to what is taking place on the screen. Listen to the way people comment upon what they see during the performances, how they talk to the flickering projected figures of light . . . Yes, probably I'm mistaken (Meheret thinks), perhaps the apparent need for 'explanation' of the French African girl is also just a means of stretching verbal intercourse, of slowing down the tempo and rocking time in its essential immobility.

The bright young fanatics come here from elsewhere, from America and Europe, they are exiles with unhealed wounds in their minds (and rolls of supermarket fat around their midriffs), and they come to criticize the local regime for having imported bad Western habits. They don't have to live here, they have no local responsibility, they will return to their white perches of martyrdom to take part in orgies of moral outrage. They have flipped. Africa is out of step, archaic, rotten to the core; Europe (or America) is evil, colonialist, dominating, racist; they themselves are the only pure ones. They are right. They fight momentous struggles in their minds. Sometimes they will extend benevolent condonation to a 'revolutionary' African state (or experiment), provisionally, on condition that . . . They are doomed to disappointment and paranoia.

In the gardens around the pool, there is the smell of dust. People are churning around, meeting and separating, shaking hands or embracing effusively to slap backs, picking up old conversations or initiating new lines of communication. Like at a cattle sale. In the air there is the thrumming pounding of drums, patterned music flowing non-stop from the transistor radios people carry. Actors, directors, musicians, technicians, journalists, politicians, students, activists, hawkers, groupies, hangers-on, a few weathered 'prominent personalities'.

Mano and Meheret managed to find a room in the Hôtel Indépendance. Who knows how many people are actually staying there? Mounds of luggage and filming equipment litter the floor of the reception area. The entrance door is guarded by a huge, sand-coloured stuffed lion with bared snarl and glinting eyes. The couches and the easy chairs are sagging under the weight of people who with glassy eyes watch other people coming and going. Against the wall opposite the reception desk (where it is impossible to put in a word edgeways) a fat lady is presiding over piles of coins on a table, exchanging money. Walls are decorated with gaudy posters announcing films, conferences, meetings. People come and go, speaking of Michelangelo.

Like all these pilgrims, they too made their way to Ouagadougou for the Pan-African Film Festival. Meheret wants him to be introduced to a different Africa ('your country may be on the same continent, but it is in another world'). He came to shop for support for the project he has concocted with Barnum. Together they started a production company, Birdflight Inc., they have several script outlines ready, and now he is anxious to make contact with potential sources of money or technical assistance. However elusive or intractable the situation, the South African one, it must be possible to translate thinking into images and rhythms and space. And however poor the continent, oughtn't it to be possible to mobilize interest and investment in such a hot subject? There is profit in pain.

There is also another reason for his being here, one he has not yet allowed Meheret to know about. As if he could fool her. Walser told him that Mumpata, 'the roving ambassador' of the Movement, would be present for the festival (corridor politics is his speciality), and he thought that they should meet. 'Go and talk to him about our qualms,' Walser said. 'He could indicate the way to pursue. He speaks with the weight of authority, of organization. You can open your heart to him. Trust him. Politics is just another form of culture. Blah-blah-blah.' In the back of his mind he knew, and Walser knew, and Meheret knew they knew, that they were already talking about the need for him to return to South Africa.

It was a long flight to Ouagadougou, winging into barrenness and heat, the huge expanses of the continent gliding away below the aircraft. Mano went to explore the cabin. When he came back to his seat he told Meheret that he'd come across a spy travelling first class. He'd been intrigued, he said, by this athletic white man with the dark glasses sitting very stiff and still and alone, a volume of Rimbaud's poems open on his lap. Behind the tinted lenses the man must have been asleep, but when Mano bent over him to have a closer look at the book, he was instantly awake and he removed the glasses to show his functional blue eyes. The agent wore a gold bracelet. One cheek was marred by the puckered scar tissue of an old blemish probably caused by burning. Mano (instinctively trying to fit himself into the skin of the other: this faculty gives one a perverse, cold pleasure) was impressed by the combination of hard and alert professionalism and the unexpected interest in poetry. He asked whether Agent liked these verses, and the other remarked in a defensive manner: 'He was an adventurer.' It was as good a way as any of looking at Rimbaud. Did he perhaps identify with the walker? They talked for a while. Agent asked Mano how much he knew about their destination, whether he was familiar with Burkina Faso, what the new régime there was like – 'What is the marxist input?' A security agent – Mano said he was sure that the man must be an information gatherer, perhaps even an executor, not to say executioner, Pierre Lecteur he said his name was – a spy has no justification for ever being without an *enemy*; generations of Western agents have lived on the look-out for marxists.

Mano said no, it was his first visit as well, he didn't know much specifically about Burkina Faso, but that the country and its rulers probably reflected a need for dignity, to be respected. They were poor? Maybe they even took a certain pride in poverty. As far as he, Mano, knew, the new government consisted of young people who didn't seem to be suffering from unduly gross hang-ups about colonialism or imperialism; all they were interested in was the intro-duction of democracy and the dissolution of corrupt entrenchments of government and administration. 'They want their own identity?' the other asked. But Mano didn't think that was the germane ques-tion at all. They know who they are and to think differently is white man's reasoning. In fact, maybe they don't even have to *know* it. It was much more a matter of power. Mano wondered what business could bring a spy to West Africa during a film festival. But Meheret told him not to be so naïve, that many plots were laid under cover of cultural activity, that Burkina Faso was a 'revolutionary' country (though far less so than Ethiopia), which like rotting meat must attract all kinds of human flies.

They stopped over in Niamey, and stepped off the plane to stretch their legs. It was like walking into the full blast of a furnace. The air shivered. The desert is a terrible beast lapping with a dry tongue at the town not far off. The ground temperature was 40° Celsius, and in the airport building where men in long dresses tried to hawk their sandals and their stones, it was hardly any cooler.

Aircraft approach Ouagadougou in a slow descent over reddish brown earth dotted with a sparse vegetation of scrub. Mano was reminded of the regions bordering on the Kalahari. The houses are mud-walled. There is an artificial lake to one side of the town, bordered by a denser growth of green. It takes them quite a while to move through passport control and customs. At their descent he noticed that Agent Lecteur seemed to be accompanied by a tall, thin African who must have been flying tourist class. They were met by two men wearing dark glasses who pilot them through the exit for diplomats.

The taxi taking them into town, to the hotel, has a radio going at the top of its scratchy voice. Immediately they were struck by the slogans painted on big banners, at the airport and on the way into town. 'Burkina Faso the graveyard of imperialism'. And later, at an intersection of several roads: 'The people thirst for their own image'. And: 'African screens for African images'. The driver expertly weaves his way among the hundreds of bicycles and scooters. The streets are lined by modest houses and what seem to be scores of shops or eating places, judging by the hand-painted signs. The radio is pouring forth a litany of names, resolutions and pronouncements in the most flowery French, regularly punctuated by choruses of 'La Patrie ou la Mort, Nous Vaincrons!' It would seem to be a direct transmission of a session of the National Revolutionary Council. It sounds like a play based on the Revolution. During a pause in the proceedings they can hear a baby squawking.

There is the overpowering sense of heat. Mano and Meheret are sitting at one of the cast-iron tables grouped around the swimming-pool. Two shy young men approach their table and ask if they may have a word with 'the South African delegate'.

They present themselves as being office-bearers of an organization called the Young Revolutionary Comrades. One of them has the standard revolutionary appearance with scuffed briefcase and intellectual glasses. He has bad breath. His friend wears a pair of dusty sandals. They draw up two chairs to perch on the edges of the seats, holding their hands folded between the knees. The spokesman shifts his glasses around on his nose and then launches into a speech which rapidly starts sinking under the weight of its own baroque clichés. His comrade nods sagely, from time to time picking up and repeating the tail-end of the spokesman's phrases, emphasizing the incantation. Mano finds himself responding with something like: 'Given the grave nature of the present situation in South Africa, blah-blah, and speaking for myself but, I am sure, also on behalf of the freedom-loving blah-blah, I wish to impress upon you blah-blah and living forces.' In fact he really only felt like saying good afternoon, I'm so happy to be back on the continent, and how are you . . .

10

A black London-based film producer, called Lion, has joined them at their table. The actress from the Ivory Coast snaps her fingers at the waiter. Her head is covered, as with a tight-fitting helmet, by symmetrical lines of plaited hair. Not much of it can be her own, black wool must have been painstakingly woven in with the rest. The waiter has a patient, glistening black face. She would like to have another glass of cold tamarind juice please, or if that is not available then a beer would do.

Vultures drift in lazy circles on the winds above the city. Sometimes they come down and hop along the ground as closely as they dare to the tables, screeching and shaking their wings, to gobble up the left-over morsels of food. There is a notable absence of flies, filth, drunks (had this been South Africa, obstreperous inebriated fellows would by now have been all over the place) or smokers, fanatics, beggars, smelly people, or American rock music on the airwaves. The music you hear has a fast beat to it, there may be some discernible Latin-American influence, and often the songs convey a political statement. (Everything gets woven into music in Africa, patterned to a beat, subjected to dancing – Aids, Nelson Mandela . . .) Many of the men are elegantly but soberly dressed in what seems to have been revived as the national costume – the *dan fani*. Since, thanks to international black-balling, the country can no longer profitably export its cotton, the fabrication and internal marketing of clothes have been encouraged. The cut is loose and simple, wide long gown without a collar, short-sleeved jacket and pants, square-necked overshirt and trousers with low seat – sewn from narrow off-white strips with a black, a green or a blue linear pattern. The *Sidwaya*, the local paper, has a small news item from Abidjan: Three US tennis players have left the country after one of them, Jimmy Gurfein, was found raving with cuts and bruises he got from jumping through a second-floor window of the Ikoyi Hotel; the three had started by reading the Bible, then they destroyed their passports, cash and other possessions, whereupon Gurfein shouted that he could see Jesus floating by outside. Watch out for low-flying gods!

Lion has the tonguefall and the attitudes of the London intellectual used to standing propped up in a brown pub. He says: 'Americans are weird. Maybe they've lost all touch with reality from having lived for too long off the fat of the fridge.' He is an old conference-addict, he has been here before, he has seen it all. He tells a few horror stories of the brutalities committed by a certain Diallo, a half-blood who until recently was in charge of the security apparatus, of people being tortured with blow-torches, of midnight raids and interrogations meant to terrorize actual or potential opponents. He shakes his head and clicks his tongue – 'these natives!' – laughs uproariously, opens his briefcase to extract his bottle of whisky, pours a round, screws the cap back on, returns the precious bottle to its hiding place. He says he's in the process of getting together enough funds to film the story of a war between two poor African states; the president of the one country has penetrated the territory of the other at the head of his army when he hears that he's been deposed in a *coup d'état* back home . . . He laughs some more (he has the supercilious British attitude to Africa) and says: 'Thanks to war we know we have frontiers. Do you know why the Burkinabé are so tolerant? Because in their vast majority they are neither Moslem nor Christian but animist.'

Mano: 'Ah, may God protect them from monotheism!'

The Ivory Coast actress says she was in Ouagadougou, right here, during a previous *coup d'état*. It would be good material for a film one day. She was acting in a play that toured several of the neighbouring countries. ('In Niger we were being wined and dined in the President's palace, and in the courtyard I saw some small people – probably children of the servants – so undernourished that they looked like slow skeletons with red eyes and bloated bellies. They had red hair and flies were crawling all over them. My food stuck in my throat.') One night, just down the road here, she says, they were attending a garden party in the grounds of the French Embassy when shooting broke out in the streets. They were told to enter the building and to lie down on the floor for protection. With them there was the Upper Volta minister of culture. The next day he left the embassy compound after obtaining the formal assurance of the new rulers that his life would be spared. Perhaps the French ambassador had negotiated the safe-conduct. A few hours later, during a lull in the fighting, they themselves were permitted to return to their hotel, the Ran. In the street, not fifty yards from the embassy front door, they passed the corpse of the minister lying face-down in his own blood. It was before all the flies had been killed. They were blocked for more than a week in their hotel, together with a group of Alsatian nurses and a delegation of Canadian businessmen who'd been visiting the country. The hotel staff used to leave at four in the afternoon, to be out of the field of fire before nightfall. So the guests had to do their own cooking and washing up. At night soldiers shattered the windows with their gunbutts and tried to break in to rape the nurses and the female members of the cast. They were probably drunk. One morning the guests woke up to find an unidentified naked dead man in the lobby. It was not the minister. Nobody dared touch him. He stayed there for three days, by which time the stench had become unbearable.

'Death comes silently on rapid feet, to go away with the morning star,' Mano says. 'We always work with death at hand. He is in fact the one we are talking to, and the props we play with - the clothes and the masks – are in fact his, are elements of his presence. Ours is the work of the night, we burn fiercely but pathetically against a dark backdrop, we splutter and then we go out and our invisible partner, death, takes over centre-stage. Nothing remains but strings, rags, cardboard and dust. In a sense we are engaged upon the creation of an illusion, and it is a matter of knowing what to leave out, what traits to accentuate. The conception of life, and therefore the illusion of life, lifelikeness in other words, is the art of seeing how close you can come to the improbable, to the absence. To death. Because the recognition of life itself is an illusion, and the mind – or the imagination – must be left room enough to make the associations, to fill the gaps, to effect the jumps. Birds are not frightened off by people but by scarecrows only very crudely and summarily representing people. The shadow on the wall is imbued with more life than the person or the object throwing the shadow. We are crafting the mechanism of memory. More precisely, we fashion the hollows in which memory can fit. Our modern age doesn't provide for memory any more: the child going to school or the scientist doing his research work doesn't need it any longer – functional memory is built into his computer. Naturally, programmed memory is dead data, it cannot be self-generating or self-inventing or self-transforming like the memory of man. But it is probably more reliable, objective, precise. Except that in this process of compartmentalization people are losing the faculty of memory and therefore of invention, and this is a pity because we are human and terrible exactly because we have memories which we cannot circumscribe or codify. We actors imitate the shape of memory. We cannot compete with artificial intelligence in the conveying of knowledge, but we can suggest the incoherent, we can apprehend the forms and the movement of time, the slowness and the uncertainty of it. We can approximate life – but it will be scripted, rehearsed, directed, repeated – and thus again an illusion.'

The Ivory Coast actress (she'd really prefer to be known as a starlet) has smiled coyly at at least ten of the men wandering by ostensibly to go and look at the opaque surface of the water in the swimming pool. Night is darkening the sky and a slight breeze is rustling the leaves of the trees. She is now scratching the furrows between the plaits on her head with a long red fingernail. She talks about a play called *Wasan Kara* (meaning 'King of Straw') taking place once a year in the town of Zinder, in Niger. The whole population will participate in the play, lasting the whole day. They'll have been practising for weeks beforehand. Quite ordinary people are chosen to incarnate the roles of local bigwigs, army officers, the head of police etc. . . . Then they re-enact some historical event, imaginary or real, in the presence of the people they're impersonating. They may decide to do the day President Reagan came to Africa to sell democracy. They dress the part, speak the part, walk or march the part. And since they are repeating all the flowery gestures and speeches, the whole affair becomes ever so subtly satirical. One cannot mouth nationalist sentiments or moral pronouncements as an imitator without it being ridiculous. The actors of course take their roles very seriously and the entire population takes part with enthusiasm, squealing and ululating, making the same obeisance to the 'false' dignitaries as they'd make to the 'real' ones, but just slightly over-doing it. And becoming so bold as to laugh at the silliness of it all. Their masters, for one day, have become puppets. History, for a day, is in their grasp. Maybe power is after all just a matter of strutting. And all of this with the 'real' actors as onlookers.

'What does it take to be a good actor?' Lion asks, tugging at his salt-and-pepper goatee and moving his shoulders like an exiled jazz-club pianist. It is just a gesture – he doesn't play the piano.

Mano says: 'Good or bad, who knows? You can say there are two kinds of poets – those who write short lines and those who write long lines. Both can be beginners of course, it's not a question of age or of experience, but of whether he dreams of maggots or of worms. But whereas the poet can say that he's waiting for his problems to die, the actor must keep them alive . . . To be an actor you need to be intelligent, gifted, and to have a problem. By intelligent I mean that you must understand what you're doing, to read the sense and the intentions of the text. To be gifted is to know how to move and to speak, to interact with the light and to respond to the pulse. And you must have a problem – be it alcoholism, homosexuality, fascist tendencies, exile, blindness. That which is lived as a frustration or a castration, to which you can relate in an effort to go beyond it, the obsession which will take your mind off the real partner, the self. The wound. The pain of the wound. The thought of pain. The abstraction you must make of the self in order to start shadow-boxing with death.'

The actress from the Ivory Coast scratches a bare leg and says the problems people have in this part of the world are rather more down to earth. 'Take witchcraft,' she says. 'There is a mental sickness now being studied in this country, called the "Ran" syndrome after the name of the railway line running from Ouaga to Bobo. People making the journey are very often attacked by bandits, robbed of their money and food, even raped. And so, to stay awake so as to see the evil-doers and not be taken by surprise, people, particularly the women, take all kinds of drugs and brews. But these eventually make them have hallucinations so that they often jump out of the train screaming that the robbers are after them when there's nobody around at all. There you have a case of illusion becoming too real . . . You can say the same of love. To be valiant in love the men sometimes take a concoction of red pepper and other stuff. It is called *cacacan*. A woman may have the hots for a young lover but be married to an old chief, say. It is a terrible bondage. So she will feed an excess of *cacacan* to her despotic old husband who will stupidly fuck himself to death!' (And she laughs the way people used to before air-conditioning was invented.)

In the evening they leave the hotel to join the others for a film show in an open-air cinema. A bus takes them there. Lion has stayed behind. When they leave he waves a floppy hand, saying that he's seen enough movies to last him a lifetime, before bending over clumsily to grope for something in the briefcase between his feet. He's found a buddy to share his philosophical thoughts with, punctuated by a knowing red-tongued laugh. 'Did you know that the baboon is called a *Cynocephale papio*?' he asks. But his buddy (who may be an off-duty waiter) clearly doesn't understand a word of English. The belle from the Ivory Coast, who has found the time to go and change her dress, has moved up in the world – she is now hanging on to the arm of a grey-haired Senegalese director with leather cap, dark glasses and pipe.

Desert nomads, proud and inscrutable, their heads wrapped in lengths of indigo cloth so that only their fierce black eyes peer out, swords with richly ornamented grips strapped to their backs, sit their tall grey camels in the street before the hotel. People fill the streets, riding two by two on their buzz-bikes, or walking as if going nowhere. Nowhere is just down the street. There are nearly no street lamps: the pedestrians flit like shadowy ghosts by the bus. Near the compound of presidential buildings, under the deeper darkness of high trees, they see an old naked woman sitting on the pavement with her legs stretched before her. Her dry, wrinkled breasts hang down to her waist. Next to her she has a few tins, a flattened cardboard box. But the vision is so fugitive that they cannot be sure there was really someone there.

A hum of people has filled the open arena built in the shape of a half-moon. The film (called *L'Ombre de la terre*, made by a Tunisian), and the site where it is shown, is like a double-take. It is an exercise in unreality. Behind the screen there is a backdrop of palm trees, just barely standing out against the night. A slow, hot moon is climbing the purple skies above the city. They smell the dust lingering in the air, the pungent sweetness of frangipanis. The film is telling a desert story of slow, economic gestures and spaces of colour punctuated by palm trees. Everything is a mirage.

Do Africans die more easily than other people? It is late when they return to the hotel. Some people are sleeping spread-eagled on the armchairs in the lobby. Others still wander around among the trees by the swimming-pool. A big moon is going to lower itself into the black water and the pool will overflow and wet the paving stones.

Mano says: 'I'm thinking of the sea. It is strange to be thinking of the sea here, so far in the interior. Singing the sea. From the beginning everything is. Every thing is its own manifestation. The sea sings itself from ever to ever.'

Meheret thinks: What is this thing that makes you feel at home here rather than elsewhere? What is it that constitutes the anguished awareness of exile? The sense of having lost the language, the daily bread of self-knowledge? But with modern means of communication there can be no real loss – you can buy the newspaper, pick up the phone. The beauty of a native landscape? But as we move we realize that there are many beautiful places, and that true freedom is a question of harmonious interaction with the environment you find yourself in. Admittedly, some coasts or landscapes or towns breathe freer and more calmly than others. Is it the security of a job? But many exiles find better conditions for living and working elsewhere, in their adopted lands. Is it the fact of never fully becoming part of your new surroundings? Such will also be the case of many indigenous categories, both at 'home' and in 'exile', all the marginalized sectors of the population of any country. Is it simply because it is 'unnatural'? Is it still unnatural? Masses of people, in groups or as individuals, have been uprooted, deported, resettled during our century. And are we not nomads at heart? Perhaps it would be more honest to propose that exile is often a lucky escape from oppressive conditions back 'home'; that the state of exile is itself a powerful boost towards accomplishment. And if sense of loss there is, is it not the general and shared loss of youth and innocence?

Mano says: 'Let me recite you a poem:

'we come in public
to scratch our sores with scabby paws
so that you may pity us,
we turn over the dustbins
and forage and ferret in newspapers
soaked in stale news
to read of riots
and people on gallows
and separate the peels
from the ink of death,
so glad that we are here:
we the exiles
we who wanted to struggle
against all forms of loneliness

sometimes a messiah comes from the interior
to talk to us about new words
and warm bread–
then we comb our beards
and disguise our wounds with unguents
and wind white weeper around our hands,
for one magical moment

we are again perfect and proud
in the eyes of the countryman

but life resumes its pageant
of begging forays
and we go slobber against your panes
to exhibit our pain to you,
we the exiles –
we who wanted to struggle
against the shape of loneliness.'

Meheret: 'You remember that we once talked of this, of being of
the centre or the periphery? Let us not fool ourselves. Why should
we have stayed here in Africa? Look at all the misery, poverty,
death, ignorance. Oh, not here perhaps, not in this town. Though
who knows what's going on in the countryside out there? Are the
peasants making a revolution? Of course not. They just want to eat
and live in peace, have a little more and not be terrorized by bureaucrats or by the spirits. Where is our democratic future? What have
the successive rules of dictators done for us in Africa?

'It is normal, healthy, good that you should want to escape. My
father was a dreamer and a gambler and he died abjectly. Where
can we live out our dreams? If I had the choice I'd do it all over
again. Maybe this time I'd have gone elsewhere, America or Canada
or Australia – Europe is going down in mud and madness. But I'd
still have left for the centre.'

The phone starts ringing. It is one o'clock in the morning. Mano
hears Mumpata's low voice in his ear, unconcerned at the lateness
of the call. Whether Mano can come out to an address on the edge
of town, tomorrow morning at ten?

They go to bed. Maybe the moon has disappeared behind the
edge of the earth. Above them there will be the void, a vibrating
night sprinkled with stars. 'And if I were to have a child?' she asks.
'I wouldn't want to be responsible for bringing a being into this
awful world,' he says. 'Each one must walk his own road. If there
is a child, what can we hope for? That he becomes a revolutionary.
That he knows there can be no end to the struggle, that blood
doesn't purify or justify, that dark forces will colour his vision. But
also that he may know the exultation of the struggle, the honing of
the mind down to nothingness, to non-being . . . It is our destiny
to rise up.'

She dreams of a vast indigo-coloured sea as seen from above. The surface is smooth and mirror-like, terribly vulnerable. There is a grey, rocky coast, and there are boats. So as not to be detected from the sky, the ships take on board huge plinths and obelisks of grey rock. They drift away over the blue expanse, like islands.

He dreams of an emblematic figure called Greta Garbo. A young couple arrive at a well-guarded house where they intend to kidnap Greta Garbo. Four men are shinning up four flagpoles outside to unfurl four green flags. Inside the fortress there are some very surprised nuns. 'Greta Garbo? She's dead, she's been dead for ages. Look, this is her coffin.' The couple steal the coffin, but it turns out to be empty. And then Greta Garbo herself goes on a visit to a museum where coffins are kept. She is a dignified old black lady. She is being shown around the museum. Her coffin is there too, as bait, as a lure. When she sees it she will recognize it and climb back in. And be stolen, hurriedly, to be carried back to life. It is not so easy to come to terms with rest. Four flags flutter in the wind.

11

At breakfast in the big buzzing dining hall, they find the same people of the previous night. They are all bit actors in a low-budget epic film, coming and going in various costumes and disguises, waiting for someone to shout 'Action!' and the shooting to start. Meanwhile they sip their coffee, wave their hands, and repeat their snippets of dialogue.

Meheret and Mano are joined at table by a couple of Whites. The woman must be in her late thirties. She has a red face, tawny hair tied in a ribbon, a rather impressive bosom imprisoned in a bright yellow blouse. She is making sure she will get enough to eat. The man – older, fatter, dressed in open-necked shirt and trousers – is not eating. He has a pile of publications under his arm.

'Excuse us,' he says, extending a soft hand to Mano and to Meheret. 'May we sit down with you? I saw you and I wanted to come over and introduce myself. My name is Mitganger. I'm German but I teach the history of politics in Toronto.' (Mano recognizes the name; he's a rather well-known socialist theoretician on questions pertaining to the Three Worlds.) 'And this is Kathy Human, a compatriot of yours. You are South African, am I right?'

Meheret says no, she is Ethiopian. Kathy Human blushes and admits they were told there's another South African in town, and she just wanted to meet and say hello. She's in films, an assistant director, living in exile in Canada, that's where she knows Mitganger from (from the way her fingers brush over the palm of his hand it is clear that they know each other with eyes closed), and actually she's only on her way through to Nigeria where she will be working on the production of a musical that's supposed to take place in South Africa.

'Africa is so corrupt, don't you think?' she says. She was having all the trouble in the world to get to Lagos. Just over 20 per cent of their budget is earmarked for bribes alone. She finally obtained a visa in London. Took her ever so long. The Nigerian ambassador there said the phone bill for contacting Lagos concerning her visa was coming to one hundred and twenty-five pounds at least. Now if she were willing to pay for the telephone expenses . . . perhaps the visa could be speeded up. 'Aren't they terribly rotten, these African diplomats?' While the story is pouring from her she's buttering her buns and scraping jam from the little containers. She licks her fingers.

Mitganger explains how glad he is to meet someone from South Africa. Could they have a talk? Does Mano know so-and-so and whatsisname? There's so much that he'd like to hear. Mano says that it would be inconvenient just at this moment, he has a prior appointment outside town. 'What sector?' Mitganger asks, and when Mano indicates the address he winks knowingly. 'I know it. Cyrille Ouedreago's place. Important, hey? Hush-hush.' But when Mano asks him who Cyrille Ouedreago may be he becomes secretive.

'This country is so complicated. Have you met the Man yet?' (The Man must be the President.) 'You should, you know. He is very accessible. We are old friends. I was with him last night, and we have long arguments. There are still corrupt elements that need to be purged. He listens to me. That is why you see everybody going around, on bicycles here. The civil servants and the little chiefs are no longer permitted free motorcars. He can surely help you. He's still young, you know. And he doesn't have any cultural or historical complexes. He is intelligent and he has integrity and he really wants to transform this society. He trusts the people, but he may be making a mistake. I think he underestimates the contradictions here, and he is too naïve. The imperialists are not going to leave him alone. Of course the real equation is the economy. I hope he succeeds, he's a friend of mine, but I'm pessimistic, you know? It is a world-wide struggle. I have seen too many disappointments when the leaders are not well enough prepared.' (He says 'vorld' and 'haf'.)

'They are four actually. Close like brothers. Discuss everything together. They used to be five, the fifth one was a Coloured, Diallo, head of security, but he's now been sacked because of his exactions. A cold fish. High time the Man got rid of Diallo. I told him so. Could only bring him bad luck.

'You'd better take my car to go out to Cyrille's place. The taxis are uncomfortable and unreliable and I have a car and a chauffeur outside. I live in the Hôtel Silmandé, but I don't need my transportation this morning. I have to go and give a lecture to the National Revolutionary Council. About the history of Africa since independence, you know? Why don't you come out to my hotel some time? Tomorrow? I'd like to talk to you.'

Kathy Human looks up and blushes. She's eating a pineapple. Already they can start feeling the heat of the day. The air-conditioning isn't functioning all that well. Mitganger's hair is plastered to his forehead and his neck is shiny and red.

When they start driving to Cyrille Ouedreago's house, they realize how spread out the town really is. Down Avenue Nelson Mandela they pass a bus stop called 'Honte à l'impérialisme'. They drive around a traffic circle which has a soaring monument to the Cinema – a coloured concrete jumble of square and round shapes, the round ones could be resembling the flat tins in which films are kept. They go through neighbourhoods that must have been flattened to make way for rows of new buildings. The constructions – shopping areas and blocks of flats and private housing units – create an attractive impression of comfort and roominess. The streets are wide, the habitations obviously built at about the same time and designed by the same architects, but the many trees and shrubs, the touches of individual colour, the good quality material used, prevent a feeling of sameness. These quarters are named after the year of construction, counting from the Revolution on – Year One . . . Year Two . . .

Could be Maputo or Luanda, but more humble. Portuguese colonial? No, not really. Built against the heat. Flat-roofed. Deep balconies. Outside walls up to the height of three feet stained red from the earth. Must be caused by diluvial downpours. Desert economy in reality. Subtle adaptations and modest expectations, but tenacity. Degree Zero of survival in stripped environment. Horizon of expectation – of awareness? – a long thin line. People no longer allowed to just go and cut down trees or pull up bush for firewood. Stern restrictions. Must have special permission. Only vehicles painted green and white may transport wood. Lorries, donkey-carts. Programme of reforestation. Any excuse good for planting trees. Too late? Ground colours wherever you look. Use of modest materials – earth, iron, grass, leather. Modesty? Humbleness? Frugality? Fragility? Poverty? Overpowering heat moving in waves over the landscape. Correlation between fragility and formalism?

Further out there are huts or rudimentary houses lying a little way back from the road. Flat land, then clumps of trees. Donkeys, goats, chickens. Colourful birds flitting through the whitish sky. Some a bright green colour, or blue. Mano says: 'Down there we have beautiful birds also, and they have such pretty names: *lemoen-duifie, kokkewiet, piet-my-vrou* . . .' Meheret asks: 'And if I were to have a child?' Mano: 'What a cruel, lovely, sad world.' Bees are splattering the windscreen. Meheret says: 'In Ethiopia we make our hives from lengths of hollow tree-trunks wrapped in reeds. We hang these from the branches. We put smouldering sweet-smelling leaves inside the hives to attract the bees, and when we have enough of them for a swarm we close up the round opening. Our honey is golden. We use it in the place of sugar. We still make mead. It is called *tej*.'

Outside the houses, a pen of dried thorny branches for the cattle close by, old men stand facing the sun. Nearly imperceptible murmur of lips. Faces the colour of night. Looking at us from the past. Oh, ancestors, gods – our forgetting obliterating your presence like darkening masks. We move by you as if over the smooth unknown. We no longer understand the meaning of your eyes. We cannot read you. We have lost the timing of your thoughts. You are decorative masks. You are too ancient to be seen from a speeding car.

Bushfires in distance. Dark blue smoke-plumes. Circling around the edges of understanding. Story is pattern of circling, is rich bowl of dust. Pattern is rhythm. Heart like fist clenching hope. Heart flooded with despair. I cannot silence despair of the heart. Heart a bowl of water. Wash the fist. The sun makes everything look white, like snow.

The car turns off the main road and immediately clouds of red dust are chased up. They arrive at a walled-in house, the walls patched with the shadowy pattern of some trees spreading their branches. Mumpata comes to meet them at the gate, leads them into the house to a cool room with a few comfortable chairs, a low table, a painting of Malcolm X. on the wall. The host is absent, Mumpata gestures, at work in town. Not a military man, but a position of responsibility. Mumpata wears a jacket and tie despite the heat. He is a man of above average height, his skin so dark it looks purple, his head absolutely bald and shiny, his eyes hooded by careful eyelids, his teeth – when he smiles – discoloured. 'Will you have tea or beer, Sis?' he asks Meheret. But she turns down the offer, says she'd like to walk around outside, let them discuss their mutual concerns; she has some notes to make.

Mumpata asks Mano whether he's ever been to this part of Africa before. Mano tells him of his first impressions, the keenness of the people they've met so far, how concerned they are about South Africa, the struggle. He talks about Mitganger and the Human woman. Mumpata knows Mitganger – 'he's a dilettante, a hanger-on' – and yes, he's heard about Kathy Human. One should be careful. One doesn't know who she is, where she comes from, why she's really here. It is too easy for all sorts of people to move around Africa. The Africans are gullible. One will have to find out more about her. What Mano thinks of her? That she's perhaps too loud. Too fat, anyway.

Mumpata has been to Burkina Faso several times. 'Have you met the Man yet? No? It is better not to get involved in political discussions here. This is not our scene, and there's not much they can do for us. It is senseless to become embroiled in this fair of radical and anarchist ideas. Too many opportunists, provocateurs, exalted ones about. I don't know how long their experiment is going to last. Mind you, I'm not saying it's not interesting to see what they're doing. But it is still very much France's back-yard. And Africa – bushfires! The Man is up against terrible problems. You can't make a revolution with love and generosity.'

'What are the dangers?' Mano asks.

'Many, many. Personality cult. Internal rivalry. Regional jealousy. Houphouet is unhappy. Big-power manipulation. Too many enemies inside and outside. The sullen and cynical opposition of the political-administrative caste – he's cut back on their salaries and their perks. He sacked too many generals. An open house for intervention by rightist mercenaries and avaricious adventurers. The economy is too weak. They are trying to move too fast – to build on what? Slogans are not enough. How long will people put up with hardship? Where is the outside help and support going to come from? Which foreign power will let them have the necessary means? The West? Integrity is a dangerous commodity. Cleaning up an administration is destroying the bed of the West. The socialist states? But the Man is too unpredictable, too unorthodox, too independent. The fragility of the system can be exploited. They will run out of breath soon. And then? It only takes one natural disaster to break their backs – drought, locusts, Aids. It is delirious now. Crawling with all sorts of leftist theoreticians attracted like flies to honey. The same ones you found in Tanzania, Mozambique, Angola, Guinea-Bissau, Zimbabwe – the failed and embittered ''professional'' revolutionaries who will try and push them too far but who really function in terms of their own frustrations and hurt. And when the house of cards tumbles, they will not be the ones facing the firing squads. No, we have too many footloose dreamers in Africa. It is dangerous. It is better to stay out of this. Don't get excited. Don't get involved.'

Mano laughs and shakes his head. Of course he is not going to get involved with anything here. He is not aching for a revolution, he's just curious, that's all. Although quite impressed, he must admit, by what he's seen so far. A lot can be said, he thinks, for the virtues of poverty. Could it not be argued that subsistence economies, when assumed consciously, allow for a dignity based on self-sufficiency, that there can be a transformation of basic realities – with earth materials and native intelligence – without the utopist folly of top-heavy and foreign-relying superstructures? Could there not be the valorization of non-Western traditions and types of learning allied to the most modern techniques the north has to offer? Surely they put up examples of modesty, integrity, sincerity? They have shown a suppleness of adaptation to harsh environmental conditions, they are resilient, they have developed survival methods and yet maintain a thrust towards metamorphosis. In South Africa now, not only are the Whites spoiled by riches, but the Blacks too – compared to the rest of Africa – are imprisoned by fancy means and fads provided for and controlled by others. Your sophisticated means may also be the chains of your dependence.

Mumpata is lighting a blonde cigarette. Slightly acrid smoke curls around his plum-coloured head. He grins without looking at Mano. 'So you have taken the bait too? Aren't you perhaps looking at Africa with disappointed European eyes, and through idealistic glasses? I think it may be time for you to . . . return home, to go and look for yourself. In what way is South Africa part of the continent? Our histories are so divergent, so particular. It is incorrect to wish to impose a foreign analysis, however generous, on our specific conditions. We are largely a Third World country, agreed, and the majority of us are black Africans just like the Africans here – but that is not the whole story. Our set-up is so much more sophisticated. It would be simplistic, romantic, to think otherwise. And not very scientific. Didn't Walser teach you that?'

'Walser?'

'Yes, Walser. He is the one who referred you to me, isn't it so? We used to know one another quite well some years ago. At the time he worked with Curiel's group, but he was never a member –

just a go-between for various outlawed organizations and individuals in . . . free orbit. The Party made use of the services of Curiel's group. Oh, not much. That was before the fiasco, that nasty business of Bernael's foolhardy trip into South Africa, and Curiel's assassination. Quite different from one another – Walser the slow dancer, Curiel of the quick mind . . . They disagreed about so many things. Still, I'd have thought Curiel's careful analytical view would have been shared by the old man.'

'But times have changed,' Mano says. 'You are talking of fifteen years ago. I never knew Curiel. He has been dead for nearly fifteen years. And there have been changes in Africa also since then. Yes, Walser was the one who suggested that I should contact you, to make the connection for sounding out the minds of some people back home. I, and others like myself, who have also been involved in the struggle to some extent, we'd like to know where we're going. You can say that we are the second generation of exiles. You know, the way one speaks of generations of computers – with very complicated dead memories . . . I must return there. I don't belong in Europe.'

'And I, we, should like you to return. Particularly since you are clean. You have no record of activism. You could move so easily in that society, under your own name, being neither white nor black. We need people like yourself to go down and have a fresh look. Not to do anything. Just to bring back your impressions.'

'Yes, and I have some personal reasons for returning too.'

'If you want to, it can be arranged.'

'Still,' Mano says, 'it is important to start from here, to get the African background right. There is to my mind a strategic importance in the attempt to break the links between South Africa and the Western powers.'

Mumpata is slowly lighting a fresh cigarette, looking at his hands.

'The whole world is our stage . . . You say: As in the case of South Africa . . . *that* is the block on Africa. How well you speak. You see, here we have another dimension to what you call the strategy of breaking the imperialist domination. I spare you an analysis of the extraordinarily complex history and actual situation in our country. You know it for yourself. Except that I should like to point out that South Africa will have to be helped to come to its senses.'

'I agree wholeheartedly' – Mano has become quite excited. 'If by that you mean that no one can do what we South Africans must

123

do for ourselves, but that Africa, can, indeed *must* help shape our consciousness. You as well – I'm talking of the liberation movements – will have to understand that the struggle, our struggle, is not an East–West one, not even ideologically so. That it is not necessarily the traditional revolutionary process towards communism. It may well be that the South African revolution, when completed, will see the creation of the most orthodox socialist state on the continent. Surely no African country can claim to be communist, although nearly all are authoritarian. Even the embryo states exercise a power monopoly over their peoples, often for the sake of a foreign instance.

'But South Africa must be brought home to Africa. The liberatory organizations should shift their paradigms away from Washington and Paris and London and Bonn and Moscow and Tokyo. Our horizons are Harare, Luanda, Ouagadougou, Accra, Tripoli, Algiers, Hanoi, Havana, Managua . . . *You* are heading down a dangerous trail. You have a doctrine adapted to other situations, another continent, another history, as your guiding star.

'Isn't the problem that you want to be recognized as a negotiating partner by the West? To negotiate with whom? On whose behalf? On what base of liberated power? With what guarantees and what means? To concede what? And what will be the outcome even if you were to succeed? What will your usefulness to Africa be then? Will we be a truculent giant, perpetuating an iniquitous relationship of unequal power with the neighbouring states?

'South Africa, poisoning agent of the world, bastion for foreign interference, South Africa must return to Africa. Agreed, you may feel that putting your trust in Africa is like pouring precious water into a rotten sack, that the fabric will rend . . . Nevertheless, it is in the strenuous and high-principled interaction between the South African revolutionary consciousness and the liberating processes elsewhere on the continent that a new awareness can emerge, that new principles can be promoted, that the lackeys can be isolated and counteracted. Zaïre, Gabon, Chile, Taiwan, Israel . . .'

There is a long silence between the two men. Mumpata is turning over a glass ashtray with both hands. His head is down on his chest. His voice is low: 'The struggle for emancipation of the Three Continents, the long and complex . . . war . . . against the rich North, flaring up in uprisings, riots, revolutions here and there . . . Smothered in blood. And you are trying to tell me what must be done? What other continent ever had as many revolutionaries as

Africa? Luthuli, Nkrumah, Mondlane, Ben Barka, Lumumba, Machel, Neto, Cabral . . . All dead.'

'Sobukwe,' Mano adds.

'All dead. The constant strategy of our adversaries has always been to behead the revolution.'

Mano: 'And yet this is still a clean war, a war worth waging . . .'

'Are you finished yet? I think we have to get back into town.'

Meheret has been there for quite some time without the two men noticing her. She is framed in the light falling through the doorway. She looks frail, the sun making a halo of her short hair, oiled and combed away from the forehead. Maybe she's frowning, but her eyebrows quite naturally grow together like that in a stern line above the nose.

They go back the way they came. Mumpata has seen them off with a veiled expression in his eyes. The same goats seem to be nibbling at the same dry acacia branches. Old men have shifted their positions. Like totems they face the sun. One or two of them have a thin, claw-like hand shading the eyes. Are they wondering who the foreigners in the car may be? Mano has closed his eyes. There is the hot smell of dust in the car. The driver has wound down his window. He wears a cap pulled down low over a scarred face. Mano takes Meheret's hand in his. 'For how long were you there, listening to us?' She doesn't answer.

He says: 'I never knew my father. My mother had an older brother. Once or twice, when I was very small, my mother sent me to her brother's, Uncle Isaiah's place, for the school holidays. Riviersonderend, the town was called. River without end. He lived there with his wife, three sons and a daughter my age. How envious I used to be of their family life! A small plot, a vegetable patch, some fruit trees, chickens. He was the sexton of the local church. When I was eight years old my mother took me with her to a hospital in a suburb of Mother City, to go say goodbye to Uncle Isaiah. He was dying from cancer. Small and brown and wrinkled in the bed. Big glasses sitting on his nose. The lenses were dirty. My mother was weeping unashamedly. Uncle Isaiah's old wife on a chair next to the bed, you could only see her kerchief, her shaking shoulders. "You have to help me, Sister," he said. "You have to get me out of here. I have to go and pick my apricots." It must have been late December. He had three beautiful apricot trees, heavy and fragrant with fruit. My mother had to promise. Before leaving, the two women sang a hymn in their thin voices, drawing out the sounds. I had to keep the rhythm, clapping my hands. My uncle was discharged from hospital, picked his fruit – it was a good harvest – and died.'

12

The night may be silent but in the afternoon there's a rustling of leaves. Vultures circle high above the city. The streets are crowded with people going to market, going to an afternoon cinema show, walking around to watch the other people walking around, going nowhere. Nowhere keeps on shifting its location. The 'blue people' of the desert sit very aloof on their camels. They have been hired for the week as decorative effect. Flashing mirrors stud their saddles, their swords look lethal. Men with dark glasses and open-necked shirts linger on the verandas, observing the passers-by and commenting with loud laughs. The odd European visitor stands out like a sore thumb, baked a brick colour by the sun, festooned with cameras and tape recorders, wearing the kind of 'native' straw hat that none of the natives will be seen dead in, and a T-shirt preaching some good lost cause. Music throbs through the streets. The women are thin, dressed predominantly in shades of brown, not half as elegant as the menfolk. Small children sit strapped to the backs of their mothers, feet splayed, never saying beep. Through trustful eyes they watch the world swirl by.

Across the street and one block down from the hotel is the central courthouse. A trickle of guests and participants are moving there for a press conference or a lecture or a meeting. All over town, and particularly in more or less secluded parts of the garden around the Hôtel Indépendance swimming pool, these meetings form and disband. The themes are obscure, the organization supple, the speakers passionate.

The main courtroom is big with a high ceiling. There's not much light. The benches and the boxes are of dark wood. Justice must be a dim affair. On the wall behind the presiding judge's table there are two huge portraits of Lenin and Stalin. They are far from home. Mano is making mental notes. If the project of filming part of Barnum's story comes to anything they would certainly need a court sequence. Why not use this setting? The pictures would have to be replaced of course – perhaps by those of Vorster and Botha, or Malan and Verwoerd. A courtroom is not so much the forecourt to death as the antechamber of oblivion. Confused pleas have darkened the walls. All rocks are ground to sand in the machinery of justice, all snow becomes water.

Mano turns to Meheret and snaps his fingers. 'That is the point I was trying to put across to Mumpata this morning,' he says. 'He asked me what I make of historical determinism then. I said I'd rather not think about it because the very notion has been detrimental to us. The Party does not *learn* from the past, it becomes the recipient, the guardian, of the accumulated *weight* of the past. The past becomes longer and longer, and we spend all our time commemorating it. So that the present becomes a comment, not a commencement. Blame us on history. No time to invent. No need to break. Past time is an investment. We can wait till the pigs come flying home and the horses shake their horns – all the while sitting on our beam-ends discoursing on contradictions and the glorious accumulations of the Struggle. Marx will be proved right . . . How is this any different from the Afrikaners' doctrine of predestination? Listen, I think this is an important similitude: Are we doomed to become imitators of the people we are combating? I was talking to him but I might as well have had an old *Boer* before me. He had the same gestures, the same mind. Have you noticed how enemies often dress the same way? And how the opponents to an oppressive system use the methods of the oppressors to impose themselves? When Mugabe came to power, he ruled Zimbabwe by the rules of Ian Smith's state of emergency. Why is that?'

'You know why,' Meheret answers. 'First of all because no struggle takes place in a void. The actors are all players in the same game, which has its rules and its characteristics. How could they be enemies unless they share a common ground? They may be opposing partners, and the stronger of the two parties will have left its stamp on the nature of the game, but both react in quite similar ways to an objective reality. Then, because it is normal for people to imitate one another. Especially for the weaker to imitate the stronger, since he would like to rob him of his strength. Opposing someone is a way of making love to him. The Struggle, the Game, Life – is a passionate affair. In French it would be: *Tout pouvoir a besoin de rapports*, all power needs interaction, relationships, intercourse . . . in order to exist. It is dialectical. You are not fighting ghosts, but your brothers. Do we not share humanity? We are linked by our differences.'

'But it has induced an attitude of waitism in the Movement. Of bloatedness. Too many freedom fighters have been forged into diplomats, into glib travelling salesmen on the beggar circuit.'

'Sshhh!' she says. 'Not so loud. Do you think people here are all that different? You are taken by them because you think they have the bit between the teeth. You think they are creating themselves. Isn't it because you don't know anything about their past? Their past is invisible to you. You are impatient.'

The proceedings have started, the purpose still remains vague. As if to echo their concerns, an African film-maker with bulging black eyes and a wild head of hair is saying into the microphone which he cradles, clutched in both fists: 'African films have a *pedagogical* immediacy. People don't crowd to our screens with their heads saturated with a cinematographical culture. Sound and the spacing of images, the play of empty and full, are tools of communication, not ends in themselves. For us there is less distance between being and acting. In fact, there is no acting. The symbols we stick in are there as nodal points of power, not as enunciations of beauty. We live in a world where spirits are omnipresent. That is why you will not see dream scenes on our screens – because people will immediately relate to dreamlike reality as the world of the spirits.'

The conference drones on. People come and go, not speaking much of Michelangelo. There are men in flowing traditional garb, women sitting with their knees clumsily together, young men in smart European 'relaxed' clothes, students with briefcases, boys fresh off the street with dusty feet and shorts and torn shirt-tails hanging out, a few soldiers in neat uniforms.

Even the most banal question coming from the floor will be written out beforehand on a scrap of paper – and then some will have trouble reading their own handwriting. How people love 'taking the word'! Words are warmed in the mouth, their outlines traced by the tongue, then taken out, passed around, repeated, held up against the light, praised, ridiculed, bargained for. They become tactile and odiferous. Anyway, you do not soliloquize, you insert yourself in a pattern of communication, become inscribed in a rhythm. The others will punctuate your words, apostrophize you, help you around the corners, bring you down gently. In the end you will not know whether you proposed or agreed. Who spoke? Mano remembers something Aimé Césaire once said: '*C'est par le mot que le moi se coagule*'. ('The word fixes the shape of the I.') He was speaking of words as masks, or masks as words – the *mot-masque*.

'*L'impérialisme? A bas! / Le colonialisme? A bas! / L'apartheid? A bas! / Le sionisme? A bas! / Le pouvoir? Au peuple! / Tout le pouvoir? Au peuple!/ La patrie ou la mort!*' Mano's musings are brutally scattered by the shouting of slogans which habitually closes every meeting. The questions are shouted by a young enraptured man and the answers mouthed by all the people present. It dies away in a murmur of *we shall overcome* . . . , accompanied by a raising of clenched fists. But these are friendly and languorous African fists, not of the American Black Panther variety showing off a shrill (and short-lived) virility. Sometimes the ritual chanting will interrupt a gathering. People will have cleared their throats, shifted their buttocks, and the parley can continue.

On the way back to the hotel Meheret says: 'Be careful to not get too carried away. Don't judge by surface appearances. Where are the opposition parties? Where is the freedom of the press? The scene may be more complex than you think. Do you know that the King of the Mossi, the *moro-naba*, lives in his palace just outside the capital? I talked to Mitganger's chauffeur today while you were inside the house with Mumpata. It seems the King still holds court. Recently the government cut off his water and electricity because he thought he didn't have to pay. They say he's not very old, somewhere in his thirties, and extremely fat. Traditionally he has to be fat, to eat all the time, and he has to sire as many children as possible. I don't know how he reconciles these two duties! Every Friday he gets on his black stallion and threatens to leave his subjects. Then all the people of the palace come out to weep and implore him to stay. He will hesitate, reflect a while, and get off his steed to return to his arduous tasks until the following week. Is he king or playing at being king? This too is part of the traditions.'

13

Being taken through the dark alleys of night to the reception. Street lighting is spotty, the African night without limits or horizons. The old naked lady, a well-used bag of wrinkles, is sitting under her tree, her head with its short grey hair in profile talking to a distant presence in another world. Her legs are stretched flat on the ground, her back very straight. She is as pure as a thought having no reference to any known substance. Around her she has the essentials of civilization: one plastic bowl, one flattened cardboard box. Baobabs and palm trees and flamboyants; they could do with some eucalyptuses.

Two streets further the headlamps of the bus pick out a young woman walking purposefully down the middle of the road, completely naked too. The sturdy buttocks and belly, the scowl on the face. Thoroughfares are thronged with a moving humanity flowing in mysterious directions. People are the dark furry lining of the night. The lights of the bus will spear the penumbra, fluorescent patches of white will momentarily emerge – an eye of wet glass, a winking tooth, a pale shirt – like moths they flutter and disappear. Low voices settle in silted-up layers over the city. From poorly lit back rooms with doors opening on the nocturnal void the mineral craziness of African jazz is broadcast. Hundreds of flickering lights dot the night-enshrouded sidewalks. Votive offerings to the spirits? These are single candles burning low, throwing a small napkin of orange light over humble stands selling three mangos, two tins of Coca-Cola, six packets of cigarettes of five different kinds, a book, a year-old magazine with a photo of the naked tits of a Monaco princess, little bottles of undefinable home-made substances, spicy meat, two jars of unpurified shea butter, luke-warm sorghum beer, a thumb-blackened copy of the *National Political Options*, another of the *Discourse on Women* with two pages missing, a watch made in Korea, a coloured photo of a Muslim saint, a cassette of Alpha Blondy, a pair of sandals cut from a tyre and its inner tube, a chicken, a copy of the Koran, seven round fruits with green peels, volume three of the collected works of Kim Il Sung, a T-shirt commemorating the Fespaco of two years ago . . .

La Paillotte is an open-air 'dancing', part of the estate known as *Year Two of the Revolution*. In the centre there's a big round dance-floor with all around it a series of smaller circles protected by thatched roofs on high pillars. Gaily dressed people are eating and drinking and trying to impress one another with a display of dazzling thoughts. A little further back, where the light doesn't reach, there are camouflage-dressed soldiers with rifles slung across their shoulders. The Revolutionary Police Band is providing the intricately intertwined music. One tune flows into the other, the patterned lyrics now and then throw up a reference to a known name or a revolution, the beat is strong and even like that of the heart. The night is hot. The singer shakes his silver legs. When there is a lull – because the musicians must also wipe their brows – a snake of tribal dancers burst forth and start circling the central area. They wear leather breech-cloths adorned with beads and cowry-shells. Around neck, forehead and arms they have decorated thongs, little leather pouches containing magic *gris-gris*, loops of trinkets – and as they frenetically move hips and buttocks (and only those) to the hypnotic beat of small holy cowhide drums, the beads and the strings jerk rhythmically with the sound of click and thwap.

Then there is a hustle, a stir, as a tightly packed group of people move from the shadow of the periphery to one of the circles, and a small flame running through the crowd: 'The Man is here. No! The Man himself has arrived. Really? Look! Where? Where? I told you he was coming. No! I knew he'd be here, he always is. Look, the Man is here.' People crane their necks, half-rise from their seats, smile at their neighbours. Then the whisper dies down, people try to look unconcerned, and the Revolutionary Police Band throw themselves into a new frenzy of glittering sounds.

The Man has a coterie of friends and colleagues seated around him. There are ministers, relaxed and joking, some stern-faced foreign dignitaries, a few age-tanned cultural or political mummies – veterans of the First African Dream. The security men and the protocol officers are hovering in the background. A small, fat, middle-aged Frenchman, his red face shining like a new apple, is darting in and out of the magic circle of power to obsequiously go whisper sweet nothings in the Man's ear. He is on the point of splitting the seams of his too tight-fitting *dan fani*. Mitganger is nowhere to be seen, but Kathy Human is moving up with Lion to be introduced to the Comrade President.

Kathy Human is blushing, trying to curtsey; Lion is shaking his shoulders and tugging at his grey goatee, his other hand nursing a bottle of beer. They don't get very far because of the language barrier. Amateur creators are standing on chairs to direct their silent red-eyed Super-eights at the hub of interest. Seated close to the Comrade President are three young French media products of the humanitarian industry. The Man laughs and the young French are stupid enough to mistake his friendliness and informality for familiarity. Any moment now they will light cigarettes and stretch their legs. They will slap the Man on his back and interrupt him. They haven't noticed the deceptively concealed pride of a genuinely humble man. A tall silent figure with frizzy hair, dark glasses and a dark-reddish skin is slowly making his way through the crowd. Short sleeves are stretched tight over his bulging, tattooed biceps.

Meheret watches with an amused smile as Mano tries to approach to within hearing distance of the Comrade President. Then the Man is on his feet, slowly progressing from group to group. The elbowing journalists and other groupies are being held at bay by a few bodyguards. Camera flashes pop their sudden white explosions. The Man is young, of medium height. He looks like a warrior priest in his simple white robe. The face is attractive, the eyes mocking and intelligent. He smiles easily, looking quizzically at the people around him. Mano is trying to catch his words. The Man seems to be curious and challenging at the same time. He must really be wanting to provoke thought.

'But the African mentality is shocked by the direct approach,' he says in answer to some remark. 'I know that I myself, although I admire the concise way of expressing ideas, indulge in long meandering explanations, often using symbols and images to illustrate the message I'm trying to bring across. In fact, we are suspicious of people with precise, journalistic answers. They are politicians, not of the people!'

Mano cannot hear the reply of the expatriate African journalist with the jeans, the dreadlocks, the granny glasses, the beret and the slogan buttons, to whom these words are addressed.

'So you are saying,' Comrade Man continues, 'that we need a cultural revolution behind all this verbiage. I'd agree – on condition that we are talking of a truly cultural revolution, thus of a modification of consciousness and perception. And then you must remember that growing awareness is by definition open-ended. It may well escape the control of its initiators. Think! It could even lead not only to a questioning of our aims, but also modify the means used. And if the vessel cracks?

'You know, racism is a subtle complex of relationships. It could express itself either through contempt or obsequiousness. We still have a lot of work to do before we will have decolonized our minds. You, an African, should know. You know what our climate is like, or you should remember – although I see you're dressed for a Parisian sitting-room of radical nostalgics. We see it around us, every day. Take for instance the young blade who will try and conform to extraneous criteria. He will take out his fiancée in a car with the window rolled up, and he will have her wear a fur coat! Just so's he can pretend that his car's air-conditioning is working! Here in Ouagadougou! We are mentally colonized, white images have blurred our imagination. Foreign behaviour-patterns and examples are flooding Africa. We eat chewing gum. We kiss in public. We forget that public kissing is "dirty" for us Africans. How many of us still know how to make love in the traditional way?'

The Man and his entourage have reached the dance-floor. He has started dancing, holding his torso very straight and moving his feet with great agility. Everybody is trying to crowd on to the circular space. It must be the Protocolar Dogtrot they're doing. Men are dancing with men, men are dancing alone, women are freeing their hips and their eyes have become moist dreams. A red-bearded European with a small hat is lost in his own primitive shuffle-and-stomp. The fat apple-faced 'white African' crony with the grey GI haircut is hopping from foot to foot, rolling his barrel awkwardly. The three young stars have their eyes riveted to the swaying bodies of the African beauties. They are having communication problems with their legs. The moon has a thin veil of dust.

14

Late at night, when there are no more shows to be seen, no shadows flickering on the taut drum-like skein of illusion, when the effervescence and the feverishness of the afternoon and the early evening have subsided, some people still loll around the swimming pool. They could be inveterate insomniacs, aged and failed spies scratching around for scraps of information that would give sense to an evaluation that has to be whispered in the ear of power, directors who haven't made a film in ten years, political advisors to obscure embryo states looking for someone to influence, or simply the odd ones, the marginal ones who have nowhere else to go, no bed or room to fit to their sleep. It is a pleasant hour – the intense heat has died down. With a bit of luck, if you have the right kind of acquaintance, you may be offered a splosh of whisky at one or other table. You could share a few disjointed thoughts you may not otherwise have aired. Beyond the perimeters of the town the African night is heavy and still, but alert. Some people never sleep.

On their way to the room Mano and Meheret are hailed by an old man wearing a blue *boubou* with silver embroidery and a white skull-cap. He lifts a peremptory finger to ask Meheret whether she was ever called Gsiaber. She is so surprised at this unexpected question that she stops to look closely at him. He must be at least seventy years old, his eyes are rheumy, with a whitishness in the corners, a smile is hovering like a very young bird around his lips. He bows slightly, invites them to sit down at his table. A moon has risen and is now bobbing gently on the surface of the pool's water. (The water is surely not clean enough to swim in.) He is very black, and as he is sitting in the dark it is impossible to gauge his expression. He has hidden his hands in the midnight folds of his robe. Has he closed his eyes? Let me tell you a story in the African way (he says), to honour the memory of your father. I knew him many years ago in Cairo. Yes – you are very surprised now. You look like him when you are surprised. You carry your head the same way he did. A nomad can recognize his camel just by the taste of its milk . . . It was at one of the first, and last, Pan-African bicycle racing meetings . . .

This afternoon (he says), in the court-house, I heard you make a remark to your husband – yes, I was in the crowd, you didn't notice me, I'm an old dry stick – you had the kindness of remarking upon the large number of bicycles, mopeds and scooters in our streets. You said that you have a soft spot for cities where bikes outnumber the automobiles, and this fact denotes a certain lack of ostentation. I thank you for your perspicaciousness. Your father had a soft face, the very same eyebrows you have . . . It is important to live as if walking into the wind, even with a gammy leg. The breeze of eternity, coming from beyond the horizons of our small mortal existence, smelling of snow and of dust . . . The night is long. In Africa we burn the slow branches of our stories to keep the darkness at bay. Did you know (he says) that we call a Yamaha moped a *mari capable*? It means 'capable husband', because the women here oblige their men to prove their worth by being able to afford a bike.

Did you know (he says) that it was here that he caught the fatal illness? I am speaking of Coppi. Fausto Coppi. Please allow me to speak of Fausto Coppi, because he was the most perfect rider that the world ever saw, a man of our time with the attributes of an ancient hero. He was way past his prime when he came here, to Upper Volta as it was then still. Forty years of age. He should have retired long before, but he was never one for knowing when to stop, Fausto Coppi, he had the heart of a horse, and he jumped at the idea of measuring himself once more wheel by wheel and huff after puff against the old and new cracks.

Yes, it was late fifty-nine when he came to pedal against Anquetil and Rivière and Hassenforder and Van Wyk and Anglade and the others. After he returned to Italy he had to repair to hospital immediately, they thought it was a stomach ailment, then a severe influenza, then a lung infection. All the while it was the bad form of malaria, *plasmadium Falciparum*. The French doctors knew it, and they'd informed their Italian counterparts, but you know what stubborn fools doctors are, the more expert the more foolish, nothing is as blinding as self-importance. And as for French doctors practising in the colonies . . . Fausto Coppi died miserably. I'm not sure, but I think malo malaria rots the liver. Let us turn our heads and spit the other way when we think of evil.

You've probably seen the photo of the hero on his bier – it is part of our century's iconography – striped suit, handkerchief in breast pocket, chin up, hair slicked back, noble expression with the closed eyes looking inward as if trying to apprehend an elusive shadow in the mind. Coppi looking like Che Guevara looking like some Caravaggio painting looking like Christ. Are you surprised that I, an old African stick, should refer to Italian painting? Never judge a man by his *boubou*.

The racer and the black ink squeezed from him by the light, fast, faster. I always think that dead eyes must be like fractured stones, a certain perfectness has been lost irredeemably. Around the corpse you see his friends with coats and scarves, it was winter in Italy, hooded eyes and down-turned mouths. Maybe a few of them were his *gregari*, his supporting team-mates. The scene could well be the illustration of a victory celebration, or some baroque Mafia ritual. I have studied the Italians. I have been invisible in Palermo. We Blacks are disembodied shades in Europe. Bartali, his old arch-rival, not to say enemy, the one whom Coppi had dethroned as *campionissimo*, and he, Bartali, Gino the Pious, *il vecchio*, fanatically religious, member of Catholic Action and *frater* in the Third Order of the Carmelites, always kneeling before Mary Virgin, didn't help him much, bad-tempered, suspicious, easily irritated, greedy Gino Bartali was there as coffin-bearer, sobbing his eyes out, his handkerchief a soggy ball, together with Louis Bobet and Jacques Anquetil and Darrigade and Kubler and Gaul and Federico Bahamontes. Hall of fame. Fragile mirrors.

He moved people's minds, did Fausto Coppi. Of course his two wives were tottering on the edge of the yawning grave. Didn't I mention far-away winds? Bruna, the legitimate, the one he'd married young when he was barely starting out after begging an old bicycle builder to knock together for him a racing bike mounted on an ancient frame, time and again he'd tread the forty-two kilometres up hill and down dale to go plead with the old man, Bruna who used to knit his wrecked body after the numerous falls, Coppi was known to have a glass skeleton, four hundred and thirty-five days in all he'd lost during his career thanks to bruised legs, broken pelvis, cracked shoulderblades, snapped thighbones, splintered shins, ankylosed ankles, slipped discs, torn ligaments, smashed knuckles and noses out of joint; tractors would run him down, one one-eyed competitor never saw his back wheel and pushed Coppi under a lorry; the sour Bruna he finally left for Greta Locatelli, wife of a doctor who was an ardent supporter of the champ and so pissed off at the hot love between his lady wife and the idol the *aficionado* was to become that he personally led an assault party on Coppi's house, big to-do, the cops had to intervene, Greta arrested,

Coppi parked outside the station to wait for her release, Greta 'the lady in white' who used to collect photographs of the lover hero, went to live in sin with him and eventually gave bloody birth out of wedlock to a little bastard Faustino, the good citizens of Monte Acqua were so upset that indignant fellows with waxed moustaches offered through the newspapers to fight the cuckoo, the arch-angel of demons, the Bernael, in a duel, and the Pope – bless his little white socks – refused to stretch a prayerful hand over Coppi's curls. Not that this bothered him. I know my Coppi backwards. I was young once.

He'd always refused to go down on his knees, not even in Lourdes where the crocks are repaired and where angels tread on one another, although he was quite willing to grant God a fifty-fifty chance of existing, always a fair competitor, Fausto Coppi.

It is believed that a woman gave birth to him during 1910 in Castellania, hard by Nove Ligure – 'the sons behead the burnt-out fathers', Martin Ros was to write about him. His father died in a firestorm. Coppi used to give his money away to the poor and he flirted with 'the people' whilst despising all politicians. 'I attach greater importance to the smile of a child or the kiss of a woman than to the warmest political hand. When I hear a politician doing his nut on the radio, my eyes mercifully close by themselves.'

Greta used to follow him through all his cruel training sessions, sitting in a white Lancia, stopwatch in hand, and it is said that even now she still expects of a late evening, sunk in sadness and shadow, with eyes of milky nostalgia, the door to open and Coppi to walk in with his narrow nose, his slender hips and his dancer's tread (if you don't count the bumps), the light metal bicycle slung over his shoulder.

How he trained! Many people wrote about Fausto Coppi – you must have come across the books and articles, I trust, if you are really interested in bicycles – Marcel Aymé, Tristan Bernhard, Martin Ros, Alfred Jarry, Loup de Montcorbier, Dino Buzzati, Boris Pasternak, Roger Vailland, Morland, Luis Nucera, Georges Clémenceau, Paul Morand, Mornas, Antoine Blondin. From the mouth of one who in his youth was a passionate admirer of the hero and who followed him for months on end, I am now speaking of your father, Guebre Gsiaber, I have the remark, probably first made by Blondin, that the essential enthusiasm for bicycle racing is born from the urge to meet up with yourself, to test yourself to the deepest level and that preferably in utter solitude. It must be remembered that Coppi was the perfect monster: a remarkable lack of harmony between head, torso, arms and legs – the head too big, a chicken breast, a slow pulse beat – and an astounding lung capacity of 6.7 litres.

He had the stroke of luck of getting to know a blind expert in massage and the arts of the wheel. This Homer taught him how and what to eat – marmalade, a lot of fresh vegetables and steamed fruit, boiled fish and chicken, a light rice custard, barley sweets to suck, huge quantities of tea without tannic acid and caffeine-free coffee, yoghurts, no alcohol, a litre of milk a day, morning and night a bowl of bran; how and when to sleep – the afternoon nap was most important between one o'clock and half-past two; how and how often and when to train; how to suss out the track or the course. You know, Coppi could easily pedal at fifty-five kilometres an hour for a whole hour without flagging. In forty-two, in Milan's Vigorelli stadium, he broke the world's hour record of Archambaud by thirty-one metres. He'd ridden forty-five kilometres and seven hundred and ninety-eight metres at a resistance rate of fifty-two by fifteen.

And he won. He wiped the track with poor old Bartali. Unforseen débâcles, like war, would come and temporarily interrupt his ascension to glory. In 1943 he was captured in North Africa and became a prisoner of war, but when he came back he was hungry for victory. His eyes were deep down in his head. In forty-six he finished off Tesseire in the race from Milan to San Remo. In forty-nine he won the Tour de France, ditto for the Tour d'Italie, and he became world pursuit champ as well. So it continued. Five times the Tour of Italy, five times the Tour of Lombardy, six times the Milan–San Remo, five times the Trofeo Baracchi . . .

Of course he lost sometimes, inevitably he would tumble, crack, gasp, wheeze like a mortal, but he took it like the man he was. It would happen that his rhythm was nearly fatally dislocated. As on that hellishly hot day during the fifty-one tour when Abd-el-Kadar Za'af from the Sahara rode the shit out of him – pardon me this crude expression, my child – just about enticing him to his death – the entire Italian crew had to sprinkle water over Coppi, egg and beg him on, flap sweatshirts before his glazed eyes, sweep the road before him, blow him on from behind, whisper prayers in his ear, all so that he wouldn't be disqualified. He wasn't. He survived for a tenth place. Martin Ros, in a famous article in the *Haagse Post*, tells of another occasion during the same race when the selfsame

Za'af came a cropper. It must have been a hot year, the strong and happy African was free-wheeling way ahead of his competitors when the French spectators started offering him jars of wine to slake his thirst, and the brave man indulged so lavishly that he soon turned tail to start zig-zagging the other way *towards* his pursuers. As an immigrant you should never trust a Frenchman giving you wine.

Eventually he started losing more and more often, Coppi, more and more badly. As he picked up years he slid back in the field. It became difficult to watch. I spoke to you of Guebre Gsiaber. Guebre Gsiaber no longer followed Fausto Coppi around, he told me many years later over a hand of cards that it had become too painful to assist at the degradation of a demiurge. He rested his hand of cards and his eyelashes became moist when he talked of those sombre days.

Let me show you the feats we *griots* are capable of. I shall speak to you of Jan Zomer, another lyricist, who tells of one of the ultimate races, in 1956, when Fausto Coppi wanted to win a last one for the road and for the lady in white, against the likes of Rik van Looy, Jacques Anquetil, André Darrigade, Magni, Fred de Bruyne, Baldini – strong blighters to a man. He pushed the pace hard, did Coppi, shaking off his followers and tormentors like autumn leaves scattered by the wind, but they caught up again, wheel by wheel, he knew he had to exhaust them, wear them down to retching gullets because at his age he could no longer hold his own in a final sprint, and all his magnificent resistance rose to the surface in a sustained explosion of effort. See, I have it here on this yellowed newsprint cutting, the way Jan Zomer tells it (the old man took a sheet of newspaper from a fold of his *boubou* but didn't read it – he must have known the text by heart, and anyway, it was too dark outside):

One more time Coppi called upon the maximum pull and push of his sheathed muscles without excepting a single fibre. He scraped to the bone or to the marrow the still present remnants of his unsurpassed class. One last time Coppi beamed the shine of a *coureur* who in fact did not belong to this earth. The human disappeared for its place to be taken by a demonic metamorphosis. Even the fastest of this moment in time could not keep tread with his wheel. Was the maestro after all to succeed in hurling his tortured corpus as winner over the white line? The spectator with the surrealist eye of the true wheelman would register this final athletic explosion of strength from the distorted limbs. The death struggle on the Milan track was of such a bizarre beauty that it evoked eery and intense emotions. At the line André Darrigade in the fraction of a second shattered Coppi's crystalline victory glow to the dullness of ashes. The fact that he'd outraced Rik van Looy, De Bruyn, Magni and the others, did not count. Coppi was inconsolable. He who had triumphed so often, now wept like a child.

He would not give up. It became a gory spectacle, the once great athlete exhibiting his broken carcass to the avid masses, a living Christ being paraded in the arenas after his crucifixion, no longer able to work miracles, punch-drunk, teetering over the track. A great man. Trying to stay ahead until the last lap against Bernael Angel Death, the thing breathing down his neck with an easy rhythm, cold song of thin wheels, Coppi pedalling as if treading water. There you are. He had been a generous agnostic and it must be said to God's grace that he too gave Fausto a fifty-fifty chance. Except that Fausto was a hundred per cent runner, a winner-takes-all.

When he died some orphans who'd been provided for by the champion left one hundred and sixty-five carnations on his grave, and a note: 'Dear Fausto, we can no longer embrace you but we offer you this bouquet as a sign of gratitude from all the children helped by you. Look upon each carnation as an individual heart from one of us. It is little, Fausto. But we are poor, you know. Keep your chin up, Fausto, we shall always remain close to you.'

15

The swimming-pool of the Hôtel Silmandé is like a big, greenish, translucent semi-precious stone. The façade of the hotel rises on one side, a flat-topped pyramid of brown mirrors reflected in the water of the pool, reflecting the pool's turquoise sheen and the clouds skidding through the blue panoply. Around the pool there are green lawns, a rockery, a scattering of tropical plants, huts for changing, a long roofed-over open-air bar, deckchairs, stretchers on which the guests can recline to tan. This pool, unlike the one at the Indépendance, is actually used for swimming. Birds twitter on the grass roof of the bar, slip through the air from bush to bush. A few eucalyptus trees have been planted, but they're still small. Greyish or biscuit-coloured lizards scuttle up the poles propping up the big umbrellas of grass, turn around and puff up their vividly orange jowls. Scavenger crows hop around the edges of the grassed area. Lines of ants criss-cross the slate-grey flagstones.

Hotel guests and visitors wait in the cones of shade provided by the grass roofs for something to happen – West African Ministers of Culture and Communication with gold-rimmed spectacles and long-legged, round-buttocked secretaries; bored West African Directors of Television with Parisian sneers and long-legged, round-buttocked assistants; very Important Personalities with camera smiles and peeling noses and long-legged, round-buttocked female interpreters; playboy businessmen from Europe with carefully careless coiffures and gold bracelets and long-legged, round-buttocked night-guides; spies and head-hunters with long-legged, round-buttocked lady acquaintances. Several pretty young ladies, black and brown, on long legs carrying round buttocks, parade around the pool. Then they slip in at the shallow end to boisterously splash water at one another. They have glistening, polished skins and pointed breasts. Sitting away from the pool, under the protection of a tall aloe, are two very white Russians. They look lost and miserable. They are too obviously foreign to pass unnoticed, and the Silmandé is out of town so that they can hardly merge with the crowds, let alone the toiling masses. It is clear that they haven't been trained in the lizard-like art of wasting time in the sun on deckchairs around a glittering pool. To be a Soviet spy in Africa must be the equivalent of being exiled to Kamchatka without a parka. The heat probably gives them the shivers. Maybe they don't even appreciate long legs and buttocks which move like otters in a bag.

Kathy Human comes down the steps of the hotel building towards the pool. She's wearing a red two-piece bathing suit. Her skin is pale. Her legs are not long but they make up for it by their substantial girth, and her buttocks have long since accepted a state of distended cohabitation with the rest of her body. She has the voluptuousness of excess. 'Hi!' she greets Mano from a distance. 'I just had to come out here for a breather. It's so hot in town. Mitganger will be down in a moment to see you. Bye now.' She spreads a towel on the grass and lies down on her stomach to start leafing through a book.

Across the pool from where Mano is waiting, he notices Pierre Lecteur Agent talking to the girls with the firm bums on the long stilts who have emerged from the pool thinly coated with silver water. Lecteur has the muscular body of a trained weightlifter. He's wearing his dark glasses. Another man has approached the pool, turning his head as if looking for someone, as if leisurely stalking a prey. He is sallow-skinned, with his tattooed upper arms even more muscular than Agent's. Although his eyes are darkened by a pair of sunglasses, it is obvious that he is very alert. He walks up to Pierre Lecteur, the two exchange a few phrases, then move away from the girls to stand facing each other stiffly. Agent turns angrily on his heel and stalks away. The other man watches him go and then saunters down the length of the other side until he comes to where Kathy Human is pinking her flesh. He goes down on his haunches next to her with a thin smile, evidently trying to chat her up.

Pierre Lecteur has stopped next to Mano. With a jerk of the wrist he removes his glasses. His eyes are cold with fury, his face flushed, so that the puckered patch under his left eye shows up more vividly. 'That bastard,' he says, jutting his chin in the direction of the tattooed man with the Afro hairdo squatting on the far side of the pool's green glass body. 'He's paranoid and dangerous. Came up to me and told me he knows why I'm here, that I'm a French agent. Said nobody will threaten this régime – he himself will eliminate all the President's enemies. Told me to get out or else to try him on. I'm going to warn the ambassador.'

'But who is he?'

'Diallo. The President's henchman. We know all about him. There's an international warrant out for his arrest. He's committed at least three murders we know of, in France and next-door in Mali.'

There's humiliation in the air. Agent must be torn between the gut reaction of wanting to measure himself against the opponent (is that what he came here for?), and the instructions to hold off, to not be provoked, of being on foreign territory.

For security operatives to be good, sharp utensils, they need to be trained to the pitch of not *thinking*, but *reacting*. They are marked by the wound of being ridiculous, and the conditioned reflex that the Other is the Enemy. What moves must be checked, is first of all a threat. Rather kill than be mistaken. There can be no security without an enemy . . . They are hunters, they need to shoot, they need the white-out of cathartic solutions, of obliteration . . .

Mitganger comes towards them in a big white towel wrapped around the senatorial expanses of his midriff. (Lecteur has disappeared into a cubicle to get dressed.) He drops the towel and slowly enters the water as if making an offering to the gods. With a sigh of contentment he turns on his back and floats to where Mano is sitting. During the course of their conversation he will paddle around, burping with satisfaction, like some aged and bleached sea-elephant returned to its native environment after years of living the sawdust life of the circus. His body is limp, his lips drooping from having to emit reservations about the politics of his African brothers, his eyes permanently softened by the admiration he has for the revolutionary leaders.

In a conspiratorial voice he asks whether Mano has met the Man yet. When Mano says no, though he did see him from a distance last night, Mitganger confides: 'It is not easy for him, you know. I went out to a military camp this morning to talk to the officers there. That's why I was late for our appointment. The Man has a real desire to transform this country. I can see it. He has a good grasp of history and he is truly inspired by Pan-Africanism. But he must continue trying to "create the facts" or else history will catch up with him. I saw it happen so often in the Third World. It is very upsetting. He has to identify in advance the reasons why people may wish to revolt against his ideas, and then take pre-emptive action. I'm here to try and help him, you see . . .'

From across the pool the brown man glares at them. Kathy Human is sitting up, she has pushed back her hair, she smiles uncertainly. The man, Diallo, gets to his feet and starts walking to the hotel. Two young sunbathers with long slender legs rounded off by bobbing buttocks follow him nonchalantly. Maybe some otters will be let out of the bag.

'But tell me,' Mitganger asks, 'how much longer before the revolution in your country?'

Intellectuals! Mano thinks, remembering a conversation he once had with Walser. Trying to reduce reality to a brilliant synthesis, mistaking it for the real thing, forgetting that it is but *another* reality. Forgetting also the deeper movements of the heart. And once a situation has been described, a new picture has been created; you can never again experience or go back to the original without reference to its image. The mind is a mirror capturing mind, the moon a shadow. How to live the Original Mind? Did the Original Face have a moustache? What is the woman in your mother like? The intellectual cannot practise non-duality. You have to have lived with cattle and crops to know what non-duality is like.

'You say you are an actor? You are so lucky, because you can observe people and creatively re-interpret them. You have the freedom of the artist. South Africa must provide you with a lot of material? There are many different cultures and customs in South Africa? It is more difficult for us scientists. We have to stick to the facts, even when the facts are cultural. We have to help these countries, you know? They need us. I know all the leaders of the Third World. We have to redefine what revolution is all about. I have to deal with history. And history has a sense. It is a movement towards the light.'

Intellectuals! Stupidity, arrogance and irresponsibility! He comes here, the intellectual, to impress upon the rulers where they went wrong and why the prophesied doom is inevitable. He moves through the poor countries with his hair-shirt on, telling everybody how terribly evil white colonialism is, making amends personally with a soft, charitable Christian hand, pretending to be the disabused but steadfast and modest grey eminence – conspiring, explaining, teaching, linking revolution to revolution. Inevitably he returns to his well-padded chair at the university, waiting for the day when he can say: 'I told you so.' If shove doesn't come to push, he covers his own faulty perceptions by a new twist in the theory. If the shit hits the fan he doesn't have to go clean the ceiling, nor does he pay the electricity bill. Is he not the intellectual? His hands must be kept clean the better to write authoritative texts with, and to wipe the mouth which has whispered dainty compliments to the powerful arses.

'Yes, Africa is a cruel continent,' the man floating in the fluor-green water says, 'and it has a cruel memory. My concern is to define how knowledge is passed on from one generation to the next, and what constitutes the fields of reference, you know, which will specify that knowledge.

'Recently I was shown some notebooks containing the thoughts and the instructions of Pierre Mulele. It was a great privilege. I can't tell you how they came into my hands, because the people who have the documents risk being exterminated. These notes were made by Mulele's comrades-in-arms, the surviving ones now live scattered in the neighbouring countries, many of them don't speak any French and they refuse to talk to foreigners. It was a strange experience, you know. The notes were copied carefully by comrade after comrade in their school exercise books. A primitive African form of *samizdat*. Can a theory be copied so many times and not be changed?

'Pierre Mulele was in the *maquis* for five years. After the defeat of his campaign in the bush, he retreated to Brazza. Of course he told his peasant warriors that he would return. And he was killed, we all know that. Ten years later an imposter arrived in the area claiming to be Pierre Mulele reincarnated. The peasants and the revolutionaries flocked to him. Mobutu had the incipient uprising squashed in blood. Then he, Mobutu, ordered the killing of Mulele's surviving brothers. And finally the old mother also was publicly executed on the village square. Her corpse was chopped up in several pieces and sent to the outposts of the land, to show that never again can Pierre Mulele be born.'

He puts a hand on the tiles bordering the swimming-pool, to steady himself. His nails are manicured and shiny. He sighs.

'Tell me about Diallo,' Mano says.

'Oh, Diallo? The man you saw talking to Kathy just now? He's not important. A sad case really. Diallo is not his real name, he took it after the revolution, it is a common Fulani name in these parts. His mother was a white French woman, his father a Mossi chief from around here. But he never knew the father who abandoned them when he was small. Or maybe it was the mother who left. Anyway, he grew up with his mother in France . . . France is a racist country, don't you agree? You live there, don't you? Maybe you, as a white African, haven't experienced it. You are white, not so? It is easier in Canada, a new country. We are all immigrants there . . . He must have had a difficult youth. I don't know how he met the Man – Diallo was never in the army, you know – or when he started working for him. Still, you could say that he is one of the lost sons of the revolution. Some people claim he acted as go-between for the Man and the Libyans. I couldn't say. Some also say that he carried out some unpleasant tasks for the Man, or maybe that he went too far in defending his interests, or what he perceived as the interests of the Man. A revolution is not a mundane dinner. Didn't Lenin point it out already? What is certain is that he is totally loyal to the Man. Nearly an obsession. And I think there's another reason for this fanatical attachment. Diallo is a half-blood. He needs to identify himself with a people, a cause, a person. The Man is, in a certain way, his surrogate father. There is a sadness there, don't you think so? Because he is psychologically hurt, he doesn't belong naturally anywhere, and so he has to be doing more, going further all the time to try and win the approbation of the father or brother he never had. They are about the same age . . . Now it seems that he may have gone too far. He has become an embarrassment to the government. The Man cannot afford to allow such an image of his power to exist. Diallo has been sacked. He is like a dog that has been punished, kicked out of the house. So he's roaming around the edges, keeping watch over the Man all the same. He wants to sacrifice himself, do something glorious to prove his unique worth. Some people think he is dangerous. I don't agree. I think he is rather sad. Like a character in a novel.'

(Barnum, the angel writer far from the scene of action, to illustrate his hang-ups and to pace himself, steps vicariously into the African dance, with two partners.)

KA'AFIR: I don't see how a White can talk about a Black. To my mind his way of thinking, which is the route of power, is too restricted. The history of conquest and domination has imposed a rigidity and a fractiousness on the white mind. For him the Black is feed, moral or economic. It is only normal because the white culture is a voracious virus looking for new host bodies. To see himself objectively, the White should have been capable of scaling Mount Meru, which he isn't.

POLICHINELLE: Let me also have a say. I'm not a parrot, after all. Nor shall I allow myself to be eaten. White has at least given a certain stylishness to cannibalism. They have evolved to the stage where the real can be described as appearance devouring substance immediately. An instant anthropophagy. It means that they have succeeded in spreading a film of modishness over the unnameable. You could say that form carries the day against content, that there is an implosion of awareness to arrive at postmodernism where actualization is always an intra-textual affair, a nod and a wink to the already existent, a staging of the event. Pain is a private joke. I should imagine that this is what is known as 'speeding up the vacuum'. Ideas, if you can call the dustbin pickings ideas, now enter the Hall of Fashion as quickly as a glossy paper simulation of orgasm. In this way – since you are speaking of black and white – South Africa, as a nerve-knot of agony, has entered the Parisian lexicon '*à la mode*'. You will notice that I speak like a very cultivated bird.

KA'AFIR: Should we even talk about it? Can we allow ourselves to be that narcissistic? Death has no style. Europeans and North Americans do not have the notion of the internal mountain.

POLICHINELLE: At least we have politicians as scarecrows to chase away the old blind birds of honesty.

KA'AFIR: Yes, you are right. The political caste does serve a purpose. They put up a norm of debonair obtuseness and guiltless immorality. And since they are paid to do so, this creates a movement of money, a fluidity of power, and thus the illusion of activity. It is unacceptable to be dead and not to have the appearance of movement. But their first and most outstanding usefulness is perhaps that they make it possible for society to marginally reduce unemployment. What would we have done with these humanoids if they weren't politicians? Exchange them against shells on the African shores? To have the monkey population of the forests infected? On the contrary, we should by all means increase the number of politicians and bureaucrats and we do have enough candidates among the young whose minds are being blown and blasted white by television. We live in a mutating society where new ways of maintaining the privileges of the powerful must constantly be developed. Luckily the means of burning off excess people are constantly refined: in creating categories of nomorerights, new poor, homeless ones; by starvation or malnutrition (which works out cheaper); making them disappear into statistical black holes or objectifying them as opinion polls; through Aids or some other genetically engineered plague; by exposure to televisual or bacterial or nuclear pollution, or the innately hostile sun (if we can get rid of the ozone protection); or simply through war. Redundant nations ought to be eliminated, like the Armenians, the Lebanese, the Dinkas, the Palestinians, the people from Bangla Desh, but the trouble is that not enough people die in wars, and famine is not what it used to be either so that too many humans still survive to grow up stunted. The culling will have to be done more scientifically . . . It is essential to retain the momentum in the recycling of money. What counts and what matters is the buying and selling of money to finance publicity and image-mongering – which doesn't need labour, so that production can finally be done away with.

POLICHINELLE: You'd still have to generate energy.

KA'AFIR: That's where Africa comes into the story.

POLICHINELLE: Africa? I don't follow you there.

KA'AFIR: Easy. It is true that Africa takes care of its own destruction, which, seen on the world scale, is a saving of economy. It is also progressively becoming clearer that Africa is too poor to be exploited properly. Furthermore, it is an established fact that the African is a species on the way to extinction. So it is perfectly profitable to leave it alone. But the Africans still have a usefulness. Oh, I know you can't employ them in Europe because they tend to faint on the job – although it is good to bring them over and have them eat the bread of the French, since it stimulates white joblessness and can help precipitate the decline which the politicians need as a backcloth for their promises and their never-

149

never solutions. The African has at least two further uses for the White though, apart from the fact that it provides him with someone he can feel superior to. The first is in the relationship between Africa and the North. African destruction should be stimulated through its outside connections. It is good, for instance, that Africans go north to be educated. Not only do they learn nothing there, but they forget their African roots and culture. When they return as intellectuals with Saint-Germain clothes, gold lighters and mock Cartier watches, they can immediately become victims – they can try and stage revolts (because they would have acquired European-conditioned appetites) and be summarily executed. This is excellent for building a state. A state is a locus of consciousness which can flourish only if watered regularly by blood. And there can be no thorough and final destruction of Africa except by the perfection in theory and in practice of the notion of state. Africa is where the memory and the guilt of man will die . . . The second benefit for the North is that Blacks could be used for fuelling the factories. The ecologists quite correctly point out that it is criminal the way the earth is being stripped of its wood and its charcoal. I am sure that we have a solution in hand, by substituting Africans as primary burning material. There may be the slight inconvenience of the smell, but then the Northerners have shown that they can live with that bothersomeness.

POLICHINELLE: Could the African not also be a politician? Or am I now talking at cross-purposes?

KA'AFIR: Of course! We have many examples of the African élite with whitened minds becoming astute politicians. Some become presidents for life and develop a taste for dialogues, monkey glands and limousines. How are we to build cathedrals in the bush if we don't have politicians? They are perhaps less adroit at the game – for instance, they must always physically eliminate any alternative power structure, which doesn't speak well of the loyalty among hyenas and may give them a bad press. But then, the press doesn't count for anything in Africa. In some ways they do even better than their white mentors and commanders. Thus they have far more of a penchant for protocol. In fact, in Africa politics is a matter, in declining order, of: Protocol, Posture, Pretension and Porruption. African politicians may from time to time have to bite their lips when rising from between the legs of the North. You see, the arse-sucker always has to follow suit, and when the host body changes its tune he may all of a sudden find himself with a mouth full of foul thoughts. But he will lift his head with dignity and in the right protocolar way.

POLICHINELLE: What you say there, you as an African, is terrible and a-historical! It is also incorrect, since you know who or what, or what combination of colonialist forces, caused the White-sucking of Africa.

KA'AFIR: I have told you that it is a dead continent, but that its death is a source of richness to the white world. And the white world needs Africa on the one hand, and the politicians on the other, in order not to sink into mediocrity. It must be allowed to dream. What I regret, perversely, is that memory had to die there. But perhaps that was inevitable, since Africa has always been a continent weighted down with far more of a past than a future.

16

The sky is a merciless blue. Not a cloud, not a smear of humidity in sight. Dust as fine as red face-powder hangs in the air above the roads leading to the stadium. Thousands of people with red faces converge on this central catchment area. Thousands of bicycles left on the open ground around the stadium form pyramids of metal and rubber. A double row of horsemen in red tunics and tarbooshes and blue pantaloons sit their horses on either side of the main entrance – the *moro-naba*'s household cavalry as honour guard. The horses hang their heads and swish their tails. The Tamachecks are there also, high on their camels, and the young pioneers with their bright yellow berets and their red kerchiefs. The stands are packed – row upon row of humanity, cheering, swaying, waving, getting up to stomp. From time to time - rarely – an altercation erupts, one sector will be in ebullition, a whirlwind of arms (maybe a pickpocket was caught redhanded) until a few figures are ejected, pushed over the low wall, hang on from the ledge by their fingertips for several seconds more before dropping with a flaying of legs and arms into the sector below. In the open arena, on the green grass, a podium has been erected, wired for blaring sound, a band is snaking and jiggling backwards and forwards, sun flashing off the electric guitars, a battery of drums snaring and kettling and rustling and finally booming chunks of blue sound, the three female singers swivel their hips and move with liquid movements three steps to the left three to the right, the lead male singer with his mike like a thrashing serpent is a jack-in-the-box, with springy legs he covers the stage, he's wearing white colonial shorts, white socks up to the knees, a white pith helmet. From the far end of the field someone has dropped over the last barrier, is jogging in a fast lope up to the bandstand, and now he is jitterbugging to the beat with all the unrestrained rhythmical joy of his body. The crowd applauds. A second man casts all discretion to the wind and comes running up to join the first one, to partake of the spineless contortions, drawing figures in the air, forgetting day and eternity. They take turns, the one attempting to out-dance the other. Then they become a couple, respond to each other, end up by doing splits and cartwheels on the grass. The stands have filled up. The noise has blown the vultures high into the upper reaches of the blue dome. Little children, dressed in their festive finery, sit as sweet as black sugar next to their daddies, their eyes riveted to the huge hollow green square exploding with sunlight and sound. The Man is there with all the ministers of his government. He is wearing an orange-coloured uniform with paratrooper's insignia, a red beret, a pistol on his hip. His guests are in the rows behind him. Rows of heads turned his way when he entered, a few bodies bobbed up and down, then everyone settled down again. A huge electronic scoreboard is flashing revolutionary slogans and announcements. Lions four, Christians nil. A plane must have flown across and circled very high, curling the afternoon light, because now thousands of necks are craned to watch the skies. And dots appear – are they vultures? are they angels? – growing bigger, multi-coloured parachutes bloom, five, six, seven men drift down wafted this way and that by a gust of air, back again, they are taking their time, now there's speed-up, pulling on the ropes to land in one fell swoop (but on their feet) as close as possible to a white chalked target on the grass. Delegations of barefoot children, boys and girls dressed in the same colours, the poor of the earth, march around the arena, the stick-like legs stiff with pride. Leading each delegation is the flag of an African state, and those of the liberation movements. Loudspeakers boom to identify the flags. Twenty thousand pairs of hands try to capture the ripples of applause sweeping by. Then silence. *The masks* move out of a tunnel into the light. From the ancestral forest of darkness where man is spirit or animal to intervene with the forces of creation. Silence in the arena. Each society of masks accompanied by venerable elders dressed in tatters, beaked faces in the air, and two or three drummers who seem to be in a trance. Stumbling, slow-moving, fixed images of death and terror, matted pelts glistening, long locks swinging from side to side, half-decayed monsters leaning on long sticks. Then waddling dwarfs, animals from the chaos of time. Striking fear in the breast of man. Striking down the thin man-made barriers of sanity. They hobble like old, old people. Close observation, close imitation, a few movements to recall all the animality of the unsayable. Huge, bumbling apes. Then tall, decorated wooden effigies. Smooth, bald white masks. Sumptuous but cheap-coloured cloths, covering the humps, like moth-eaten dream material from some theatre dressing room. Our dislocated memories totter and twirl through the arena, heavy with dust and indifference.

When humans still dwelled in heaven they were immortal. And, being playful, they became too numerous. God, with the help of the Iron Smith, sent a number of them down to earth where they were organized in two groups: the Earth Masters ruling over cold and dry, the Rain Masters ruling over hot and humid. Thus the earth was perfectly balanced – when the Rain Masters increased the heat it caused drought, and then the Earth Masters increased the cold to untie the rain. Similarly the Rain Masters, called upon to die, had no contact with their dead, and the Earth Masters, the immortal ones, were the grave-diggers. Those who could die were happy with their lot and never complained – when one of their number passed away they arranged for a funeral feast and regaled themselves on *lalso*, the food prepared by women for the dead. But the Earth Masters were jealous, they too hankered after *lalso*. So they sent two messengers into the bush to go and buy death for the price of a cat. They finally made a deal for the price of an ox, and in this way became the equals of the Rain Masters. So what if the world's harmony was upset? In effect, from now on they had to live with the fickleness of the seasons, the dry periods and the wilted harvests. This was the real price paid for the privilege of enjoying death.

17

The urgent slap-slap-slapping of naked footsoles on tiles, raucous shouting, confused questions, local languages, more feet running, sounds of doors opening, excited or awed buzz of voices. Mano wakes up with a start, immediately alert, Meheret rolls over shading her eyes. 'What's up? What's all that noise about? What's the time?'

Mano hastily pulling on trousers and shirt, going to the door, it is not yet properly light outside. Meheret: 'Don't go out there! Stay here, watch out! Mano, where are you going?' But Mano already at the door, out in the corridor on his bare feet, down the passage to the big open walled-in space with its swimming-pool.

People running up to where other people are gathered at the poolside, half-clothed people, guests, domestic servants, the sleepy-eyed hotel manager. Someone calling: 'Police! Call the police!' Someone else: 'Fool!' Mano trying to get closer, to see what it is all about.

Turgid, brownish surface of liquid in pool. Smooth, undisturbed. In the middle, too far to be reached from either bank, the floating body of a female, face down. Calm position. Like having congress with the mirror. Body – pinkish stripes of sunburn – naked, long hair aureole around the head. Head in water. Nothing to be seen down there, no ultimate sense of life. No feedback. No movement. Body very dead. White woman, light-brown hair. Big shape. Foetus-sized cloud of darker liquid spread underneath body. Keel. Tendrils lazily stretching and curling in the water. Blood. Even keel. Home port.

Voices: 'Jesus, she's dead! Who is it? Who did you say it was? It's a white woman. Anybody here know her? Is she dead? Who found her? Look, she must be dead. Whyn't somebody get her out of there? The management, where's the management? Call the police! You fool, can't you see she's dead? Oh God, the blood, the blood. Don't stay around here. Just what we needed. Ah, shit. What's this, a scene from a movie? Does anybody know the woman? What a way to start the day! Oh hell, oh hell, oh hell. I think she's been eviscerated. One doesn't see any wounds. Is she dead? Belly cut open . . .'

Somebody, a hotel employee, with long pole with sieve on end used for scooping fallen leaves from the water. Poking at body, pushing it to the far side. Bobbing progress. People walking around to the other side, some without shoes. Advice. Warnings. Confusion. Two uniformed men rushing up, roughly making a passage through the crowd. Several men on bent knees, grabbing hold of the corpse. Slippery. Sweetwater fish. Dream eel. Dead weight difficult to handle. Police pushing people out of the way. Corpse half-lifted from water, half-rolled over edge of pool on flagstones, dripping water and blood. Wet sound when rolled over on back. Inert limbs, one arm slipping back into water. Ghastly slash running at a slant from just below left nipple to beyond the navel. Gaping red. Not bleeding much. Pale around edges, dark inside. Wet hair pushed back from face of corpse. White face starting to swell. Glazed open eyes not bothered by sun which has risen over trees. Eyes have seen the night. Meheret tugging sharply at Mano's shirt-tail. 'It's that South African woman, what's her name, Kathy Human.'

A blanket has been brought up to cover the body. More officers, thin men in civilian clothes not saying very much, have arrived. The body is lying on the floor of the reception area, between desk and stuffed couches. The body is being removed, carried out of the hotel and put into the back of a private car. The crowd has split up in small groups of gesticulating people. Voices. Who? When? Nobody knows her name. No traces of blood in the water. Clean as a mirror. A wet spot on the flagstones, drying rapidly, where the body had lain after being dragged from the water. Soldiers with rifles at the street door.

At breakfast Meheret and Mano sit down at a table where a knot of people have their ears hanging from the lips of the Ivory Coast actress. Her complicated, well-patterned hairdo hasn't changed in the least. Her dress accentuates her breasts and their breathing. She is talking excitedly. Saying that the white lady was lodging in the room next to hers on the second floor of the back wing of the hotel. Last night, late, after the final ceremonies, she was having a last drink with Lion by the pool, the deceased came home. She must have been a little over the moon. Was wearing her shoes in her hand. Was accompanied by that other man, Diallo. Somebody was saying something about the moon on the water. No, she didn't really pay any attention, she didn't hear any funny noises. Did she go up to her room? Yes, much later, she's sure of it now. No gurgles, no giggles, no nothing. She thought Diallo must be up there giving the woman a thorough talking-to with his prick. Nailing her down with African truths. She didn't think much of Diallo's taste. She'd always considered that Diallo must have something weird going on in the head.

Later in the morning they see Lion at the reception desk, trying to place a call to London. His eyes are red and his beard is ashen. He goes into the jazzman's stance and asks them whether they'd heard about the murder. Seems that Diallo – here his voice goes softer and he glances at the other people in the lobby – Diallo, the security supremo, knifed some poor woman. Maybe she was an agent. We are living in strange times. He, Lion, thought he heard a man screaming in the night. But probably it was the whisky. Funny place. 'Man, oh man,' he says, 'I'm getting out of here.' What happened to Diallo? No, no, nobody knows. Heard it said that he was seen leaving the hotel early, before daybreak, no rush, unconcerned. Probably holing up in some military base. Or already left town. Lots of police around. Not asking any questions. Tight-lipped security men. 'I'm leaving. Not a minute too soon.'

It is already very hot out on the street. Outside the front door of the Hôtel Indépendance there's a mountain of luggage waiting to be loaded on the airport bus. It's going to be quite a problem getting on the flight.

18

Low scrub, greyish. Some rare enclosures, round or oblong-shaped, of greenish shrub, protecting two or three green trees. And then expanse. Nothing. Expanse of nothing. Brown nothing. Red nothing. Ochre nothing. Grey nothing. Whitish nothing.

And when the plane stoops over the pale pink desert, everything stops. Neither movement nor shadow nor relief. A timeless sunstare.

This is it: eternity cracked open. Spined sand-dunes like icebergs floating on a sea of oblivion. Deeply gouged plateaux, black, basaltine, castles shaped by the careless and playful hand of God. Rivers of sand. The sparkle of death. Imprints, a hundred miles square, as documents explaining the origin of being in a long-lost script. Vast and wild silence. Wind creating grimaces.

· People, there must be people living down there, if only they could be taught how to bring down the flying machines. Not many – one here, one there, from time to time. We are not greedy. A small sacrifice for the West – more people than a Boeing could carry die on an average weekend on the roads in France or Germany. But what riches to the poor! It would be like putting a small village, or at least a hypermarket, within their reach. Provided the carcass is not too charred the fuel could be recuperated for energy and light, the metal could be recycled as implements and medals, the food and drink thus saved and redistributed would constitute a feast for the gods and their camels! The trinkets and relics which had been bought from pedlars at the airport would be taken back into circulation. The tourists' money, clothes and other bric-à-brac? Well, some use could perhaps be found. But what a stimulation, what powerful injections into their subsistence economies these occasional crashes would be!

Legends will be fashioned, the campfires will crackle with excitement. And for as long as the transistor batteries last, the whole wide world will be but an ear away.

Mano leans over: 'What are you writing?'

Meheret: 'Notes. Dreams. About how disembodied we are. How alienated by our riches and our comfort. As if we are moving on a totally different orbit from those below us in the sun and the sand. I must write my African book.'

Mano: 'We must wage guerrilla war against the opulent North. Raid their larders, strip their outposts, make them pay tribute, harass them, attack at night, liberate their techniques, cut their lines of communication, merge with their populations to become invisible, hiding in the light, and distribute the stolen loot to our poor.'

'And we sweep their streets, become objects for the satisfaction of their erotic fantasies or their moral guilt. We oppress and corrupt our own for their benefit.'

Mano: 'We must remain alert however, to the temptation of seeing Africa through white eyes. All this hand-wringing and sobbing over the fate of the continent. Sick Africa, if you read their books. Says who? Say all these "sympathetic" Whites and the whitened Blacks. By whose standards? In terms of what virginal utopia? Africa will absorb that too – the good will of the Third Worldists will be turned into song. Africa will multiply her structures, aping the Whites, but leaving room for the past, for a revival of the night. Sure, we shall have our lackeys, our rogues, our fools. We shall have confusion. But Africa will muddle through – by magic, if nothing else!'

Why hasn't anybody thought of making glass-bottomed aircraft? Leaving the sun. The sun is leaving us. This is where I want to die. Here in the desert, in the soughing void. I want to walk here, burnt to white flame by the sun, and then, in a fold of vastness, find a trickle of water. I want to die, day by day, wiped clean in this land which has the knuckledness and the white sounds of a skeleton.

The day remains clear. The day accompanies us over the barrenness and the cryptograms of this vast continent. This is not imagination. The land with its rhythms below us is beyond the realm of dichotomy. It is. The day will not leave us. The heart shrivels with anguish and pain at the thought of going north, back into the cold of sour minds. How long? Two, three, four days of living with clenched teeth and reddened eyes, before 'adaptation', 'insertion', before we again harness the straps of paranoia and distrust to become functional in the Parisian milieu. Welcome to Dogshit City. The land of the law . . . My heart, you are like a child in me – how will you survive there? Will you be like a shell on a shelf which has forgotten the sea?

Mano, the nomad, next to me. Sleeping now with shallow breath, mouth open, the slanted sun striking small sparks from the stubbles on his chin. Strange how he reacted to the murder this morning. Kept on asking after that man, Diallo. Wanted to puzzle out what Diallo's motivations, feelings, might have been. Wasn't at all interested in the woman. Poor woman, being emptied of her guts so far from her home and her people. Mano is too passionate about Africa. What is the origin of this sense of loss, this not-belonging that he must compensate for? I can feel him reaching out, for a resolution, an absolution, a dissolution. Is he trying to get away from me? Africa will swallow him. This morning at the airport, on the tarmac before departure – Mumpata must have some diplomatic clout to have been allowed right up to the gangway – Mumpata saying: 'Next year in Johannesburg?' And Mano answering: 'Of course! I refuse to accept that I've lived for nothing!' I know the hollow of his back, the scar under his left ear, the first swelling of his double chin, his bright, green, eel-smooth eyes, the intensity of his longing. He must be dreaming Africa. Poor dream of sand and dead trees.

Other passengers in the plane. The African (from the Cameroon?) freelancer with the glasses, the long hair, the beret, the jeans. P., the old reactionary reporter from *Le Monde*, Africa is the property of his French pen, it has flown from his analysis. Next to him the brassy woman with the platinum-yellow hair, the rightist assistant to the Minister of Cooperation. Their bags full of souvenirs and secret assessments. Leeches! Mongo Beti in the row behind us, saying to his neighbour: 'I work for the consciousness of the people. So that we may no longer need politics.'

We shall descend through successive layers of darkness. A small sickle moon there, the prophecy of some seer. I am bringing back a cowry-shell, small and smooth and white – a moon with a vaginal slit. What if I brought back more with me, a child like a heart starting to grow, a blackbird, a flute, a future revolutionary?

And the evening star preceding the moon, following her, accompanying her. So often have I thought that these two, moon and star, illustrate the ancient fable of how the angel comes to announce her pregnancy to the Virgin. The angel will guard her, watch her grow big to give birth and become dark. (Give birth to what?)

Grey blanket over Paris. We bank and start drifting down. Afterglow of the setting sun on the wind. Like the tattered remnants of a once flamboyant African toga.

19

You see, down this succession of paragraphs do I fashion you. It is like opening doors to rooms, letting you have a good look around and then saying – now, let's move on, since what you have just seen is all yours.

Already you have the attributes of a personality, you have a future and a past, you have a lion to serve as your guardian angel, you have *things* which, in their relationships to you, will flesh out the impression of a separate being. Because of this, of your singularity, you will die one day. It is said that one becomes so used to living that you wonder how you are ever going to go about dying.

But death starts even before birth. Age will be the implacable accumulation of the echoes of death. Maybe death is when the things become too heavy, too numerous to be ordered – and no longer being able to control or count brings about the withering of the controlling agent. Things fall apart, the centre cannot hold.

Silly that I should be speaking of death to you when you are not yet born! But it is because I'm starting to have a sense of who you are. I can picture you. Today the doctor moved an echo-finder over the ant-hill in which you lie curled up and confirmed my dream: that you are a girl . . . You have a flower – the carnation, the rose-coloured one. Your father's was red (because of the revolution), mine is white, yours will be the product of ours. You have a shrub, the laurel, the symbol of victory, and when you burn the dried leaves the smell will embalm the house and the hours. You will have a totem – the chameleon, an African actor like your father, a messenger of life. You have a name. Soon you will have a name. I think I'll call you Mona Senedu.

There are echoes in the name. *Senedu* means: she who has prepared herself for being born. And as for *Mona* . . . Your father is Mano . . . Many months ago your father had a conversation with Barnum who'd been requested by some German publication to take part in a series of writings on the theme of the quintessential painting, the one of greatest importance to the guest writer. The two of them, your father and Barnum, bantered about the possible choice.

What, Barnum asked, could be the *one* painting, the nexus of images, for a South African, for someone coming from a stitched-on culture? He meant, I think, that painting in his country is a foreign and imported mode of expression, easel painting that is.

True, Africa has a rich iconography, but taking other forms and perhaps with a different intent. Of course we have paintings too - in Ethiopia, the oldest Christian kingdom, you will find them all over the walls of the churches, and there are the painted scrolls rather like comic strips illustrating some adventure or attribute of a biblical character, or a king or a hermit or a saint or an angel, or a mythical situation, serving as talismans against the evil spells. Then there were the famous coffin paintings of the dead in Egypt, where the deceased person's portrait, perhaps slightly idealized, was painted on the lid often long before his demise: the idea was to leave a recognizable depiction of the identity so that one could be owned and claimed in the afterworld. It was not a bad idea, because death is present at any age and at all stages of a person's life. But, by and large, Africa did not know until much later – and then it was imported as a cultural aspiration – the development of painting.

In the West, painting, quite apart from the progress in aesthetical reflection, must also have been the result of the relationship between artists and religious authorities; then, later on when the art object acquired a mercantile value, of the interaction between temporal powers – kings, patrons of the arts, merchants – and the creators. (How depressing to arrive at the point where I can be only to the extent that I know what I have.) And still later, with the accent ever more on the individual in Western societies, the alien-ation brought about by the disruption of their traditional mores, and the concurrent rise of the role of the artist as sensitive outcast, as interpreter of the disconnected one-walker's dark lonelinesses – the results of the decay of a communal culture, and the enrichment thereof through decay. Painting became the outprints of tortured or ecstatic souls. We Africans didn't know this road, not in the same way.

The two of them, your father and Barnum, laughed and drank some wine. 'But what are we,' Barnum asked, 'if not cultural hybrids? Particularly we the South Africans. You, Mano, certainly more than I, although you try to escape the confusion by being an actor, by definition a man without a defined identity!

'Never can the lines be untangled again, and I doubt that it would be beneficial were we to try and do so. Our bastardization was our most potent antidote to apartheid. In fact, one could say that apartheid was the horrible fever accompanying the slow forging of a new culture, perhaps even facilitating it! If it hadn't been for our protracted identity crisis, we wouldn't be so aware of the different strains going into our make-up. We are awareness rubbed raw, and we try exactly to supersede the iniquity of the system and its dogmas – and its dogs – by our expanded cultural awareness. We are the mirrors created by the system. The monkeys also. I once read somewhere, I can't remember where, that mirrors have a personality to the extent that they absorb and digest certain particularities which they then subtract or reconstitute, totally transformed, after a rapid combustion.'

(Mano, thinking: Speak for yourself, fellow. Not all of us can escape the system through the cultural door. And if the reality and the relationships of power are changing, slowly but surely, it is not cultural awareness bringing about the changes, but a hard struggle – political, military, the people, the trade unions, the international community . . .)

'Just take as an example our music, our beautiful mixture of blues and indigenous rhythms, just listen to that great coloured pianist, Dollar Brand, who now calls himself Abdullah Ibrahim and who has become a fervent black nationalist! Or the blending of gospel, negro spirituals and traditional African chanting mellowed in the voices of the Ladysmith Black Mambazo. And theatre. People tell me we used to have traditional African theatre. Maybe. But I'm not so sure. More likely the telling and the reciting of dramatic events in the life of the clan, glorified histories, praise songs, myths of creation. And look now how vital South African theatre is with the grafting on of a European tradition! The transformation into something alive, corresponding to local realities and aspirations. Not blackamoor playlets, but the revitalization of modes of creation that Brecht and Beckett would not have disavowed. There is something for you to look at as an actor.'

(Mano, thinking: How nice it sounds. How elevating. How positive. How enriching. How enthusiastic he is. How much he still believes that history, mixing, interaction . . . are forms of progress. How 'voluntarist' he is. How he believes in the perfectability of the human experience, if not the species! How desperate he must be!)

'And the same goes for painting. The Whites brought canvas painting to the country. Poorly equipped people! When I visited Canberra once with my lady wife, we saw a similar process illustrated there in the Australian Museum of Art. When the means of perception of a society are narrowed down, no, when they have started *seeing* or even *experiencing* through the narrows of a given medium, they cannot come to grips with a new and vastly different environment except through the now accustomed means. We saw how the European immigrants tried to absorb or understand their new environment through the known forms of painting. Painting became an eye, a sadly restricted one. Not just to record, but also to order the new experiences, and this could not grasp the already existing but *different* structures and spaces and rhythms. So, when you are taken through the museum, you see how they struggled with the visual matter. The earlier paintings look like English landscapes. The language is too genteel, the frames too small, the mind's colours still too soft.

'I'm not saying you cannot invent the unknown, like Dürer's drawing of the rhinoceros! Successive European fashions of seeing, arriving with a delay of several years, ships were slow in eating the winds of those days, brought new attempts at coming to grips with what they saw, with what kept scratching at the eye and just refused to be encompassed – impressionism, expressionism, cubism, abstract action painting.

'Only gradually, after generations of dying, did they start to expand, and to embrace the vastness, and slowly they saw that other people there, the Aboriginals, had their own blueprints of reality, their dreamprints.

'So too it must have been in South Africa. People like Thomas Baines and other early annotators at first wandered to the limits of European knowledge as if through paradise, seeing through the mindsets of a Jean Jacques Rousseau . . . Our painting, after a protracted period of muddy Englishness, early on developed a strong Germanic streak. It must be because the strong local painters – Irma Stern, Maggie Laubscher, Katya Hamman, Wolf Kibel, Pranas Domsaitos, Jean Weltz and others – were either of German descent or went there to study. And now our black painters are all pure expressionists! The height of irony is that some of them, those who have reached summits of visual expression, in exile since decades, still stubbornly continue painting "South Africa"! Gerard Sekoto, Gavin Jantjes, Serpent . . .'

Your father had his head to one side while he listened to all of this, and then he said: 'Well, if I were you, if we take it then that we have the heritage of several continents as our due, why do you not choose the archetypal European painting as an example to write about?'

Barnum seemed to be taken aback. 'Yes? What do you mean?'

'If I were you I'd write about the *Mona Lisa*.'

'What a weird idea. And why, pray?'

'Well, if I were you, which I'm not, thank God, I'd choose the *Mona Lisa* for two reasons which may in essence be the same. One – because it is an autoportrait. I mean *your* image, not da Vinci's. Doesn't it become you when you appropriate it? It only needs the act of taking possession, of recognizing it as of yourself. You said something about mirrors. Where could you find a clearer mirror than this *Joconde*? The second reason flows from the first, or explains it: Because it has been seen by so many people, been looked at so much, it has become invisible. I'd say the 'Smiling Sphinx' is the original invisible painting, the effaced face, blinded by exposure. The wing of the bird eventually wears down the mountain. *Mona Lisa* has no privacy, no one unique individuality, no family, no history. Looking is weathering. If enough eyes – and minds – rub over the surface for long enough, if enough smiles lock in on it, it becomes smooth and empty. No relief, no perspective, no mystery, no attachment. And I'm not even touching on the fact that it must have been scraped clean many times, restored, varnished. When you write that story you can add something about how every generation furthermore inevitably sees something or someone else – we know less from death to death – so would the true Mona Lisa please stand up . . . ? There you are . . .'

Up on the heights above Addis Ababa there is a village which became famous during the war. When the Italians invaded our country, they went up there and castrated all the boys for some punitive purpose. Years later, when the Emperor returned to his throne via Eritrea – he'd sat out the war under the wings of the British – he came through that place and he was shocked by what he saw.

So he took two of the maimed boys with him to the palace where they grew up. After the revolution they escaped the country. There had been much in-fighting and bloodletting among the members of the royal family too. The Emperor's daughter was his toughest, most rigid supporter. She was also the fly in the ointment, scheming with a few hard-line aristocrats to stiffen their backs and to knife in the soft parts the members of an opposing faction of liberal aristocrats. This made it impossible for the *Negus* to pre-empt the revolution or to negotiate a compromise solution with the rebel officers of his army. The princess is called Tenagnework – meaning, 'there where she sleeps nothing but gold is produced' – and she was arrested with her three daughters. She is still in prison – oh, a comfortable gaol for sure, since it is the old imperial palace, but she is old and blind and infirm now, suffering from the shaking disease, and her daughters are as aged and sick with chronic hepatitis, cancer, tuberculosis . . .

The two castrated young men made their way in the world. One, looking a lot like your father, Mano, became a priest. He shrivelled rapidly and died before old age, or even middle age, could grasp him by the cassock. Towards the end, it is said, he became delirious. He was put up in a hospice in Rome, an asylum for indigent ecclesiastics, where he raved and shouted all the while refusing to speak Italian. He always carried a small pocket mirror with him in the folds of his robe, and would spend hours speaking to it about the horrors of the African night finding refuge in the palace corridors, and about blood running down the legs of people. He died on his side, looking at himself in the mirror held in the palm of his hand.

The other one, called Golden Mouth ('the mouth which could only say good'), became a very good and a well-known painter. He is an extremely beautiful man, but bitter and bitchy, as one may well imagine. He is tall and straight with his thick hair combed back, a very fair skin, huge oval eyes, a strong and aquiline nose, and delicately shaped hands. When he walks into the room you'd swear it was an angel coming with a message. In a sense, of course, he is indeed an angel. He still paints in the supposedly primitive Ethiopian way.

If I ever finish this book I shall ask him to design a cover for it. I want him to paint a motor car with my father driving and a lion with crumpled ears perched on the back seat. And many little children running after the car, waving their hands and shouting. They will all have these big oval eyes, as if they're carrying birds on their brows.

One could be as silent as invisibility.

166

20

Your father and I were made for one another, we were comple-
mentary, like honey and butter. But now he is gone. The days are
short and grey, and yet they go by ever so slowly. I am terrified of
losing you too. I was born under the sign of the lion. We believe,
traditionally, that a woman such as I risks being attacked by the
evil spirits which cause premature births and bloody abortions, the
death of babies, illnesses of the throat and the lungs, wracking
coughs, chest pains, vulnerability to the potions of the jealous. If I
were back home in my natural milieu, I'd have gone to consult a
dabtara – an expert in song and in poetry who can identify the evil
and combat it by traditional means. I am afraid. I don't want anything to happen to you. The *dabtara* would have helped me prepare a
protective scroll of light grey sheepskin, with the prayer of *Susenyos*
written on it, the prayer against blood. The *dabtara* would have
requested the *zar*, my spirit, to reconcile himself to his horse, to
me. If I were inhabited by an impure *zar*, he would invite it to leave
me. This would call for ritual and sacrifice, because the spirit needs
to slake its thirst for blood. We would slaughter a sacrificial sheep
of the right colour, I would have been washed with the blood, I
would taste a few morsels of the scorched meat before my immediate family, and only they, consumed it. The bones would be buried
in a hole too deep for the animals to get at, and the skin used for
making the scroll. Thereafter I would have kept the prepared and
inscribed parchment with me, around my waist, except at times of
sexual congress.

My little one, I feel the need for us to be protected against 'the
eye of the shadows'. We need to be wrapped in a story, a prayer.
In the old days there were the *Masters of the Name* who knew all the
secrets, the attributes of God. Maybe they would have given me a
scroll with the prayer known as *Solomon's Net*. The *dabtaras* don't
know what they're doing, they only copy and repeat. Man used to
be on speaking terms with God, he knew the names and the nick-
names. The old knowledge has been buried, ancient professions
have fallen into disuse, the bone with the secret formula of memory
is covered by ignorant flesh.

Mano used to say that the theatre too will disappear. Actors were once the intermediaries of the gods, they spoke of them and to them, they imitated them. The theatre had a religious function, and when that broke down, the state had to step in in the name of culture. But culture always goes against the grain, it doesn't come naturally. Admittedly, people will have the atavistic urge to communicate with the unknown which they sense around them by means of ritual and trance, but this need in itself is not strong enough to justify the survival of the theatre. Your father, Mano, thought that such a desire could eventually be satisfied amply by crackpot mediums selling the presence of a god at 300 dollars the session, or even quite simply by the television altar. But now, when the state's sense of cultural responsibility has crumbled and creation is left to market forces, now that individual life has been reduced to a statistic hedged in by bureaucratic taboos, now that society's cohesion has been shattered into corporative micro-egotisms so that there could no longer be any generosity or solidarity – now the theatre was doomed to die. Literature, Mano said, could perhaps still survive for a while. Publishing had created a commercial circuit independent of the state, and publishers, some of them in any event, still had occasional twitches in the dead body of the old-fashioned guilty conscience; some of them liked to walk about with the appearance of a love for literature and cigars, so that they could afford to smuggle 'difficult' literary works as clandestine passengers aboard the train of selling merchandise.

In the prayer it is described how the blacksmiths appeared in a dream to Solomon. They took him to their king who was seized by fear when he saw Solomon. He asked Solomon what he had in his stomach. Solomon said that he was filled with the mercy of God, and this grace would protect him against all malefic spirits and intentions. He thereupon started reciting the names of God. The King of the Demons became so angry that he ordered the killing of the offender. But Solomon said: *'lofham, lofham . . .'* and the King's mouth was shut. Some of the ironsmiths were drowned, the majority went up in smoke and flames. The King survived. Solomon grabbed him by the collar and started shaking and beating him until his teeth clattered. He ordered the man to cough up his secrets. It was a real interrogation. This is what the King of the Smiths confessed to: bringing about miscarriages, stealing his victims' hearts, making monks and nuns fall down staircases, planting little bastards in the stomachs of princesses, appearing under many disguises – the face of a donkey, a horse, a dog, a lion, a tortoise, a crocodile, and many more. The face of the author. Again Solomon thumped him, and prayed, and the terrified devil spat out its tongue.

Everybody always remarked upon the stinginess, the avaricious-ness of your great-uncle Talsam. Sometimes he had bad luck – he would be foolhardy enough to risk gambling at cards with my father, Guebre Gsiaber, and leave a season's earnings on the table. Once he was so broke that he had to borrow the car of his niece, Werzelia, for a trip into the provinces. Weeks went by and Werzelia asked in vain for the car to be returned. Then one day, to her utter amazement, she saw her car coming down a street in Addis Ababa with a complete stranger behind the wheel. She thought it must have been stolen and ran to tell Uncle Talsam. 'Oh that,' he sighed nonchalantly, 'I sold it. Had to.' Poor Werzelia was aghast. How could he possibly have done so without even asking her! But Talsam was quite unrepentant, in fact he convinced her that he had done her a great favour seeing the excellent price he sold it for. Of course she never received the money . . . But this story caused such a stir in the family (your great-grandmother was still alive) that Uncle Talsam was convinced a demon must have taken possession of him. He went into the mountains to the hermitage of a monk renowned for his ability to drive out the bad *zar*. The monk advised him to fast for ten days. After the period of fasting the old monk told the penitent to undress and to throw a bucket of cold water over himself. He then took a bundle of green twigs and started beating your great-uncle mercilessly. 'Do you see the devil? Do you see him?' he shouted. 'No! No!' poor Uncle Talsam wailed. 'Go back then, and fast for another ten days,' the monk ordered. After ten days our bedraggled and half-starved uncle again stood there naked and shivering to be whipped. 'Do you see him?' the monk insisted. 'No! No!' Talsam started protesting, but it hurt so badly that he suddenly changed his tune: 'Yes! Yes! I see, I see, I see him! There he goes, the devil! Look, he's getting smaller and smaller!' He pointed a finger down the mountain. The old monk put down the twigs, looked disgustedly at Talsam, and said: 'Well, it took you some time to understand, hey?'

You, my baby, are getting bigger, you are moving inside me. I am also growing bigger but more hollow, and there is a gurgling in my body as from faulty central heating pipes. My baby is hollow-ing me out from inside. What a racket there must be around you –

my aorta, the digestive tubes and sacs, the tinkling of water in my bladder, the urgent throbbing of my heart like an engine pistoning a ship. I glide over the mirror, leaving seagulls in my wake. But it would seem that the foetus has the ability of screening useless and disturbing sounds. My belly is a tightly stretched drum, and you a living tongue in this resonant calabash.

Now, when I take my bath, when I'm totally relaxed and afloat in a state of weightlessness, I watch the rippling of my abdomen and I can see you moving your position. I know where your head rests, and where the feet. I can now feel my body from within because you knock against my stomach, you nudge my organs. When I need to pee you get all agitated, egging me on, hurry! hurry! Are you feeling constricted by my swollen bladder, or is it a game? Is my baby getting restless? I sense you arranging your nest, looking for the most comfortable place.

Soon you will be born. I have decided to move house. I have to, there are too many memories here, too many eyes watching from the shadows. My heart is heavy. Mano will not know where to look for me when he returns to Paris. But will he ever return? We are separated. It is death. And when I go laboriously about my tasks, deciding what to keep and what to do away with, what to pack and what to throw out, I feel you getting all excited, wanting to help. When I bend forward towards a cardboard box or a suitcase, you start scrabbling around. I stop. 'Now, child,' I say, 'you have to let me do this. Don't get in my way. We can't both be trying to do the same thing.' Ah, if only you were out already, tied to my back, slumbering peacefully.

The phone rings. Cigale talks to me, a calm voice, at first I hear only the sounds and not the sense. And then I find myself sitting on the blue chair still clasping the telephone to my ear. My hand on my bulging stomach. Be calm, my baby. It can't be true! Resnard dead? I hear Cigale's quiet voice and I know that tears are running warm and salty into my mouth. Tears for Resnard, for Cigale, for Mano, for us, for you, for the day outside the windows. When? How? Last night. They fetched him, took him to the hospital, he died, it was all over. Ah, poor Resnard.

Why am I crying so? When Mano left, did we know it was to be the final leavetaking? I held his hands in the traditional way. I submitted to our fate. Aren't we Africans supposed to be fatalistic? I did not know it, I could not see it, but I must have been crying because he looked at me in surprise and then down at his hands, and said: 'How warm your tears are.'

Yesterday, it was Sunday, I still talked to him on the telephone. He asked me for news of Mano. He was one of the very few people who knew that Mano was gone, who worried about him, who remembered him. Paris is the place of forgetting. There was a huge march-by through the streets not far from his house, to protest against the racist politics of this government. Perhaps he heard the clamour. Life. Life outside. Banners, drums, songs, slogans, bands, scarves and fists, thousands of shuffling feet. Maybe he was envious. It is hard to die like this on a cold April day, with snow whirling in the wind. Rage, rage against the dying of the light.

But yesterday he did not know how close the angel Bernael had approached; he could not know that it was crouching on the landing outside his door, uncomfortable with its heavy wings in the restrained space, blowing on its cold hands, meticulously going through the list of names taken from its briefcase, moving a blackened finger down the alphabet – A., B., A. . . . R. – then listening for breath at the keyhole. Just to make sure it didn't come all this way for nothing.

He wasn't feeling well, Resnard, he could hardly speak. Told me to hang on a while. I heard the deep soughing of his breath. He apologized. Said that the doctor had had three bottles of oxygen delivered to his flat and that now he could breathe, that he needed to breathe in order to talk.

Did I think that he would live? 'Yes, Resnard,' I said, 'of course. Why else would they make you do it? I swear to you, you will live. Don't give up now. Clench your teeth and see this through. Actors don't die, they're not noble enough! I shall still see you do Lear, and Mano will be there to cheer you. Just think how jealous he will be . . .'

He said he was ashamed of it, but that he felt unrelated to death. There just hadn't been room for the old devil. One can't be taking care of everything. He had rejected the darkening of the mind. And yet, over the last ten months his two closest friends had died. Aids. Accursed house! The second one barely four months ago, homosexual, a needle case, horrible white death with skin turned black, and Resnard had to take care of all the arrangements. The family wouldn't come to the cremation, too ashamed of their wayward son, the disease of shame. Seven in the morning. Grey winter cold. Don't come to the crematorium, he said then. It will only upset you. Don't worry, he would have understood, you with child. There is time enough for the little one to learn of the horrors of the world.

That night I saw him. He was so funny. We had a dinner party at Osiris's house. Resnard couldn't quite understand why he'd been invited – he didn't know Osiris personally. It was one of those worldly gatherings, the human market where new connections are made and old scores settled. He wore a silk jacket, a leather tie, his cheeks were flushed, he laughed a lot. He went down on his knees, careful not to spill his champagne, and embraced my belly – nothing was showing yet – to say hullo to 'the little one', and then once more 'for the absent father and the son and the holy ghost'.

According to an Ethiopian legend Solomon had a labyrinth with seven concentric rings built to house his many wives and concubines. Sirak the Sage was close to the King, he could come and go as he wished in the palace. He, perhaps inadvertently, seduced one of the beauties and then, like a worm who has already been at the apple, he dug a tunnel between his house and the palace so that he could take the beloved to his bosom whenever the fancy thickened his tongue. Rumour would of course, in due time, have stained the palace walls. Solomon was curious to meet Sirak's 'new wife', and so Sirak invited him over one day. The King sipped his coffee, looked her over, thought he recognized one of his own women, how extraordinary, and scalded his tongue in his haste to rush back and count his herd to make sure it hadn't been tampered with. But already Sirak had smuggled her back in through the underground gallery . . .

What a racist Resnard was! He lives – my God, already I must use the past tense! – he lived in the rue des Rosiers, smack in the heart of the Jewish quarter. Beautiful apartment, immaculately kept, on the top three floors of a filthy, decrepit building. When I first knew Mano, he had a room there, and he kept it even after we started living together. It was from there that he left for the land of absence. The house was open to all comers, many of his actor friends could be found there – one having brought a bottle of wine, another a wheel of cheese, another his blues, a sad story and an empty purse. Homeless players would spread their cloaks on the floor and doss there. It was a place for the gay and the morose and the desperate. And how Resnard used to amuse us with his hilarious imitations of the orthodox Hassidim with their bobbing locks and their spaded beards, the hands on each other's shoulders, mewing on Kippur Day. Yet his first lady friend was a Jewish girl.

Poor Resnard. At home in Africa we have the custom to gather after the death of a friend for each one of us to tell a funny story about the deceased. I remember now an incident related to me by Mano, of how Resnard turned up at the theatre one evening all covered in blue bruises and welts. Seems he'd returned home early the previous morning only to realize to his dismay that he'd forgotten the house keys. So he tried to shinny up the water pipes of the courtyard. The ash-cans were kept there, a source of continual conflict with the ground-floor neighbour, a Jewish spice merchant, because of the heaped-up rubbish and the rats. What could have been expected, did happen: Resnard fell off the wall among a clatter of bins, cracking a rib. He dragged his battered body to the back door of the Jew's shop, croaking for help, and the cursing merchant came out with a stick and beat him some more, mistaking him for a burglar. When he finally recognized Resnard he gave him a few final stinging thwacks for good measure, for trying out his stupid actor's pranks at that time of the night!

He was not a good actor, Resnard. He was too intelligent not to know his own limitations. He was always researching some or other complicated philosophical or historical treatise, trying to extract material for a play from it, and it never worked. Maybe he felt obliged to aspire towards intellectualism, coming as he did from a proletarian background – his father is a butcher with heavy cheeks and watery eyes and hams for hands. He never even completed high school, and started life as an apprentice barber. The fact that he'd broken off all contact with his family, that he'd rejected them was a great source of shame. Often he would bend over with anguish, clutch his stomach, and say how well he knew that it was wrong, despicable, but that he could not behave differently. It was the shame that made his innards ache. And now, who is to bring the tiding of his death to the bereaved and stupefied parents? Who is to run down the dusty road with the burnished shield? They didn't even know of his illness, thought he was off somewhere making a film.

Tubes were put down his chest to drain off a litre and half of liquid. He had high hopes, working on some impossible new scheme – directing a comparative history of religions or trying to turn Heidegger into theatre material. Then, two days ago, they discharged him from the hospital. Sent him home. Just like that.

New health policy. Home treatment. Doctor and nurse would come by at regular intervals, they promised. And he living all by himself in the big apartment.

God help us, what heartless bastards the French are! Whatever you do, when you see the curtain coming down, make sure you don't die in France. They chased him off like a mangy dog. Don't disturb our harmony, they said. We don't want to know about death. Go, go die your own hole!

Yesterday I talked to him on the telephone. I listened to his gasping. I wanted to say something ridiculous, inconsequential, anything to cheer him up, that Mano would soon be back and certainly would want to replace his dead Japanese canaries. Wait, wait, he whispered. Just give me a moment. Don't talk to me about canaries. Explained that he'd called the doctor. Told him that he could no longer make it from the table to the bed. Not to worry, the doctor said. I'll send you some more oxygen. And now today. Alone under the cold sheet. Dead, and his last role a flop. This world, my poor child.

Grey skies, flurry of snow outside. It is difficult for me to sit on this chair by the window with my huge drum. Be still, my baby. I must inform his friends, on your father's behalf. Who is to tell his parents? The dumbness of bereavement. Tomorrow, next week. We shall forget. You will be born. I saw a cat walking in the tree in the back-yard, stalking a bird. Death. The tree has green buds, like flames in the snow. How I miss Mano.

21

This morning the telephone rings. Whenever it rings now, I get a shock. What will the bad news be this time? Another death? Another disappearance? My mother calling from Rome to complain about my brother? She never talks of our young sister . . .

As people grow older so their horizons seem to lower. The cloud-bank gathers girth, becomes a more threatening blue; outlines are hazier, birds fly away from us, the language is poorer, the silences are more strident, the bones start to ache. Weaknesses which seemed to be dormant or minor now become major obstacles. With us foreigners it would appear that, as you move into dimmer regions, your exile becomes purified, more of a conscious state. The illusions of integration fade away, it is too tiring to keep up the pretence, the sadness of a lost youth recurs. Young *émigrés* who step out in the morning with shiny eyes to go and split the big wide world down to the kernel of truth become a shuffle of living exiled ghosts in the evening – the way bright young revolutionaries grow up to be old functionaries.

Since the child in me has started to show, I have noticed a wider circle of emptiness around me. In the race for survival a pregnant woman becomes dead weight. Nothing to be gained from that quarter. My friends seem to be otherwise occupied, and I have no news from Mano's accomplices and acquaintances either. I'm not even sure that Barnum knows about Mano's arrest. I recently saw a picture of him and his wife in a newspaper, attending a gala for the victims of civil war in South Africa. They looked healthy and unconcerned and happy. Probably they had just returned from a holiday in Spain. They never contacted me. Ka'afir disappeared at about the same time as Mano, though I don't think there's any link between the two departures. (Ka'afir is much too cynical to be involved with anything relating to Mano's activities.) Apart from Resnard, none of Mano's theatre mates have looked me up. Walser didn't call. There is wind and rain and sometimes snow.

The wind is cold. When I go out shopping for Mona Senedu's layette, I have to put on the heavy black coat which gives me the appearance of a corpulent bear. I think my skin has grown darker too as I gather my strength around this African child in my body. Two days ago I heard someone calling my name on the boulevard. I turned around and saw two *clochards* coming towards me. The one, the younger of the two, was leading his companion by the hand and making signs at me with the other. When they were close enough I had a fright of recognition: the young man was my cousin Haile, Uncle Talsam's only son, and the other was my Uncle Ganen, the film-maker! I hadn't seen him for years, didn't even know he was still in Paris. Both of them were dirty and drunk. How could Ganen – the dandy, the darling of bohemian Saint-Germain – have come to this? He was nearly unrecognizable, his hair flattened to his forehead, his nose squashed, a crust of blood caking one nostril. Then I saw that he must be blind, or nearly blind, because Haile was explaining to him who I was. They were speaking in Amharic, which was strange too because I'd never heard Ganen use his mother tongue before. His past had caught up with him. Perhaps he had murdered the young dreamer in him and this crime forced him into permanent exile, or maybe the final impossibility for a *métèque* to be integrated beyond a certain point stared him in the face. Paris was no longer a world centre allowing for the free association of foreigners and locals in an exciting cultural or political project. The power is now elsewhere and so is the culture and the money. As for a foreigner wishing to make films . . .

Ganen stank of stale alcohol. He let his hand slide over the big shape of my coat. The fingernails were black, but the fingers were still slender and sensitive. I shivered. 'What's this then?' he asked. 'Is it King Solomon or a *zar*?' I explained that I was expecting, that it was due soon, a girl. 'You poor fool,' he cackled. I was unwise enough to give him my telephone number, because I learned later (my mother in Rome knew more about Ganen than I did in Paris) that he was now quite often out on the streets, sometimes spending the night in a luxurious toilet of one of the 'palaces' that he used to haunt in better days. He could become a nuisance.

But it is Walser on the line. His voice is even and soft. He enquires after my health, makes a few trite remarks about the weather – 'the third bad winter in a row, the heavenly harmony must have been disturbed' – and then asks me whether I'd like to go to Africa. Africa? Whose Africa? I, in my condition? It takes me a few seconds to remember the pre-arranged code, to realize that he is in fact proposing an appointment. We agree to meet at seven o'clock.

The Place de la Cathédrale has an unseasonal sheet of white snow over it. The steps leading up to the entrance of the church are shiny and black. I think about going in (I have Fanuel, the little lion, in my handbag; I always carry him with me now). The door opens to let in two fugitive silhouettes and I glimpse soft candle-light inside, but hurry on because as it is I am only just going to be on time for my seven o'clock meeting in the Café des Anciens d'Afrique, on the other side of the square.

It turns out that I am late – I'd forgotten that the time given is always meant to be translated as half an hour earlier. Walser is sitting in a corner, facing the doorway through which I am to enter. He has finished his cup of tea, and some coins are neatly stacked next to the teapot. Lying by his side on the bench he has the evening paper, his hat and coat and a scarf. His eyeglasses are steamed up – it looks as if he has enormous white eggs for eyes. He rises from his seat to brush the back of my hand with a surprisingly warm moustache. We sit down. His thumb and index finger start tugging at the thick growth on his upper lip.

'I have no news for you,' he says, speaking softly but with emphasis from the corner of his mouth, 'but someone will be coming here in a minute and he will have something to tell. We are waiting for Victoire – the man you met with your, ah, husband, in Ouagadougou. That day outside town. He should be here any moment now.' Victoire? I don't know what or whom he could possibly be speaking of. Walser chuckles briefly. 'You perhaps know him under another name. And you also met a friend of mine there, Baba Ndiaye. Do you still remember? An old black man with grey hair talking to you about bicycle racing? Baba Ndiaye is in fact from Senegal originally, from the coast, he is a man of humidity and of winds, but he's been travelling all over Africa to promote the sport. Blah-blah-blah. He knew your father as a young man.'

'Yes, I see who you mean, but how do you know that he knew my father?' I am excited.

'Because I also knew him,' Walser says, as calm as an egg.

'Please, tell me,' I start asking, and then we are interrupted by the arrival of Mumpata, who turns out to be the 'Victoire' we've been waiting for.

I feel sorry for Mumpata. He probably often goes on missions to colder climes, and he is still ill-prepared. He has on a suit of a thin, summerish material, and a raincoat; his shoes look as if they could be made of bad quality cardboard. Obviously the Movement, or the Party – who knows where his true loyalty lies? – does not issue its agents with adequate clothing, or enough money to buy the necessary. His face is purplish and inscrutable, but his skin has lost its shine. Maybe the cold air gives it this ashen hue. He pulls up a chair and asks for a cup of coffee. He lights a cigarette. His hand is trembling imperceptibly.

During the time in which he tells me the story that he wants to convey, he never once looks me in the face. Walser, next to me on the bench, is silent, scrutinizing the clients at the other tables, watching the passers-by outside the plate-glass windows, like wraiths in the snow they are, with white flags growing from their lips. 'Speak like a patriot,' he murmurs. Was it my imagination or did I hear 'like a parrot'?

Mumpata says they now have precise information from their 'contacts' in South Africa concerning Mano. He says (carefully removing the ash-cone from his cigarette tip) that it is very difficult to communicate with 'inside' – the country is in turmoil, many aspects of the normal functioning of a state now escape the illegitimate authorities, but they are still powerful enough to camouflage certain events and to manipulate information. He says he cannot at this very moment tell me of all the implications of this intricate game: security considerations demand a lot of discretion. What he can tell me for certain, though, is that Mano has been arrested on a trumped-up charge of murder, some sordid crime that he obviously had nothing to do with, and taken for trial to a town in the interior, called Bethlehem.

It happens often now that prisoners are taken for hush-hush trials in inaccessible districts, he says – the Security Police do not want any public event, that may cause the gathering of a hostile public, to take place. 'You cannot believe how mobilized our people are at this stage of the struggle.' Security Police? Yes, because it is obviously a faked proceeding and Mano, by all accounts, has sensed the trap, and bravely turned the trial into an exemplary political platform for the cause. There has been a lot of solidarity around the case. Mano, Mumpata says, has denounced the farce and then went on to pitilessly expose the rotten ideology behind the repression. This must be another reason why the Greys are trying to cover up what really took place, they must know they are facing dynamite! The comrades have managed to make a transcript of the entire proceedings, and as soon as it is deemed safe for Mano – his safety must remain the primary consideration – the transcript is going to be made public.

The verdict? (Mumpata's coffee has grown cold.) Well, as was to be foreseen the state had a corrupt judge presiding to make sure that the verdict was guilty, and death the punishment. But I am not to take undue notice of that. Although it will be as well to be prepared for the worst. Anything can still happen in the present period of chaos and confusion in the country. He personally knows of people condemned to death who will never be executed. They wouldn't dare. But these are bloody, uncertain times. Besides, the Movement has members even on the Prisons Staff. So there is really no justification for being despondent.

Then he asks me if there is anything I want to have transmitted to Mano. A letter perhaps. They have the means of getting it through. He feels it necessary to insist nevertheless that all of the above information be kept confidential. It is important, for Mano's safety, not to confirm by hasty declarations the suspicions the Greys may have had concerning his activities. Bigger interests are at stake.

Walser is clearing his throat next to me. He suggests that we part company, that it will be advisable not to tarry unnecessarily in this place, one never knows who may be watching, what magnetic ear may be pointing our way. He suggests that Mumpata should see me again before leaving Paris, in case I have a letter I wish to forward.

We leave. Walser is blowing into his hands and asking me if he may walk me to the bus-stop. It is difficult walking with him – I am clumsy in my big coat, he tries to be courteous by taking my arm, but it is clear that he doesn't see very well and that I have to guide him over the street. The snow, slushy in parts, does not improve matters. We are quiet. Walser is embarrassed, doesn't quite know what to say.

'I told you I'd known your father,' he suddenly announces. 'I'm sorry. I don't want to intrude. When Mano first told me about you – these are the things one has unfortunately to be informed about in the activities we share, you know, the bare essentials about personal relationships – I immediately recognized your family name, Gsiaber.'

'Yes,' (we pause, ostensibly to look for the safest and shortest way to the bus-stop, but in fact to allow him to gather his breath) 'it was before your time. Your father hadn't married your mother yet. She was such a pretty woman. I was in Ethiopia on a political mission, blah-blah, and I even tried to recruit your father to help us. Can you imagine? But he was not interested. He was all taken up by bicycle racing at the time. He couldn't be an athlete himself, because of his leg, you know, although he was such a graceful dancer – but he was going to train a champion team, he said.

'Maybe just as well that he refused to become involved with me. You see, I fell in love with your mother. Were they already married? I'm not sure now – it is such a long time ago. They were meant for one another, like honey and butter. Could you imagine me as your father? Blah-blah-blah?'

He coughs and makes a great show of pulling his scarf closer around his neck. Advises me to be careful in this weather, not to catch a cold, particularly in my condition. He is fussing over me, like an old hen who has produced an egg late in life.

'A good man, your father. An entrepreneur, of course, but a man of the people, and with a heart of gold. He once saved two of our agents, two trade unionists we had to have smuggled out of Egypt in a hurry. He put them up. I'm sure he never told the family anything about it.

'I would have liked to know him better. But I never went back. Not till much later. I was in Addis Ababa at the time of his funeral. It was after the revolution, of course. I was there to discuss some affairs with the new rulers, and I'd gone on a tour of the city to see what was left of the dancing halls of our youth. It had been raining. I could smell the eucalyptus trees. You must know how popular he'd been . . . Well, this is where we part.'

He tries to kiss my hand despite the gloves I am wearing. I think he is going to fall, put out an arm to steady him. He takes off his hat, tugs at his moustache, puts it back on again.

How kind he is in trying to take my mind off Mano.

22

It is high summer and even the Paris birds are singing when Mano takes Meheret to his place of work. These are old raucous birds, pretending to remember the tunes of nature. Paris is quiet and somnolent. The native population has taken to the beaches or the mountains. Suddenly there are far more foreigners in town – tourists, but also the proportion of African or Asian or Latin-American Parisians who cannot afford to go away on holiday. The tourists wander through the streets on sore feet, from time to time gathering to try and all squeeze together into the same photo. Towards nightfall black families drive down the boulevards as if they are people who belong here.

Both Mano and Meheret are getting more involved in their various projects. The magazine to which she occasionally contributed articles and interviews – *Les Voies de l'Afrique* – has folded, the *directeur de publication*, a fat man named Prospère Dakité from the Ivory Coast, has absconded with what little money was left. He must be sitting shiny with perspiration in some bar in Abidjan, telling his cronies and his cousins and the flies about his stupid creditors. This is as good a time as any, she thinks, to settle down to serious writing. She even starts plotting a novel in which the two main protagonists will be somewhat like Mano and Barnum – the half-black and the half-white, half-brothers as it were, both alienated because born in a mad country on a dying continent, but each in his own fashion expressing it differently. What will interest her, she thinks, will be their interaction, the extent to which they project and fashion one another. It will be clear, she intends, that they have to *invent* one another in order simultaneously to *ape* each other. Maybe she will call the book *The Monkey's Mirror*.

Ever since they returned from Burkina Faso Meheret senses a new restlessness in Mano. Somehow it is as if he's made up his mind to move, to go places. She knows that he is seeing the old man, Walser, more frequently now. What could Walser's influence and attraction for Mano be? That of a surrogate father? She knows that Mano misses not having had a father – 'that is the condition of being a bastard', he often quips – but she doesn't imagine he'd want to invent one just to fill the absence. He now talks to her more often about his past. What he holds up are images, like flashes from a long-hidden mirror. He obviously adored an old blind neighbour, called Oom Sampie, whom he knew as a child. This Oom Sampie lived in great simplicity according to Mano, the sparse furniture in his two-roomed house was smooth and polished from the touch of the groping fingers, and he made the most beautiful multi-coloured kites that could whistle with the wind. Does he see a replacement for Oom Sampie in Walser? Maybe Walser is blind too – it is difficult to be sure – and his dreams of political action are most likely also just red paper stretched over arched reed constructions, like kites . . .

Sometimes, too rarely, Mano will tell her something about his mother, Magriet. He says his mother must have been a pretty girl, brown and well-shaped and happy, maybe working as a domestic servant for some white family in the town of Montaigue. His father, he says, cursed be his name, begat him in the dark of a servant's room and then went on to become an important man in the district, the political representative for the constituency, rising to the position of minister. But he, Mano, was born when his father was still a nothing, a 'son of the family' only. Mano describes himself as a by-blow, the bitter fruit of illicit love, of stolen Sunday afternoon backroom love, what you'd get if you crossed an apricot and a horse. Ministers have no memories. They cannot afford to. His mother would never talk about his father. Mano says: 'I have no father; I am a son of the land.' Later there were one or two other men in her life. One at least had left a nasty imprint on his mind. His mother, Mano says, went stark raving bonkers. That is why he left her, left the country with the desire to invent himself over and again. And he holds this man responsible for his mother's madness. They took to drinking together, and then would repent in maudlin religious ceremonies. 'Jesus loves me . . .' Once Magriet emptied a bottle of bluish-purple methylated spirits over the man's head and then started scratching for matches to put the man alight. 'Kill the devil! Kill the devil!' she slobbered. He spent much time on the streets as a kid, Mano recounts, but the one thing Magriet was adamant about was that he shouldn't associate with Whites.

These snippets of information – these mummies of memory, as Mano calls them – will be woven in with their lovemaking late at night. They lie next to each other on the bed, whispering, the window open on the small garden with its broken-down toolshed, its lilac bushes, its gnarled cherry tree. Their bodies touch, and sometimes there'd be a discreet cough of wind outside. Ever present in the background, like a huge turbine or a sea passing by or a humming mountain or a mind in cogitation, there is the distant rumble of the city. He will go down between her thighs, lift his head and say: 'Whispering moon.' They take great care to muffle the sounds of their bed and their bodies – and maybe this secret communication helps Mano confess – because they now have a guest sleeping downstairs, a man with the name of Ka'afir. Mano says: 'Whispering moon. My love. We must not wake the African. Let sleeping philosophers lie.' Later he says: 'The moon is the memory of the sun.' Still later he goes away on a dream and she will be awake next to him, awake and still, imagining her man's body. Since their trip to Africa he has grown thinner, more tense. He has let his hair grow. 'I shall be white,' he jokes. 'I shall pass unnoticed. Nobody remembers me.'

Mano brought Ka'afir home one evening about a month earlier. He explained to her that he'd met the fellow in a public park. He explained to her that he'd been there for an appointment with old man Walser when he saw this black man on the next bench. With the black man there was another character, very drunk, a Palestinian as it turned out. The two of them were passing a bottle of cheap red wine back and forth, and discussing politics. Mano says he pricked up his ears when he heard mention of South Africa, and then he was impressed by the moderation of the black man's discourse and the excellence of his French. Later they parted company – the Palestinian, who wore a dirty cloth wrapped around his head, kissed the black man on his forehead and both cheeks – and out of sheer curiosity Mano followed the Black. He heard the man singing a song in Zulu (this made Mano very nostalgic), and he saw him skip a few traditional steps. They were going down the stairs of the same métro station, Mano trying to look uninterested, when the man turned to him and said in Afrikaans: *'Ons is ver van die huis, né?'* ('We are far from home, hey?')

Mano says he was absolutely astounded by this. He still doesn't know how the man, who introduced himself as Ka'afir, knew that he had a compatriot facing him. Is there such a thing as a South African look, Mano asked himself. They started talking. Ka'afir was very forthcoming about himself, and yet also totally mysterious. He said he'd been travelling far and wide, that he'd been studying in Poland of late, that he had to admit to the incurable weakness of being African, that he was a philosopher by profession ('because it is a profession, not a search'), particularly interested in poetry as a way of philosophy to the extent that the two disciplines are supposed to be so diametrically opposed. He thought that poetry could expand philosophy, but he was not at all convinced of the contrary.

It turned out that he was on the bum. Mano invited him home, thinking that the man would leave after a day at most. He did leave, but he's been coming back every time, staying for two or three nights in a row before disappearing again. Ka'afir is a tall, well-built man, with the very beginnings of a soft Zulu bulge around the midriff. ('My authority,' he says.) He has a mocking, gap-toothed smile. The two of them, Mano and Ka'afir, sometimes spend hours laughing and teasing one another, or playing with Polly, Meheret's parrot. She has never seen Mano as relaxed and convivial, and yet, there is the underlying watchfulness – as if his bantering with Ka'afir affirms some purpose, some plan. Ka'afir is a heavy smoker. This is the only objection Meheret has, so that he every so often will have to go and sit on the steps of the staircase leading down to the garden, in his underpants, smoking and singing under his breath. He also drinks heavily at times, consuming what he can lay his hands on, and then he will lash out in the most violent monologues, shouting at the parrot – to make a compatriot of him, he'd say. Meheret and Mano nevertheless feel that the man is basically sane. They have the strange impression that Ka'afir is preparing, somehow already poised for action. 'Now we have a philosopher in the house,' Mano whispers in Meheret's ear, 'to keep the parrot company. And the moon.' Why is the man so attached to Mano? Meheret asks herself whether there isn't some unconscious physical attraction involved. Are they aware of it?

She is happy. She has no prospect of work, not in the foreseeable future anyway, and yet she is unconcerned. She now often wears her one and only traditional Ethiopian dress, white with a colourful pattern embroidered around the hem and the short sleeves. This shows off her slender black arms to great advantage. She's cut her hair even shorter. With summer her eyes become bigger and brighter so that the stern eyebrows growing together are less noticeable. Often now, when the two men are out – either together or each off on his own, Mano to meet with Walser, and Ka'afir to go 'read the stone of the times in the dust' – she will stand facing herself in the tall mirror of the living-room. Birds are flitting around the ceiling, perching on the sills and the table or in the branches of the big green house-plants. These are Resnard's Japanese canaries which Mano is supposed to be looking after. She keeps the windows closed to prevent the birds from escaping. It is like being in a glass cage herself. There will be a dark light in the mirror. The depth of the dark surface, the fluttering of the birds and their song, Polly in his coop further back, the scintillating leaves of the tropical plants, she herself moving her hands over breasts and hips, the dark eyes looking out at her and the slight smile of the full mouth like a fish coming to the surface to sun itself – there is a dim but quiescent past there, and something waiting to happen.

This book – if she ever finishes writing this book, and if she were to try and structure two characters like Mano and Barnum – what kind of a past will she invent for them? Maybe they would have had a shared childhood, and perhaps she will have to finish off the tale with the one killing the other. She thinks about this as she watches Mano slowly assembling the elements which are to enable him ultimately to impersonate or to interpret Barnum. She resents this way they have of walking in each other's shadow, she feels that Barnum is somehow sucking Mano's lifeblood like a leech. Then she drops the idea: to invent what exists already is to be totalitarian, she remembers somebody saying. Barnum cannot possibly have had a past. He is still writing one.

With Ms Delanoy he left Paris several weeks earlier, not long after Mano and Meheret's return from Burkina Faso. For some time Barnum had been working on a verse-play, and he now gave a copy of the text to Mano, with this enigmatic remark: 'I think the two of you should have a child.'

Meheret was used to Barnum's strange observations. He liked to pose as some Svengali, concocting their lives for them. Whenever she met him to let him see a further instalment of her *récit*, he'd snort a few comments and then suggest a new twist, a novel departure. 'Why don't you take Mano to Africa,' he'd say, 'to prepare him for what I have in mind?' She felt like asking which Africa? His or mine? Anyway, it was as if he proposed that Tuesday should follow upon Monday.

Mano leafed through the manuscript. He was intrigued. What is this story about a child? And why is the work called a lament? Wasn't he, Barnum, supposed to be engaged upon writing a screenplay, the one they still intend doing together?

'But what you have there will be incorporated in the screenplay,' Barnum said. 'I must create some drama. I must flesh out your role, give you more substance. In other words, I had to imagine a sacrifice. Unless I can subtract something from you, you will not have enough weight. When you leave, as we agreed that you should, then your departure must be a painful break, it must be tied to something terrible staring you in the face. Otherwise there is no point really. Oh, I haven't made up my mind once and for all – maybe I can produce some other horror. But, as you know, I have been fascinated for a long time now by the process, the mechanism you may say, of the transmission of remembrances from one generation to the next. How do we do it, and what does it do to us?

'So I had a look at the Greek tragedies. I'm not an expert, I'm rather a self-taught reader – but what struck me in the fragments that came down to us, from Aeschylus and Sophocles and Euripides and Pericles, was exactly this theme of the passage. More precisely – the fact that the passage from one state of awareness to the next, which is unavoidable, can only be achieved at the cost of some terrible offering, a fatal choice, a renunciation. The gist of tragedy must be the play between free choice and fate. The cruel play. Take your time, read the play, learn the words. You will see traces there of the authors I've mentioned. And then excuse me for thus merging the different figures. Isn't it only normal when you have a memory of the myths moving through your subconscious, when you have a passage consciousness?

'I tried to build two people, the father and the daughter. My mind immediately shaded Oedipus and Agamemnon into the father, and Electra and Antigone and Iphigenia for the archetypal daughter. Those old scribblers also borrowed characters from one another. In all of their stories there is always the murder of a brother or a daughter, there is of course too the cry for revenge intermingled with the howls of lamentation. Add to the general mayhem the argumentation around the public role and responsibilities of the citizen. What interested me was that section of Pericles' funerary exhortation where he postulates that the citizen who knowingly gives a son to the war does so to the honour of his city. You must be willing to do violence to your most intimate self, for the sake of society's well-being.

Agamemnon, when he kills his own daughter, Iphigenia, believes that it is the sacrifice needed to permit the fleet to leave port for the conquest of Troy. Death will be the soft breath of wind. If you read it against the historical context of the times, I think he is really talking about the passage from an uncodified society, maybe a matriarchal one, to that of the Rule of Law, of democracy.

'Then I asked myself – how do I weave the mythical pattern and its implications into a modern cloth? Just imagine, I said to myself, how a person of our time will react when faced by this need to offer up a loved one in order to open the way. I tried to place myself in the position of someone like you, Mano – a modern warrior due to go and do battle for law and justice. But he does not have a child, I said . . . Let that not be the obstacle, let me make one for him from the threads of memory and imagination – history, in fact. Let it further be made possible for him to lean upon his past and look back over what he has done, as also to peer forward into the fog of the future. Sacrifice, we all know, gives second sight. Let him be several stories in one, several people, as we all are. And then let there be intersection of these stories so that he can start to dialogue with the child he left before its birth, present now as a grown woman on the stage.

'Confusing? Yes, perhaps. But there it is.'

Meheret shuddered when she listened to all the above. As if someone had just been walking over her grave. One shouldn't taunt the shadows. Mano was embarrassed by the gift. It was intended that the play should be directed by an old theatre director with an atrociously disfigured face: Zob – 'the Mediterranean shark' was the way Mano referred to him.

And then, ever since Africa, Mano found all kinds of reasons not to go ahead. He was not old enough to be that kind of father, it is too solemn a part, he really hates verse-plays, it will be ridiculous for him – a Cape Coloured – to be cast as a mythical figure. (Really, why should he be acting out another man's fantasies?) Undoubtedly his reluctance was the cause of the tension between him and Barnum. It was as if he wanted to free himself of Barnum's influence, and the latter resented this. The only valid explanation he could offer (or was that too just an excuse?) was that he would henceforth be too busy getting the Birdflight Inc. film project off the ground. He said he feared being too scatterbrained and too thinly spread. He said it was becoming abundantly clear that he'd have to go to South Africa in person for on the spot research. Wasn't that more important, for Barnum too, than his strutting around a French stage with cloak and shield and sword, a dirty cloth around the forehead and the lips wet with weeping? Now is the time for all patriots to come to the aid of their country. Why not offer the part to Resnard?

Resnard was only too pleased to have the job. His only request was that Mano should please look after his flurry of rare Japanese canaries until the night of the première. Resnard was such a serious actor. How could one hope to learn one's lines with birds singing their lives around your head? Mano and Meheret carried the birds home in three perforated brown-paper bags.

And today they are going by bus through the half-empty streets of Paris to the Théâtre de l'Ombre where Resnard and the others are going through the final stages of one of their last rehearsals. They enter the building through a side door past a poster showing a man with dark glasses and a bloody sword, and make their way up the staircase to one of the loggias. The auditorium – the stalls, the bays, the galleries – is clothed in thick darkness. Nobody knows they are there, high up against the wall like birds flown in from some storm outside.

Mano is standing behind Meheret. 'The darkness is impenetrable,' he whispers in her ear. She leans back against him, he smells the warmth of her body. 'And made of velvet,' she answers as softly, stroking the back of a chair she cannot see. Below them the stage is starkly lit, a pool of white light, shadows like black knives, beyond the edge the blank void. Resnard as Agamemnon – in jeans and dirty T-shirt – is crouched front-stage, his head between his arms. Next to him there is a crumpled grey blanket. Iphigenia, a mass of red curls, shapeless shift and sweater, is moving forward into the light centre-stage, obliquely towards the man who is balled in the position of a foetus or a buried ancestor.

Mano (in Meheret's hair): 'He has finished his long speech. He didn't know she was there. He's blind, you see. And they have been playing several lives telescoped into one act. Now she will start speaking to him. Listen!'

IPHIGENIA: Father . . . Father!
What a joy . . .
Let me kiss you after our long separation. Look, I've poured wine and oil as libation . . .
Father?
It's me, your little bird, your chameleon, your own carnation.
Don't be angry, let me light up your eyes.
I've put on my wedding gown.
MANO: (*Softly, his hands moving down* MEHERET'*s back, down over her*

buttocks) My moon, my bird, my moonbird . . . Shall I slip you an eel?

IPHIGENIA: But, but you're crying.

AGAMEMNON: A crossing awaits you too.

Without your parents. All alone.

But first I have to make a sacrifice.

You'll see, your place will be close to the sacred urns . . .

You, Iphigenia,

your beautiful locks will be crowned, like now,

the way the spotted doe is crowned

when as a virgin she comes down from a mountain cave,

and from your human throat must spout black blood for the goddess, Artemis . . .

(MANO's *hands are snaking up* MEHERET's *thighs. He has undone his trousers which are at present down around his ankles. He is bunching her dress up above the hips with the other hand. She has grabbed hold of the armchair in the dark before her, is now arching her back while bending forward slightly. She is biting her lower lip and whispering:*)

MEHERET: No, no. Mano, you can't, we cannot . . .

MANO: You are quivering like a kite smelling the wind.

IPHIGENIA: Don't let me die before I have lived the life of a mother.

The light is so sweet. Don't make me go to my wedding bed

in the underworld in this gown! I was the first to call you 'father',

the first to abandon herself on your knees,

to give and receive the pleasure of caresses . . .

Remember, you called me your little bird,

you whistled for me.

Let me be married. The sun is there.

Underground there's naught but void and all those unintelligible

bones. He who wishes to die must be mad.

Is it not better to live in shame than to die in glory?

(*The actress with the flaming hairdo and the tired breasts has gone down on her knees next to* AGAMEMNON. *He has half-risen, is kneeling on one leg. From underneath the blanket he has pulled a sword. During the following exchange of words she will gradually lower herself until she is reclining with her head on his thigh, her throat exposed to the light.* MANO *has penetrated* MEHERET *deeply, moving back with her until he feels the chair behind him. He sits down with her on his lap, her thighs spread wide over his. She is butting rhythmically against the lower part of his belly. As if trying to dislodge the watery snake.*)

MANO: (*His lips on her neck which is damp and warm*) Don't be afraid. It is as if we do not exist, and yet we are here for all eternity.

AGAMEMNON: Girl, daughter, woman – look how I tremble over this act, and how I shiver at the thought of not doing what must be done.

Do you not see that army lying at anchor, all those soldiers with their standards, their hoarse mouths, their breastplates of bronze, whose route to the walls of Troy will be blocked if, like a weakling, I cannot sacrifice you?

I don't know what frenetic force pushes us into barbaric countries to bring civilization and peace.

Yes, it is to the Mother City, whether I wish it or not, that I offer you. We must remain free, my daughter.

Never again must the Barbarians be allowed to steal our wives.

MANO: We are the Barbarians. We have always been here . . .

IPHIGENIA: Unfortunate race of ephemeral beings, how cruel necessity is! Woe am I to die thus on the sword of my father. Never will my body know the hands of another man. Never again will I see the day, the primeval explosion of sun!

Hush, Father, here I am. Since you have so decided, I am willing to die. It is done, let no one touch me. I shall be quiet and offer you my throat without fear. Please don't dirty my virgin vestments.

O happy day, luminous disc,

O ray of Zeus, I am leaving

for another life, another destination.

Beloved light, I bid thee farewell!

(MEHERET *stifles a cry. She is lying back, limp against* MANO's *chest. His thighs are trembling. She turns her face to his in the dark, kisses him. Her cheeks are warm and wet.*)

(*On the stage* AGAMEMNON *has slowly pulled the blanket over the supine* IPHIGENIA *covering her body. He gets to his feet, resting heavily on his sword. His head is down between his shoulders.*)

AGAMEMNON: My snail, my chameleon, my spotted doe, my poem . . .

(*He lifts his head, listening*)

What is this rumour of wind

I hear? Whence this *puhpuhpuhpuh*?

The birds! The birds!

From the second or third row where he has been sitting in nearly total darkness, they hear Zob calling out: 'Not bad! Not bad! a bit too solemn though. Don't be so serious, Resnard. Let's take it through one more time.'

(The text Barnum wrote with Mano's movements in mind and which is called:)

Lovesong to an Unborn Child
a lament

There is no death!

It is not natural for a father to mourn his daughter.
There are accents which die in the throat,
wounds which the white robes of bereavement cannot purify.
I listen for your heart in the hymn of the bird,
my back is on fire,
I turn and your eyes are questioning me like flames on the
 skyline,
my snail, my small chameleon, my doe . . .
Quiet! Be quiet!

A word only lives when spoken aloud
and when there is absence it must be silent.
Where then does this song come from, this voice?
Is it the gods trying to direct me as if I were
some old sweeper of sentiments in an abandoned theatre?
When I was young I dreamt the symmetry of the world
and now I no longer know whether I'm senseless laughter
or a foul curse in someone else's sad anonymous mouth.

Quiet!
This ink must dry, this heart close up –
when I slit your voice it was to seal your eyes,
for it is not possible for the citizen to take part
in the making of laws, fully, from man to man,
unless, like the others, he is willing to play
the lives of his children.

Why do you look for me?
The illustrious warrior has the whole world for his grave.
No need of a fading name on a crumbling memorial to the dead
to recall his existence. Even in foreign lands
where nothing is written down

192

each native has an eternal flame of memory
speaking of attachments, if not of action.

Be silent, my love. With these hands I grope for the words
and under my fingers I feel the trembling artery
pulsing in your neck.
You are so confident and vulnerable to my touch.
You put your hand in mine. You trust me. You guide
the steps of my swollen feet.
And you are gone.

In a crowd, on a bustling street, suddenly I see
the shape of your walking
and the veil between life and death is lifted.
Dust rises from the plains. The city is in smoke,
The rumour of decay reaches the temple.
People scream and scream for democracy or peace
and are ground to silence under caterpillar tracks
of the victorious. Reverberating through the ceaseless corridors
of our labryinthine history there come
the hoarse imprecations of freedom fighters,
the furious commands of captains of capital,
the inchoate stuttering of instruments of killing –
like so many hearts being torn from their rhythm
before the silence of sanded memory.

And then the silence.
Broken down to silence.
Listen, I must talk to you.

Echoing through the desolate reception halls and courts
of our palaces the volumes of silence.
Where is the daughter who will snip off her plaits
and mourn for me when I'm through?
Memory of snow and of dust.

It is not natural for a man to weep over the future!
I am the old dog holding down my whimper of despair.
At night I turn and toss this aching sack of bones
honed shiny and salty and smooth with the mumbling of tooth-
   less gums –

now lying on my heart,
now on the liver –
trying to eclipse the moon from my dreams.
Give me symmetry! Give me sense!
I must bury the rotten carcass of the doe,
drown the loquacious face of cold fire:
and your image sails behind my empty eyes.
If only I could get shot of your eyes!

The room is dark. I am a ship launched
to go free the trading routes of the Mother City,
and I drift off through the night
which becomes the sea, the moon a whale.
This breath must be mine! I hold my breath,
curl myself in the oblivious snail-shell listening
crouch of the foetus
and ringing through watery chambers of time
and time your lonely chant floats to me.

No, oh no . . .
How deep you lie buried . . .
Through the amniotic past tense of amnesia
your pale shape swims. I search for your limbs,
I long for the innocent movement of your hand
when you fasten your hair to be woman.
And you are not there.

My shroud has the sweat-stains and the stench
of an old man's body.
Over my head the heavenly hunters pursue their prey.
Stalagtites drip their ice-invisible light.
I shall go out on the roof and rend my clothes
to shout: you are not there!
Do you too hear a barking dog?
No, I cannot die . . .
Must I live to the end of this rhyme
knowing I killed innocence?

THERE IS NO DEATH!

To travel alone

through the dictionary of another dry desert land
where consonants rattle and stars coagulate
and snakes of sound stealthily
slither like water over the suffixes,
to suspend all prejudice and disbelief
and hold on till the next refrain,

is to be dizzily cupped in the hands of the gods.
The walls of the world become cheeks warmed by a sun
tossing through wheatfields a light head
of shimmering horns, the countryside
has the crimson smell of breast-beating,
foreign beggars shriek by, mouthing their orifices of pain.

There everything can be imagined: even a change
in direction and diction and never to return to destiny;
lock the door on neighbours' silly chatter;
jump through a window into a sea;
transmute the multiplication tables of loneliness in song.

To move from underground terminus to airport
with the bag a little lighter from station to station,
from mild sadness to pout-mouthed elation,
and reach under another name any destination.

To travel alone
where mirages thrum and shipping lines lie slack,
to let slip the long silences,
string the heart from a darkening moon,
sit with writing on the knees
brooding on dreamdeath until one is left
with a fly-trap full of inkspots in the lap,
and then hold out for a free refrain . . .

My voice will mingle with the wind and the laughter of oracles.
Look, for one who has known the drunk-making pleasure
of the mother's orgasm, whose blade is stained
by the blood of the father,
it is not necessary to peer into the future.
I killed the owl!
I stuffed the fountains of this earth

with the slain bodies of state enemies.
I am blind the better to look for ever
upon the black face of justice . . .

Oh, I know, I know
this role is corrupt, rewritten every time a hand
was poised in killing, sung whenever a voice winged up
to plead for mercy.
A red tide washing over the stage.
But ever since the memory of mankind I have erased you,
ripping apart the sounds of your throat
to make you dance upon my knee.
My eyes don't have to see.
I know the words by heart, I can count on my fingers
the tiny intelligent wristbones of the chameleon
to spell out the meaning of metamorphosis.

Listen – one hears nothing: neither bird nor the wash of the sea.
The winds have died over Europe.
And yet, only yesterday, it seems like yesterday
the season of the blackbird's mating call,
the lilac blooms, the cherry blossoms,
the horses prancing in the courtyard, the burnished shields,
the young studs toasting their loves in champagne.

This sea is like a night which has lost touch
with its coasts of dawn and dust . . .
Happy are they who pass without glory
through a life without peril.
How I envy them, and not him who has the honours,
not him who hobbles on three legs to the end of the line
and the one leg a bloody sword!

I am the history of myself.
I am the white mask of the law, the actor of my script,
the lover of life. You could not have lived without me,
and it is not possible to shut up war
except by demolishing the enemy.
I recite my lines, I spend my life
repulsing those who rise up against us, be they Greek or
Barbarian.

Ah, and now I honour on my cloak
the snailtracks of dust and of snow.

Could I refuse to participate in the duties of a Citizen?
A lowly birth has many advantages:
It allows you to bewail and mourn
what a nobleman must keep to his mouth.
We are ruled by honour, my child, making us slaves
to the multitude.
That's why I'm bitter to be crying
and ashamed to be holding back the tears
now when I so much crave to rinse the heart.

Do not think it easy to structure order and law,
rushing from conference room to assembly
to television studio in order to promulgate conventions,
reshape morality, install the abstract
and promote the state:
To keep chaos at bay.

Legitimacy must go to them who make the laws.
Law is form, is shape, is tractable destiny
for the common well-being. But no law without exclusion,
or else the state itself will wither away.
Did you really expect us to build on women,
bastards, gypsies and Blacks?
How could we let the chameleon have its ponderous way,
its ancient colouring, its naked soul, its weighted
walk of the embryo?

Our principles brought us to this station.
Our political régime does not imitate foreigner's laws –
no, we are examples, not mimics.
We constitute a democracy
to cultivate beauty in simplicity, and the things of the soul
without letting go of our firm control.
If we are rich we are not arrogant.
As for poverty: it is no shame to confess it aloud,
though it would be a dishonour not to attempt
improving your situation.

On shield and on cloak we bear the signs,
witnesses exist to our power, holding us up as paragons
for the admiration of present and future priests.
We need no Homer to praise our glory.
We have forced sea and earth to open up
before our audacity, and everywhere we left
imperishable monuments as souvenirs of evil and of good.

Contemplate and love the power of our city
and know that it was a question of honour
to construct it in action.
Even when we left our white bones clicking on the ramparts
we knew we would never be the dust of snow,
but proud syllables in our city's book of glory.

Why do you look at me?
The illustrious warrior has the whole world for his grave.
No need of a fading name on a crumbling façade to the dead
to recall his existence. Even in forlorn lands
where nothing is written down
each native has an eternal flame of memory
speaking of action if not attachments.

Don't look too closely upon death.
It is much more terrible for a man who has some pride
to sense a weakening of the grip and a veiling of the eyes
than to face Lady Death with all his strength intact
as shareholder of the hopes of the people,
not knowing where she of the white breath will pounce from.

For it is not possible to take part in the play of history,
fully strapped in the city's machinery,
unless one is willing, like the others, to bring
one's children on the stage.
Only the honour of having sacrificed and suffered will survive!
There is no death . . .

To be there must be the final curtain.
There must be a law, or else we shall go on killing
one another for all eternity. You were what I loved
above all else in myself, you the hand writing me.

You made me go beyond the sepulcral rhythm of the self
for the sake of us all.

Listen, my daughter:
I must tell you urgently about life:
In Africa too there are birds at large
singing a secret night of love and of hunting.
But here on this dark stage I heard for the first time
the blackbird's warbling of hesitation,
and knew again how trembling and sweet
one note of happiness can ring in a penumbra of space:
ah, the earth of exile is not only bitter.

Is it not strange my eyes and heart should be dry,
that I can weep only in tracing and reciting
to keep down the howl of madness?
This is why I shall hold you like the goat
with a knife at the throat,
to muffle the singing,
your cursing society for all ages to come.

Your blood will be my ink.
This heart must crust over . . .
Sometimes I turn and I see in the glass
the blind memory advancing.
A cold wind blows down the corridors of the underground
where vomit and old bodies dry . . .
We enter the mirror.
People are bathed in the white light of whales.
People study dim maps for confirmation of the station.
From a dark tunnel a train comes screaming its wrath.
A bearded man with dark glasses shouts,
the face caked in blood, barefoot, fetid breath, the body
    unwashed;
a bearded man with black eye-holes shouts:

Ladiesangennelmen please excuse me for the bother
I have to tell you it's only hours I was released
from prison I want to go home to my wife
my three daughters and of course my job I'm a sailor
I want to return to Mycenae and put out to sea

199

since this morning I am standing along the highway
and no one will stop help me give me a coin
from your hearts ladiesangennelmen so I may go home
before nightfall to kiss my wife and of course
my three daughters I thank thee . . .

No! oh, no! No!
Is it already this late? Already the end
of the night? Wait, I am not ready . . .
Last night, only last night I dreamt your face
more pinched than a writing hand,
furtive and white like a bird spinning flight
in a blurred beating of wings.
I saw you as the conception of the sun
between the legs of my beloved.
Nightbirds sang a sweet obscurity.
How I longed for you, how I envied that drumming
of life in the body, the growing of warmth.
I, a man, stupid, with trembling hands keening
for the intimate knowledge of freedom.

I caught your first cry
like a word whose circle of flight
can never be circumscribed.
And there was blood all over my knees.
Do you remember I kissed you? That I
brought breath to your mouth, named by touch
your tiny shoulders, the crumpled fists,
the swollen petals of your sex?
Nightbirds sang a sweet complicity.

Yes, I knew you would fill my home and my grave.
There must be beginning and there must be an end. There must
be an end. There must be a law.
I walk out on to the roof and I look
towards the hills which harbour the darkness:
From the gorges day will break, swelling,
sweeping over the ridges and flooding the plains,
ah no, and I must write
and this writing will kill you.

You came forth from my loins and yet
you precede me and I shall never see your face,
ancient one, countenance of flight, the hidden Africa
of my bones.
I shall write to give birth to my love
and flesh to my flesh, I shall flesh out
the small ideogrammatic puzzle of bones
from which the flesh will be torn
to forever make an end to death.

I hear the murmur of generations
invading our land, flooding our hills, rising
to a wail like the ultimate white mushroom
bird of oblivion . . .

It is cold in the courtyard. Last night
I heard the cry of your birth
and I was cold with the fire of silent
emptiness between words.
Day will come and my eyes will be blinded
like birds looking for the sanctuary of love . . .
What is that *puhpuhpuhpuh* I hear?
Is it already this late?
No! No! No!

23

At first he stayed only for the night. He wanted to retain his freedom of movement, and during all the time that they lived together he was seeing people and doing things that she knew nothing about. She'd met Walser only once, in his company, in a dark café somewhere near the Gare de Lyon – and yet Walser must have had a strong formative influence on him. As for Barnum, she saw more of him, sometimes together with Ms Delanoy, but they so obviously moved in different worlds that the contact was superficial.

She implicitly welcomed him to stay longer. He'd entered her life on a bed one rainy night near the lake of Mont Aigu, and she took it for granted that he was there to stay wherever she went. It needed no solemn love declarations. Their rituals were African. She'd had other love affairs, naturally, but the attachments were not lasting.

She had room. She had this house – that is, she was lucky enough to have been asked by an old gentleman doctor and his wife to look after their Paris house while he, the doctor, was on a two-year teaching tenure in Montpellier. The doctor had worked in Ethiopia during his youth. She got to know him when she was researching for a documentary film on humanitarian aid to Africa. They became good friends – when she could get hold of the right ingredients she'd come over here and make *injera* and *doro wat* for them. The house had been neglected and probably it was due for demolition, but it was roomy and pretty. It was situated in the Impasse des Impairs in the 20th *arrondissement*, not far from Ménilmontant where the Arabs were getting rarer. The house was built on three floors, but the ground floor had been blocked off. Its charming characteristics were the long living room covering nearly all of one floor, where the doctor's collection of tropical plants was concentrated like an erupting dream of forests, and the garden at the back. It was a small, untended garden, with a toolshed demarcating it from the neighbour's property, and it had an old cherry tree, two huge lilac bushes and a wild vine feeling its way up the wall of the house. When it was warm enough she could open her bedroom window and pretend to be somewhere out in the country far from the bustle and the stress of Paris. In early spring crocuses grew under the budding cherry, and there was even a snatch of grass where she could sun herself. Sparrows often visited the branches of the tree, and a blackbird seemed to have made its nest in a secluded spot where the grass grew high. A neighbourhood cat – nearly all white and without a tail – would come prowling, stepping delicately over fallen twigs on the toolshed roof before lightly jumping down into the garden.

She'd been happy here. Maybe more even than his infatuation with her, the openness and the calm of the house enticed him to stay longer. But he was like any animal that had to familiarize itself with its new territory and so he came and left several times before settling in. They never formally discussed their living together. He kept the room he had in Resnard's apartment in the Marais, an extra-territorial base as it were, but bit by bit he moved his books and clothes and few souvenirs over to her house. He preferred the upstairs workroom to her bedroom, and when Ka'afir came to stay they'd let him have the bedroom and both sleep upstairs under the roof.

He was not the only animal in the house. For several years now she'd had a parrot called Polly, a pearly grey with a flash of red in its tailfeathers. It was supposed to have originated from the rain forests of Gabon, and was of a species reputed to learn the human tongue quite well, but Polly would only squawk and squabble and preen its wings no matter how hard she tried to get it to imitate her. 'It is convenient,' Ka'afir remarked wryly. 'It means you can safely tell it all the secrets of the world as if to some Polichinelle.'

But from the outset there was mutual distrust between Polly and Mano, nearly as if the one thought the other to be trespassing on its dominion. For some or other reason he insisted upon wanting to teach the bird an Afrikaans ditty. Sometimes he would spend an hour or more outside the parrot's cage in the green-shaded living room, singing:

Ma slaap vanaand alweer by Pa
Pa slaap vanaand alweer by Ma
Ma raas, Pa raas
Die kinders krap in die koskas
Dis meatless day
Of course ja

All to no avail. He prided himself on his rapport with birds, and through the Uncle Sampie of his youth he imagined that he knew something about the secret of flying, but this one would only cock a beady unblinking eye at him, walk the length of its perch with the uncomfortable gait of a horseman on the ground, and try out its beak on the bars of the cage. Ka'afir couldn't help teasing him with the lack of response.

She'd been happy here, and now it was all over. As summer drew to a close, he was getting more and more tense. Was the break-up becoming inevitable? What break-up? Breaking with what exactly? He wouldn't tell her what was eating at him and as far as she knew he didn't confide in Ka'afir either. Some weights were shifting in his mind, moving to new alignments. What was it that he was afraid to tell her? They'd been to Africa, and that experience precipitated something in him. They still had their moments of euphoria, of intense joy, of lightheadedness – like that afternoon when they came out of the Théâtre de l'Ombre and decided to walk all the way back home to Ménilmontant, drinking beers in whatever cafés they could find open along the way, and both of them laughing uncontrollably. He had her panties balled up in his pocket as if they were a flag wrested from the enemy. But often now she woke to find him already out of bed, downstairs watering the plants or (when it was hot) naked in the garden. His face was closed, his thoughts too far away.

She'd been happy, looking back, perhaps until that day when they brought Resnard's birds into the house. Ever since then they had to keep the doors and the windows of the living room closed. The canaries were free to fly around at will. But it was as if they too were now living in an aviary. The birds sang quite prettily, no doubt about that. He liked them – 'at least they make music,' he said, 'not like that one there,' referring to Polly. And he said that not many people had the privilege of seeing themselves in a mirror with birds flapping around their heads. 'One could imagine oneself in heaven here.'

But then one late afternoon they returned home to a scene of carnage. Some branches of the plants were broken, a lampshade was overturned, there were feathers all over the place – and blood: streaks of blood on the carpet, bloodspots against the walls, and especially a smear of blood running down the swordbright length of the mirror. They came upon the mangled and mauled bodies of the canaries, and then only did they see Polly sitting in the top of one of the plants, cleaning its feathers with a bloody beak. Somehow it must have escaped from its cage and then there must have been a terrible fight between the canaries and the parrot. Was it jealousy? A question of territory? The pent-up frustrations of alienated birds? Or were parrots and canaries programmed to attack one another whenever they had the chance to do so?

He went absolutely berserk with fury, knocking over furniture to try and get at Polly. She screamed at him to stop, to leave her bird alone, that the bird had been there with her long before he came into her life, that it would never have happened if he wasn't so complicated and finicky that the poor incompetent Resnard had to play in his place and then they wouldn't have had to look after the shitting canaries to start with. She'd had enough of putting up his friends and warming his soul. This was no zoo! They'd never had such a terrible argument before.

That night they slept upstairs again, even though Ka'afir was absent on one of his 'missions'. They didn't want to be too close to the deathfield living room. They talked into the small hours of the morning, his mind roaming as he told her about the family he never had – 'my father must have been a bloody parrot,' he whispered – and she taking him through her memory of other hills and white plateaux.

In the morning she woke up with a start. He was sitting bolt upright next to her, saying: 'Listen! Just listen! Will you believe it? One of them survived after all!' From downstairs she could hear the distinct trilling and warbling of a Japanese canary. He was already going down the steps, naked and excited.

Suddenly she heard a roar of fury. She was just in time to see him with his hand inside Polly's cage, grabbing the bird, dragging it out and flinging it against the floor. He was blind with anger, one bloodied hand (where he had been clawed) reaching down for the twitching bird to throw it against the wall again and again. She screamed and screamed and screamed. Then she went for him, lashing out at his face, pulling his hair, kicking at his shins.

And it was all over. In a few minutes' time he was up the stairs, dressed, running down with a bag in which he'd rammed some possessions, and he was gone. She was sitting in the kitchen with the dead parrot in her lap. She couldn't understand the violence of his reaction. How could Polly have known that it was going too far when it started imitating the song of a canary? Did he lose control when he got downstairs and saw that it was the parrot singing, that there was no surviving canary? Was he angry at being fooled?

Or because the bird never wanted to talk to him? Did he take it that the parrot was mocking him? What was it that upset him so – his own credulity? The theft, through imitation, by one bird of another bird's life? Was it death?

She took the dead bird down into the garden and buried it in the shade of the cherry tree. A thick finger of brown gum was bleeding down its trunk.

Two days later a telegram arrived at the house, addressed to Mano. She hadn't realized, didn't know, that he had apparently retained some link with his family, maybe to a half-sister, at least to the extent that they knew where to find him. The telegram was to announce the death of Mano's long-forgotten father, and saying that they were waiting for him to return for the burial. Why were they willing to let him attend the funeral? Was it some deep family guilt that needed expiation now? She couldn't possibly tell him about it – she knew that he had it in mind to return, but these fatal tidings would knock him completely off his perch, would have him recklessly precipitating his plans. On the other hand, for how long could they possibly keep the old man's corpse before getting a sniff in the nose, before being obliged to lower it into the earth?

She telephoned Resnard and asked to speak to Mano. She wasn't going to say anything about the dead birds. Mano was not in. That night he returned her call. His voice was distant. She asked if she could see him, said she had something important to tell him. Was he now going to leave for the land of the white barbarians? He wouldn't say. No, he preferred not to come to the house. They would meet by the cathedral. Soon it was going to be autumn, winter. The nights were already long. Ka'afir also had disappeared into thin air. Often she asked herself why she'd ever let these bloody South Africans into her life.

She would keep the house, but it was empty now. She would keep it, because certainly he would return and things would be as before. And meanwhile she would spend the colder days in the upstairs room, writing down this story about Africa.

24

This will be the last time, maybe the last time, I don't know. I only know my time, our time has come. You are due. You have moved down, head first, ready to be born. Maybe you are beginning to see a crack of light. I think it will be tomorrow. The fatal day.

After that I shall not write to you again. You will be born with an ancient memory. In the beginning you will know everything, all you have been, and coming into this world (again!) will be like being torn from the light. You will suffer the tear, you will howl with despair. Luckily you will be consciousness only in a ball of flesh, too weak to abort its own existence. And then, day by day, this perfect knowledge will fade into your subconscious. It will never disappear, no, it will inexplicably inform so many of your gestures and emotions, but you will become stupid again, a little child, and new, more tender and fragile figurations of awareness will be acquired like an overlay. Your body too, which has been shaped through the dreams of the ages, will impart to you certain expressions or movements and the feelings and attitudes which go with them.

I wanted to write this last letter to your father – to tell him how much I love and miss him, and of how big you've become, how you have been treading water for the last week. But it would have been futile. I'd have had to impart too much despair to him. I'd have had to tell him about the treachery of his friends and of his begetters, of how his father's corpse may for all I know still be rotting in a morgue, of how even I became unfaithful.

Though I'm not sure it can be called unfaithfulness. Ultimately we are joined by our impurities and our inconsistencies. When you are close to another human being, even to a killer, you are somehow close to the one you love.

I'd have told him, your father, that the house is empty now, that Corbeau and Cigale came over to help me move our few belongings to an apartment in the suburbs, I don't even tell you where, because Dr François and his wife will be returning soon from Montpellier. It makes no sense or difference now for him to know where we shall be going. All I have left upstairs are our two suitcases, mine and yours, and the food I need to see me through the night. I am sitting in the garden, writing this. I'd have told him, your father, how beautiful the garden is in the falling afternoon and the gathering gloom of twilight. At home, when the year turns, thousands of people will walk the forty-two kilometres up the mountain through the night, with burning sticks to keep away the hyenas, to go and pay homage to the angel Gabriel.

Here I sat when Mumpata brought me the news. That there was no more hope. He insisted upon coming to the house. He told me they had inside information that the game was finally up. Nothing could be done now to save him. We talked for a long time, about many subjects, but mainly about Africa. He said he couldn't explain to himself what had gone wrong with Mano's mission, but he speculated that the collaboration with Barnum may have been for something. He didn't want to go any further, he said, except that they'd warned Mano not to become too closely involved with Barnum.

A blackbird was acting strangely, hopping from branch to branch on to the low roof of the shed, flapping its wings and screaming. We couldn't understand what was happening until we noticed the white cat stalking some prey in the garden. The mother blackbird was frantically trying to distract the cat's attention, to lure it away from a nest where we saw one young bird unable to fly. The nest was almost exactly over the spot where I'd buried Polly. We chased the cat away.

Later we lay down on the grass in the sun and I cried. Afterwards, the grass was flattened, the way it can be trampled by elephants near a river.

He said I should think about returning to Africa, that life was too hard here in Paris. What was I going to do all alone with a child? But no, how could I go back to the poverty and the terrible illnesses and the hunger and the repression? It may be difficult to live among cold people, but have we forgotten what we fled from?

I shall miss this house, this garden. When you were just three months old in my stomach I once woke up to find the garden white with snow. It was as if the sky had made up its mind and a poem overnight. Even the bowl with seeds that I left outside for the birds was filled to the brim. I held in my hands the cup of purity, and I knew it would melt to nothing. How light it was. We mustn't be attached to this life, to houses and gardens and affairs of the heart. We mustn't become attached to words, for it is like hanging on to a robe stitched in pain. At night I hear Mano's voice in my hair, softly talking of love, telling me about the ancient kitemaker, or saying how close he feels to my wrists and my tongue – 'secret and essential like those of the chameleon'. The snow will disappear, the chameleon will die too, and one day it will become clear that the garden never existed. We shall be the memory of the future.

I must finish my book on Africa. But it will be so much more difficult than I thought. Perhaps I'll just pretend that I'm writing it for you. I once heard Margaret Gardiner, a friend of Barnum and Ms Delanoy, say: 'Unless you're incredibly talented you can't just spew out a book. You have to devote time to it, especially if you're writing a book with depth.'

Nine months full. You are not a book. And yet you are nearly written. You have come with me such a long way. Now the detachment must come. Tonight will be a wake. By dawn, I know it must happen at daybreak, the waters will break and you will come down from the mountain to slip from my thighs and enter the sea, my little dolphin. You will lift your blue, smothered head to the light, tied to me with a rope of blood. The rope is the connecting link between death and life.

May you go out the good way. May you walk well.

PART TWO

ON THE NOBLE ART OF WALKING IN NO MAN'S LAND

Si je vous dis que sur les branches de mon lit
Fait son nid un oiseau qui ne dit jamais oui
Vous me croyez vous partagez mon inquiétude.

PAUL ELUARD
La Poésie doit avoir pour but la Vérité pratique

1

It is a cold morning. You may think you already know all transformations of the celestial space at the break of day, but it is never true. Even if you were to isolate the elements and the components – the darkness, the stars and the planets, the blinding wreckages of space vehicles, the moons, the clouds, the mountain, the light, the looking eye, the looker, the faculties of the observer, his frame of mind, his pre-conceptual prejudices, his memory. Even then the variations of combinations are inexhaustible, for these can never be captured. They are eternal (whatever 'eternal' may mean); it always is, but the essence of that is, is becoming: it is forever getting to be day. And it is only in that evanescence that you, yourself, in a state of deliquescence (fugitive to boot), may capture the essential. Of course there will be the simulacrum of inherent structure since there is the repetition of circles, the antiphony of day and night, the dawn and decay of the moon, the sundering and the run of seasons – and for you the awakening and the sleep, the fade-out of realization and the stylus of experience, the lie and the shriving, the feint and the block and the acceptance. None of this will remain constant. Nothing is ever again as it always was. There is no progress. There is no past. Only coming into being remains. Always an inside shelled and shucked as the outside starts seeping in. You are ink on paper. Clever like the pen. Like the wagging finger. The spacelessness of space, and then man, or prison of being (perpetual movement) in there. What makes you think transformation doesn't have a structure – that it isn't structure itself?

Take, for example, the mountain. Mountain as hunk or as wall or as city of refuge or as thing or as portal. Mountain dead, with all its life. Greta Garbo is in the mountain. She's waiting for you up there.

Today it is winter. Above the eastern rim climb a play of fleece clouds, purplish blue, silvery pink, the colour of fishes. Faintly up high the skimpy scraping of pallid moon, a geometrical proposition: perfectly at the frontier of invisibility. And then Ukwezi, the morning star, moist with fire. And other points of light, drill-hard, against an etiolating backcloth. (Emblems on a religious banner.)

A V-formation of geese greying a line to the green shelter of the mountain. There is still life up there.

Go lie down half-way up the mountain's first incline, on your side, legs curled up, in the folds of your clothes the dew will be cullets. The drab fog-bank resting on the extinct city in the plain is darkened by ancient smoke leaking through. The city is full of faults. Where the coastal land starts climbing gradually to the heights, the Place is waking up also. Black digestion pollulates like plumes from the boiler's high chimneys. Light flies through the naked trees, over the carcasses of helicopters, over turrets and reservoirs, crashing against the ramparts of the fortress. The phantoms in the watch-towers put on their silhouettes, they have white breaths and heavy overcoats. A bell rings in breakfast and all the dogs start to whimper. An inner courtyard is unlocked. Up the slope float notes of some sad ditty. Loud-hailers crackle to life. People are hiding in the mountain, listening. Green ones? Black ones?

I am here. I fold my hands tightly. (Perhaps this is too much information to start with.)

2

The point is to start anywhere. To continue then in the direction opened by that start. Whatever the way may be, wherever it may lead. Can you believe I don't know where I'm going? But this I do know now: I cannot reach anywhere except by beginning here at this instant. It is important to *begin*. Thus to take hold of a loose thread and to unravel the pattern – for to travel is to lengthen the road, also to destroy the wholeness of it. (In the first instance one sees the man among his friends in the crowded room, clinking glasses, comparing smiles. He is well-dressed, *très comme il faut*. One notices simultaneously the blackish string or cord coming through, it seems, a buttonhole of his waistcoat. One sees him turning around, gathering up the lengths of string. Still clutching the cocktail glass awkwardly. Following it. Perplexed. Careful now not to entangle the feet of the fellow guests. Out through the adjacent room, then the next, fewer people here, finally the entrance, still attached. To be attracted is to be attached. With the bundle of draped string in his arms he clumsily disposes of the dirty glass on a small table by the front door. Opens same. Vehicles swooshing by in the distant night. He is alone. Steps out. Wire taut. In the street outside there lies the cadaver of a donkey in an advanced state of decomposition. Quite bloated (look closer) but already the flesh is rooting away from the structure. The black line disappears in the innards of the animal. Very likely it is part and putrid of the twisted intestines. Flies are everywhere, crawling big and blueglass over the carcass.)

The method I've decided upon is to move forward. In this way, I should say along this way, I trace a memory. But memory is a faculty of the imagination. To imagine, to create images, is to regurgitate. To regurgitate is to complete. For you must not think for one moment that the process is haphazard. (You must not think for one moment.) I don't expect to have a choice. Inevitably there will be false starts. I'm not to know if a clear line will ultimately describe itself. Those who continue will see. But there will be repetitions: it is the simplest way I know of to make patterns, and patterns bring about rhythm by which (an image of) life is ensnared.

'Life is a story.' So a story you will get. Why else would you bother to read? Why would I care about reporting this to you now that I have so little time left? Time is detaching itself from the bones even in the present line, like this. Therefore time, to last, must be compressed. The effort of not seeking must be concentrated to an intense point. (Of explosion. Letting go.) It is rather like a *Che-hsin*, destroying time-consciousness down to the final purity of causeless and ceaseless sequence. The joining of mind to mind.

Even thus my report is a story. Which, by definition, must have a beginning, an opening up and enduring to an ending which is in the beginning.

Start with the immediate: one can't go wrong there. One can't go wrong in any event. And immediately there are flies, too many flies; which is strange because unseasonal, it is cold after all, the night is early. Outside there's a mountain. That is, I know there's a mountain. I see it when it's still light.

(Pattern as prototype, primitive form, protoplasm, precedent, criterion; cynosure, exemplar, paradigm, dummy, matrix; likewise design, nature, condition and period; then too orthodoxy, assimilation, adjustment, practice; also inscape, formation, formulation, fashion, outline, lineament and even morphography; to lead to scaffold and skeleton or perhaps just surface; flower, mirror, background, wreath, buttonhole. Which as rhythm will be iteration, ditto, harping, revenge, plagiarism, cuckoo, creature of habit, atavism, curtain call, ding-dong, counterpoint and syncopation, song.)

3

The Characters

NOMA, the cock of the roost, Master of the Game, Prince of the Place.

ANOM, the protagonist.

GRETA GARBO, his beloved, an agent.

KHADJIA, her aged mother.

BARON SAMEDI, DR YAMA, partners in undertaking.

GUIDO DI PIERO DI GINO, a painter.

R. NOORDHOER, a dealer.

KA'AFIR, poet and manifesto writer.

SCHLOCKMEISTER, a Samaritan.

MASTER BASIE, a brachycephalic disciple of discipline.

STOEL, a furniture.

MORLAND, resistance leader, chairman of the Waterworks Commission.

UKWEZI, the morning star.

READER, the normal, probable reader.

APOKALIPS, a tame mouse.

PETE, a warder.

BIRD PARKER, a jazz musician.

SESHA, AMO, NXTATSHISWITI, JOHN MILES, ELEPHANS, ZIKALE, MALAPI, passers-by, also members of the choir, crowd, and the Waterworks Commission.

MR VAN WYK, a cyclist.

HIPOTALAMUS, a loathsome fat Greek philosopher.

HAFIZ, a drifter.

LAZARUS, a dead.

REALITY SOUL ADDICTS, a rock group known previously as 'The Mind Movers', before that as 'The Soul Suckers'.

ESPEJUS, a cabinet-maker.

WRITER, a pen pal.

BENJAMIN PÉRET, the image-maker.

KASHYAPA, a reference point.

MOUNTAIN, a mountain, an *alter ego*.

SUICIDE ARTIST AL. SHIVA, a suicide.
THE BAFALADI, strangers.
PLAYERS OF THE GAME . . .

4

My dream is heavy water. The whole night long I wander along canals burbling darkness, vehicles (swooshing) on mountainridges spear and spar, and it is so urgent that I return, and choose the way – can my feet go wrong? – and I don't know where, how borderline is confusion, but day becomes me near thee, seated in the bus, and traversing suburbs of the rose and cement wastelands away away to that glow-encapsulated city.

Dear Noma,

For the first time I allow myself to write to you. Or for the first time since that one other occasion when I was, I remember, barely nine years old, when I learned the painful truth of who you are, and thus of where I come from. That letter I wrote with the utmost calligraphic concentration – in *skoonskrif*, 'clean hand', the way our Afrikaans mistress taught us – and I had to slip away from home to go mail it. Why did you abandon me? It was a long way along the dusty roads to the post office. Of course I knew exactly where the building was, all Victorian with turrets and scrolls half-way between the city hall and the police station and just below the stern and cold church on the hill of the pink people.

We would run the gauntlet of those streets on a Saturday afternoon, I and a gang of urchins all my age, and the pale kids living in the sector would drive us off with stones and dogs. Whenever my mother found out about our escapades she spanked me for having been into the white town again.

'What business do you have with those people? Do you think you're too good for us, you little runt?' she'd yell between the blows raining about my head.

Don't ask me what the letter said. I don't recall; the experience is blocked out in my mind. I must have felt a mixture of pride and shame and hurt. And, as always, the longing. (One early morning in Paris, after a long night's carousing, a drunken friend of mine stepped out on the sidewalk, looked at the swaying sun and said: 'Now I long for people I've *never* met in my whole goddamn life.')

Distress and shame because of the cruel fashion in which I was told about you. Uncle Sampie, our neighbour, had neither child nor crow, just a nephew called Janneman who often came to taunt the old man, rummaging around his drawers for coins. This Janneman was five or six years older than I; already he was a hard-case *skollie*, regularly getting stoned on cheap wine and *dagga*. That Saturday Janneman and his pals 'borrowed' one of Uncle Sampie's kites, and after filthying it up by dragging it along the street – they couldn't be bothered to coax it gently into the air – they jumped on it in pure vandalism. Then they had the cheek to return the broken-backed bird and to lay it out on the kitchen table.

I saw what they did; I was forever hanging around the old man's small house. When his blind blue fingers discovered the broken reeds and the torn wings, tears started running from his nose and there was a small funny sound in his throat, as if he were a sick dog. Janneman grabbed me by the collar, wrestled me to the floor under the table, and shouted that I was the culprit who'd done the foul deed. 'What else do you expect from a white *hotnot*!'

Uncle Sampie tried to intervene. He stretched out his hands, bumped against the workbench, knocked over the chair. 'Hush,' he pleaded, '*nee*, Jannie, don't say it. Leave the child be. Hush!' But it was too late. 'You old fool!' Janneman screamed furiously. 'I tell you, that's the thanks you get from warming a half-breed adder in your bosom. The little bastard is nobody's child. He's just a spy. Why don't you send him back to Baas Niemand? Mano is a mule! Mano is a mule!' (For weeks afterwards the kids at school would goad and taunt me with their *Mano Mule*!)

I wanted you to recognize me. You never received the letter. I folded the page carefully to make it look like an envelope, and on the outside I drew a stamp in the top right-hand corner. Underneath I wrote *Meneer Niemand*. Then I thought better of it and scratched out the *Meneer* to write *Baas* in its place. (Please permit me my sentimentality.) On Monday some clerk in the course of sorting the mail must have come across the letter; he took it to the editor and sole employee of the local news sheet, and by Tuesday it was the laugh of the town. Did it embarrass you? Surely many of these self-satisfied white scavengers were pointing whispers at your back? Or didn't you even know of it? My people, the Coloureds – who on earth are 'my people'? – were not at all amused.

You will not receive this missive either, for the simple reason that it will never be posted. If the *Boere* were to find it in my cell they'd hand it over to the Greys, the political police, and all the beans I've been trying so hard to keep out of sight will be spilled. Or am I foolishly hiding Polichinelle's secret? Do they already know the true story? It is one of the questions I keep asking myself.

I have this urge to write to you now in the hour of my need. It is after all your land still, your laws, your institutions. You are, as we say in our slang, *die nek van die plek* - the boss of the Place. It is in your power to intervene and save me. Irony of ironies, if you, the white master, could explain who and what I am they'd have to admit my innocence because the murderer, it has been proved, could only have been a White. And I'm not a White . . . Do I really want this to be known? Can it be a valid plea for the defence? Have I not been passing for white ever since I came here?

You are my only family, my last link, the father that could claim me – and I never knew you! The woman who bore your child, that lithe brown girl, became a shapeless old dark muttering vegetable; she is long since dead and under the ground. I know, I killed her as surely as if I'd done it with these two hands. Oh, not directly, no. But my leaving the country the way I did, making sure my tracks were covered, and her never knowing whatever happened to me, certainly destroyed first her sanity and then her health. I left her with the worm of anxiety gnawing at the innards. I thought I had wiped her for ever from my thoughts . . . Now she regularly visits my dreams with her white Sunday hat bobbing its flowers, and the awkward handbag, although I sometimes confuse her features with Meheret's. But you don't know Meheret either. She is my dark love.

I *had* to reject her, I *had* to escape my false past. I disappeared and became a nobody. Perhaps my mind was made up for me the day of the breaking of the kite. (I am pursued by broken wings.) Till then my origins were a hushed scandal. I swore that I would one day become someone else, a *real* person. It can't be said I didn't succeed. And in the process I precipitated my mother's senility.

I must write, I must talk to someone out there. Before I die I need to get off my chest the whole truth of what actually happened to bring me to this impasse. I don't want to disappear before you've known me, acknowledged me. (But I shall not die. THERE IS NO DEATH. Somewhere there will be a solution! The mistake will be realized and I shall be set free to continue the imaginary and inconsequential life of a mask!)

I don't dare make contact with Meheret or with Walser, and certain not with Mumpata. The only person I could perhaps correspond with would be Barnum, and how could I trust him? For the sake of the cause (what cause?) I have to continue playing my role to the hilt. How ensnared I have become in my own fabulations! I need to write and to invent.

Since I've been sentenced and brought to this Death Row, I even started drafting a memoir. I thought to call it 'On The Noble Art of Walking in No Man's Land'. It is fragmentary, and as I advance it becomes clear that it is a possible description of the undertow of a given surface, a piling up of images like the break-up of an ice floe. The ice of experiences and impressions becomes a slough of water. In due time this will evaporate to become a cloud in the heavens, rain, rivulets, stream, sea – to be frozen over with winter. Death must be deep-frozen. Excuse me. I'm not totally honest now. This work that I spend my time on – of which even these letters are a part! – my making water of my memory, is the screenplay of my movements that I imagine Barnum to be writing. You see, I am still imagining myself in his place. (But you don't know Barnum either . . .).

Can it ever be the screenplay for a movie? Still, words become images when penned down on paper. And words are steps and steps constitute movement and movement is walking. Walking is a story. The story is a walk. Through history? Isn't life the process of filming and editing a long walk to nowhere? Cut!

It is not enough. I shall continue my dance of writing towards you, although you won't know of it. There is the need to clarify my way. I want, for the first and the last time in my life, to be in a position where I can whisper intimately to someone: *Father, Father, here I come.*

Your son
A. Niemand

5

It is dark, pitch, black, blind, blunt. With hand-palms one may stroke the darkness, fur staining skin. In this big ship we move up river, in land, deeper, not knowing. Neither knowing where we are nor what the where looks like. We bend, grope, pick up any loose object on the deck: wrench, bar, bolt, grape, grass, monkey, gullet, stone, brass. Which we cast in silence on to the banks to hear the sound be it muffled or sharp of impact. The echo, the distance, the ultimate direction, the substance. We do wish to remember where we are. To establish. To make contact. To be circumscribed by rejection. To hit the darkness and limit it. To find what we are. Also becoming. 'And consciousness when it doesn't clearly understand what to live for, what to die for, can only abuse and ridicule itself.'

Dear Noma,

When I decided to *mayibuye*, to let Africa come back to me, there were two considerations for the trip, and in fact the one served as a pretext for the other. I intended to do background research for the film in which I was to play the part of this Barnum. Where did he grow up? What was his youth like? And then, later, during his disastrous erring through this limbo, who were his contacts locally? What did they make of him? Who, if anyone, gave him over into the hands of his tormentors?

The second excuse – the ostensible reason as far as the Movement was concerned – was that I had to make some assessment of the Party's impact and implantation as an underground structure. I furthermore carried some mouth-messages and also undertook to see to it that a letter from Ka'afir reached his sister, Nomzana. The search for Barnum's tracks was to bring me into contact with the Organization; sifting through the grids of the Organization was to help me find the traces of Barnum's passage.

Even so the real motivation lay elsewhere. Barnum never realized that I knew full well who he was. I told him I was from the hinterland, and then left the exact location up in the air. He never probed any deeper, probably assuming that I had a miserable past to hide under my frayed actor's cloak of anonymity, and that he should refrain from asking for uncomfortable answers. How proud these Whites can be of their considerate restraints!

Once, during a conversation with Meheret, I heard him remark that the writer obviously discovers in the process of writing the story he's trying to pen down, but that he should also know beforehand exactly what it is that he wants to tell so that from the word *go* he can start judiciously leaving out certain parts. He said the art of writing is to convey the known *without* stating or describing it, or also that only the transcription of a fragmentary awareness can bestow an impression of veracity upon reality.

In a sense he was right. You see, I never told him I grew up in Happy Valley. Was there ever any place in *your* memory for that 'location' lying like a dog full of sores and scabs kissing its flanks and paws just outside the back-door of Montaigue? More, I never let on that my mother worked in the kitchen for his family when I was small. He was already a young man at the time, I only a small boy sifting through the dust of the yard and vroom-vrooming around with some of his discarded toys. I recollect his going off to court a sweetheart on his bicycle, wearing his first pair of long greys. There was nothing wrong with his left hand then. When, many years later in Paris, he came back-stage to congratulate me and my friends on our rendering of Fugard's *Bloodknot*, I instantly recognized him. True, in the mean time he'd made his name and his photo, without the glasses, had been in the papers. In the exile community his imprisonment had been a subject for conjecture for a time, and then we had more serious matters and prisoners of a different calibre and feather to worry about. I have since read his own dramatized and self-exculpatory account. No comment! Had I spoken to him at an earlier stage about our intermingled home towns, it would have established between us a ground of unspokeness too sore to the touch.

Using him as a fool's mirror I came to search for the blotted-out self I'd abandoned in Happy Valley and in the dusty back-yard of his parents' home. Your household must have been something like that one – the extended family, the dependants and attendants. I cannot recollect ever seeing Barnum's father. Did you know him? You must be about the same age. To tell the truth: I need to outline *you*, the gap in my life. At last to lay *you* to rest in my imagination if not in my memory. My writing will be your grave.

When it was later put to me that I had to change my identity as my 'real' name was most likely burnt since the Greys were now looking for a certain Mano, and when I was asked to suggest a new neutral monicker, the spur of the moment brought *Niemand* to my lips. Let me be *Anom Niemand*, I said. It would do, Dr Yama opined; many Whites in this country are called Niemand. My friends could not have known of its private meaning: namely that it was the father's gift never entrusted to me. (But you have still to meet Dr Yama.)

Let me go back in time. By way of my efforts to explain to you the sequence of events, I may perhaps understand what happened.

At first everything went off without a hitch. From London I flew into Johannesburg's Jan Smuts Airport on one of those SAA flights which now stop over in Abidjan. Brazen backstabbing if ever there was any; I mean, Houphouet-Boigny allowing a feedline into the besieged citadel at a moment when we, elsewhere in Africa, were trying our damnedest to quarantine the evil.

From Jo'burg I travelled to Mother City. That was the area where Mumpata had arranged for my link-up and there, furthermore, I was going to start looking into Barnum's antecedents. I immediately telephoned a man called Van Wyk, as agreed upon before my departure from Paris. Two days later he came to fetch me at my hotel and took me into Crossroads One where I first met Dr Yama in a modest private home. On our way there we passed through several road-blocks, manned by very young white and black conscripts; there were armoured vehicles patrolling the streets, and from time to time gunfire rattled and rolled in the distance. Surprisingly some semblance of 'normal' suburban activity was maintained. Van Wyk advised me to relax jaw muscles and buttocks – not the sphincter though! – my papers, he said, were above suspicion. Life goes on!

Dr Yama was black, a medical man. With him he had a pale-skinned white woman with pimples and glasses and hair reaching down to her shoulders in rat-tails. I never caught on to her name; Dr Yama simply called her Girl. I did learn that she was a student activist, probably one of the hard Lefties of bourgeois stock whom I seem to have problems with.

For a few minutes we exchanged little cows and calves, as our saying goes. Van Wyk repaired to elsewhere in the house, from where he could presumably keep an eye on the tense street. Two flies were twirling a ritual love-making around the lampshade. (The curtains were drawn.) Girl sat on the sofa, chain-smoking, directing suspicious glances at me. I was too close to white for her comfort. Dr Yama had a thin face tapering off to a wispy beard. His eyes held the intelligence of humour, and his perfectly toothed smile sent a shiver down my spine – it could alternately be a flash of affability or a chilly threat. When he needed to consult a name or an address pressed between the pages of a minute notebook, he fastidiously positioned a pair of thick-rimmed glasses on the tip of his nose. Doctors have the hands for delicately removing the skeins from the flesh of an orange. He confirmed that my arrival in the zone had been ground-laid by Mumpata, 'our roving ambassador', and then he enquired after the true purpose of my visit with a quizzical lilt of eyebrows and lips.

I explained that as the liberatory struggle and its concomitant repression flared to new levels of intensity, an essentially ideological debate raged not only in the ranks of exile groups but also among other potential supporters of our cause. The Movement itself was starting to show the strains of divergent analyses inevitably expressed in different and oft contradictory strategic options. The debate, it risked being more than a debate, I said, was about ancient, practically millenary questions: the relationship of Party to Movement and those to People, it being understood that each entity would articulate the struggle differently given the nature of its historical stirrings and structures, and to some extent the peculiarities of its aims. Although we all take freedom as a mountain to be scaled, we may still disgrace ourselves in our differing assessments of the dialectic relationship between our organizations and our goals; we may not be choosing the apt moment to go relieve ourselves behind the bush: in other words, we may not share the same reading of how and when to walk. Take freedom. It was a matter of movement, I said; how to coordinate it for maximum effect, how not to be out of step, how especially not to be tripped up, how most especially not to walk away from the work. (And while I was speaking thus memory echoed through my mind – Ka'afir saying: Why do mountaineers carry ropes? To hang themselves in case of a bad fit of altitude depression.)

It had been decided, I said, by those called upon to make such decisions (meaning the committee of the Party), for me to come and sniff the wind and sift through the signs in local sands; perhaps I was not the only envoy or eye on an errand of this nature, but conceivably I was delegated to play the part because of my clean record, and in fact I had no past of militant involvement. As I was no sore thumb I could move in several milieux with the ease of a blender assured by chameleon camouflage. Treading softly. I had no axe to grind, no thesis to defend, was neither judge nor protagonist, just the concerned observer. The passive actor. (I did not confess that I had become very critical of the Party, that for the sake of broadening and deepening people's power I was inclined to underwrite demands for far greater autonomy and initiative leeway to other components of the Movement, in reality that I was all for the People taking over the struggle. Neither did I admit to my growing intimate penchant for Black Power, to my ever greater distrust of Whites, my disillusionment with Europe and its dominant albocentrist ideologies. All of this I played close to my chest, but maybe Dr Yama guessed my mind. I sensed that he must be a subtle diagnostician. I similarly did not think it politic to touch with words on my film research project. Wouldn't such an interest be perceived as spurious or incongruous? As petty bourgeois? And how could I ever explain about you, Noma? This land is our land.)

Dr Yama permitted me to perceive the barber's razor of his smile, sharpening it on a lower lip. 'True enough,' he said, leaning back comfortably in the armchair before throwing three wingbeats of an eye at Girl. 'These are momentous issues. We on the inside sometimes consider it a luxury to indulge in such . . . matters – not to put too fine a point on it – and we comprehend that it may be of more urgency for compatriots in exile than for us here where we daily have the fetid breath of the beast on our faces. For us on the ground the alternatives are more urgent, probably also because we are caught up in the dynamic workings of the struggle. I am not suggesting that we give less prominence to the pre-eminence of pure reflection, but in our daily tasks and campaigns – with people dying and the mountain on fire – we tend to have a more physical experience and appreciation of these somewhat . . . theoretical – should I say theological? – conundrums.

'What's more, it has been our experience that individuals who become too fractious in their quest for ideological purity can so easily end up as sacrificial goats. There *is* such a phenomenon as the martyrdom junkie. Let me tell you' – he suddenly leaned forward urgently – 'and this may surprise you: the revolution is not necessarily pliable to leftist ratiocination. Nevertheless we think you have a valid mission, even if we sometimes wonder why Headquarters – you must have your instructions from Headquarters? – multiplies this species of caper . . .

'We are too much in a hurry not to take our time. Here we are in the thick of strikes, boycotts, guerrilla actions, all under extremely difficult conditions and lowering skies' (his voice had an edge of irritation to it) 'and we *do* have democratic if slow means of letting our brothers and sisters out there know of the application of directives and the evolution in our thinking . . . We are, in a figure of speech, the very digestive organs of thinking. And you out there do know how rich and developed the internal dialogue is . . . Still, the state of emergency and all, and imperilled communications . . . As we say, there are never too many flies if you want to come to the end of the dead elephant.' (I couldn't help but feel that he was sceptical about the outside sending such an obvious lightweight on a wild-goose chase: he had more important matters darkening *his*

229

mind!) 'Naturally we shall arrange for you to meet the comrades. Will you see to it, Girl?'

I then said – and probably it was a mistake – that before leaving the country again from Johannesburg I also had to give X. a letter from Ka'afir intended for Nomzana, and if they could please put up the meeting. A mistake, I think, because Girl nipped her cigarette with one nicotine-stained nail and muttered what sounded like *'shit'*, or perhaps *'mixing sand with shit'*, and Dr Yama was rapidly putting on his glasses when there was nothing to be read or noted. 'We know no one by the name of Ka'afir,' he said in a low voice. Then, as if snapping for scissors or knife during a surgical operation: 'Van Wyk!' And to me: 'It is not wise to stay in one place for too long. Van Wyk will escort you back. We shall be in contact.' (As an afterthought: 'She'll be coming round the mountain when she comes.')

I was taken to my hotel. The next morning I went into town, to the main station, and took a train for Montaigue. On the platform soldiers (not policemen) were checking the identity documents of some passengers. I saw three nondescript individuals being led away with firm hands at their elbows. But there was no atmosphere of panic, or even of tension. The Whites were leafing through their bland newspapers or scrutinizing the station's roof-pattern; at the far end of the platform Coloureds (the women in colourful dresses) were quietly airing their tongues and teasing one another. I had with me a morning edition of the local *Mother City News*, and a brown paper bag of deliciously flavoured, yellow-peeled *nartjies* (*Citrus reticulata*). A drunken old poet had once written of all the ladies of the heart evoked by the oily spray from the snapped *nartjie* peel umbrella-ing over the hand. My heart was heavy with memories, like a sac of water. I longed for Meheret's smile, her wrists, the caress of her fingers on my cheek.

The train left on its three-hour journey. So trains still ran, despite the intermittant fighting? Although apartheid was no longer practised on public transport, the *de facto* situation was unchanged by the simple expedient of having Whites travel first class and Others in the other classes. My compartment reeked of stale smoke. The landscape was in the slippery grip of winter: the suburbs all wet, the shanty-town streets mud-flooded, the oak trees bare. One slope of the mountain, where part of the city had recently been burnt down, was smoking oily feathers. My paper shouted in hollow headlines about the SADF's latest military prowess in Zimbabwe, smaller items reported a number of acts of sabotage on the Witwatersrand and inferred that a police station had come under terrorist attack. I was quickly re-adapting to the South African art of reading news: between the lines, from the corner of the eye, with sections of the mind whitewashed. Ours is the magical land of vanishing realities; we live in the kingdom of invisibility. The *nartjie* slices were refreshingly cold on the tongue, the skins on the floor like fragments of a winter sun shot up by terrorists. These fingers did know Meheret's body.

The town of Montaigue hadn't changed that much. The white sector seemed to have shrunk somewhat, the church on the hill digging in its heels even deeper. Barnum's parents' house had been demolished and an office-block rose in its place. I looked over the gate into the back-yard – so little altered! – and before my eyes floated the vision of Barnum, in profile, nonchalantly sitting his bicycle, clips keeping his turn-ups free from the oily chain, letting go of the handlebar to rub his hands together. I skirted round the limits of Happy Valley, thought it senseless to run the risk of entering. A foreigner would have no business strolling those streets. Besides, chances were that someone would recognize me. 'My people' have the stubborn memories of mules, and mockery comes spontaneously to their lips. I could just hear them poking fun at me, 'the foreigner'! I could see down to the first intersection where soldiers in typical South African browns hunkered atop a Casspir. The area was more developed now, at least one street – the one nearest the white part – was lined with fancy bourgeois residences. Collaboration does guarantee a measure of upward social mobility. No, I didn't look for your house. It must be in a sore place of the heart. (My father has a mansion with many rooms.)

Back in Mother City, on the second day if counting from my first meeting with Dr Yama, I took a taxi-cab to the house of a certain Oupa Coetzee living in a suburb called Newlands. The driver of my car wore a cap pulled down deep over the pock-scarred face which kept on spitting out the window. I had to turn up my collar against the fresh draught. Oupa Coetzee normally taught Afrikaans at the Western Cape University, but the campus was now off-limits to staff and students alike, and all activity had been banned since the sacking of the buildings during the February riots.

It was Barnum who had provided me with the address. That

man, meaning Oupa Coetzee, knows me like an open book, he'd told me in Paris. Go talk to him if you want to read me clearly. 'But watch out – he has a very sombre mind and a bitter laugh.' I found him with three students in his book-lined study: it would seem that cause-committed lecturers were trying to continue instructing the young privately. He had a big head of white curls, dark bloodshot eyes, and a straggly grey moustache. When I explained the purpose of my visit, namely to flesh out my feeling of Barnum the better to portray him in a film we had the intention of concocting (part fiction, I emphasized), he laughed and shook his head. 'Oh no, not again!' What did he mean not again, I asked. No, I was told, it just reminded him of other times when unexpected news of Barnum always brought bad luck and calamities and red-handed guilt. Why? 'Why? Because he uses his friends as if they were figments of his fertile – no, febrile – imagination, caring not a fig for their opinions or their security, or even their private lives or appearances. We are just toilet paper to his plots and his dreams. I remember that time when – '

But I knew what he was going to relate: I'd read the book. I asked whether he thought I could pass myself off for Barnum – what with the beard, which you will have to imagine, obviously, and rounding my shoulders like this? And making of the one hand a white mouse that has been sniffing its way through too many mazes? He laughed again. 'If you really wanted to, probably yes. You have the same accents, I must say. Perhaps you've eaten the same kinds of food giving the mouth a similar shape. But why bother? Why imitate a relic from the past? Do you believe that appearance should try and re-enact being? And what about memory? A person is what he remembers. That snow and dust cannot be imitated.'

We thereupon had a long discussion – his students joining in – about the crafts of adaptation and dissimulation, the quest for survival even at the cost of destroying the identity, of the dialectics between a thing and its image. Image could be read as an anagram for magic, someone suggested. All part and parcel of the actor's bag of tricks, I thought to myself.

Then we talked, but only obliquely so, of the political situation. They weren't forthcoming, playing out their thoughts parsimoniously, treating them like foreign objects, and I wondered if it was because they were uncertain whom to trust and whom not. Oupa's mouth drooped despondently. 'Deep and dark days await us, because we didn't want to learn about the dying of time.' He fished out a precious bottle of Roodeberg '82 – 'One of the last joys left.' (The hectic hedonism of eating and drinking before the death of the morrow – all the rage till recently – was now something of the past, I was given to understand; but this seemed to be belied by Oupa's precious belly-bulb and the flowering of the vine on his cheeks.)

He told me how his son, Marco Polo, had skipped the country not long before, for all he knew to go join up with the guerrillas. To top it all off, he sighed, his wife had gone and got herself pregnant to the eyeballs again, like mustard after the meal, her time was close, nearly to be weighed on the hands, and this time around it was to be a girl. 'Bad timing, but God, in whom I don't believe, has devious ways. The chameleon is the oldest serpent on earth.'

From a shelf he took some back numbers of a magazine, *The Marginal White*, he once helped edit. 'You may find some birdseed for thought about your model B. Bird in there. Take them,' he said . . . Then I was advised that it would be better to leave before curfew fell. He saw me to the street, shook my hand, laughed his wine-rich breath for a third time, and spluttered: '*Fok maar aan! Fok maar aan! Waar ons nou nog niks sien staan, gee God goue graan!*'*

Early on the morning of the third day someone knocked at the door of my hotel room. I opened and saw Girl in the passage, ludicrously disguised in a red wig and dark glasses and coat dripping water (it was raining on the esplanade). For one mad second I thought that perhaps, but nix, she seemed not even to notice my pubic hair or my tousled bed, I breathed easier, she said she'd been sent to fetch me for an appointment, and for some unfathomable reason my breathcage became more constricted.

This time round I was driven on her scooter to a posh palatial house in Kloof View. Two fully grown Doberman-pinschers with shiny coats were belling and bawling as they patrolled the walled-in perimeter of the property. When we entered, Dr Yama was standing by the bay window, his back to us, looking down upon the rain-shrouded city and the gleaming harbour. He turned his face to us. 'Sometimes one forgets about the island out there,' he said. And: 'The city is actually an ancient woman of long ago, a grey *karos* embroidered with nacreous tears slung over her shoulder. It is a quotation from one of your mad poets, named Marais.' Then: 'Do sit down.'

---

* 'Bugger on! Bugger on! Where we will see nothing now, God gives golden corn.'

Girl removed neither coat nor glasses; now she could presumably look me over at will. It is always easier to scrutinize someone when you think that you yourself are unrecognizable. She remained standing. Cheap dramatics, I thought.

Dr Yama plaited his fingers fastidiously. He was sitting forward on the edge of his easy chair, the sharp smile nesting in his mouth behind puckered lips. It was as if tongue, lips, teeth and smile were having a drafting session behind closed doors. The words will in due time emerge as a resolution produced by consensus.

'Something new has come up,' he said, not looking me in the face. 'You never mentioned that you were here for other purposes also . . .' Only now did I feel how the rain outside must have cooled my body. I thought a shiver – if he takes out that smile of his he will slit my throat with it.

'We have advised. And ahem, it is imperative that you get out of this town immediately. We . . . have . . . learned that the Greys are on the trail of a certain Mano. So we shall provide you with new papers. Is there any name you have in mind?'

'Niemand.' I spontaneously uttered the one name which was forever lurking in the darkest alleyways of my memory. 'Make that . . . eh . . . *Anom* Niemand. Nobody will know my name.'

'Fair enough,' Dr Yama said. 'Common name among the *Boere* too. I once knew a General Niemand in the Prison Service, brother to the Minister, both retired now . . . Listen carefully to what I'm going to say. You will have a new identity the day after tomorrow. Don't go out on the streets until then. Consider yourself naked. Leave that same afternoon for the North. A commercial traveller will take you up the line as far as Matjiesfontein. From there you take the night train for Johannesburg. When you arrive, go to the Southern Cross Hotel in Hillbrow and book in under your new name. Wait there. Someone . . . will come (for you) to give you further instructions. Be careful. We know that Colonel Williams himself is coordinating the search. Watch out for him . . . He's a bas-tard!'

(It rang a bell. Hadn't I come across that name somewhere else? Must be a well-known flatfoot.)

Girl left the spacious sitting room and returned with a camera, a tripod and a lamp. I was directed to stand with my back to a neutral partition. She fixed the lamp to the tripod, directed the hot spot on my face, and started snipping off impressions of my image. My eyes were blinded by the glare; Dr Yama was a silhouette in his chair.

'So it's Barnum,' he unexpectedly snorted a sneer. My midriff tensed painfully. 'That must be what set the lines jangling . . . Foolish endeavour when the city is on fire . . .' And softly, as if gently slicing open a self-evident thought: 'You don't even *look* like him.'

The rain outside must have been colder than I thought; even my mouth was twitching.

And so, at exactly noon on the fifth day – it was the eighth of September, I'd been in the country eight days – Van Wyk came quietly into my room, greeted me, remarked upon the fact that it was bracing to be another nippy day hard to ride a bicycle against the wind off the sea and springtime is goddam slow a-comin' in, but what else could be expected of Mother City this period of the year seasons aren't what they used to be wars and rumours of war there will be wailing and a gnashing of teeth in the outer darkness, and handed me a yellow envelope. Inside I discovered my new foolproof identity: ID-card, driving licence, passport – all in the name of Niemand. The documents looked authentic enough, slightly used, the passport pig-eared, surely only the photos had been switched around. The strange thing, which I didn't notice at first, was that the driving licence photo was of a much younger me than those on the other two documents. Where on earth did they find it?

Now I was no longer the foreigner returning invisible to the land of his birth, to where the corpses were buried. For the first time as an adult man I felt that I now had an integrated, non-hostile administrative status. I had the funny feeling of being *home* – finally completely adopted! The lineage was established. I had your name, our name, in my breast pocket close to the heart!

Van Wyk stayed with me until four that afternoon (we drank some bad brandy from a plastic toothbrush glass, and the day became less dismal), when he walked me across the esplanade and down two blocks from the hotel, insisting on carrying my bag, to where two men waited in a cream-coloured Toyota parked before a pharmacy. The one on the back seat introduced himself as Noordhoek Van Meegeren, a Dutch expatriate travelling salesman in toilet articles and plumbing fixtures – 'Anything to do with waterworks,' he sniggered. The chauffeur sitting behind the wheel wore a cap pulled low over a severely blemished face which kept spitting out the window. He must have had a touch of bronchitis.

I spare you the details of my trip lest you think I'm trying to take you on another metaphysical journey through a never-never mountain range of mists and myths deep into the heart of the country. My spanking new identity easily withstood the scrutiny of police and soldiers at road-blocks. I unabashedly spoke Afrikaans to them.

I thought I was safe!

I was
Your son
A. Niemand

6

The account so far. You see, Anom is on his way to security, to enlightenment and relief, to redemption, to requital. Is he a traitor? Has he been smoked from his ultimate foxhole and will he now be brought before the bench of judgement of his comrades? The question is being put. You assume that Anom is a delegate, a courier, a contact agent sent out to pick up the dropped stitches of the network of resistance remnants in the city and displaced persons in the countryside. Reconstruction efforts must be envisaged. You move from the understanding that he is an underground infiltrator, small common mole in the mighty garden, slowly to undermine the field of power. You are correct. (Seen from your angle.) How dare Anom survive? With what cheek is he playing blind-man's buff? You see, all control centres, all initiative knots have been decomposed. There is fire and no fire and again fire: the cinders of being. This is naturally establishing cognisance. Taking notice of cogs. Noting notice, right? Notes of nothingness.

Anom is lying half-way up the mountain. He is on his knees, aching for Greta Garbo. He writes Greta Garbo a letter. He writes a second letter to Greta Garbo. Khadjia, her mother, is the fly in the apothecary's ointment. (Her father dies in the run-down hotel on the shoulder of the hill, with a song drooling from the lips.) He must effect the junction with the Waterworks Commission. Greta Garbo is the link permitting the connection. He writes a letter of resignation (and acknowledgement) to the WC. He has meetings and he has conversations, *inter alia* with Ka'afir and Master Basie, and he has to laugh at the artless flapdoodle.

At the foot of the mountain the Place lies, like old puke. The Place is full of doves. Further back, in the background, the smouldering city. This takes place during the period following immediately upon the Denouement and there is a fair amount of confusion; defeatism too. Grey geese cut the sky on the wing and Kashyapa turns his nose in a dolorous way. On that day a million flies show up. The land harbours a multiplication and a host of inkscapes. Everything, also that which is veiled, will be directly inveigled into a book, because a writer roams and learns how to lean towards walking in his pursuit of fixture. There are rituals – in the gulches, in the arenas, on other sports fields, along the line between sea and land where the sounds of communication are bellowed. The Greens and the Blacks confront each other – the remembrance of reflexes from primordial times. The Greys supervise and know better – as in olden times, as ever. As it must always be, for the sake of the weight which must liberate the scales. Philosophers rinse their robes and above and below a search for Noma has been launched. The dogs have been let off their nooses. Undertakers toil in their attempt to erect structures. In a ditch an aged drunkard makes use of his own wooden leg to bash in the skull of his own concubine. Thieves enter private properties by climbing through windows which they've knifed open. City dwellers and other idiots crouch with mournful dark lips to concentrate on the crackling emanating from black plastic containers. In short, all are drawn into the game which may also be called 'life'. You expect that it will all ignite to erupt in some conflagration? Maybe.

Anom meets Greta Garbo. (Not yet.)

7

Naturally the neck is long like a step-by-step stick. Rather use a rope – it is by definition the primary appositeness of 'rope' or 'noose' – but you don't always have the necessary at hand and are obliged to fall back on whatever may be handily within reach of the fingers. Belt may do the trick provided you still have yours and can justify your having kept it. Forget laces; they are seldom strong or long enough. An article of clothing torn into strips and tied together may be your best bet. It depends on whether you've been issued with winter or summer apparel, and on how intimately the raiment has been used. Usually, when it tears easily, it is already not sufficiently resistant to bear the weight. Remains, if available, the cord or the washing line. If you dispose of enough time and liberty you may try bedding. You do have bedding? A length of sheet or the torn-off edges of the blanket, wound up, soaked and then twisted tightly – ideal. Then: any solid crossbeam, bar, shower pipe, or even the door knob should do.

Impressive and tender the purple flanks of the mountain, but very far away as is to be expected (though close in the heart), so that your lips cannot caress the rugosity; and white birds flying towards the night; so sweet the slight cooling of earth falling by the window; soon the moon a pretty unschooled embroidered shoe for a club-foot. A swain dressed up to the nines with staff and hat for spooning with the sweetheart, a grimace thrown in free of charge.

Man lugs along his time in a clay jug. Who knows how much he has and what would happen if he were to go into the water with it? That is why, when time flows over the hands, you should rose the mother knot, the number one, the one which is as important as an eye, carefully and lovingly precisely below the one ear. The left ear.

Keep in mind the necropsy in the room of sorrows, pathologists dressed in mourning white and with surgical gloves thinner than the epidermis softly stroking over swelling and abrasion, the cut in the abdominal wall, the snippets of spleen and perhaps liver for organic analysis. You ought to be considerate enough to others not to be exaggeratedly contradictious.

The symptoms in order: brain showing a loss of blood (far away the dreams); self-evidently red or raw chafings around the throat; the epiglottis cracked, vocal cords tied off, uvula stuck to palate; parts of body below neck bloated, swollen abnormally with blood since the irrigation will not have been interrupted instantly as with the brain; the neck need not be 'broken', feet may touch the floor, and vulgarities such as grotesquely twisted body attitudes, the obscenity of protruding blue tongue and goggling pop-eyes and head-on-chest and smile-for-birds and spittle and blood of burst vessels staining noose, of grume and effluvium – these should be avoided; traces of spermatozoid and gamete in underpants are allowed: it is common knowledge that an irascible urge to penetrate and paint *white* the heavenly gates may take possession of the body.

No height worth speaking of is required: after half a minute (barely the time needed to read this) blood-flow to the brain will be blocked if more than six kilos were to dangle from the implement. Small tears, contusions, perforations of the skin, bruises – these will have been caused by a rubbing against the walls; indeed, attention should be drawn to the exiguous space, the primitive means, the ineptness of the subject. Feet can evidently not be firmly flexed against the soil; with entanglement of the thing being hanged a whirligig effect comes about.

Quite possibly a further inquest may be suggested by this or that body, during which the flesh will be pinched between the fingers, a search will be made through the magnifying glass for needle-marks or the after-effects of shock therapies, the telephone's breath, the longing of the leopard. All watertight. Coloured skin, like tempera, will be more resistant to the begriming of thumbprints. Devotedness counts, and the quality of the leap.

Mention should be made that although a measure of experimentation may be allowed for, it is finally a unique occurrence: something which it will be foolish to fuck up (or let come to grief) because of ham-handedness or butter-fingers.

Do you really mean to tell me you don't know about the mountain? Were you never told? That you shouldn't go there at certain times of the night, on certain nights in any event? That it is sacred then, particularly along the summit when the big horses cast in their reddish bronze come alive, look at the glow on metal as your path twists on and up, swirling fog deflecting the light, enfilading beams, sheen of copper and coals, they stand lining the route, and rearing, hissing, grunting, high the enormous hooves that they may stomp on you? Where they come from? No one knows any more. Long before we are born and those before us are born they are there already, huge shapes worn smooth by time passed in rain and wind and mists and dust. Fitted into the mountainside as if molten from the traces of metal in the rocks. Flanks or a rounded belly eaten away in sores with green edges. Missing a limb maybe. Accentuating the sinews of a neck or the tendons of a leg. An eye stiffened, an ear gnawed blunt, the hollow of nostrils picked out, slashed, gouged, etched, eroded. And isolated perhaps skull-immediate the grin of teeth with flesh withdrawn. Hollowed and eternal. Yes, you make your way up the mountain. You take your offering to the giants or to the council of the Waterworks Commission. You go sacrifice your fears. Lay down words with both hands a-tremble. On certain nights in any event. When crag and peak are bathed in light and scarlet fingers stab over the horizon. Alive to the sacredness of the heights. There is no other time. Don't you know?

A large portion of my past lies behind me. (*He remembers*.) The land is crooked, running obliquely to the white towers in the distance. They are all present, a large group of them, an expedition from the dovecote. That is what the cooing is all about. Blessed and peaceful is the day, fresh but damp, the earth is sludgy. Perhaps it is the afterstay of rain from preceding days. The sky is cool. They are here, lodgers from the Place, on an excursion. He doesn't recall the Place – doesn't know it – the Place is dead.

There they are arrayed in sitting and reclining postures on the embankment of the fast-flowing river. The river breaks forth from the mountain and the water is browned by ooze like a throat worded with fury. But here there's no anger. The walls of the river are slippery and where an acceleration in the stream makes an elbow, the contours must be undercut, slabs spill into the flow, there are slip-ups, a crumbling of coherence. Limits are displaced. Everyone is gathered at present, including the cleaners, the musicians and the corridor polishers. Some of the day-trippers plunge into the swirl. Some flounder and go quack-quack. Some gesticulate with the arms or thrash the viscous liquid. Others are simply carried off with their clothes billowing like parachutes around them. Bees also get stuck in the calyxes. Here there are no flowers. Mumpata floats by swathed in a grey blanket. Look at the bobbing head. The head is bluish and bald. When the head pops up, the mouth snarls to reveal three yellow fangs. The picnickers enjoy themselves no end. Look, there goes Mumpata's smile.

He falls into the slurry and pokes deep holes with his arms. The water is heavy, his saturated garments weigh him down. When he crawls out on the river bank once more, he is as heavy as water. He takes everything off. He puts on a blue coat. The coat is of a rough fibre and wide but short. It is Mumpata's coat. Mumpata has no more need of the coat. He slides his feet into the wooden sandals. The leftover possessions he stuffs into a knapsack. Look how he slings the muck-stained bundle over his shoulder. Anon we shall return to the contents of the tucker-bag.

He walks towards the settlement. How incredibly deep of chest the air is, humid but house-broken, all rinsed, so that feet go sliding over the smooth riparian land. All is changed. And the town bigger. Now we are at once upon a time towards morning's end when clarity is a hand's breath above the horizon. 'All rinsed' refers to colours. It should be: colours are washed away, all is changed. Many new residential cages have been added. There is aggrandizement. It is called a township. Pools of water are shattered mirrors to the grey. But at the far end of the agglomeration of greyish knocked-together lean-tos there is as ever the house, the one with the green shutters and the shadow of a tree etching along the one wall. When wind moves. The wind-home is built in a style similar to that of the golf clubhouse on the other side of the road crossing the railway line. Behind the house the chicken-run with coops. In one of the coops a snake, could be a puffadder, standing on its tail with a throat browned by mud so as to hiss with the flicker of wet-fire tongue. The chicken coops are empty, grass growing right up to the framework where chickens would perch. Golfballs dot the garden, eggs nest whitely. The people of the house are deceased. In the one room a projector of images with blown fuses. In the parlour coffee with cream could have been taken. Over the floorboards a carpet with desert patterns and in the air the remnants of a radio serial's sounds which used to fill the room. The serial would have been about little Emile and the detectives. The back stoop is closed in with wire gauze which can capture the convulsions of steam engines whistling by. Wire gauze must allow dust and soot to pass unhindered. In the back-yard a round pool with a high wall around it the better to drown unnoticed. Chagrin has deteriorated the cement embankment – were you to slip and slide and hang on desperately, your finger would be cleaved right down to the white bone. The dam is not empty. At the bottom a squalid mattress, three golfballs, a blue overcoat, some black water. The mattress is stained a pee-colour. No wind capable of a blow. The green shutters too are tightly locked. The atmosphere is wet and oppressive.

On his way to the house there is a man with a blemished face. What is he mouthing? Is the man barring the route? The man with the lesions asks: 'Where are we going?'

He says: 'I'm going home.'

The man with the wounds says: 'Go to hell.'

He decides to take a short-cut, winding his way through the grey scaffoldings. Red beaten earth roads. Red with the slitheriness. Around a curve in the road he happens upon a group of people draped in yellow blankets around the shoulders. The deep yellow flames cause the blanket-bearers to stand out spectacularly against the grey walls. It makes natives of them. They are drawn up in a circle, the hands with palms turned downwards stretched out before them. The skulls are shaved close to the skin. Within the circle there is a large perforated drum. In the drum there are embers and flames and heat. No smoke. Smoke is in the one cloud high above in the skies. Nor any vibration of hot air. When the blanket-bearers notice him, they emit deep growls from the throat. They are the unemployed. They are the war veterans. Some more obscure people are standing among the blanket-bearers, also the scarred man can be noticed.

(But when you know the way through the maze, you soon hit the main road, it is just down this turn-off, no further than the throw of a stone or the flight of a chanticleer, turn left turn right, stretches will even be tarred. Listen to the glow and the blare of traffic down the asphalted main artery so close back-stage. And the white pinnacles towering above make the town seem to tumble.)

The fellow with the lesions advances upon him. The damaged man has something in his hand, I can't see what. The disfigured man says: 'Have you ever seen this smile somewhere?' I drop my shoulder-pack to the ground. Behind the damp cloud the sun once again appears, a silvery kiss. Suck me! A bird tweets. How strange, since birds are all dead. Hate is a mutilation when it makes of the head a scar-tissue of ink and paper, and still no confidence. Come now, Reader – where are you when I need to curse you?

10

It is the Ascension. A sad and swinish time. I have this dream of better days. The train has broken down in the desert. Hot, so hot and sticky and uncomfortable. The minuscule grains of sand will work through the gaps and slits and joints to grey the surfaces and crunch under the soles. The air-conditioning is still functioning. Soon it must cease and we shall be absorbed by the heat. People descend from the carriages and hunker in the trench of shade. Off-colour shadows. Couples take off their clothes to wriggle in the sand. Half-buried lizards, the sluggishly moving tails. I wander down the corridors towards the diner. My little dog scampers around my feet. He is spotted and alert with big upright ears tapering sharply to points. He has sensitive and trusting eyes. I call him Apokalips. Sometimes I also call him Lord Byron. A dog empties itself of all dogness to affect part of the human owner's character. Only on the primal level though, because it doesn't learn how to hide and scheme and be duplicitous. A dog is therefore at a disadvantage, vulnerable . . . In the passage I meet the lady and her two obscure companions. She is fresh and virginal. She is also very attractive with curves and big eyes. The mind smells the heat of loveplay. The men with their impenetrable dark glasses reflecting images must be pimps. We go through some formalized manoeuvres. (The passage is narrow.) When I turn my back, when I'm out of earshot, the threesome pass derogatory remarks among themselves concerning my attention and my posture. They make some snide hints about the putative size of my procreative glands. They pass it from palate to earshell. But my small dog hears sharply. I approach them again. The lady looks me up and down with smokiness in her eyes. My dog goes down on his haunches before them and starts talking woof in a hoarse voice. This gives them such a fright. They are unveiled. They are bared to the navel! I fondle my silence although I want to bark a laugh. I get off the train to walk down the length of the coaches. 'Come, Apokalips. Come!' Passengers are scattered all over the immediate vicinity. Along the tracks going in the opposite direction a down-train comes roaring a white blur and dust. Some people manage to flee out of its way in time. I see one woman crouching low between the rails hoping that the speedspewing monster will pass over her no touch. I hear another woman shouting a warning shout. A boy, her son, scampers down the tracks meaning to escape the metal. But he is too slow and too dull. The train touches him and tosses him aside. The mother running up on knees half-bent. The train decreases in a tunnel of howl. The mother falling in folds by her son. Whose body, though apparently unfingered and immaculate, is utterly broken. He is dead now. Now he is dead. Dead is now he. The howl vowelling in the woman's throat. Pale bodies thrashing in the sand. The heat grows. I re-enter the train, my compartment. Soon the strength of this barren region will overcome us. Last touches of civilization will be obsolete. I mix and shake a drink in a glass. With the ultimate coolness in the hand I go down the passages again. And I ask my dog ('sic-sic' I say, and he flicks his innocent but sharp ears – 'sic-sic. Apokalips baby') to indicate to me the compartment of the lady and those of her agents two. My dog shows that she is alone, now. I slide open the door. I enter with the glass in my hand. I offer it to her. She has large and knowful eyes. When she accepts the glass she comes right up against me, hard and soft and shapely. I say nothing, but she must have sensed the growing echo, for she whispers: 'Not here; *outside*.' Shall we go outside? Is there any hope for rescue at all? The sand obliterates the tracks. A wind is rising from the depth of the dead land, rasping and hot without any humidity. She withdraws, her fresh fingers holding the glass breaking shaped. She returns to me. She is attracted because I am the Mystery. And she says, here, she says close to me: 'I want you to deliver (me from) the child in me.'

11

Where there is land, there is earth. Where there is earth, there is fertility. Where there is fertility, there's time enough to linger and put seeds down into the ground. Where seeds are put into the ground, there will be gardens. Where there are gardens, there will be flowers, showing off, tubers, chronicles and other neoplasms. Also insects, birds, fruit, and at night the *kalong*. Where there are insects and birds and flying foxes, there will be humans to labour the soil. Where the land is cultivated, it multiplies. Where there is multiplication, there is life and death. Where there is life and death, there is structure. Where there is structure, there is appearance or semblance or simulacrum or glow, and thus the riddle, and in this way labyrinths, and so the wiping out of borders, and therefore heaven. Where there is land.

Where the land starts climbing up the slope towards the mountain, there it must be fecund, a fruitful earth fattened through the ages. At a pinch one could have plotted a garden if only there were permanence, even temporarily so, that the toiling of hands may leave the prints of thumbs, so that the growth teased from fingers may be remarked upon. Here colour can show up in patches, beds and fields of *ageratum, lobelia, petunias, alyssum, nierembergia, pansies, dianthus* – blue and purple like regal rituals; the plumed *celosias, bougainvillaea* as climber. One could lay out acres of lush grass – several varieties of *Acorus gramineus variegatus, Pennisetum cuperum* purplish all around the fountain, *Cyperus haspan viviparus* to have papyrus leaves to write on; and bamboos, the yellow *Arundinaria viridistriata* or *Phylostachys nigra* with the black calves . . . But where the hero reclines, the soil is scorched grey. Too many variations of the Game have been played here. This you have to accept. Not that which you see is of importance, but that which you remember. You have to sculpt yourself to fit the truth, obviously – the alternative would surely be unethical. And what about eternity? What *about* it?

I hum a land
I hum a land
and where is my country's turning?

warbler is a troublesomeness in the reeds
down by the marshes the lapwings wrangle
to lure one away from the burning

Here Anom lies in the foetal position, quiet petrifact, clean as the conscience of a firearm without the merest whiff of gunpowder-smoke in the barrel, clean as a tooth from which the last fibre of meat has long since been sucked, silent as an upper lip with neither inkling nor education of moustache, silent and clean as a human in prison and that prison the concretizing of inner life. Above him the celestial canopy is a cloud, behind the cloud a sun, below the cloud a flight of grey geese with the trilling of thrashing throats. Next to Anom his wooden leg. On the peg a story is carved. Inside the story an inkscape. (Also a theme, or core-string . . . in manifold reflections.) In the inkscape – where steps matter – there is a coming and a going and a staying put. What remains is the man on his back with the sun like a hairy upper lip in the welkin. There is mirroring, and so multiple intimate insights.

A procession moves by. Up front Baron Samedi walks. He wears a black suit (with golden watch-chain in the vest pocket), dark glasses, a black umbrella. The clothes are somewhat the worse for wear from all the putting on and taking off and the frequent kneeling or heel-squatting to crap the rural way. The umbrella is a small shelter where the sunbeams may splash. The idea is to treat non-sense intensively. Next to him Dr Yama goes in deep conversation. Dr Yama is fat, his spectacles grey like swine-pox. He's dressed in a grey robe with a frayed hem, he has newspapers stuffed in his wooden sandals (all the death notices), he has a carrier bag over the shoulder. Dr Yama guffaws and wipes the giggle off his face with a greasy sleeve. Behind them a youngster sits his horse. The horse is small and dun-coloured with long hairs and long limp ears and a blue prick as long as the fore-arm of a twelve-year-old orphan groping along the earth in search of a stone with which to kill or stun to a stupor the animal that has swallowed him and now has this slight problem of evacuation. The youth is crying with neither relief nor mercy. In his thorax he has a rose. He is the Suicide Artist. In his arms he cradles a Golden Syrup tin full of pebbles. When he wants to make the steed walk, he shakes the tin to set the contents rattling. When he holds the tin firmly, the riding-animal comes to a stop. (From fear of the darkness we wander on.) Suicide Artist is the after-rider of the two savants. He is the recruiter.

He is the Handler of the Mirror. He keeps the tin still, the animal stops, he slides off the hackneyed back and puts the tin between the forelegs of the beast (between the hindlegs would be inviting murder). The mount starts munching the pebbles. 'Will you lay off,' the lad sobs.

Baron Samedi again goes down on his haunches alongside the corpse. 'Give over,' he says without looking while holding out a hand to Dr Yama. 'One moment,' Dr Yama says, a pudgy paw in the air. Then Baron Samedi switches his umbrella from the one hand to the other and hands it over to Dr Yama who in turn entrusts Suicide Artist with it. Suicide Artist advances a pace and removes the mirror from the doctor's shoulder-bag. He takes the mirror from its sheath. He gives the mirror to Dr Yama, Dr Yama passes it on to Baron Samedi, Baron Samedi holds it up for the sun to dazzlingly look into its surface. Suicide Artist advances even more in order to spread the black wing of the umbrella over Baron Samedi's expressionless black face. 'I bring you the image,' Baron Samedi says. This is the end of the beginning.

'I bring the image,' says Baron Samedi, 'and you are quite alone at this moment. Death laps up your marrow. She always catches you off your guard when you are alone. Look, your life is for nothing. All grass, all *Pennisetum cuperum* at this the instant of your death.'

'But his life bore fruit. Tell him his life bore fruit,' says Dr Yama.

'Your life is barren,' says Baron Samedi. 'What do you have of it now? Who appreciates it? Who has any feeling for you?'

'His family,' says Dr Yama, and shakes with repressed laughter.

'Your family, you say?' Baron Samedi sighs, bringing his lips close to the corpse's ear whilst gently stroking the wooden leg. 'Your family couldn't care a dove or a schnorkel or a linen shroud for you. Everyone is trying to squeeze the last drop of juice from what's left over. They're throwing you to the dead – not consciously, no, for sure not – anyone will wipe out his own tracks for fear. What have you got behind you? Nothing. Where are you going? Towards a greater consciousness, you say. Ahead there's nothing, my dear chap. It's not worth the hardship.'

'Show him the image,' Dr Yama says.

'I bring to you limpidity,' says Baron Samedi. 'What do you see here? A moustache? How foolish you are! It is because you have hierarchy on the mind. I shall hold your forehead for you. You can spit out your smile in my hand if you want to. No, it's not a moustache, it is structure.'

'You are putting him wise to labyrinths, Sabbath,' Dr Yama says. Suicide Artist sobs and turns his head away to stare at his tears, that way, up the mountain.

'No, I bring him succour. Anom, I'm unveiling to you the laws of metamorphosis. Look into this clarity. One cannot grasp the concealed structures with bare hands. Noma can approach IT directly. It is exactly the roundabout way that will get you there.'

'Tell him about the bypasses. We are telling you about the detours, corpse.'

'Use the poem as example,' says Baron Samedi.

'Ka'afir would have explained to you that the verse is a reality, and a method or an alley or an opening on reality,' says Dr Yama. 'On the first face of *sham*, of meaning and of message, it is the primary thwart against which comprehension or memory or the projector must bump to be dislocated – the more harmless the surface, the greater the shock – and in this fashion be allowed to penetrate to *being* or cognitive structure. Put differently: your confrontation with the initial unit or premise, as totality and in its substitute components, is the tripwire; the deviations from the expected or reproached or normal grammar, the lapses and lacunae or codicils and affixes, the tension, bonding, styptic, bandages, nature and sheets which all together constitute the such-ness of poetry, this is the explosive charge which will blow you open to another *niveau* of reading.'

'Tell him the way it is, James,' Baron Samedi murmurs. 'Relativize the side-shows and the subsidiary issues. Tell him how he is dead. Quote, gather, give hell, spell it out for him with capitals.'

'And your investigations of the above-mentioned transformation will be ontology, or the teaching of structural meaning,' Dr Yama says. 'The first law of metamorphosis is that the matrix, be it life or death, cannot remain unchanging once and for all. We don't have time – do we have time, Sabbath? – no, we don't have time enough to enter upon all the actualizations of peeling the skin. Everything you've ever been acquainted with is there, all the crises and the denouements and the catharses. But there is a second law: It is only to the extent that you recall the original surface and accept it as valid, that the deeper-lying *actual* will obtain the right to existence and space and thingness. You must be absolutely credulous. And the more you blind yourself to it, the more there is to see and the easier it becomes. And a third: The more direct the path you take, the smaller your chance of finding something at the end of it. You must walk the long way around. Labyrinth – that's the in-thing, the name of the game. It's the dead-ends that count.'

'What are you showing him now?' asks Baron Samedi.

'It's not me who's doing the showing. *You've* got the funthing mirror.'

'I show him nothing,' Baron Samedi says. 'I'm letting you see this nothing.'

'Which doesn't imply that we wish to drag you screaming into some ideology,' Dr Yama says. 'It is more like life getting an outline.'

'And yet, James, you know – these hypotheses, these low methods, I'd say, whether pertaining to poetry or the game of *Go* or theology – that which always derives from skeletonism written with a big white (the Big Void?), aren't they all leftist disciplines? You giggle? Isn't dialectics a key component? To have penetration (or progress) you must have exchange, for reciprocity there must be development, for development you need opposite poles, or paravents, even if the prerequisite barricade or obstacle is a ghost image. This is the process and procedure of walking. It certainly indicates that transformation and metamorphosis are intrinsically concepts of the Left, for your primary point of departure remains that the one structure shapes (deconstructs) the other – even if you don't hold that there is one immutable Noma behind the façades – and herewith you jump into the arena of social engineering. Or rather, the substance of manipulation. You play the Game, are played by it, you object, objectify, you become a pundit. Let alone that you must be the *jongleur* synchronizing the chuck and the catch, exactly for the sake of Structure.'

'Ah-ah,' says Dr Yama with a smothered giggle. 'Ah-ah! It is precisely the opposite if you don't mind! Who is it that swears to high heaven by technique and knowledgeability? Who is forever foraging for clear, concise, exploitable accounts? Who absolutizes communication? – its techniques, to the disadvantage of its humanitarian and humanist implications for society? Who rips out the innards and throws away the carcass? Who makes of the tool, the means, the medium, an idol – because it can help bring about smoothed-over adaptations which will eliminate the need for metamorphosis? Who? Why, precisely the Rightists! The Liberals!'

'People, good people – don't scrap like that,' Baron Samedi says. 'Although it must be part of the image we bring you, Anom. All these fragments, you ask? Truly necessary, the shards? Yes, rather. It is like a fellow sickening to write a book. How could there be a core of mutation or a pure central stem except you have all the shreds, all these pages like leaves on a tree?'

'What trees are you talking about?' Dr Yama asks. 'There's no tree here for days around.'

'Here there's nuffink.'

'We give you that nuffink.'

'But we do create the illusion of relationships. And we are the barrier.'

'We bring you the image giving on to the image.'

'And the most important theorem. That you should live in accordance with the mirror image that you already are.'

'Will you lay off it,' the youngster sobs.

'Come with us,' the donkey says. 'We shall find something better than death, wherever we go . . . We are tired of our conditions. Winter is too rotten, there is no spring worth spitting about, the summers are stifling, and the beer as weak as bourgeois morality. They've fucked us around enough. We are all going to the beach of Tunix so that the police may choke on their chewing-gum from boredom. We want something different! And we want it now! If you will be so kind.'

12

The murders continue, the weather is pleasant. Alienation is a form of incompetence. Anom Bird awakens in the Place, grey light of dawn, grey desert colours. Doors slam sounds. Occasionally someone steps out into a corridor to shout a long, lingering echo. This reminds him. It takes him to another time, as real, a black cry of pain caroming off the cement walls down the narrow passage.

The passage is always narrow, isn't it? The holding spaces are crawling with life – the crippled, the lame, the halt, the grubbies, the fourteens, the coats, the hawks, the one-eyed, the grocery rabbits, all manner of *onnagata*, the big fives and other *amapimpa*, the *malletjies*. They bill and they coo. Their knuckles are white. They perch on the bars, hunched, puffing. There are layers of life. This is the Place. There must be a pecking order, there must be allotted space, there are contracts and contacts. Briefly a fluttering fight will erupt, snarl and squawk and lips lifting slowly to bare teeth and gums, the smear of blood bright so quick, like new roses. The occasional flash off spike and blade. Bile in the throat, briefer even the fire in the eye.

Ah, but there is also vanity and slime to the outside. The new day brings its show. One must groom the feathers of those who are going to be on display, one must wax the legs to a high sheen. See them prance and preen – Brahma, Dumpy, Sumatra, Dominique, Old English Game, Rosecomb, Houdan, Crèvecoeur, mFushana, Hamburg, Mottled Frizzle Cochin, Favarolle, Red Jungle, Polish, Sebrights, Spitzhauben, Belgian, Cubalaya, Cornish, Sultana's, Japanese, Bony, Silkie, Kasjapa, Mille Fleur.

The door to the inner courtyard is unlocked. Menboys on the walls thud their feet warmed by newspaper in their boots, and shift the firearms from one hand to the other. Fine mist dusting their overcoats, the peaks of their caps. The noses are red, the moustaches wet. Swirl of fog obfuscates distances. A greyness rising from the land – it is as if the very earth were a smouldering mountain of ash. Bird can see neither the mountain nor the shiny lips of the sun nor even the hooded moon far above. A short way higher in-country a man may lie, also waiting for clarity. In the dark one crosses frontiers. And music flows from inside as part of the rites marking the day's passing.

Inmates are out in the yard – some parading, strutting, others reclined against the walls, inert, the eyes half-shadowed, watching the fog lifting to cloud, sucking deep into the cavities of the body the blue smoke from hand-rolled torpedoes. They absorb the music. The Reality Soul Adepts are dead but the sound is on tape. It is blared out, scratchily, on black squawboxes. The menboys lower their chins to listen. The cocks spit to one side and move their hips in time to the throb.

> How would you like to be
> A baby white whale wailing in the sea
> Salty so salty the tears there
> Foamhumpéd the years where
> You have to sink deep to ever fall free!

And: 'Yeah man, oh ma-an,' the *jollers* sigh. And: 'Take it away now.' Or: 'Move it, like,'

> Know thy tree Thelonius
> The wind the branch melodious
> Atwitter the dolphin high in its nest
> Treefire at sundeath always commodious
> Burning to bone everything odious
> Leaves just the twitter high in the crest
> Who you? Who me? No, no –

In the afternoon the people go down, ragged and hungry, past the dingy grey constructs, past the house with the closed shutters, past the dilapidated zoo where mangy animals pace the delimitations of their cages or coops, over the railway tracks, left down the main road to the outskirts of the smouldering city. They fill to overflowing the mounting tiers of the forum. In the arena the two teams are drawn up, the Greens facing the Blacks. The players strain forward, resting knotted hands on waxed knees, staring at the opponents with dull eyes under puckered brows. The crowd speaks in many tongues. But by and large the aficionados of the two teams mouth their obscenities and their pain in either Prolog or Bos. The tension mounts. Mountain blocking background. A cloud also, obscuring the sun as a mouse of a whisker would dim the lips.

Then the dark girl appears, lithe, a flow in her hips. Her breasts are pointed stiff with the tips touched blue. She has paint or chalk on the cheekbones. She wears a dunce's cap with a tiny bell attached to the point. Under the cap the hair is a frizzy halo. Her eyebrows meet in a frown. She walks the line between the two teams, a bump and grind of the pelvis holding the backcheeks high, slender hands just about stroking the fleshcones and columns of tits and thighs.

And stopping at one end of the Green frontline: she produces with a flourish of hand and twirl of fingers a small and bright red ball from her mouth. (Round like a lover's cry.) Oops she moves, fluttering to the next man, and the ball disappears somewhere. To be fetched from the ear of the player fourth from the end in the Black row. In this way she continues until the dryness in the players' throats becomes a growl and now she pirouettes on the centre-star of the field, equidistant from the two lines of adversaries, perspiration streaking her flanks, the envelope of musky odour, and throws the wet red ball high, high, high. Where it disappears as if swallowed by a mouth covered with a moustache. Releasing the teams in a blind charge and scramble. The roar from the spectators all trampled on their feet now avidly following every feint and subtlety of chop and appreciating the finer ruses and tactics of the Game.

The point is to see how long it can last before the last one succumbs. And whether the rules are properly adhered to. 'If the truth is too weak to defend itself, it must go over to the attack' – Galileo.

Bird is breathless. The coat he wears is too wide for him. He must make contact with this girl, but where has she disappeared to? The deads are carried up the mountain in a snaking procession. The chant goes:

> Früher ist es uns hier gut gegangen
> Jetzt geht es natürlich viel besser
> Es wird uns aber noch viel besser gehen
> Wenn es wieder gut geht.

Up front walks an old geezer with sunglasses and black suit worn to a shine, Homburg square over the shades; he carries a folded umbrella holding aloft Greta's tinkle-bell cap. The corpses are pushed over the rails into the cages of the animals. And they shuffle forward to sniff and to lick and to snarl with blind marbled eyes reflecting the light. The light lighting up the wet red gore, the occasional sheen of bar and spike. It is the grey light of dawn. Doors slam sounds. Someone steps out into a passage to relieve himself of a whisper.

Dear Noma,

My real case was never argued. Nothing was brought to light. Was that – is this – the sum total of my existence? As poor, as insignificant? I was not to be given the chance to enter wide-eyed into my dream of heroism, self-abnegation, freedom struggle. Instead I was backed into someone else's second-class, shopworn nightmare of cowardice and inexplicable criminality. I was angling for a premier role in an uplifting work of art and I got stuck with a walk-on part in a miserable matinée show in a country at war with itself.

In a larger sense too my case and my cause was never argued in the light. Without my knowing it my life was directed and manipulated from the dark. From the wings, as the saying goes. I was written by some unknown unimaginative pen. Then, after having served as page-filler, I became dispensable: too many characters were crowding the stage. The page had to be turned. There is nothing more useless than to carry a dead bit actor from chapter to chapter. But, you may well ask, is this not the true destiny of the comedian, to play whatever role is written for him, however humble, to the best of his ability? Isn't that his greatness, the real laying down of the self? His professionalism is not in becoming another character, but in being the perfect vehicle for the written page-thin projection or reflection or image of a person, or even of a fleeting feeling in a universe where heaven and earth are words. The veritable actor stinks of ink and sawdust.

One becomes used to everything. It is quite possible to die while nominally still alive. The hulk is there, it reacts to stimuli the way a live person might; the pattern of primitive emotions and desires is still present, you are capable of anger and elation and you feel hunger and cold – though *cleanly* now. Without any coordination, except as mechanical programmatic action and reaction. Without any central control, therefore with no real interest. The days and the nights have an inexorable rhythm. Since they will always be, they stop being. The armature of restrictions become as many reference points inducing a sense of normalcy, of security, exactly of rhythm and pattern that have no purpose or sense outside their own manifestations. Light grows and wanes within the walls, the days become longer and then they will become shorter again. I am an integral part of a self-repeating whole. I am in prison, I have always been here, I shall always be here, even beyond my death.

The story, the play, will continue. At most I could say that had I not been here it would have been slightly different. And since no real change can take place, everything becomes conceivable.

I am not a writer. Not even an apprentice reporter. I cannot invent myself. But I have been writing, working away on my *Art of Walking*. I intend this – I surely mentioned it in a previous letter – as a scenario. I set out to complete Barnum's dream, and thus incidentally to direct my own life. But I see that it has become something else. What I conceived of as an *alternative* to incarceration, another world to escape into, piling up details and fragments (of images and words) in order to simulate veracity, to establish a counterweight to the dead weight of my immobile days – all of this has turned out to be graffiti on prison-stained walls, an aftertaste in the mouth of real experiences. Where I crack the ice, all manner of characters surface to clamour for attention. My limbs weigh me down. It is not possible to walk away from prison. Or rather, yes, you are free because you have interiorized death and therefore the dichotomy is dissolved. You will become the internal shadow of the flame. Again, I played at being God – dare I say Noma? – and in the process became aware of the limitations and the ultimate impotence of being God (you cannot write yourself free because your very essence is ink, or the condition of being black on white), and in that consciousness I became God. Or his photocopy. God hated mankind so badly that he sent his only begotten son, his inheritor, his self-beyond-the-self, to be killed so that mankind would have neither God nor successor to God. All of which was to be replaced by Guilty Conscience. By this 'sacrifice' God made mankind accomplices to murder. God also must have had an all-devouring hatred for his son. He could not suffer the idea of being replaced. Dare I say Noma? Perhaps it is better to cling to atheism – that at least is a state religion.

I arrived without any mishap in the Gold City. (A misnomer; it really ought to be called Murder City.) I took a taxi from the station to the hotel. When I gave the address of my destination to the driver, he rolled down the window and spat out a saturated thought, turned around to face me, his face was one big pock-marked leer, turned his oily cap to face the same direction he was, and said: 'Sorry man, you must be mistaken. Ain't no Southern Cross Hotel in Hillbrow. It's Braamfontein you want.' Whether he was sure, I wanted to know. Yes indeed, he was very certain, it is his job to know what he's doing. Hell, I thought. What now? Wrong hotel or wrong district? More likely the district, the hotel's name was precise enough. Dr Yama could have been mistaken. Or maybe I heard wrong. 'Get me to the hotel,' I said.

Nothing happened for the first thirty-six hours. I strolled the streets. In an Experimental Cinema Theatre I was surprised to come across an old picture Meheret had told me about in Paris, made by an Ethiopian film-maker: the story of a young exile roaming abroad after having killed his fiancée in a fit of passion; how he cuts out the photo of some model advertising a soap powder because she reminds him of his beloved dead: how, delirious with hunger and the Africa blues, he ends up believing that it really is the picture of his sweetheart, and how he starts writing long letters to her, mailing them as it were to the Underworld; how he makes enough money to return to his home village with a dowry and a ruby on his pinky, only to find it deserted except for one old blind black man who curses him. How he breaks down when he cannot find the girl of the picture . . . I thought it very dated, very sentimental. Then, late on the second day, the purple shadows soon to be washed away by a thunderstorm, I returned to the hotel, and as the porter handed me the key to room 42 he informed me that a man had been in to ask after me, Niemand, not long before, that this man had with him a photo of me which he'd let him see, and that he said he'd be back. I felt a fluttering of butterflies in my stomach, a sense of pleasurable anticipation; I was sure it must be a comrade making contact the way Dr Yama had promised. Relief was at hand. It was all a God-almighty mistake of identity and of purpose. I should soon be on my way 'home'.

I crossed the foyer to the foot of the staircase and a silhouette rose from one of the deep armchairs and stopped me with a hand on my arm. He had broad shoulders, curly black hair, a sallow face, slightly protuberant eyes, a pencil-thin moustache. 'Anom Niemand?' he asked. 'Yes,' I said, 'at present.' Then he said: 'You're under arrest,' and his hand upon my arm became very heavy and compelling. It was all so sordid and commonplace, like a sequence from some sleazy movie. Dated and sentimental.

Two other men stepped forward from the shadows of the hall – the one with the raincoat must have been waiting on the stairs, the other near the street exit. They didn't say a word but their eyes never left my face. The butterfly in my stomach had become a stone. It is miraculous the way flight can turn into dead falling. It all went very quickly and yet as if in slow motion, with each action precisely defined and senseless, dislocated. We went up the stairs to my room – a firm hand guiding me by the elbow. I was to stand in the middle of the floor. The man with the bulging eyes showed me something that could have been an identity card and said his name was Captain Dino Felis. His two colleagues rapidly but methodically went through the wardrobe, stripped the bedding off the bed, flipped over the mattress, shook the pillows, inspected the lamps, felt along the ledge half-way up the wall, palmed and fingered the curtains. As rapidly my belongings were gathered, and down the stairs we went with Raincoat carrying the suitcase, across the foyer past the reception desk (the porter talking quietly to some customer, his hairy-backed hands in the splash of yellow light on the counter, he never even looked up: to this day I don't know who settled my room bill), out on the street and into an anonymous car. The waters must have broken during the interval – the streets were wet and aswim with etiolated reflections of street lamps and shop-signs. The air was beautifully fresh. There is nothing quite as heart-breakingly pretty as a city street at night after a shower. We drove through the night. I was reminded of Ouagadougou.

I was taken to Brixton police station – for decades the head-quarters of the city's notoriously cruel murder and robbery squad. Why didn't they take me to John Vorster Square? My mind was running away with me, but more in the way of a rat running the treadmill. Somehow I must have been admonishing myself to run to form, to cling to the acquired instincts of the trained actor. Here I was being given an unscripted role, just a virgin character as point of departure: it was up to me to improvise within the narrow boundaries of make-believe and verisimilitude, in such a way as not to leave indelible imprints on anybody's mind and especially not to harm any comrade's vital interests. Ah, my comrades of the Shadow! I was ready, I was going to make a real person of flesh and blood out of Anom Niemand, I was going to carefully cut out and hide away the Mission, to protect it through forgetting it like fog, all the better to bravely fight for the Cause. (I'm good at forgetting, have to be, the actor's art is more one of forgetting than of learning by heart.) I had to play my lines carefully until such time as I knew what the plot was all about.

Captain Dino Felis and one of his men – not Raincoat, but his mate – took me through to what I assumed to be the interrogation room. I didn't even have handcuffs on. He went to sit behind the working table, I stood under the cone of harsh light splashing from a bulb suspended from the ceiling. The backs of his hands were smooth. He said, quite formally, that I was charged with murder. What? I think the clean and totally innocuous white laboratory rat forgot to keep on running and started screaming with disbelief and confusion. Was I to laugh or to cry? Was this comedy or tragedy? (And I still don't know, although I'm so much closer to death now.)

Immediately the trap became visible to me. Did they lay it for me, baiting it with my neither-nor identity, lure me into a possible projection of myself? I no longer know. I didn't think so then. What murder? That of an old white woman, reputedly rich. Where? In Bethlehem. Bethlehem, good God! Of all places! Isn't, isn't that in the Free State somewhere? I've never been there, don't even know where it is. When? Ten days before. But I was in Mother City then, I had hardly arrived, in fact I now remembered reading in the *Mother City News*, a minor item tucked away on an inside page, about an old woman found hanged in her own house, she had befouled her underwear, one more death as a statistic in our tabulated total of stabbings, brain-bashings, burnings, necklacing – the grist of the civil war. I saw that I couldn't expect to defend myself by producing my real false identity – wasn't this what they were trying to drive me to? It would have been like denying a theft because terrorists don't steal. It would also have meant implicating and bringing down a whole network. What the hell was going on here? Coincidence? Did I by inconceivable bad luck get stuck with the papers of a murderer? But what about the photo Dino Felis flashed at the hotel? Was I so wall-coloured, so much of a chameleon, that I could resemble someone I'd never seen in my life? Were they just looking for any scapegoat to close the case? And if it was a gigantic mistake? If I played along too easily, admitting to the murder (to keep the hounds off the scent), and they found out that they'd made an error – wouldn't they then want to know even more fiercely what I was really covering up? Police are stupid by definition – but they have all the time and power in the world, and they work within the eternal human framework of vulgar treachery and weakness and fear. I had to play for time not knowing what the final sentence would be.

It was a long night, so strange that I thought I must be dreaming. At other times the proceedings struck me as utterly farcical. Careful, I said to myself – let's not bring the house of cards down, let's choose our metaphors carefully, let's tack as close to the wind as possible. Raincoat's mate had shed his outer garment and was sitting under another light, pecking away at a typewriter to record questions and answers. I had to provide some answers, some cue-lines, didn't I? How else was I going to be innocent of what they thought me guilty of whilst not being so innocent as to become guilty of something they didn't even suspect! Barnum had once told me of a dotted tattoo he'd seen around a fellow-prisoner's neck: *My last words are a rope around my neck.*

As interrogations go, as I'd been led to believe by the hair-raising tales one hears overseas, this one was soft. Dino Felis had a file in front of him to which he referred often. It seemed to contain diagrams and photos and, I presume, local police reports. He was courteous, infinitely patient, gradually rounding off his 'picture'. From time to time his globular eyes would weigh me up without batting an eyelid. His gaze was unfathomable. Sitting behind my back, discreetly smoking, was Wordpecker, quietly grasping the thin threads of supposition woven into a pattern of probability and then into the pages of conviction, and these he covered with indelible black ink.

Where I'd been over the past month? Travelling. Doing what? I'm an itinerant . . . actor. The strolling player, that's me. Where? Ah, here and there, you know. Playing what? Oh, whatever the hand finds within reach, Shakespeare, yes, Brecht, the Greek tragedies, Pirandello (careful, just now he'd want to know about those characters in search of an author), everything really, a soldier of fortune and a man for all seasons. Where did I perform recently? Eh, no, not really; we actors are so often out of work. My address? On the road. Where I got my money from, how come I could stay in a grand Braamfontein hotel? . . . Why I went to Bethlehem? No, but surely there's a big mistake somewhere, honestly. I don't even know where the place is, it must be somebody with the same name, it is a common name, isn't it, I believe a general and a minister? (Careful now – watch that mouth!)

But he had the proofs, right here. Anom Niemand had stayed in the Bethlehem Inn (dear Jesus, this was getting altogether too biblical!) on the night of 31 August, the night of the murder. That night, at about half-past eleven, an old lady living by herself in the white sector of town (her name was Mrs Katya Hamman) was killed by hanging from the neck in her own house, it couldn't have been suicide because she was found dangling high from a chandelier (she was frail and old) with no kicked-over chair or stool anywhere near. She had not been sexually molested – he looked at me for a long

262

moment without any expression whatsoever – so the motive must have been robbery. At first they suspected that it might have been a coloured housebreaker or a black maniac from the Location, but it would have been impossible: because of the curfew all the Blacks are out of town by eight at night, there is the *aandklok*, the evening bell, the streets are well lit and regularly patrolled by police and vigilantes. No, it could only have been a White. Only a White would have passed unnoticed through the night. Anom Niemand must have left the hotel before daybreak, precipitously, he never paid for his room. There was no theatre performance in that town that night. Or anywhere else near. Nobody goes to the theatre any more. This is war.

The night was nearly over, but I couldn't have known it. Other policemen entered the room, maybe looked at me from the pool of darkness while sipping at paper cups of coffee, and quietly left again. Down the corridor there was the indistinguishable and dis-embodied crackling of radio communications. Then there was the matter of the letter. The one meant for Nomzana (but her name never came up). They'd of course found it in my luggage. Who was this sister? And the Ka'afir who signed the letter? No, ah, er, it was only part of a script. A script? What script? A film I was interested in becoming involved in. Oh yes? Yes, ah, some simple Black-and-White story, to be shot in black and white heh-heh, and I was, ah, to play the part of a policeman, hah-hah! You learn as you live. Sympathetic portrayal, of course. Where the rest of the screenplay was? Well, it was still to be written, partly, mostly. The title? Ah, er, mm, On, ah *On the Art of Walking in No Man's Land*. What kind of a film is that? A kung-fu thriller? No, er, finally about how important it is to find a way out of the impasse, the maze we find ourselves in, the spiral of bloodletting, to a brighter future for one and all, I believe in the potential of our fatherland, a little good will and give-and-take, a lot of sense . . . (This was taking the skiff dangerously close to the reefs.) I could let him see the rest of the book as soon as it was written. I'd like to have his opinion. Captain Dino Felis didn't want to know about politics. We were here to solve a murder case. We have solved a murder case.

I found myself in a cell. Nobody bothered me. I didn't know what to do. Should I insist on being allowed to contact someone? Who? And how then not to let the cat out of the bag? I allowed myself to be lulled by the general indifference. The country is mad. Nobody is really looking for me. I'm not even a monkey, let alone

263

an organ-grinder. They will let me slip away as simply as they caught me.

After a week I was taken, handcuffed in the back of a police van, to Mother City. They drove me through the gates of a huge prison where I was put into the White Male Awaiting Trial section. This was Pollsmoor! I was being given the chance, incongruously and ironically, of seeing from the inside part of the place where Barnum had been imprisoned during his stretch – material for my memoir! But it was redundant information, our film project no longer interested me. It would never get off the ground. Not every bird is meant to fly. Though I was willing to write a novel if needs be. Outside the complex of buildings, a prison farm really, the majestic mountains reared their hoary heads. Birds often flew over the exercise yard, drifting by on the high white winds. One had no view over the city from here. Was it still burning? I didn't even dare make friends with my fellow luckless inmates. They were mostly petty thieves and drug addicts anyway, and a-political to a man.

And then it went quickly. So quickly that I was in a daze. I was told that the investigation had been completed, that my trial was due to begin on the first day of October. A *pro Deo* advocate was designated to defend me. He came to the prison to interview me, to prepare the case, and obviously he didn't believe a word I said. Without really looking at me, the lawyer riffled through the contents of his fat briefcase. He asked me if there was any family I wished to have informed or contacted, and I said no, I had only a father who was once a prominent politician but who'd committed suicide over a woman. By hanging? he asked. Yes, by hanging himself, I confirmed. (I don't know why I thought up this lugubrious lie. Wishful thinking? Or because I wanted both to claim and to deny you? Conjuring fate?) Did I have any alibi? Well no, but I certainly was not the one who had done in old missus Katya Hamman. He said I didn't seem to realize that I was risking my neck. Couldn't I be more forthcoming? Then he sighed and said he only hoped we didn't have to appear before Judge Tshwete who felt obliged by his precarious position to send every suspect up the gallows-steps. (Yes, we had our first black judge sitting on the Cape Bench!) Because of all the political trials, ordinary criminals were no longer getting a fair deal, he muttered. Justice was becoming too summary.

What were my friends doing? Surely they must have known by now of my predicament. Were they suspicious of me, scared that I'd cracked, that this trial was all just a trick to cheat them into thinking that they were still safe? Were they too busy doing other things? Had they perhaps been arrested too? Were they even now planning my escape? Or did they simply lie low, knowing that I was covering up for the Movement?

The trial started before the Cape Bench of the Supreme Court, Judge Breytenbach presiding. It went on for three and a half days, the time needed to straighten the cuffs peeping out from under the jurists' cloaks, to indulge in some abstruse legal crossing of swords, to pay lip-service to the idea of justice. In the well of the court I noticed, sitting among the case officers, a man in dark glasses and a flowery tie, his face unnaturally white and stiff, his hair apparently dyed (I should know the tricks of the trade), who looked long and insistently in my direction. Captain Dino Felis, Raincoat and Wordpecker treated him with great deference.

Very little evidence was presented. It was hardly necessary. The prosecutor painstakingly took Captain Dino Felis through his story. He described my stay in Bethlehem (!), how I was arrested in Johannesburg, that I had with me a large sum of South African money in new banknotes – probably the result of my selling off the objects I'd stolen in Mrs Hamman's house, but how I nevertheless had claimed to be a poor out-of-work actor. (How could I tell them that I'd quite legally exchanged that money upon entering the country?) He said that I could provide no credible explanation of my movements during the two weeks preceding my arrest. The hotel register of the Bethlehem Inn was produced with the entry of my name and the date of my arrival. Evidence was led – this was totally new to me! – of smudged fingerprints on a table-top in Katya Hamman's house which seemed to correspond to mine. The prosecutor got Dino Felis to say that I'd shown no remorse, and in answer to a question from the bench he said that the motive for the crime was obviously robbery. A medical expert testified about the state and position of the body, the approximate hour of death, and he speculated about how the crime might conceivably have been carried out.

My advocate – why even bother to give his name? He probably forgot mine immediately after it was all over – my advocate made the mistake of having me testify. He had no other witness upon whom to practise the skills of puppet-master. I no longer knew what line to take; I'd thought that by now the absolute silliness of the set-up would have become self-evident, and it was certainly too late in the day to blurt out the truth – the truth? – as a defence

265

stratagem. Who would have believed me? As a witness I was cross-examined by the prosecutor, and taken to pieces. This was no play. These people, although they were dressed up in theatrical robes and using the studied gestures and inflections of the stage, were not play-acting. Death, for them at least, was not a shadow to be dialogued with ritually every night and then discarded. The prosecutor demanded the maximum penalty allowed by the law, arguing that we were living through terrible times and that we had to punish in an exemplary way these scurrilous crimes perpetrated against defenceless old women, from *within the ramparts* as it were. That it was, practically, a matter of safeguarding the morale of our besieged country, if not actually the species. Could we allow the rot from inside? A mad tirade, if ever there was one.

My defender, in his final plea, drew attention to the fact that I'd grown up an orphan, that I was obviously an unstable character with profound psychological scars – the fact that I'd chosen to become an actor was ample proof of my identity and affective problems. But, he claimed, I was quite clearly neither ignorant nor stupid, I had no criminal record, and had I wanted to steal or kill (this is no passionate crime we are examining, m'lord) I'd certainly have taken the necessary precautions of covering my tracks, of changing my name perhaps. These are known tricks. He rejected the validity of the evidence against me as being circumstantial only. He said the fact that I could give no satisfactory explanation of my movements was no proof of my guilt. The country was in turmoil, many people could not even prove their existence any more. It was incumbent upon the state to prove their assumptions – *that absence of verified innocence did not yet constitute guilt* – and he ended by asking for my acquittal so that it may not ever be suggested that South African justice has become summary.

Judge Breytenbach adjourned the court (it was late morning) until the following day. I felt nothing. Not any more. My nerve-ends were deadened. My advocate was plunged in conversation with some colleagues, like him parading as crows. I must have known that I was ripe for the trapdoor. I was taken down to the cells below the court. An indescribable murmur rose from those dungeons: bees in a tomb. Hundreds of 'political' cases – rioters, strikers, rock-throwers, pyromaniacs – must have been awaiting their turn to be processed through the punishment mill.

The judge didn't even look me in the face the next morning. He read his summing-up in a monotonous drone. He had big ears and

266

red jowls and dandruff on his sleeves. The senior officer who'd been sitting with Dino Felis was no longer present. Dino Felis glanced at me expressionlessly. My advocate seemed tired and hung-over – had he been drinking the night before? The judge said that I was an untrustworthy and contradictory witness. He felt that the state of the land could not be advanced as a valid argument (although we were living through terrible times). He considered me as sane and responsible for my acts. Justice must remain the same under all circumstances. He resented Defence trying to advance extra-legal considerations. He detected a biased attitude to Court in Defence's plea, and he was also struck by the discrepancy in trying to show psychological irresponsibility whilst simultaneously claiming innocence. There were too many coincidences. Only a White could have done the deed. The accused was, in a manner of speaking, the White for the job. On the balance of evidence presented, he had no doubt about my culpability, and subsequently no option but to sentence me to the ultimate punishment of death, to be hanged, to be hanged by the neck until death ensued, the court is dismissed.

This I had to hear standing up. I turned to descend the steps. My ankles and my hands were chained. There were four or five spectators in the back of the hall. Was I mistaken or did I notice Girl among them? It seemed hardly likely – the woman I glimpsed was smartly clothed in a two-piece suit, her hair well combed, and she was without glasses. And yet, there was something only too familiar in the truculent bearing of her shoulders, in that I-told-you-so attitude. Could it have been Girl after all, wearing contact lenses? What for? Could beauty be that artificial?

I went down. Dino Felis was waiting just outside the court cell in the company of my advocate whose face was livid. They talked to me, but my mind was numbed. I thought – a spool of flashed images jerked through my mind – of Meheret, of you, Noma, of Uncle Sampie the kite-maker. It was urgent that I should get to the toilet. The guard wouldn't let me – I pissed against the white-chalked wall of the chapel-like cell. My body was cold and stiff. The voices of the detainees crowded in their dungeons became inaudible.

They returned me to Pollsmoor. Time had come home to me. I was probably supposed to be moved rapidly to Pretoria Central Prison, to Death Row, but evidently the accrued control necessitated by the intensified state of emergency in the country paralysed the normal proceedings. In my cell – now permanently shackled as is the case with all condemns – I quite forgot the art of walking, I became impervious to the outside world. Sometimes rumours filtered through of attacks on police posts, particularly in the North. It was as if these things, the things of the world, no longer concerned me. I was privately weaving an actor's cloak of words, something to flesh out the drama of my impersonation – the way the clothes we use on stage are the requisites and the props of death.

Then, in March of this year, a week ago today, I was brought up to Pretoria in a convey with other candidates for death. The shock of travelling, the break in routine, suddenly jerked me back to life. This has gone too far. I don't want to die!

Noma, father, somehow I imagine you as God. This much must have become clear to you by now. Forgive me. I see you as benign, with a wise face. God, in this bleeding and burning country, must certainly be an elderly white man. And you have, as far as I'm concerned, the discretion and the powers of a god. You now know my full story. Only you do. You could intervene. You could save me. Save me!

Your (loving) son
Anom

PS But if you are indeed God, you will be cruel and indifferent.

268

In this dark space, murky and musty, they sit ranged behind the long table the kings and their queens. The time is indeterminate. The venue is a large room rather like a place where communal prayers are said amen. Outside off to one side the land climbs away to the glittering mountain range. And along the skyline a haze where the corpses of dead angels are cremated in the open. The air is open. The distant stench of burnt feathers. On the other hand through the window in the background quite close by clear and foaming the sea. In the sea a shape. This here is called 'the holy office of kings'. They must congregate regularly to reassure one another that they still exist. Dressed in sombre finery and burnished breastplates. The kings have camouflaged the bruises about their eyebrows, the queens the cold sores around their pouts. In the gloom the patches on mantle and slip may pass for embroidery. And they murmur regal mutterings while they displace the hands and incline the heads sagaciously. The conduct aims at being impressive. But behind their backs against the wall an assistant stands all clothed in black and he is weak-kneed from laughing so much. He is the commoner. The hanger-on. His knees go knack-knock and he has to cling to a pillar overcome by gusts of gasping. His weak knees may also be ascribed to his ripe old age. Age ripens in the joints after all. The sea is heard gurgling by the window. The sea is a flash of noon brightness. The sea is a blind spot for the sun.

(Read a little way back about Yama and Samedi, the two clowns' visit to this place while the holy office of kings is in session, of the men in the cage on the marketplace, clothed in yellow blankets, of how the borders are broken, of how easily you go missing, and in due course about the horses' cemetery too.)

The senior king present clears his throat and raises his sceptre to say: 'Yes it *is* lonely in the head, but we admit that the mind is capable of great beauty. I make a vague gesture thus flying my hand. You must get a flash of what I mean. I'm hinting at what's already set down gained and at that which still may come!'

Page 42. Sunday, September? Meeting of the Waterworks Commission. Writer is summoned to take notes, *nolens volens.* Morland decides right from the word go that it should be so. He furthermore proposes, in his capacity as chairman, that Writer should not only jot down what is being mouthed, but interpolate the notes with personal impressions, observations, sideshows, thumb sketches – or thumb (dumb) mice, as he calls them – even if these were apocalyptic. It will be of historical value, he says. In all vagueness, this is a bilingual country, he says (*Bos* and *Prolog* are spoken, please leave *Afrikaans* out of the story), so you will make your notes partly in the one furrow and what's left over in the other, this is the way of the matter, core-truth escapes us. Or the dark stone of limpidity. The notary is a translator. All notes are translations, alas, Bertolt Brecht says. How can it be different? Writer takes notes. Writer also makes notes. Minutes are made by me. Right at the outset, Morland says, we must have a citation to head the report as it behooves. Flag nailed to the cross.

> *Pero yo ya no soy yo*
> *ni mi casa es ya mi casa . . .*
> *verde carne, pelo verde . . .*
> *y el caballo en la montana*

And Lorca too is dead, says Morland. People die from lack of dreaming, the Marquess Pubol murmurs. Mourning? Morland asks. Good morning, says Pubol. Now I shall declare the proceedings open, Morland says. The proceedings have been declared open. With a motto beforehand, to wit: *Dura lex, sed lex. Ek sekondeer*, says Master Basie. Forsooth, says Shiva.

Are present: Morland, Antonio Conselheiro, Bob Marley, Elephans, Marquess Poopbowl, Sexton Blaking, Shiva aka Suicide Artist, Khadjia, Noma, Han van Meegeren (or substitute, R. Noodhoek), Stoel, Mr Van Wyk, Master Basie, Lazarus, John Miles, Amo, Writer, Bertolt Brecht. It is a quorum. A good attendance, solid gathering, largely a quorum, says Morland. And: let it be noted thus.

Before we take on the roll of court Writer is asked to read the minutes of the previous meeting. Writer reads. Morland criticizes the minutes because they do not reflect (the light of) scientific exactitude, diverge from the spoken image, install a gap 'twixt the spoken of and the written about, so much so that the more delicate in fact gets all fucked up, containing also impressions and some-such, swarming *inter alia* with thumb-mice. He asks if anyone in the present gathering has remark or observation to make. That it isn't true, John Miles says. That I wasn't here, am not here, don't belong here in another man's story. Stoel groans. What is truth? Amo asks, carving a smile into small white incisors. Truth is the offspring of time, not of authority, B. Brecht proposes. Our ignorance is limitless, do let us reduce same a touch or more. But we do at least have a maggot, the Marquis Poebol says. Leave me be, Lazarus protests. Can we thus move the motion that it be accepted without dissentient vote? asks Morland. (With minor modifications.) *Ek sekondeer*, says Master Basie. Of course, it goes without saying, says B. Brecht – isn't it literature? Let it therefore be noted thus, says Morland.

Morland has filed-down teeth and also the appearance of a well-fed statesman. Subsequently we come to the matters in hand, he says. This Parole Board has options, he says. Hear, hear, Lazarus moans. Not that it should be item one on the agenda, says Morland, only a principled position within a general framework of reference of what was, is, en shall be. The beginning of sorrows. One: What to do about Anom. Relevant to same we have here a letter from him, a petition in the disguise of a letter. It will be read. Shiva has the long face of a bazaar bread. Two: What ought to be done about the despicable and horrifying murder of Greta Garbo. Khadjia shouts: Revenge! Revenge! She is so big she looks like a woman on a mule, or like *Andansonia digitata*. The old crow has grown too fat to either sob or sink, says Elephans. Khadjia hisses. Stoel creaks. The dragon is an oriental tradition, says Amo. Soulshack, Shiva sobs. We have to avoid judging pianists by their playing, Pubol remarks. Since when does a battered baobab tree play the piano? B. Marley asks. Order! Morland says. Will you come to order! *Ek sekondeer*, says Master Basie. In my capacity as drill-master. The third point, Morland resumes, is that we are to define a given identity. You know who I'm talking about. Private? Public? Amo asks. And is there any difference? B. B. says: Look, the private individual is a mutation of the public one, and he doesn't survive despite this dichotomy, but because of it. We know who we're referring to, says Mr Van Wyk (very timid); should we not indicate Him with a capital Aitch? Sexton Blaking doesn't say a work. Cock has been kicked to death in the arena, says Marquess Poopbell. Because of an excess in literalness. God knows, says John Miles. Ekart says: God who has bared his true character sufficiently once and for all by combining the genital organs with the urinary tract. But why are you now taking to your heels? J. Miles asks (his beard atremble with grey ash). No, hang on, I must get out of this; I thought the intention was to class the symbol under the third heading and now you're chasing up ghosts. To pass from the intuitable to the non-intuitable is to negate the function and the meaning of the symbol, says Han Van Meegeren. People, you are skinning the bear before you've sold the pelt! says Morland. I say order! People, people, don't quibble this way. *Ek sekondeer*, says Master Basie. If you would ask me, I'll give you a quotation, says Antonio Conselheiro 'Man makes a superhuman/Mirror-resembling dream.' But we'll get to that later on, says Morland. First this – discussion point number four, again and ever to be broached: How shall we do to provide with water the Place as well as the city of flames and all the discursive outlying areas? Five: As, I mean since, the Denouement is with us, what ought to be done to coordinate the resistance effectively? And against what authority? Can this point be summarized under three? What lucidity should first be achieved before we can go over to action? Or does lucidity (as in a mirror) make all action obsolete? Is clarity therefore in itself action? Is walking an unnaturally acquired habit, an awkward gait? Is Pheidippides a nitwit? In the sixth place we have received a petition from Ka'afir, a kind of manifesto in which he puts in a good word or a preface for *Patantra*. I don't know that we'll have space and time enough to get that far. Says Morland. Lazarus just sits there invested with authority like a king, in a threadbare (see-through) mantle. Sexton Blaking has swallowed his tongue. The marquess has knobbly buttocks like a white ant.

15

'So what are we to do about Anom?' So what are we to do about Anom? asks Morland. We have to teach him about the noble art of walking, says Lazarus. One two three. Which is essentially the faculty of letting go of the called self within a specific environment. The inexhaustible outflow. But I remember reading, remarks John Miles, years ago in some enduring factasy, that man exists in an essentially hostile environment. (As I do here, sandwiched between a spluttering of spooks.) Do you want him to be run over? So what? queries Morland (he uses talcum on his hands). What we wish to instil in him is immaterial to hostility or accommodation. His relationship with his environment is not a compromise. It is more in the nature of a symbiosis. (There lies the soul of walking, which is a relationship. A *camouflage* really.) Together he and his surroundings and his perception of the interplay and the *dépassement* form reality. Do we really need a reality? asks Carl Rogers. Sure we do, says Han Noordhoek – there must be a reference or else we're unfocused and lost parable and in-existent like a particle in or of someone's mind before the theory of the indestructability of matter! Don't worry, for whatever you fear: a particle, my friend – says Carl Rogers – is a tendency to exist. Nothing more. Or more nothing. Forget about one-ness. (Forget about being.) There is no satisfaction after action. The universe is not a collection of pieces but a web of interrelationships. That is, if there is a universe. What makes you think Anom is alive? Footsake, Shiva sobs. The Mark de Pooball: But he must be, since he's here, entangled in our words. Or do you suggest we're wasting time, just licking a tune, slobbering over the *dépouille*? Writer, scratch that last remark, Morland instructs. It will contaminate the clear water of our reputation. *Ek sekondeer*, says Master Basie. Writer obliterates the words from his mind. Writer chases them to catch and destroy them, but he has to climb over other phrases to get at them. Listen, says Carl Rogers, living things are self-organizing systems; a self-organizing system is living. One effects, therefore one must be. The effect can create the cause. Call it reciprocity. You are quite right – Anom is now and for ever more. And because he is, he walks! How could he be without walking,

since there's the eternity of decay? But we're concerned / indeed upturned / about the *art* / of his walking *part* / says Bob Marley. Carl Rogers: Yes indeed. Systems which exchange energy with the environment don't follow only the law of entropy. They are self-enhancing and creative as well. So the movement flows from the exchange of energy for movement? asks Elephans. And to exchange he or it must be an entity, a system? He or it *is* always a system, a structure, says Carl Rogers. The more complex the structure, the more likely there are to be fluctuations in the system. Fluctuations? Shiva objects. Fluck the Eulopeans too! Carl Rogers: I mean, the structure which cannot take the fluctuations as they become greater, is forced into a more complex and integrated organism. You cannot go alone. I'm saying that walking is a loss . . . The change is not gradual. Various small changes converge into a large change. That is: the jump. Walking, the outflow, the sequence of small changes, peak in the jump over the precipice – or from the stool, if the rope is strong enough to bear the connection. Hang on! Hang on! Khadjia shrieks. Where does this Carl Rogers come from all of a sudden? Stoel creaks. Why can we not just leave him lying there? Morland asks. Lazy *skelm*! Master Basie says. Foolshack, Shiva whimpers. Why must we mind him at all? R. van Meegeren asks. Because the mind is greater than the brain, Carl Rogers says. He is with each of us. The whole is contained in each part. Aren't you jumping the discussion now, professor? Morland asks. Aren't you wading into Noma? No, says Carl Rogers, all reality is contained in each of us and each of us is a part of all reality. In fact we make him walk – because we are changing by jumps in the mind. After all, conscious-ness is an important part of the web of interrelationships. Certainly no experiment (or experience) can be conducted without taking the consciousness of the investigator as an important part of the *findings*. What we need to study is the processes of change that come from within. What I want to find is my daughter, Khadjia howls. Or how, Poopall reflects, we as a commission assemble the camel to look like a horse, with strings attached. True, Carl Rogers says, true indeed – it is a science of tendencies, possibilities and not hard facts (faction, not fict). Of understanding, not control. Ultimately reality is a series of approximations. Going towards, says Lazarus. The noble art of walking, says Amo. Since that is the case, since we are his steps, he doesn't have to walk at all, says Han Noordhoek. More, to walk he needs to not escape our attention, he must remain immobile, says Amo. Which is where we want him, says Morland, since we need the bait, we need the vomit, we need the point of re-entry. And we don't want the old woman to scare off the flies, says Bob Marley, putting his hands over his ears. *Ek sekondeer*, says Master Basie. We thank Carl Rogers for the experience-expanding citations. And we agree that Anom, as bait for decomposition, has to stay where he is. This we propose and we accept without showing our hands.

16

There is silence. Writer moves. 'We, the people, the oppressed . . .'
No, Morland bangs the table; scratch, delete, suppress and unquote!
This is not the vehicle for subversive literature and we aren't Anom.
I rule the introductory paragraph out completely of bloody order
and out of mind furthermore, as also the next and the next. We
resist but we do not dig up skeletons and we don't gather wool.
We are the Players. The Denouement has come. Continue. 'But if
I am not a criminal, I beg to be permitted to go abroad . . . temporarily, for at least one year, with the right to return as soon as it
becomes possible in our country to serve great ideas in literature
without cringing before little men, as soon as there is at least a
partial change in the prevailing view concerning the role of the
literary artist. And I am convinced that this time is near, for the
creation of the material base will inevitably be followed by the need
to build the superstructure – an art and a literature truly worthy of
the revolution.' No! Nein! Mistake! Bertolt Brecht comes awake and
takes off the grey pebbles of his spectacles. His eyes are wonderfully
vague and large like little owls. Little naked owls sprouting their
first feathers on the wings. Mistake I say, he says. This letter is
written to the Moustache. And this isn't that. I know, I recognize
the drift. It is written by my old friend the drifter, Yevgeny Zamyatin. We are indeed in the wrong story, says John Miles. *Ver van
die huis*, says Master Basie. My daughter! My daughter! Khadjia
shouts. Forsooth, Shiva moans. Yes, B. B. says. He fits his glasses
around his ears again, and the eyes become more pointed. Owls
can see thumb-mice in the night. He eats a cigar. His hair is cut
baldshort. He wears a shabby suit similar in style to that of Amo.
But Amo has an inscrutable expression. Are we considering Ka'afir's
Patantra manifesto? Elephans inquires. Yes, B. B. says. *Ja*. We need
writers who fear nothing. This Zamyatin claims. Heretics are the
only (bitter) remedy against the entropy of human thought. It is the
tradition of Gogol, of Leskov, of Bely, Remizov, Babel, Bulgakov,
Walser – and Fedin, Bruno Schultz, Kaverin, Ginsberg, Céline,
Zoshchenko, Lev Lunts, Jarry, Vsevolod Ivanov. The world is kept
alive only by heretics: the heretic Christ, the heretic Copernicus,

the heretic Tolstoy, the heretic Ras Tafari, the heretic Ka'afir. Our symbol of faith is heresy. He says so. And further: True literature can exist only where it is produced by madmen, hermits, heretics, visionaries, rebels and sceptics. Whoofft, Puble snorts. Better still – fffttt, Han Noordhoek adds. But: Art has an enemy called ignorance, B. Brecht concludes. We Poets in our youth begin in gladness: / But thereof come in the end despondency and madness. W. Wordsworth. A burden for what it's worth, says Stoel. Words? Warts? Swords? It's tworth more at Woolwords, says Sexton Blaking. Worlds? the marquess asks. Woolswords, replies H. van Meegeren. I rule all the above and preceding swoolishness and wordweights out of existence, Morland says. I refuse to admit the letter, the phoneme, the seme, the seeming or the whorl. We shall overcome.

Dear Noma,

I have learnt, I think, some of what it takes to be an actor. Perhaps I have no view of the whole, but there are details that I understand well. It is enough. You must have seen the actor on the stage (then again, perhaps not – have you ever been inside a theatre in your life? – and anyway, what function does theatre have in this country?) – but imagine, and what you see are aspects, isolated acts. The lighting may have made you aware of the shivering flesh on an upper arm, a clumsy waist, a white-powdered neck and cheek – to the exclusion of the total person or picture. Or you may know how actors learn to make certain gestures particularly well, with great concentration. Disjointed actions – and absurd, because having no follow-up, no reason to be – but therefore beautifully free: crumpling a paper, eating an apple, laughing at a mirror, lacing up first one boot and then the other. That too is a reflection of the actor's specificity, or essence: to be a man of parts. If there is one role I should have liked to play, one character I'd wish to impersonate, it would be that of the story-teller. But outside the need to play, to activate a part of yourself to the detriment of the rest, *when the biggest part of you is dead*, at least held in abeyance; in other words, when your craft of actor is taken away from you and you are left naked – then, strangely, you don't know who you are. You are only yourself completely in being someone else. I wake up in the mornings and I see bits of myself, older versions, more or less complete, lying dead all over the cell. The mirror is shattered. They all have swollen faces, thick tongues sticking out, bulging white eyes. This dissolution and scattering, this way of not being anybody, is a true liberation.

I think I realized this was for real, that all was over (but for the shouting), that it makes no sense trying to figure out what they know or do not know, that the time of weaving and feinting is finished, that night when they brought Ka'afir into the section.

You get used to the sound of your chains. It can be a friendly clicking sound, like worry-beads run through the fingers, like birds telling each other the history of creation. Whenever you move a limb, when you turn over in your sleep, you are reminded of the fact that you are alive and that time is like a chain of eyes seeing you to the end of the line. The blind man needs to hear his stick go tickety-tock. And the man condemned to die in so and so many days' time, and that is his only punishment, *to know in advance exactly when* he will inexorably move one way from the state of being to that of nothingness, that man has the privileged sensation of being allowed to know his skeleton. The chains are your bones, to be recited cold and clicking and smooth in your hands. Somewhere on one of those bones may be scratched the unspeakable formula of memory.

Already I dream as if I am not here. The courtyard is one hollow square of dazzling white light bringing a veil of tears to the eyes. I have to cross this blind exposed area to get to my cell, but I have to walk on my hands. The ground consists of a layer of small sharp-edged pebbles eating into the palms of my hands. There is my cell, in the opposite wall. It is small and green and moist. The death-ship of a pharaoh was always painted green. On the floor a series of doors are laid out, twelve in all, with Ka'afir among them. He is the twelfth door. The crocodile is finally a chameleon.

The sharp light fractures and fragments my vision. I dream that my name is Anom, that I'm travelling with two companions (the most intimate family?) in a train through a slow landscape. It is strange but familiar territory. When we arrive at the station of Montaigue the train is prevented from continuing its journey. Rather, the train may eventually be allowed to leave but we, my two companions (one big, one small?) and Anom, are told to get off. We are taken through the streets some distance away from the station and made to wait outside. It is hot, the sun is pouring a square of sunlight over us. We face a blindingly white building with a bland façade without windows. There must be cool green cells inside looking out upon a walled-in exercise yard. A man, firm but polite, with tinted hair and dark glasses, by the name of Colonel Grey, has taken away the only luggage I had, the manuscript of a play. It was a fragmentary version. 'Where is the rest?' he asked, and maybe I said that it was still in the process of being dictated or distilled, but that I'd let him have the rest as soon as it was ready. 'Wait here,' he intimated, and disappeared through a small door into the building. The sun and the heat have given us a white façade. In the distance the train is hooting, two engine-drivers with swarthy faces and black moustaches will be peeping out of the locomotive before bringing it in motion with hissing cheeks. They will snake their way through the mountains to the sea. Or was this the end of the line? My thoughts are waiting like a train of sealed coaches in a dark station – inside the skeletons would have become indistinguishable. The chains are free. This is the place – in this street in the sun between nothing and nowhere – to meditate on a bowl of dust. Think of the glory that once was. Think that every mote of dust is a rock with shining facets. Montaigue must have a very pleasant climate. Several men in grey suits appear around one end of the building. One man, Colonel Grey, brandishes a pistol in his black-gloved hand and he shoots without even peering around the corner. Bullets zing off the hard white dust-surface of the street like angry bees, with a terrible velocity. Small explosions erupt on the bodies of Anom and the woman and the child, and red liquid splatters the lenses. A force is throwing them back. They bite the dust. These are the facts: (1) Montaigue must have a pleasant climate. (2) Streets wind leisurely up the mountain. (3) The silver silence of sleeping birds. (4) *Nobody back home will ever know*! (5) Where is home?

Before they brought in Ka'afir, there was only one other poor bastard apart from myself awaiting execution on Death Row. I didn't know what his case was, still don't, probably an obscure mess of aggravated rape and robbery. He got himself inextricably trussed up in the ropes of fate. He is white – his name, ironically, is De Witte, everybody around here calls him Whitey – I saw him once or twice as he was being led down the corridor for a medical visit, his head bowed, his shoulders stooped, his wrists and ankles weighed down by the shackles. Now it only needs a Jesus to go with us two thieves and we can have a dandy crucifixion, I remember thinking.

Death Row is a spotlessly clean narrow corridor with six cells on either side, the bathroom at one end, a heavy door barring it off from the rest of the prison. Here the outside has ceased existing. In the distance, as if in a half-forgotten past, you can sometimes perceive the rumour of prison life, the hum of many voices, a chant on Sundays, a shout in the night. But we live as if below the surface of life. We do not communicate with the world. For all that we are not dead yet. Execution is a ritual and a ritual needs time. We need to feed and fatten time, to make it ripe for slaughter. Common sense tells me there must be many more condemned prisoners in this complex labyrinth. Are there more Death Rows beside ours? We deduce from the frayed ribbon of conversations we overhear that the execution room – the High Jump it is called – is in regular use. Do they separate the 'criminals' from the 'politicals'? But then they brought in Ka'afir . . .

The lights are left burning night and day. We are looked after by six warders working in groups of two. They are functional in their work, quite indifferent to our lot. We are, after all, 'one-way customers', not to be seen again. The worst one of the lot is a cruel brute, a Black I refer to in my mind as Polichinelle because he echoes the emptiness in which I now find myself. I need this echo so as not to lose the thread of my past life. He will be Polichinelle, a memory of the character I once encountered in Meheret's notebooks. He would taunt us, or be a martinet suddenly insisting upon searching the cell from ceiling to shithole. I notice that I keep on saying 'we' or 'us'. It can't be Whitey I'm including – though we're in the same boat – because we've never exchanged a single word. But everything becomes a companion here, the slightest memory, the dream coming in the door to breathe its sweet presence over your bunk, the pair of shorts you are allowed to wear, your toothbrush left in the bathroom.

Food is brought into our section by a prison orderly, a young 'rabbit' (homosexual) I call Shiva. He is only a petty criminal. A melancholy vein-shooter. Polichinelle says he's finishing his time up here serving the dead because he's got Aids anyway. That's what you get from dropping balls in the wrong hole, he sniggers. Sometimes the rabbit rapidly tries to communicate with me, dribbling syllables from the corner of his mouth, but I never understand a word he's saying. He once smuggled in to me a small chameleon – I think the warders must have known but they turned a blind eye. ('It keeps away the flies. You will have enough flies soon,' one of them said.) I don't know how old the little animal was. It clung to my finger and its eyes were still swollen shut. It made me think of a small, ancient, nearly transparent foetus. My days took on a new meaning and rhythm because I was now always on the lookout for flies. I had to catch three a day to feed the chameleon. Now I have a real worry – who is going to feed the *chamaileon*, the dwarf lion, once I'm gone? And will a lizard growing up in these surroundings, where he will never have to change colour, eventually lose the ability to adapt to life?

But life is a knack. Where there is so little light, the small beast is of a whitish yellow colour, 'the colour of dreams' it is called. As the light grows it becomes progressively darker. Melanin in the cells of the epidermis will provoke the changes. The females go greyish brown, the males don a greenish brown garb. These colour changes, I know, are not really so as to blend with the leaf or the finger or the wall. They are rather inspired by the need to be sexually attractive, by aggressiveness, by working up the adequate hue for combat, by fear and submission, ultimately by weakness and death. Ah, my friend! The death colour is either a dull black or this same pallid 'dream' shade of obscurity, but then you will keep it even in bright daylight. You will be white for keeps! Is death the inability to change colour?

How will I ever know whether it was male or female? If there were two of them it would have been easy. As the couple prepare for copulation, the sleepwalking gentleman will put on his best bright and busy colours for the performance – waistcoat, garter, hat and tails: the green of the moon, the yellow of the marshes, the white of keening; all spotted, striped and besotted – and the lady will flatten her body to comfortableness to show the sexy pulsation of her flanks, she will inflate the folds of her chin to make room for the thicker tongue of joy. He will outflank her tail, with slender hands grab hold of the pleasurable nether regions of her body, and initiate the rhythm of that joytide which is to last from three to seven minutes, repeatedly repeated for days on end – not for nothing are you called a little lion! Which is more than can be said of many humans.

And after the coupling she will adopt the dense but tender glow of pregnancy. This I shall never be able to check – what will *my* colour be then? – but after a gestation of eighty days my grey lady will open her carriage to lay her eggs. There, in some tunnel which she would have dug and covered up again, the six-centimetres-long offspring with the ideal detective eyes will be born three hundred days later. They will never know their progenitors. Didn't Ka'afir, long ago in Paris, point out to me with a sardonic smile that chameleons are transparent at birth? Was it something that slipped out of his dream? And immediately and instinctively they know how to shift the shades, how to swing from the tail, how to patiently stalk a prey, how to use the pincer-like hands to stuff down an awkwardly dislocated grasshopper.

I noticed that when the fly still sported a head my companion's aim was as infallible as that of Tarzan's – the tongue whipping out at 1/125th of a second to thwap and stun and glue and haul back the food. But when the fly, for whatever reason, had been beheaded, my friend was wobbly on his knees and elbows, swaying with indecision, and the lopsided intimate weapon spewed from the jaws as often as not fell wide of its mark. Why does it need a victim with a head to be accurate? Must it go for the eyes?

It is said also that whenever a chameleon has to change colour, the ageing process is accelerated. May you never know the stress of battle, humiliation, or climbing with a thumping heart on to the body of heaven, I said to my ponderous little companion. And: It is true, you do walk with the movements of a very ancient blind beggar with a broken back, but may you go well.

They brought him in late one night. When you are due to die it is as if you become invisible to outsiders. Provided you don't make too much noise, they leave you be. You are kept under a disinterested surveillance though, the electric eye never blinks, to make sure you don't do to yourself what only time in its fullness is meant to accomplish. Don't pick a fruit unless it is ripe. Maybe they knew I could observe them and just didn't care. I stood right up against my cell door and at an angle through the chicken-wire over the bars I saw four warders carrying some oblong sagging shape in a grey blanket. Before the cell slightly to the left and opposite mine, they lowered their load to open the door. A corner of the blanket fell away. Rolled inside they had a half-naked human. The part of the body I could see – torso, neck and face – my chameleon would not have been disorientated – was a tumescent mass of bruises, some obviously quite fresh with blood still seeping from the cuts. The human, a Black, but impossible to judge his age or make out his features, was unconscious. They left him in the cell and locked the door.

For the next twenty-four hours there was more than the usual coming and going. At one point the doctor, I think, spent quite some time in the cell. It was clear to me that the man had been severely tortured, but what was he doing here on Death Row? Only on the third day did it become evident, by an occasional groan, that he was still alive, but the food Shiva left in front of his door remained untouched. 'A terrorist,' Polichinelle said. 'Blew up two police stations. Sentenced to death.' How come he arrived here in such a terrible state, after his trial? Polichinelle thought that maybe he still had a few minor outstanding matters to clear up with the police. 'Or else an accident,' he said with a sneer. 'South Africa is lion country.'

A week later I heard, repeated several times, a soft whistling coming from that white hole in the wall opposite mine. At first I didn't associate the simple tune with anything known to me, and then, suddenly, I recognized it! *'Ma slaap vanaand al weer by Pa . . .'* The ditty I had tried to teach Meheret's parrot, Polly, to sing! And as far as I know only one other person had shared that experience with me! But then it must be Ka'afir! It came to me in a flash that the battered human across the corridor was Ka'afir.

I don't rightly remember what happened next. I must have gone berserk, or maybe the realization that Ka'afir was here, with me, on Death Row – and thus that *there was no hope of ever getting out of the trap* – was the mechanism releasing months of cropped-up aches. I found myself banging against the walls and the door and bawling, incongruously, at the top of my voice, the liberation hymn, *'Nkosi sikelel' iAfrika'*, What a fury of freedom I felt surging through my whole body! No, I was not a common murderer of old women – my life had a political meaning – my death would be seeding the future! For the first time in my life I could weep and sing without it being an act.

The *Boere* couldn't have cared less. They must have taken my antics for some delirium, the hysterics of someone about to be shortened by a head. There's a prison term for these outbursts usually accompanied by on-the-spot dancing: the 'High Jump jerk'. Or maybe they knew better, and still couldn't be bothered. At some stage several of them must have burst into my sanctuary, the womb, to calm me down. Polichinelle was roaring or laughing a shout as big as a white barracuda in the mouth. My lips were swollen and sore for a week afterwards. It was only hours later, after they were gone, that I found the chameleon squashed to death under some boot on the cement floor. Did it happen accidentally during the scuffle, or was it deliberate, to spite me? And it didn't even have the time to fade into white or black.

Indeed, Ka'afir was in the cell opposite mine. Somehow we were reticent to ask each other questions – we knew our conversations (when not interrupted by the warders) were overheard, and even now we didn't want to divulge anything that may still be used against others. Why bother about the worries of the living anyway? At the same time there was no point in trying to hide the fact that we knew one another. The surge of elation stayed with me. With Ka'afir there I felt that my impending death had a purpose. I would rush up to the bars and shout: 'I'm a revolutionary!' And always there'd be a soft chuckle coming across the shiny corridor floor, and Ka'afir saying: 'Oh man, man – what a fool you are, *Mfowethu*!' Never mind, my joy was augmented by the fact that he called me '*Mfowethu*', meaning 'Brother' in Zulu.

Am I really his brother? Does it matter? Naturally I had my doubts. If I now understand, deep down in myself, why I'm here, I still don't know *how* I got into the dead-end street. Was I betrayed? But betraying what? Was I considered a risk? Surely I was no danger to anybody. Certainly not to the Movement – to the Party perhaps, yes. Or was I simply offered as a pawn in a bigger game? What – the terrible thought did cross my mind – what if I were used as a decoy to deflect attention from Ka'afir's mission, which I'd known nothing about? But here he was, building up for the same apotheosis that would strangle with excitement the voice in the throat. Was there no betrayal at all, but simply the police taking the precaution of clearing the table? Or was it more cunning, more personal, Mumpata excluding me because of the quarrel we had in Ouagadougou? Was it Yama, or Girl without Yama knowing, throwing me overboard to keep the wolves off the scent? Was I a test-case? Who was testing what? I even wondered in my madness whether I wasn't mistakenly taken for Barnum. But more likely it could have been Barnum shooting off his stupid mouth during some delirium of inspired creation.

Ka'afir laughed softly behind his door (we couldn't see one another): 'Come now, Barnum is not such a bad bugger after all. Give the devil his due. He has the word-sickness, yes, but he is going to survive both of us. And maybe he will write about us. Let us wish him well, *Mfowethu*. All that the world may know about us will be of his invention!'

Once and once only did I ask him whether he knew Dr Yama. There was a long silence before he eventually said: 'No . . . No, not at all.'

Of what use is it to speculate? Why is it so important to know, to understand? I'm reminded of something that Barnum once said to Meheret – that it is better to stop a story before its natural ending because it is too painful and too final to see it through to its ultimate convulsions. 'Give yourself a break,' he said. And what could I speculate on in my case? I know – I'm reconciled to the fact – that I'm the chameleon waiting for the flies of life to come within reach of my sticky tongue. I am aware also that my true mission was to come to grips with the twin notions of Mountain and Movement. Everything is resolved and encompassed by the immobile mobility of scaling your own life – the mountain will be snow and the movement will be dust and I will have moved across the stage like a memory. I know why Anom meditates on a bowl of dust.

We talk to flavour time. Ka'afir would say: 'Between sitting or standing up I still prefer lying down.' I would retort: 'A company of riot police were savagely attacked by a fourteen-year-old black girl. The assailant was killed. Luckily none of the policemen suffered any injuries.' And he would say: 'The cheek of a woman! Just because she's been making the bed which she shared with a man for twenty years, she now considers herself entitled to some compensation?'

We don't need to be coherent. Only now do I have the chance of getting to know the real Ka'afir. He's not bitter at all, not the slightest like the man I knew in Paris. With an even voice he banters and jokes. 'It's so much easier to let the words go their own way since they've knocked out my teeth,' he says. And I always took him to be a cynic! I ask him about it, and whether he sees himself finally as philosopher or poet. He has no preference, he admits, but it is true that the two disciplines – or attitudes – tend to be mutually exclusive. Whereas it may be worth trying to make philosophy more poetic, it is certainly fatal to poetry when you introduce philosophy, he decides. 'But what are we talking about?' he hums, as if making up a simple song. 'We are part of the dream and our dream will survive. Our people will be free. Already they are walking the road. This is all that matters.'

Sometimes we help one another to scale the barriers of our grey tomb. 'Now we know what it is like to live in a pyramid,' Ka'afir says. Mostly it would happen just after Shiva has brought us our midday meal which is nearly invariably the same beetroot, rice, some meat, bread. 'How is your trout today?' he would shout across. 'Not bad, not bad. Deliciously tender,' I'd respond – 'and your chop-suey?' And so we go through the dining halls of memory and of imagination. For dessert I'd offer him a cloud. He'd propose

Mozart's *Magic Flute* in exchange (and sing part of Papageno's aria: *'Der Vogelfänger bin ich ja'*). 'Would you care for some Belgium?' I ask. 'With pleasure,' he says. 'And here I have for you a 1950 Buick, three nights in Dar es Salaam, real silk underpants, a dream of eternity, moonlight, Marilyn Monroe . . .'

Inevitably we often speak of women. We make a tour of Africa to sing the praises of the continent's beauties – black, blue, brown, reddish, coconut-coloured, mixed, even white. Then we remember the French, and agree that on the whole they tend to have oily hair, thin mouths and sharp noses in angular faces; the best sector may be their buttocks, we propose; the necks aren't very nice, the shoulders may sometimes pass inspection, the wrists are harsh, and aren't the fingers too bony? As for the Italians, we find that they have excellent busts, but that the bellies are often rather softish; furthermore that they sport good and vigorous hair and strong flat feet with long heels. Ka'afir says: 'When I was young I went for sad women, those with the down-turned mouths and the melancholic shadows under the eyes. I thought they were mysterious, that they had a secret ache which I could soothe or rub away and that they'd love me out of gratitude for taking them away from themselves. Now I'm attracted by gay young females with wide smiles and comfortable hips. By those who grab life to eat it until the juices run down their chins. There is nothing as pretty as the cheek of a woman.'

'We are male chauvinistic pigs,' I say. 'Yes, that is why we must hang,' he answers. 'Did you ever meet Greta Garbo?' I ask, and listen for his embarrassed silence . . . 'Sometimes I was so sad that I went to the cinema all by myself, to sit there weeping in the dark.'

As our time approaches – we don't know when it's due, but we expect it to be soon – we get more light-hearted. We are sure we haven't done all we could, but maybe we weren't intended to do more: Polichinelle has taken to hanging around Ka'afir's cell, asking him questions, exchanging deep-throated confessions. I once asked Ka'afir whether they ever discussed politics, but he says no, they talk about sport, and there are people they both know. 'I've been away too long,' he sighs, 'and it's too late now. But we Blacks are like one big family. And he asks me about you too. He wants me to explain to him what it means to be an actor, and whether it's true that stage men are *'moffies'* (homosexuals) wearing silk underpants. I think he fancies you!'

Noma, I now know that I shall never know you. This is the end of the road. I am light, light as a footfall in the wind. Soon I shall enter the limitless no man's land of death, the South Africa of the shades, the colourless dream of the chameleon. I'm in a hurry for it to be done. My fate is sealed. Maybe I'll find you over there in the forest of spirits, and then at last you may finally recognize me as part of you, some dream you once may have had.

Any day now, any day now, we shall be released.

Your Loving son
Anom

17

He sucks on his cigarette down to the ultimate draw like a man intending to realize his last wish before the execution. I die therefore I am. This is no joke. Today, when the sun reddens the dark mountain, it will be his execution. Already the window is a whiter square of pallor, the crossword puzzle more clearly etched. In the inner yard the first smothered sounds, like blossoms. Fruit, which are noughts and crosses on the dark square tree, will gradually fade. These are fruits for show only which will never be eaten. Further image: nailheads of starpoints are knocked deeper into the mountain, until they disappear utterly, as does also the mountain. He doesn't sleep that night, but walks – the four steps up and the four steps down – looking at his hands. Full of stars. His human-keeper didn't sleep either. Long shirt. He folds back the collar of his jacket to feel the morning breeze caressing his neck and chest, oh, oh, the white-breasted crow. Is it nightwind or breath of morning? Sweet and fresh in any event. And the inner-eye floodtide of sea. (Sea with caterpillars, bicycles, grand pianos, skeletons of prospectors.) 'Got a fag for a man?' – thus he asks the warder. His human-keeper growls half-words in the throat, shifts the boots with their stuffing of old censored newspapers, the stomach is a knot and the kidneys are a joke, the moustache bristles, from a coat pocket he fishes a packet of cigs, flips it open, offers one. And: 'Lexington? The one . . . For satisfaction before the action. You know I didn't smoke?' he asks the guard. The warder has the peak of his cap pulled low over the eyebrows. He has a scar-puckered cheek. He's keeping a weather eye on the reference field. To nod now would be to be sucked under by the endless sweetness of forbidden territory. To give in to the breeze. 'S'true. Check, my fingers ain't even yellow, Master. Why, it's a shit habit, makes a man's lungs suffer blindly. I don't wanna pick up the cough. When I was a lighty, together with the smokers and the mugs, I had my fill. Since then I move sharply, clean of tongue and lung. I do it my way. But now, this morning, the smoke and the smell – wow! Thassa way it must be, am I right? One for the road, before I line to heaven. Something for the chest, to open it. Can a man then not have his little pleasures? Not that I wanna be hooked. S'good, yah. Makes me feel real grand that I walked the good way. Yeah, thank you, Master, thank you nicely. Makes a guy look more casual up there, a man of the world, you know . . . Look at me, here I go. Why, I'm knocking on Whitey's gate. I'll pass the time of day with him. Dontcha want a draw, Pete? . . .

'It's like in the movies . . .'

> have the upper hand;
> take a knife
> with a grip
> fitting slipperedly like a hand
> in the palm,
> and an adequate tract of silence.

> in order to palm in these words
> you may have to cut deep
> and extract the bloody moles,
> suns will bleed white
> on the page.

> sheathe the sounds:
> and you will be hand in glove
> with silence feeding
> out of your hand.

18

Easy. Easy. It is at last easy. Swung by the neck over the pit. Jerked into absence of light. Which is not darkness. This is where it all starts. It is a cold morning. You may think you already know all the transformations, but it is never true. Even if you were to isolate the darkness. Coming down from the mountain.

For the story to get off the ground you have to grab hold of one end of the rope. It is at last easy. The Place is erased, the Game is over. Is the Place gone? Is the Game finished? Denouement. All the words flow back to the point of origin, to the suspended hand, to the twitch in the mind.

Anom gets up to walk, easily, one leg swinging after the other, like scissors cutting up distance into immediacy. It is not far, about fourteen kilometres to Heaven. Dust in the air. Sky written in big blue letters. Warmth on the neck and the hands. Particularly warming the neck, how pleasant, where rope left its old significance like a naked snake. Where the head used to be joined to the shoulders. It is easy like birth, being born, cutting from the neck the rope which cut into the neck.

White road. More and more birds the closer he gets to his destination. Easy check-out formalities, the file no. 42 closed, the letters returned, a new pair of wooden sandals, knapsack, blue coat: 'You can go as you wish, Mister Niemand. Here is your notebook, hahhah. Take it to the old man yourself.'

Inside the walls familiar figures of times bygone laying about, Dr Yama fanning his fat black face ('Well done, my boy; you have seen the light'), Shiva starting a fire with small stones, Reader immersed in a newly published book, Bertolt Brecht munching a cigar and playing a piano, Mona dancing in the dust with lifted hands and closed eyes . . .

Barnum and Ms Delanoy. He grey hair and beard, wilted violet eyes, forefinger of left hand with white scar ('Written to the bone, all for your sake. Petitions, whatnots'); she tiny as ever, her black hair cut short along the jawline, a twinkle in the black eyes. 'So glad you made it. Thought for a moment we'd lost you back there along the road. Was getting messy and mystical.' A tinkle of laughter.

'Where is Greta Garbo?' (Will fix *his* goose by and by.)

Barnum: 'She'll be along just now. Over the hill. She's been looking for you all over, has an important message to deliver. Telegram. What has kept you so long?'

'I missed her so, I missed her so. Especially her wrists and her tongue. You are asking *me* why I'm late? Where am I?'

Barnum: 'You mean to tell me you don't know? You are home, here, in Heaven.'

'You mean this is the Place?'

Barnum: 'All of it! Sorry about the tribulations.'

'You bastard!'

Barnum, bowing, congratulating his weak hand with the strong one: 'Thank you for the compliment.'

'Why did you do this to me? Why *me*? Why did you want me to walk the rope to get to this stage?'

Barnum: 'Please, please accept my apologies. I know it was a long road. Did it never occur to you that I wanted to be *you*? Desperately so. It hurt me more than it could ever hurt you. Oh, you were often in our minds, believe you me. But come now, put your head down there and tell me all about it.'

(A sob.) 'I had to outface the slippery nihilists, the verbose agitators and other rascals and bigmouths of the flowery reasoning. I was alone. I think I can show now beyond the shadow of a doubt that consciousness does have its structuring, even if the acknowledgement of same is fractured. I became a monkey, I attempted to find my way out of the maze (only Greta Garbo could have pointed me in the right direction, the female sex doesn't lie), and found myself at sea. Luckily Kashyapa, my *alter ego*, smashed the chains of illusion by explaining to me that there *is* no way. He encouraged me to take the gap. It was like telling me to *walk on*! I saw a magical landscape opening up before me – so becoming, like an instant, a batting of the eyelid, an insight, a slip-slit, a life at last.'

Barnum: 'So you got to the top of the mountain?'

'It is a she. It is a dolphin which lugs you, seated on its hump, to paradise. Sagarmatha – that's her, and with her the heavenly orgasms: Nuptse, Ama Dablam, Khumbila, Cho Oyu, Lhotse, Kala Pattar. Who can walk where the dolphin slithers on slippery belly, where snow seams the secret cracks? Who can even actualize it?'

Barnum (sob): 'Where *we* come from they are called Table Line, Silver Mine, Elephant's Head, Skeleton Gulch, Flag's Wish, Devil's Hat . . . You lucky devil.'

'And I saw the Big Silence.'

Barnum: 'Then you saw it as the narrative description of a subject in the light of – no, under the illusion of another which shares with it certain suggestive likenesses, something which can be applied as the illustration of a moral lesson, a salacious lifting of the skirt perhaps? You did see the lifting of the skirt, am I right? Please let me be right . . . And then there was enlightenment pertaining to the country way in which, along which, you walked in order to encounter good rewards, and along that other way lay contrariness and precipices. Death lay on its side? Ah, but compared with dead bodies, don't you think pubic hair is an awfully friendly thing? Didn't you also see it as the life which the pilgrim is trying to escalate? As the marvellous ribbon unrolling under Hafiz's old wandering sandals? As an *escape* where every rock miraculously becomes a horse and *taschenspielers* nonchalantly throw the flame from one hand to the other? You saw it as Noma's parlour, didn't you? - where immorality could be negotiated on the deep carpet? By the way, do you wish to meet Noma? Or Mona? You saw it as Greta Garbo's maze smelling of love? You saw it as a drawing lesson? As anything but . . . Mountain . . . You see, you saw double. If that is what you saw, you haven't seen anything at all yet!'

'Bullshit! Don't *you* try suggest to me now a separation between destination and the road leading there. *Here*, I mean to say. I wrote! All by myself I wrote! I needed no ghost to scare me into writing. And I know the Mountain is what came forth from my pen. Something was bleeding from the dark nib. Must have been the dead mountain of trying to communicate with angels like Reader and other inhabitants of the Place, also with donkeys such as yourself. You have bitten off more than you can ever chew. That person whom you devoured will in due time use a stone to smash your brains to a blubber. I wrote, I wrote the terrible trapdoor between me and the tender omniscient sadness of the dolphin. The obtundent, the obduration and the alienation I wrote stone by stone. That death to which I'm attached through the navel string. That was the writing lying before me, on its side if you wish, which I had to eat up to reach you. But I got there at last, easily. And I ascended it as sense, as unity, as structure. Oh, I observed all the . . . definitions, shreds and fragments dotting like grey geese the I's on the page.

Up here everything will have found its place, I know now, hypo-grammatically ordered, as it always was, and it too will fall away and cease existing. I know that the path is a way of walking. And meanwhile – no, don't interrupt me and don't you walk on my head! – meanwhile everything has been smashed to smithereens to emerge purified from my stutterings. I have come to memorize the dust. And I see all about me the low-lying land so familiar to me, which I recognize like the map of my hand with its beauty spots: Zanj, Al Sind, Misr, Al Hind, Kapaai, Champa, Al Sin, Big Silence, No man's land!'

Barnum (again bowing deeply): 'At last! Please once more accept my apologies and my congratulations. Welcome to No man's land!'

Now they shake hands. Ms Delanoy laughs. Barnum takes Anom for a walk through Heaven, shows him the bars ('and don't try going in there,' he admonishes, 'why, you can't even make it to the counter the way people squeeze you'), the bullring, the workshops where writing is done, the residences with the wide patios, the enclosure for the donkeys, the whorehouses for the angels. What he does with his spare time, here? Gave up writing in any event, he says. Too predictable and too dangerous. Tells of how he now spends his time painting with the good hand. What? Oh, subject matter. Come again? Oh, time, and whatever passes. Sometimes he goes looking for subject matter. 'Come with me.'

They walk to the back of the settlement. Barnum has a long loop-necked stick. 'Watch me, and you will be happily surprised!' He chooses a spot and starts digging with the staff. The soil is white and crumbly. They come across something moving under the shifting sand, big and fat. Slow thrashing movements as if trying to hide. Barnum down on his knees, scooping away the last handfuls from the shallow grave to reveal the huge, dusty, pale, chameleon.

Greta,

Now, when it is nearly over, I have difficulty in putting my thoughts in line. So much to say, so much to recall, so much to remind you of, but it is as if there's no longer any urgency to make sense, to subject the detail to the bigger whole. No one thing is more import-ant than the others. The restrictions are gone; I'm marking my remaining moments with images, words, silences. This is what life is really like. And this is the true liberation: to live up to the white-out as a skin vibrating to the alacrity or obtuseness of interaction with the surroundings. I am a passage imperfectly aware of what passes through me and of the fact that I'm a passage. By surround-ings I mean also the past and the present – the present is only the outer layer of the past, and the present keeps adding to the past – people, air, things, smells – layer upon layer. And the future? It must be the past's hunger.

This is the unthinkable, the inconceivable. The cut-off. Oh, I tried to move around the block by writing the afterwards, about what must be on the other side of the passage when, I presume, one has lost all sense of origin or past. I am like the angler fishing from the edge of the continent, casting my hook and sinker way beyond the froth of the breakers, and hoping to reel in my own wet struggling corpse. Is there a double purpose? If it is true that death is nothing, am I attempting to colour it, to furnish it, to give it context, to make of it a welcoming and familiar place, to *create* it? (Not leaving anything to chance?) That would be the first aim. The second one: by describing it *now*, by bringing it *here* into this life, to pre-empt it, to negate it, to forget it by making it *part of the past*. I thought it would be stimulating and even funny to imagine that I'm dead. In my notes for a possible memory I went over the steps through the passage towards our execution – mine, Ka'afir's, Whitey's. It is for tomorrow morning. You see, already I can make it of the past.

(As a final jump, swinging by one hand from the rope over the abyss, I remember a last, desperate, impossible dream: It is very unfair that I should be kept here – again. Briefly I have the guts-wrenching sense of having *returned* to this predicament, this gaol – because it is a put-up job, surely the injustice of it will be realized for all to see and my innocence will be vindicated. Any day now, any day now, I shall be released . . . But the world being what it is, it is stupid to wait for justice. Luckily there are people outside who have my interests at heart, if for a price. I don't remember how to remember. I don't remember how I learn this, but at a given moment it is made clear that 'they' will come from outside to spring me. Of course I don't trust them, nor can I have any confidence in the run of events. Prison makes one totally apathetic though, you enter a certain immobility in yourself, a grey no man's land. Whatever happens, must happen – good or bad. Death becomes very easy indeed and there is no longer any moral outrage – at most a low, vacillating flame of querulousness . . . Polichinelle, the black keeper, passes along to me a message with the detailed escape plan. I will not have to do anything. But he is such a callous brute – is this not some elaborate and sadistic scheme to push me even deeper into the shit? . . . I am in a ward with many other inmates, all of them white, who move ever so slowly from bunk to table to barred window and back again. They are dressed in loose white garments of a thick material, caught at the back with small loops. We live right on top of one another: for the needs and duties of nature one has to withdraw behind a white plastic sheet draped over the toilet, but one risks suffocating to death there with the sheet plastered to the face . . . And then, at last, the door is unlocked by Polichinelle. A long, white, tiled corridor opens before me. Polichinelle leads me down the tunnel into the courtyard. Suddenly the sky is blindingly blue. Two elderly gentlemen are outside waiting for me, positioned strategically to cover all the exits and entrances to the courtyard. Both carry small, compact machine-guns. They are fastidiously turned out, like mellow bourgeois bankers. One of them has grey hair, a dark leathery face, widely-spaced teeth when he grins to shake my hand, the sun lighting up to a silver shine the black fur of his coat. The second old man (how could they look that respectable and yet be professional hit-men?) wears a pair of friendly glasses. Behind them, a little withdrawn, a young fellow with the sad visage of a half-dead Christ stands, incongruously cradling a black umbrella in his arms. I don't know how the break has been arranged, but I sense that it was made possible by large sums of money greasing a few select palms – eventually, I know, I shall have to pay over and above the bribes – also that these gentlemen are cold-blooded foreigners from a distant country, carrying out a contract. Or is it nothing but a cruel game, an elaborate *mise en scène* to madly raise my expectations . . . and transport me to the place of execution, to High Jump Hill? . . . A helicopter comes skimming low over adjacent roofs, hovers a while above the courtyard, churning up a whirlwind of dust and small pebbles, causing the melancholy lad to clutch his umbrella even tighter, and settles. We all get on board. I'm expecting at any moment to hear the rapid *puhpuhpuhpuh* of gunfire exchanges, to see the dun-coloured walls erupt in many minute fountains of sand. But no, there is a sureness about the whole operation. And then we have lift-off. When we tip over precariously in the air above the asylum complex, I see Polichinelle down below looking up, a hand to the peak of his cap to protect his eyes against the flying grit and the piercing sun carooming off our carapace. What will now happen to him? Why didn't we take him with us? He will be all right, the old man with the blind smile assures me. We have paid heavy money into his bank account . . . even if only forged dollars. Of course he is in plenty trouble from this moment on, ripe for the firing squad, but he'd be useless anywhere else. Out of his depth. If we took him away he'd be as sick as a homesick dog . . . Our helicopter now swoops over the suburb, the Place is rapidly falling behind, the tanks in the streets seem quite harmless from up here, the surrounding countryside is burnt brown, farmhouses like charred eggshells, a pillar of smoke above the mountain . . .)

They come early to the door of the cell. Polichinelle unlocks the door. With him there are three other warders, also the commander of the prison (wearing his gold-braided cap) and the chaplain. It is a cool, invigorating morning. The other two cells are unlocked. Now I can *see* Ka'afir. His face is calm and smooth, no traces left of the bruises caused by his torturers. His lips are folded over the absence of teeth. His eyes are so confident, so warm. He says: 'Thank you.' And then he says: 'It was good.' And then: 'We are home now.' Whitey is whimpering, he can hardly stand. Last night (tonight, now while I'm writing) they gave him a sedative. Shiva has not been in this morning with our breakfast. Our hands are shackled before us. Everybody knows his role. No nervousness, no bumbling, no precipitation. The voices are pitched low. The passage opens on the long glowing corridor. We walk in the shadow of the valley of death. Around us, all the way down, from the cells on either side, the singing of the other condemned ones. A sweet hedge of harmony as of birds of paradise. How springy are our legs, how open are our chests, dawn is beckoning us, freedom is touching a pale fire to the skyline.

Through the gates, through the gate, through the door at the corridor's end, and up the steps to the room without a view. Behind the other door lives the High Jump. You only need to jump high enough to make it to heaven. Our hands are unlocked to be tied behind our backs. Time for the dance. Whitey has slumped – two people are holding him up. The commander has taken off his cap. The chaplain is praying in a hoarse whisper. Nobody can hear him properly – maybe he is reciting his wife's shopping list. Ka'afir is looking and looking into my eyes. His lips are shaping sounds, he is saying something about 'brothers'. He is talking of the people accompanying us. What am I doing? I don't know. I am absent. My mind is with you. I am describing the eternity of these and all the other moments to you. The movements of the singing below us are muffled by the walls. Already we are hearing less and less distinctly. Then the darkness of the hood over the head, the smell of the material, the hand guiding me by the elbow. And the fumbling of another hand (two hands?) fitting the noose over the hood, over the head, around the neck, the knot below the ear. The left ear. The rope is the connection between heaven (the past) and the earth (the future). Death is absence.

What a long walk to heaven! Being led there by a rope around the neck. I described how I met Barnum there and how we went hunting for lizards. How are we ever going to film this? Has anyone succeeded in filming life after death, fixing the dark movements in passages of light? I mean – on the one hand – the life of the mind? Since one can imagine it (this deathstate), dream about it, it must exist. Or it can be made to exist. On the other hand – why can we not allow death to enter by filming it, by keeping the camera focussed on the corpse for as long as it takes to become transformed in its slow liberated shifts and sighs, seeping away, being absorbed by birds and mice and maggots and flies?

Some people say we have two shadows – the one, the big one, clear and distant, follows us even unto the night; the other is opaque, it becomes smaller, it is the soulbird which disappears with the cadaver. Others say that the body becomes earth, the shadow (or the double) disappears and the soul becomes an ancestor (*mzimu*); sometimes this ancestor reappears in the shape of a snake and then the people say: 'Our father has come to see us.' You will know it as the ancestor since it will have no shadow. I am my own ancestor. Somewhere the female sex is called *son*, meaning grave.

The body must be left alone long enough on its bier, wrapped in the cerecloth, for the juices of death to accumulate and seep into the earth. That liquid will be the ink.

Some people say that dying is but the casting off of the old skin. The serpent lives on. You once told me that there were those Ethiopians who believe that the dead return at night as monkeys to go celebrate religious services in the churches. Do they sing? Do they rest their chins on their cleft sticks? Some Ethiopians, however, do not believe in eternal life, and then it is claimed that old people in the ripeness of time will shrink smaller and smaller, until they are as minute and as white as ashes. They are then put in the gateway to the enclosure for the cattle, somewhere on the plains, to be trampled to dust and snuff by the animals' hooves . . . Small and slow . . .

The chameleon. (Excuse the flickering of my thoughts.) He is hated and despised. In some parts of our world he is often killed by having a handful of tobacco thrown down his gizzard.

God sent Bird to announce to mankind: 'You will be immortal. When you are old and weak and whimpering, you only need to slide out of your skin to be rejuvenated.' God gave Bird a crest on his head, like a crown, like a judge's hat, as the sign of his divine mission. Bird flew forth *puh-puh-puh-puh*. On his way he met Snake. 'Give me a bite of meat and I'll tell you all about God's message,' he said, but Snake refused. Bird insisted: 'Please, I'm telling you, when Man is old he will die, when you are old you will change your skin and be young once again.' So Snake – who is all gorge, all gullibility, all gormandizing – he who lives longest will gobble down the most – took the word to mankind while Bird was having his fill of meat. To punish Bird, God made him sick, and to this day (and night) he is lamenting his fate from the tree-tops. 'Oh how I hurt, how I hurt!'

God gave a message for Man to Chameleon: 'When people are old they will die, but they will be resuscitated.' Chameleon was so slow, his shoes were so small, his heart so heavy, his trip took him such a long time, he had to change into his travelling colours and that was a bother, he was so intent upon attracting flies, that he'd forgotten the end of the line by the time he arrived there. He said: 'Man will die when he is old.' Then Man sent Chameleon back to God with the request: 'We don't want to die. If we die you must let us be born again.' When he arrived before God (*Ata Emit*), Chameleon twisted the message around – maybe his tongue was too long and anyway his eyes couldn't both look in the same direction: 'We want to die, Man says, and when we are dead you must leave us alone.' Ever since that day all people pass away down the passage of nothingness to the High Jump, and the chameleon is a hated beast.

His slowness, it is said, which brings to mind the spitting image of death, must be because he walked in the mud before the earth emerged from the primordial waters. His ability to take on the colours of the rainbow means that he is related to the sky-gods, which is also why he looks like he's been struck hesitant and scorched by lightning. A *mina* proverb claims: 'Chameleon says: slowly, slowly. And it is death. He says: 'quickly, quickly. And it is also death.' His dragon-like dorsal comb, the slope of his body – these are the proofs that he takes strength from the earth whilst his head reaches heaven. The rainbow colours of his body constitute the road between earth and heaven, the axis along which souls progress to the Other Side. He embodies Man's fate: to be born to death, but with the promise of immortality and rebirth in Another World. For cosmic energy to be regrouped there must be dying. Chameleon is a messenger of the Invisible – a guarantor to the harmony of the world . . . All of the above I found among the papers of a dead man who was astonished that death should thus take him by the neck.

The weighted, poised, poisoned, infinitely slow jump of changing colour. But I am young still. My memory is not worth any papering over. I have no message for mankind, and no longer anything to ask of Noma.

I remember once in Rome – it was not long before I came up to Mont Aigu, where we met for the first time, remember? – an old theatre director from Alexandria, he'd been imprisoned during the war as a resistance fighter but his father was rich enough and could therefore buy his freedom, his ears were standing away from his head and he was so deaf you couldn't possibly interrupt him, his body smelled of old goat – slowly explaining to me that we ought absolutely to make a taboo of death, as of incest. We now know that the species can die. This knowing is a black flood invading our thoughts. Death has entered our minds the way ink sinks into paper. We can never again make undone our knowledge of dying and bringing about death, we can destroy our arsenals of arms but not our knowledge of how to fabricate them – but we must make dying such an unspeakable taboo (or sin?) that we shall pass it by in the same way that we do not sleep with our mothers however much we may crave to do so. We shall turn our heads the other way, and whistle like the birds. He also said – his thoughts were not more related to one another than mine are – that there can be no such notion as collective responsibility, and that there are quite simply problems which have no solutions.

Rome. That was the time I found Fanuel lying all limp and dislocated on a pavement with his nose in a puddle of dirty water. Some child must have thrown him out of a window. He was soaked through. It wasn't much, just a brownish stuffed toy lion, but it reminded me of Another World, of Africa. I picked it up, kept it, forgot all about it until I was clearing out my room in Paris before coming here. Maybe I needed to distribute my earthly belongings. You'd told me that you were pregnant, that day in the cathedral – remember? I pretended to believe you. (Tomorrow we are going up like three thieves to High Jump Hill. I have before my mind's eye the smooth body of the grey bird-like figure on the cross, the one we saw that day, lifting off towards the light.) So I decided to send you Fanuel before leaving. A patron lion for my unborn child, the one that will never be born, because I know you were only trying to keep me from going.

I'd been to Rome, that city the colour of old stone, and the stones warmed by years of sun and passing time, to look up Corbeau. We'd played together two or three times; I wanted to recruit him into the project of Birdflight Inc. He was a good stage actor, although perhaps a touch melodramatic. The poor man, for more than a year he'd been working in Italy. His wife, Cigale, was very beautiful and talented, and then she developed cancer of the breast. First she had to have the one breast removed, then the other, and immediately she underwent plastic surgery to have the scars attenuated, some silicone ersatz flesh fashioned to hint at swellings. To walk in the wind with.

Just imagine how expensive these operations and treatments must have been, and they but a couple of struggling actors. So they went to Italy, and Corbeau – who used to be an acknowledged master at declaiming Racine and Corneille – started performing naked and with a clenched mind on the stages of every conceivable sordid pornographic cabaret or nightclub show, his flesh sometimes blue from the cold, travelling all over Italy in a beat-up van, so as to scrape together enough money for their medical debts. I have always held back from telling you this tale, ashamed to have you see the humiliation of being a *saltimbanco*.

The holy number is not One, but Two. It is in the relationship between One and One that the ineffable is established. Can there

301

be any awareness of the fugacity, the furtiveness, the impermanence of life, except with reference to the other? One is self-fulfilling, is perfect. Two contains in it the break, the breakdown, the absence which will take you over the edge of yourself. How can there possibly be life except in relation to its cut-out, to stoplife? You can have no feel of the transcendental except by carrying with you the dark clay, the double, the face turned away from the moon, the slow messenger, the treacherous chameleon, the shrinking bird. It is true that the one grows from the other. It is true also that the mother is the skin of the child. I am talking to you.

Once, long ago, before I knew you, we played differently with the notion of growth – or with the idea of the magic pass linking the ordinary to the extra-ordinary. I don't like the French, although I have lived my adult life among them: I think they are too pretentious and too stupid – in fact they are victims to the terrible demands of *appearing*, of *style* – and this makes them cruel in their egocentricity and superficialness, but I have known a few funny or brave ones all the same. (And here I am writing, writing to you, to fill this terrible, limitless night.)

Together with Corbeau and Resnard I was rehearsing a play for the Théâtre de l'Ombre. We were poor as always, and we used to go to the same café down the road from the theatre, barely able to afford a hard-boiled egg and a glass of red wine each. Resnard somehow knew that the slovenly old concierge with the varicose-veined legs in care of the building next to the café had a tortoise in the tiny garden outside her loggia. Whenever we came for our early afternoon bite, she was already propped up at the bar with a tot of calvados.

I don't know who conceived of the diabolical plan, but one day we went down to the riverbank where live pets can be had and bought a tortoise just slightly bigger than the one in the concierge's garden. The next afternoon, while she was in the bar, we replaced her tortoise with a bigger one. The small one we took downtown to sell to the puppy and kitten dealer. Three days later we repeated the operation, exchanging the old lady's pet for a bigger one. By the third time (in the space of barely two weeks), we heard her talking about it to the barman, about how her tortoise has finally taken to growing, eccentric things these little buggers are, don't budge for ages and all of a sudden they get bigger, must be the salad that does it. The nuclear dust. The barman, looking at her with a vitreous eye, continued wiping the glasses.

So we carried on – learning our lines, eating eggs and drinking wine, swapping tortoises. After a month the old woman was delirious – she now regularly had a clutch of customers crowding around her while she told and retold her story. Was it magic? A *marabout* living in the quarter tried to profit from the situation by explaining about how the tortoise is a holy animal in Africa, and darkly insinuated that he was in contact with certain powers . . . Or was it a miracle? The Virgin Mother has been known to work in mysterious ways. Awed customers would leave their drinks on the counter to go and have a look at the miraculously growing tortoise. (Not that there was all that much to be seen.) Naturally the whole neighbourhood became involved, gossiping, laying bets, bad-mouthing the excited concierge, hinting at black magic ('we always knew that . . .'), weighing and measuring the animal, even calling in the fire brigade.

By the sixth week we thought the story was getting out of hand. The old concierge had had her hair dyed and started wearing stockings to hide the blue knobbly veins. In her garden she exhibited the biggest tortoise in Paris, and she was getting gloriously tipsy on the excitement and far more than the normal ration of calvados. The bar was rapidly gaining in inquisitive customers. Everybody took to calling her 'Madame Tortue'. (Some wit changed that to 'Tata Tordue'.) And then we started doing the reverse – taking away the big beast and leaving a smaller substitute to struggle with the heaps of salad and cabbage leaves.

We thought the old woman was going to go up the wall with frantic worry. She was desperate (how big did she expect a tortoise to become anyway?), until she realized there was as much attention to be raised by a shrinking animal as by a growing one.

Our play opened – it was called, of all things, *Les Pas de tortue!* – and promptly folded. A journalist came to the café one day and refused to believe the concierge's story. By then we had the animal back to its original size, though of course it was not the same one. Who knows how to recognize one tortoise from another?

I am swapping one thought for another, and I suddenly realize how much there is still to share. Am I trying to ward off the unthinkable? What does my coffin look like? I've always been particular about the vehicles I ease my body into . . . There is a town in a certain country where it is the custom to bury people very publicly. The coffin with the deceased is first of all carried from the morgue to the house of the bereaved family, and from there to the cemetery, and all the men of the town will consider it an honour to be allowed to help carry the coffin on their shoulders for a little while. It is like a dinghy on a choppy sea. A pharaoh's death-ship.

One day one such coffin left the morgue on the shoulders of some young men. Soon a crowd formed, with more and more men jostling one another, passing the box from shoulder to shoulder. Down the main street they went, and then it was as if the procession lost its direction. 'Which way should we go?' one of the bearers asked, looking at the crowd with the long faces. No one knew the answer. 'Whose body is this anyway?' People consulted each other in a perplexed way. Soon there was total confusion. The bearers who had most recently inherited the load went with it to the police station. To do what? To report a found object, a lost or discovered corpse? The police had to investigate. They opened the lid and found a cist filled with stones. The unfortunate and completely bewildered bearers were charged with sacrilege.

I haven't been to a funeral in so many years. It doesn't seem as if anyone ever dies in Paris. If they do, the dead must be evacuated at night, or else shovelled into the earth nearly surreptitiously while the cars caught in a traffic jam blare in the streets all around.

The last time I saw a funeral, it was quite by accident, a few months ago, probably around the third of September last year. How distant it all seems now! I'd gone to my hometown, Montaigue, for the day, from Mother City – actually the location where I grew up, Happy Valley, lies just outside the white town; it is now called an 'estate'. I heard the bell of the austere church on the hill tolling mournfully. It brought back so many memories – we always instinctively knew when a bell was ringing and rolling for the freshly dead. We believed it was to let heaven know that someone was on his or her way. For them to get out the clean sheets up there. A cortège of limousines was forming behind the hearse, and the procession came slowly down Botha Avenue. There was an ample mound of wreaths with ribbons to be seen through the glass sides in the back of the black-and-silver van. In the first cars there were women in black with bowed heads, holding scented handkerchiefs to their eyes and their mouths. I didn't recognize anybody – I've been away for too many years – but judging by the number of cars the defunct obviously must have been a prominent citizen, maybe a rich farmer or a retired bank manager or the school principal. Maybe a boy blown up on the 'border' of a township. Maybe a retired general, or a minister. A White in any event – after all, he or she was carried feet first from a white church accompanied by white mourners.

How incongruous that these ceremonies could still take place! The country was going up in smoke, there were control points on the roads and at the stations; outside Mother city, along the mountain flank, unclaimed or too severely damaged corpses were aligned in shallow trenches, doused in gasoline and put to the torch. And here, in Montaigue, a community went through the slow dance of committing one of its own to the soil of eternity.

When I was small a burial meant best clothes, pinching shoes, the undertaker with his white cuffs and black gloves, people needing to be half-carried, much weeping, impassioned harangues addressed to the Saviour looking down dimly from his abode up above, whining songs by the side of the grave, people fainting, smelling salts and eau-de-Cologne, clods falling with soft thwumps on the chrysanthemums and pigs-ears covering the coffin, men twisting their hats in their caloused hands. Then the interminable feast, meats, potatoes, cucumber salads, rice with raisins and turmeric, the confused inebriety of those who'd drunk too much and were nevertheless trying to maintain their solemnity. People were tipsy with sorrow.

And tomorrow I shall enter that memory intimately. Black is the dust and white is the snow, white the petals where the tears will grow and the wind blow black . . . Who will come to my funeral to entrust me with a farewell message?

Two is the mystical figure. Man and woman, you and I, the I and its double. You don't really know me. You can't. I've been to the mountain. And beyond the mountain to a country where, when evening falls, men with hats and ties still go down on their knees to whisper echoes of love through round holes in the fences along the principal street, cat-holes they are called, for the benefit of their fiancées squatted in a rustle of white on the other side. I know of establishments with neon signs where men line up facing a mirror as big as the wall – a truly 'blank' wall? – drop their pants, shove their penises through holes not much bigger than eyes in the mirror, to be masturbated by unseen deft fingers on the other side. Maybe that is the sum total of what I've been trying to do, the destination of my hesitant steps. It is said that the brief shudder of ecstacy is existential, not physical. And I seem to recall now that Captain Dino Felis testified in court that the murderer of Mrs Katya Hamman had put a mirror on the floor below the gently swaying body, that

305

someone – the murderer? the victim? – had written in red on the surface: *'Niemand'*. Maybe I have imagined all of this.

Writing is like plaiting a rope. And the rope is the present linking past to future. The guide-line across the chasm. The world is a mirror.

I don't want to die, and I cannot live on. I am a traitor. I would have betrayed all my friends and comrades and enemies had the masters but asked me to. Anything as a trade-off for breath. A rope doesn't breathe.

Ah, for the pleasure once more to wake up with the morning in a room with painted beams and the white wash of first light rippling over the slanted ceiling. To hear you pottering about and doing the dishes in the kitchen. Let it be a small house with tiled floors not far from the slow digestive swishing of the sea, three flowers on the windowsill, two books on the staircase, a scroll on the wall showing wide-eyed saints. It needn't even be Africa.

Last night, I don't know how late it was, Polichinelle came into my cell and without saying a word he raped me. All he said was: 'I have a letter for you, Mfowethu.' Did I resist? I know that my hands must have been trembling. I know, because I was biting them until I tasted the blood as salty as tears. He didn't bother to take his cap off. He must have known that condemned men don't wear underclothes, let alone silk underpants. You see, I am not a man any more. Did I shout? I asked him why he'd killed my chameleon. There must have been a scuffle. From across the corridor I could hear Ka'afir sobbing.

One should be happy to take comfort in the immediate. The song of the bird, the way the ant moves heaven and earth into its nest, the birth of a child.

When you arrive thus, so to say, at the end of the line, you owe it to yourself (and to those close to you – your cousins, the butcher, the Director of Information, your agent, the card players, the body-builders, Nina the mole woman) to turn back one last time and review the prophetic vision which brought you to this sarcophagus. Has your life been a deployment, an accomplishment of that dream? You put your shoulder to the green morning star and your back to the wall. It's been quite a way, winding up the valley through the vineyards, by the sandy patches where the pine trees grow, past the copses, along the perimeter where dogs always barked, over the moon where you lost the matchbox and your innocence, where you stubbed your toe, where you shot the crow. And where you were rocked by a dream of happiness when you saw the green morning gauging its depth perpendicularly above the mountain wall. There the prostitutes came to bury eggs. Here a man knocked on a window-pane with gnarled knuckles and a sooty smile. In that other here, the clearing in the forest, children promised each other eternal loyalty and kissdom by the red of their noses. A dog tottered on its legs and fell down dead. A motor car harrumphed basketfuls of blue smoke. Uncle Sampie ran on tip-toe as fast as a heralding of the arrival of a king along the street, his eyes like coins worn smooth and illegible with counting, playing through his fingers the string of a sun-devouring kite wafted high above the chalked white fortresses, singing out: 'Watch out for history!' There you staunched your ruminations under the blue, bee-filled, perfumed cupola of a loquat tree, it had stars in its branches, and you brought your mumbling down to the bowl of snow in your hands. You dipped your bleeding hands in the snow. Nothing we are. So rich.

I turned around and saw my mother sitting under a frilly-edged parasol. She was scrawny, but alive. The best Sunday dress, her dark woollen stockings and her shiny shoes, her hat with the nod-good-morning flowers, on her lap the sempiternal worn going-to-church handbag. Her face is a crow. Her face with all the folds of the night and a polished brown earnestness. In her old age she'd lost nearly all her hair. Where did the breasts go? She sings, the voice quavering to reach out and catch the fluttering notes by their tails: '*Jesus min my salig lot, Weet dit uit die woord van God, Al is ek ook swak en blind, Nogtans roep hy my sy kind . . .*'

I am so confused that I have to write about myself in the third person. This shaky spider's progress will entangle my hand, capture it and make it a mummy of rot as if my thumb were a fly.

What remains? Some images. My love. My love, your sex is like an apricot and mine is like a horse. The horse must eat the sweet, juicy apricot and suck the small brown stone. It is easier to kill a woman than to leave her. You will live with the treachery and the pain.

I had a dream when I tried to sleep. I dreamed I was in a swimming-pool. I dove to the bottom and found a half-drowned little child there. I came to the surface, clutching the baby to my chest. It spoke to me, saying how disappointed its mother is because it doesn't want to become a researcher after truth. I cried and I cried, holding its small head tightly, the hair was lying flat on the skull and there were stains of a rust-coloured liquid down its throat. 'No,'

I said. 'Don't! You can be anything you want to, you can be a bus-driver, if you so desire. Or a chimney sweep. Or a keeper of birds. As long as you live!'

These images will go with me. A white shell, smooth and rounded, with a slit – the moon in the desert. The dead black bull lying in the town square where all the roads cross, alone, and all the shuttered windows. On the hill the body in its grave, perfectly preserved, it will never decay. The smile puckering the lips and the droning of flies. The cold and smooth light over the landscape. The city steeped in a terrible stench, and small tongues of flame flicker-ing under the doors. The ancestors, blindfolded, smiles puckering their lips, lined up against the wall of the fort. One is shouting: 'Watch out for history!' Another is singing: 'How I hurt, how I hurt.' A third is saying: 'Ah, it is better to live today than to die tomorrow.' A fourth is beckoning me on.

I must leave you now, my heart. Now, when it is at last too late, I can say how much I love you. I love you. Please forgive me for forgetting. It is growing light. This is where my role ends.